The Lady
of the Tower

ELIZABETH ST.JOHN

Published by Falcon Historical Press 2017

The recipes featured in
Chapters 2,4,6,8,10,12,14,15,17,19,21,22,25,27,28,32,35,38,45,49 are reprinted courtesy of the The Library at Wellcome Collection, London.
Lady Johanna St.John's Recipe Book Ref: Saint John, Johanna MS. 4338
Lady Johanna St.John was the daughter-in-law of
Sir John St.John, 1st Baronet, and Lucy St.John's niece by marriage.
The letters featured within the book are both authentic and fictional versions. Sir Allen Apsley's will is the author's transcription of a copy at the British Library.

Other books by Elizabeth St.John

The Lydiard Chronicles | 1630-1646
By Love Divided
A Novel
Counterpoint: Theo Howard, Earl of Suffolk
A Novelette

Praise for The Lady of the Tower
BRAG Medallion Honoree
"Elizabeth St.John has brought the early Stuart Court in the years before the English Civil War vividly to life."
Historical Novel Society

"The Lady of the Tower is a beautifully produced novel with a well-crafted story that will keep you both engaged and entertained."
Writers Digest 24th Annual Book Awards

" Elizabeth St John brings these years of Stuart England to the fore, bringing the known facts of her ancestor's life together with richly imagined scenes creating in the process a believable heroine, an intriguing plot and an enjoyable novel. "
Discovering Diamonds

Author's Note

For Emma, who got me started; Charles, who kept me going; Deborah, who unmasked me; and all my friends and relatives who have kindly tolerated my excitement over obscure historical discoveries during the writing of this book.

I especially want to thank my Second Tuesdays Saloniérres, my Scribophile.com critiquers, Dr Paul Sellin of UCLA, Dr David Norbrook of Oxford University, the Yeomen and staff of the Tower of London and the British Library, the historians at the Library at the Wellcome Collection and Nottingham Castle, Sir Brook Boothby of Fonmon Castle, the staff of Lydiard House and Friends of Lydiard Park.

Many years ago, I came across a copy of *Memoirs of the Life of Colonel Hutchinson* by Lucy Hutchinson. Contained within is *The Life of Mrs Lucy Hutchinson, Written by Herself, A Fragment.* The story of her mother, Lucy St.John, served as inspiration for this novel. Many details of Lucy St.John's life are unknown, but enough is recorded to serve as markers of her journey. The rest of her path is historical fiction.

www.ElizabethJStJohn.com

Lydiard Park and House

The St.John family home of Lydiard Park and House, along with St. Mary's Church, is located just west of Swindon, England. Set in more than 200 acres of beautiful parkland, the house is open to the public, and contains many portraits of the St.John family featured in The Lydiard Chronicles. St. Mary's Church, one of the finest small churches in England, is full of extraordinary monuments, including the polyptych containing life-size portraits of Lucy St.John and her sisters.

The Friends of Lydiard Park is an independent charity dedicated to supporting the conservation and continued enhancement of Lydiard House and Park

www.LydiardPark.org.uk
www.FriendsofLydiardPark.org.uk
www.stmaryslydiardtregoze.co.uk

Main Characters

Sir Oliver St.John, Viscount Grandison
Joan Royden, his wife
  - *No issue*

Sir John St.John (m) Lucy Hungerford
  - *Sir John St.John*
  - *Katherine St.John*
  - *Eleanor St.John*
  - *Barbara St.John*
  - *Lucy St.John*
    And others

Lady Anne Leighton, gr. granddaughter of Mary Boleyn

Sir William St.John, a descendent of the Welsh St.John family

Theophilus Howard, heir to the Earldom of Suffolk
Frances Howard, Countess of Somerset, his sister and wife to the Earl of Essex,

George Villiers, Duke of Buckingham, King James's favorite
Sir Edward Villiers, his half brother

Sir Giles Mompesson, a businessman

Sir Allen Apsley, a friend of Sir William and Sir Oliver St.John

Sir Walter Raleigh, a friend of Sir Allen Apsley

PROLOGUE

God, who holds my fate in Thy hands, give me strength, I implore, for today I enter a prison like no other on this earth, and perhaps one that even Hell does not equal in its fiery despair. Give me fortitude to walk through those gates where so many traitors have gone before and never left. Give me compassion to hear the cries of forgotten men and not turn my head away. Give me, above all, Heavenly Father, courage to bear myself with dignity and Your grace when I am inwardly trembling with fear at the horrors that lie behind those walls.

Lucy

23rd March 1617

Silver drizzle veiled the stone walls rising from the moat's stagnant water. To the north, the White Tower glistened but bade no welcome for all its shining. Gabled roofs with ornate chimneys pierced the mist and hid again, hinting a house within the fortress. I was not comforted, for it reminded me that the kept must have their keepers.

Thunder resounded through the fog from water swirling around the center arches of the bridge, just upriver from our tethered barge. The first time I was rowed in a shuddering boat through the narrow span of columns was terrifying. "Shooting the bridge" the locals called it, the currents created by the arches manifesting river water into whirlpools. Recollections of impaled traitors' heads grinning from the pikes appeared before my closed eyes. What hell's gate was I approaching?

"Ho! Tie here!"

A clash of metal resounded as the pikemen stood to attention on the wharf. I pulled my mind back to the present.

"Aye, make way for the lady."

Roughened hands guided me from the rocking boat, and I carefully picked my way up the water steps. My heart beat faster as I gazed up at the sheer ramparts. They loomed over my head, broken only by a low arch with an iron portcullis. Blackened bars jutted forth, a reminder I entered a prison.

I shivered from the damp air, and not a little from apprehension, and stood still on the wharf. Behind me, the Thames ebbed now, and the ferrymen urgently called patrons to catch the running tide. In front, the moat lay impenetrably black and still. The cold seeped through the soles of my shoes, for in my anxiety I had forgotten my pattens. Out of the gloom, a man appeared beside me.

"Princess Elizabeth paused here," The Keeper spoke quietly, his words brushed by the lilt of an Irish accent. "She declared she was no traitor and refused to enter through that arch, for those who arrive through Traitors' Gate do not leave again."

The dark water gate, its walls defining the width of the ramparts above, did not welcome guests. I thought of the young princess defying her guards, perching on a wet stone on a rainy day similar to this, her own future cloudy with doubt and dread. I recalled the moment I heard I was to enter the Tower, and how my stomach twisted with fear at the news.

"When I served her, none could see the frightened girl behind the majesty," he continued, "for we were all in love with her, each one of us outdoing the other in deeds and poetry to gain her favor."

The Keeper waved the bargeman away, and the boat was quickly untied and pushed from the wharf, the crew not looking back as they rowed rapidly upriver.

"Her 'adventurers,' she called us, and all through her life, she played us one against many, declaring her affection and encouraging our competition—who could sail the farthest, dance the longest, fight the strongest." He pulled his black leather cloak closer against the cold. "She challenged us, and she baited us like dogs to a bear."

I looked at the Keeper, his faded blue seafarer's eyes gazing toward invisible horizons as he sailed into memories. Briefly, I glimpsed the queen's man in his prime, standing tall and strong, bronzed by foreign suns, his white beard a rich chestnut brown, his shoulders broad.

"Another woman whose own sister betrayed her, who knew not whom she could trust." My voice competed with the rushing water; there was no telling if he heard.

"All the princess recalled that sorry afternoon was her mother, who entered the gate at the king's command and never left." He turned away abruptly and hailed a guard standing by.

Just as I am commanded.

"Escort my lady to her lodging. Ensure my steward is there to greet her and introduces her to her household. I shall be at the armory."

He strode off, leaving me lonely on the wharf, my skirts heavy with the weight of the rain water, thoughts swirling. I followed the guard along a narrow path to a bridge across the moat and toward the gabled house I glimpsed earlier.

Married to a man I trusted not, parted from family and friends, I entered the Tower of London. A bleak March morn in the year of our Lord 1617, and I was the new mistress of the prison.

1

Sweet Sister Eleanor,

I beg to be remembered to you, for it is almost five years since our family dispersed, and I pray our blessed mother continues to find peace in heaven with our brother Walter and Father. I hold on to your kerchief as a keepsake of your words when we saw each other at Michaelmas two years past and hope that one day we will all be reunited. My life here in Battersey continues as before, and I still have no comfort in Aunt Joan's supervision, and indeed she doth still treat me with the same degree of malevolence. Barbara is no help, for you know how she feels about me. I give this to our messenger secretly, for he is well pleased with the coin you have provided for my letter. I have no news, for nothing happens while Uncle Oliver still commands his troop in Ireland. Each day, I dream of a life away from here, but I know not what my prospects will be, especially if Aunt Joan has her way. Remember me to our sisters and brother. I always keep you in my prayers.

Lucy St.John
19th March 1603

Her slap shocked me, for until now she dared not strike where a mark might be so visible. We stood at bay as combative lurchers, motionless, wary of a next move. I refused to drop my eyes, although they were tear-blurred, and she eventually turned away. Her frizzed hair lay thin on her crown, her stained velvet gown stretched taut across stout shoulders.

"You ungrateful wretch, do not talk back to me again." She strode to the chest and dragged out my gown and kirtle. "You will wear these and be thankful. If your uncle were here, I would demand greater punishment for your insolence, and he would, for once, see you in your true light."

"They don't fit, Aunt Joan. I cannot breathe in the bodice. I have worn this since I was ten years."

She flung the petticoat at me, its faded green fabric light and threadbare. "It has served you well these past five years, and you will wear it five years more if I say so. I am not made of money. Fostering an ungrateful orphan is not my choice of where to spend my coin."

I refused to catch it, and the old robe fell to the floor. My aunt stepped toward me, her face red, thin lips pursed, arm raised again. I sighed, and as I retrieved it, I glimpsed Barbara's feet, clad in beautiful fawn leather shoes adorned with crimson tassels. I looked up, my cheek still stinging. My sister, who observed our whole discourse, smiled triumphantly at me. She crossed the room to Aunt Joan, her new heels clicking on the wooden boards, for no lavender stems sweetened the floors of my room. They both stared, united in their common dislike of me. The unfairness gave courage to my voice.

"But Uncle Oliver left an allowance for me to be used when he served in Ireland. It is part of our inheritance. I am entitled to that money."

"Entitled? Entitled?" Joan's voice rose a level, her accent coarsening under the duress of her emotion. "'Od save us, I'll give you entitled, you proud wretch. I'll not forgive Oliver for casting you on my doorstep when I had the pick of your sisters. I told him to bring one who would mind me and have a use, older so we could wed her sooner. Barbara was a perfect pedigree. And then he added the runt of the litter."

"My uncle chose me. He told me so. He saw more in me than you—"

"He brought you because no one else would take you. And no more sense does that man have to pick the worthless child than to be soldiering in the Irish bogs rather than attending at court, leaving me to manage here on my own. Now with two orphaned girls, who I have to make matches for. One I can work with. You, however . . ." She snorted, contempt souring her lips. "I did not marry him to be a penniless widow to his military ambition."

We stood, facing each other, the gulf of mutual dislike widened by the cruelty of her words. At times of confrontation, she always repeated this story, a litany to my childhood since Oliver brought me to her doorstep.

"Come Aunt, be not upset by her inconsequence." Barbara took Joan's arm. "She is not worth it. Let us breakfast and talk of our day together. A dressmaker arrives today with a new French fashion. Our maid will find a way to counterfeit without having the services of a London seamstress."

My aunt turned to my elder sister, her face brightening.

"You are clever, Barbara, always finding ways to save me money. Unlike your ungrateful sister, who does nothing but complain and run to Oliver, whining of her plight."

I gave up my rebellion at the unfairness of her statement. Uncle Oliver spared meager time for me on his infrequent visits home, and I had little opportunity to talk of myself. His wife disliked me so that, in her mind, anything I did affronted her personally.

Joan gave me a foul look as she left the chamber, and I slumped on the cot, the faded gown wrinkling where I clenched the fabric. Although I was still small in stature, I had developed much in my fourteenth year, and with my courses, my figure filled. Stable lads threw me second glances, and I knew I was a child no longer. Perhaps this caused Joan even more annoyance, for I was not so malleable as before, and she so ill-natured in her fits that I knew not where the next rage would come from. Her subtle cruelties exceeded the tales of any stepmother.

I struggled to pull the too-small kirtle over my head and fled to the garden, where I always found relief, for neither Joan nor Barbara would follow.

The soft burbling and cooing of the birds, stirring in the wooden dovecote as the dawn light broke downriver, bade farewell to the ebbing night. The Thames, lapping the gravel bank, added a soothing rhythm to the morning wakening. As I made my way along the path through the orchard, the familiar harmony of nature quietened my spirit. Here, my memories of Lydiard lingered strongest, and in the five years since my exile to Battersey, my old home survived as my talisman.

The knot of anxiety in my stomach slowly unraveled. Although I was resigned for Aunt Joan's next slap or pinch, I knew her favorite pastimes of Barbara and dressmakers distracted her, and my garden provided safety. Her unpredictable outbursts discomposed me, and I avoided her wherever I could find excuse.

I would rather dress in rags than play Barbara's counterfeit games.

Reaching the elm gate with its unyielding bolt, I climbed over the rough-sawn bars and jumped down. I paused and looked back at the manor house, partially screened by a row of elm trees yet to bud in the chilly spring, its sinking roofline and untidy thatched outbuildings softened by the translucent river mist. From here, the old house dominated the surrounding countryside, rooted, its place in the history of the land secure. Closer up, the decaying wood, crumbling bricks, and broken roof slates proclaimed its gradual abandonment by Aunt Joan.

For her, appearances should be maintained at all cost, and pride was her daily bread. Her father bequeathed her the manor house and its lands, making her relatively wealthy in the small world of Battersey. Alas, the income from the market gardens did not stretch to the cost of maintaining the house, or, given her preference, of tearing it down and building a new, grander structure.

Although our family held significant wealth and land, all was entailed upon my brother John, who had yet to reach his majority. Even we sisters had substantial dowries set aside to satisfy our future suitors' families. Concealed from Oliver, Joan laid upon me every jealousy provoked by her mean life.

I brushed my fingers across a tightly furled pussy willow bud.

Canker . . . her cruelty hides like a canker in her disposition.

"Make way! Make way!"

A shout interrupted my thoughts, galloping hooves pounding through the holloway and silencing the dawn chorus. Dewy cobwebs clinging to black hawthorn twigs trembled. A rider appeared on the narrow track. The peaceful March dawn was shattered by the jangling of harnesses, the creak of leather, and the labored breathing of the steed.

I shrank against the hedge, dropping the primroses I had picked by the gatepost. Catching the grim expression of the messenger as he galloped toward Joan's house, my heart quickened, and hollowness bloomed in my chest. Please, please don't let this be more news of harm or death in my family. I recalled the still-raw pain when news of our brother Walter's drowning reached Battersey, and the disbelief and anger I felt at such a meaningless accident. Please, no more hurt to my family.

Hampered by my dew-soaked skirts, I scrambled back over the gate and followed the messenger to the house. My garden played tricks on me, brushing cobwebs across my eyes and snagging my sleeve with rose thorns. I struggled free and ran.

In the stable yard, the rider's horse was being walked, its sides heaving and spit-flecked as the grooms cooled the animal down. Pulling with both hands on the cold iron ring that served as a handle, I flung open the side door to the old house.

Inside, I paused, my eyes adjusting to the dim light within the passage, illuminated only by an open doorway in front of me. Voices were raised, and a sharp exclamation rang out from within the hall.

"What . . . what news?" I cried, out of breath and disheveled, my cheeks burning with anxiety. My fists clenched in my skirts as I stood in the doorway and confronted the group in front of me.

"Comport yourself, girl," snapped Aunt Joan, glaring at me. "Fie upon thee, when will you learn to have any restraint, any modesty? You are fourteen years of age and no better than an apprentice."

Standing next to her, Barbara stared at me. "Out playing in the fields again, Sister?"

I ignored Barbara and brushed the remaining cobwebs from my nose.

"Please, good sir," I implored the messenger, stepping towards him. "Please, what news?"

The messenger looked at me and ducked his head. My face must have betrayed the worry in my soul.

"'Tis expected news, for all that it is unwelcome. I come from the Palace at Richmond. The queen passed early this morning, leaving these earthly bounds, God bless her soul. She left no named heir, and we know not James from Scotland, who now crosses the border to rule over us."

Joan emitted a strangled shriek again and dramatically carried her hand to her forehead, dabbing at her eyes with a small lace handkerchief.

"We're ruined!" she cried. "All is lost!"

"Aunt, calm yourself," soothed Barbara, patting the older woman tentatively on her plump shoulder. "Why would you say such a thing?"

She turned to the messenger. "You may leave us."

"I was told to bring the news to Sir Oliver, by his kin at court." The messenger stood, uncertain for a moment, perhaps hoping for an invitation to visit our kitchen or receive a groat for his troubles.

"He is not here. You've told us." As Barbara stared at him dismissively, he shook his head and left.

"All is lost, our connection, our family ties . . . her patronage . . . our influence. The Scots king has no truck with our English ways." Joan's wailing turned to a croon.

Barbara gasped and paused her patting.

"I think not . . ." I began tentatively.

"No, you don't think," retorted Joan. "You never think. And nor do you care to understand the advantage of your breeding."

"Uncle Oliver's perquisites won't continue, Aunt Joan?" Barbara's voice acquired a sharp edge.

I think not that anyone cares about your selfish lives right now.

"He shared a granddame with the queen. The ancestry with the Scots is not so direct. Now all is lost . . ." and here she began to wail, shaking her head fiercely, "the Scottish king has no more loyalty to your uncle than the devil himself, and by that I mean that it is hopeless, for without our connections, we have no advancement."

Joan sobbed harder, her face turning bright red and her coarse cheeks trembling.

I drifted to the window, glazed in the old way with wavy green glass that let little light into the gloomy chamber. Rubbing on the dirty diamond-shaped panes and peering outside, I wished I walked still in the orchard, soothed by the soft cooing of the doves now fully awake and flying from the cote. I thought of Lydiard again, shutting out Aunt's moaning.

Pushing open the stiff catch, I looked out across the water gardens that sloped gently down toward the River Thames, shining silver in the morning sun. A pale slate sky, illuminated by streaks of rose-colored clouds, arched over the river and blended into the distant horizon of pastures and woodland surrounding the village of Chelsea across the water. Boatmen steered their small ferry boats to our landing steps between the manor house and St. Mary's Church.

Gradually, barges and wherry boats set forth from the banks and crowded the Thames. Those carrying the news called it across to others and brought yet more citizens onto the water, fragmenting the silver liquid into shards of gray. A deep toll from the church made me jump, the death knell ringing to confirm the news that the messenger brought.

The queen was dead. Long live the king.

2

Antidote for the plague

   Take conserve of wood sorrel and a scruple of saffron together with the syrup of the juyce of citrons, as much as will make an electuary. Take with a quantity of a large nutmeg every morning.

My recipes
Lucy St.John
31ˢᵗ July 1603

Through that hot summer of the succession, our days passed slowly, enlivened by rumors of fierce heathen lords from the north descending on our towns with strange, thick accents and wild hair. I considered it might be quite exciting to encounter them, but Barbara thought differently and refused to venture outside Battersey's crumbling walls for fear of abduction or worse.

July progressed, and a strange silence descended on the land around us. The rumbling produce carts from our abundant gardens weren't traveling as frequently down the rutted lane, taking our fruits and vegetables to London's markets. Never one to receive many visitors, no callers attended Joan in weeks, and I chafed at the stillness surrounding us. Moreover, the water traffic thickened sailing upriver from London, and fewer barges steered for the city. An uncertainty tainted the very air around us. Suspended between one age and another, we waited for the king to arrive, but he did not come.

As I walked early one morning by the banks of the river, seeking newly sprouted mushrooms in the wet grass, a shape in the water swaying and shouldering against the bulrushes in the shallows caught my eye. I looked more closely and turned away sharply, bitter bile gorging into my throat. It was a man—or what was left of him— bloated and blackened, trailing green weeds garlanding his head, beneath which his brow was pustuled and bruised puce. I struggled up the bank, shouting, and Vicar Ridley, who was just leaving the church door, came running.

I sobbed out what I had seen, and he quickly made his way to the water's edge. When he returned, his face was grim.

"'Tis the plague, poor soul, no doubt of it," he announced. "Mistress Lucy, you touched him not?"

I shook my head and swallowed hard. The metallic taste of fear joined the bile in my throat at those dreaded words.

"We've been hearing accounts of the sickness in London these past weeks," he continued. "It's been challenging to find men who will take the carts to London's markets—many refuse to leave home at all. It is said the new king declines to enter the city to be crowned, after all his waiting, for fear of the contagion that creeps in London's alleys."

I looked up at Vicar Ridley, and although his words were frightening, I found his presence comforting. He was a quiet man, bent over, perhaps by the cares of his world, his face deeply lined. But when he looked at me, his eyes were clear and sweet.

"You'll be steady, Mistress Lucy?" he asked gently. "'Tis not a pleasant sight to see a man's death mask from the plague."

I nodded, soothed by his familiar calmness.

"The plague rarely chooses just one," he continued, his face sober. "I fear the contagion is brewing in London, Mistress Lucy, and with this summer heat, it will be swift to spread. Plague season is upon us."

"Can Donna Anna make us the pomanders from her gardens?" I asked, my faith in his wife enhanced by the secret days I spent in her stillroom, away from my miserable house. "Aunt Joan will begrudge every penny spent with an apothecary, even to guard against sickness, I fear."

"She will," he reassured me, but then his voice turned stern. "But they are no more than simple herbs that are found in every knot garden along the river. Although she brings the ancient healings from Spain, she has no magic to ward off this devil's messenger."

"I would not presume—"

"Do not say more."

Ten years had passed since Aunt Joan had encouraged the parishioners to bring accusations of witchcraft against Vicar Ridley and made him stand trial, accusing him of being responsible for the death of a man from witchcraft. She was convinced that his Spanish wife, Donna Anna, with all her knowledge of medicines and herbs, was brewing potions and spells, and by association, he was discreetly a harbinger of witchcraft himself

By God's good fortune, our parish also held enlightened men who petitioned Lord Burleigh for his acquittal. They swore that Vicar Ridley was more likely to hate witches, and that his wife lived quietly and honestly. Suspicion of the old faith still lived in chambers of many villagers' memories. It wouldn't take more than a miraculous recovery from a plague to bring those tales of the Ridleys' past to the forefront of gossip again.

"I must warn the parish the plague has reached our shores," Vicar Ridley said wearily. "There is bound to be more contagion, more deaths. Summer has not reached its peak yet, and I fear the worst lies in store for us."

"You knew?"

"The accounts prove unreliable. Many have left London to join the king on his progress. There is little governance in the city, for those who are left have reduced authority." He straightened his back. "We do as we must. Our village will be on alert now."

"I'll tell Aunt Joan," I volunteered, knowing that she would not take kindly to the vicar's calling on her.

"Your brother?" His eyes were still drawn to the dark shape now caught in the rushes just a few feet away. "John is away still in Guernsey with Sir Thomas Leighton?"

I nodded, knowing that the vicar's thoughts flew to the remaining heir and the tragedy if John succumbed to the plague.

"We hear that he and Anne Leighton are to be married," I responded. "With their court intelligence, they will not yet leave the Channel Islands and risk England's contagion."

"And Sir Oliver? What word of his return?"

"Any day. The advance messengers arrived yesterday."

"Good. He will be safe here at Battersey, where we can guard against the infiltration of those who may carry this pestilence from London-town. Donna Anna believes 'tis the tenements of the cities that hatch the infection and breed evil humors. After that, any man could brush against another and be brought down in an hour."

The plague man now appeared vulnerable, lost to death, no one to mourn him, his mortal remains a danger to us all. My tears presented

13

suddenly, for I did not cry much. I wept as the poor dead man twisted in the river eddies, the water playing a macabre joke of giving his lifeless limbs motion.

"Fear not, child, for if your time has come, it will be God's will."

He smiled sadly at me and briefly laid his hand on my head before turning toward the church, his shoulders stooped under the burden of plague threatening his community.

"'Od's blood, fetch us ale, you wretched whoreson!" The man's voice roared above a hubbub such as the old manor had not seen in all my years.

"Bring meat, for Christ's nails I have not tasted any but maggot-ridden mutton for months . . ."

"Ale first, for my throat is parched and my belly empty."

A soldier stumbled out from the open doors of the manor and vomited on the stone steps, a steady stream of ale that splashed up against the weathered wall. Stepping carefully over the stinking puddle, I entered the hall, now filled with a crowd of soldiers reeking of noisome sweat and resounding with their loud voices and shouts of laughter.

By the dais stood my uncle, his face ruddy and his beard white above his weather-stained leather jacket.

"Uncle, Uncle," I called, struggling to weave through the thickly packed groups of men.

He heard my voice, and his face broke into a smile

"Lucy, darling girl," he roared, causing the nearest soldiers to look swiftly to see what distracted him from their stories and joking. "'Od's wounds, you've grown since I was last home!"

I broke through and ran into his outstretched arms.

"'Tis a marvel you're home, Uncle. I was so worried about your safety."

"Ha, it would take more than a rebel army of motley Irishmen to keep an Englishman away from those he loves."

Oliver turned to the man on his right, many years younger than he but just as battle grimed and raucous as the rest of them.

14

"William, your cousin Lucy. Sweeting, Will St.John, one of our Welsh brethren. A seafaring man. I persuaded him to join me in Ireland. He's never reluctant to pick up a fight."

"Aye, and between the rain and the bogs, I've seen more water and been wetter these past months than my last three voyages to Cadiz."

Oliver roared with laughter and thumped his arm in approval.

Will swept a bow.

"Mistress Lucy," he acknowledged with a grin and turned back to the group, picking up his story. I caught a glimpse of a gold earring in his curly brown hair and a flash of white teeth in a tanned face. My heart jumped, and for a beat I was curiously short of breath.

I turned to Oliver.

"Uncle, 'tis so fortunate you have returned now. There is a plague-man, dead, on our land, washed up from the river. And the vicar says there is contagion in London."

Oliver's face turned sober.

"Aye, sweeting, there is a pestilence abroad. The king delayed his coronation for the dread of plague. Many have fled the city—doubt any men would show to greet him."

"Did you ride through London?" I asked, aghast that Oliver would place himself in danger.

"Carried the news to the king of our Irish victory. Had an audience at Theobalds." He paused, pondering. "Hoped to see the queen to tell her myself. With her death, an age has passed. So many changes. Ireland no longer our enemy. Scotland neither. Seems the flags of St. Andrew and St. George no longer war over the borderland. So much bloodshed, including the Scottish queen's, for naught."

He looked at me and reached out to pinch my cheek.

"Yes, we came through London. Nothing to worry about, my dear. The city is prepared. We'll be safe at Battersey." He turned back to his men. "Now, more beer, and where is the food? Joan . . . Joan!"

Later, I sat in the garden, the distant clattering and laughter of the soldiers in the house the only disturbance ruffling the silence of the afternoon. Even the insects droned quietly, soporific with the heavy summer fragrances, and there seemed an expectance in the air.

"The plague is here," I whispered Oliver's news to the bees, superstitious that if I did not share our gossip with them, they would leave and bring us bad fortune. "Save our souls and protect us from the death that approaches on the wind's breath."

I thought of John, far away, safe in Guernsey, and of my other sisters, dispersed amongst relatives. I observed myself, holding on to these moments, suspended in time, not wanting to hear the sound of messengers with news of more loss, more emptiness. One day, I hoped my mind would not go to the worst of news first.

As the afternoon slowly faded into evening, the scents of the white flowers emerged, the blooms glowing in the dusk, holding the light in their curved petals. The thrush sang its evensong, the liquid notes settling around me like soft dew falling. Even in the house, the noise of the men was tamped by the advent of night. Surely many of them had drunk themselves into a stupor and now lay snoring by the hearth.

It reached that soft half-light, neither day nor night, which we treasure in the summer, and shadows bloomed around me in the darkening garden. I walked to the house, passing by the open windows of the hall.

"'Od's Blood, Will, I have seen some fearsome sights in war, but to see the tragedy in the city today."

It was Oliver's voice, hushed, drifting through the gloaming. I paused to hear more.

Will's response was choked.

"'Tis one thing to face a man across a battlefield with death on his shoulder, knowing that it is his end or yours. 'Tis another to see a man, mad with grief, trying to breathe life into his dead wife and children."

"This evil scourge strikes swift. Men sleep with their wife by their side. Children are safe in bed. He awakes, his woman lifeless, children dying, servants gone, house boarded up and no escape." Oliver's voice was so low I could barely catch his words.

"Shuttering prevents the spread of the vapors. Should we purchase plague masks, Oliver?"

"The merchants are no longer open. They have fled; physicians too. The town is dwelt in by ghosts." His voice rose. "For the love of Christ, in all my years, I have never seen anything like it."

"'Struth, the playhouses are closed. Even the Southwark whores are locked up. I did not expect a silent London—except citizens' cries begging for release from quarantined houses."

"Aye, it'll be a long summer. We can only rely on ourselves. Those left in the city will not help. We need to organize labor for the harvest, check stores, prepare to survive in isolation. You'll stay, Will?"

"I have nowhere else to go. If I can be of use here, then put me to work."

One of them reached out to pull the window closed, as if to shut out the evil humors of the night. Pressed against the plaster walls of the old house, I drew strength from its uneven surface, still warm from the setting sun. The manor had witnessed plagues before and withstood them all. I prayed fiercely that it would protect us from this summer of death.

From that night on, the plague days bound our lives, one blurring into another. We were imprisoned, helpless, waiting for the tide of contagion to lap at our door and recede again. I was forbidden to leave the house and its lands, and even my gardens offered little respite. The Thames delivered to our banks carcasses of all kinds, indiscriminate in death between cats and dogs, culled to halt the disease spread, and babes and children who had slipped unnoticed from the death carts. To the east, a pall of thick smoke landmarked the city. The rising sun turned the air around us an unnatural orange, as those who remained lit fires day and night in the hope of burning away the contagion.

Our sentence was measured by the numbers of dead declared by the plague masters in London. While Barbara spent her days fussing over her clothes, making our poor sewing maid pull apart and re-stitch bodices and sleeves till her eyes popped from her head, I lost myself in my writing and recipes. Now that the prospect of the plague stealing into our home terrified Aunt Joan, she encouraged me to brew my concoctions. I spent hours in the stillroom, and more in the solar, writing down all I found.

Mallow and nettles to burst the abscesses, rosemary to strew on the floors instead of the rushes, all I collected in my stillroom, fierce in my acquisition to keep the pestilence at bay. No charnel pit did I want dug in Battersey, no communal burial for our servants, our family. The bells tolled the death knells across the river, and each day, I waited and watched, the sun rising and setting upon the city of death.

Will's presence shifted Joan's attention from me, for she and Barbara found distraction in the presence of a handsome man with his stories of adventure and foreign shores. Their interest cooled when Joan discovered that his wealth depended on privateering rather than inheritance. She redefined him as a poor but useful relation, and although Barbara continued to practice her arsenal of flirtations on him, it was apparent that she viewed him as a butt on which to practice her skills rather than a real quarry. At the same time, he really had little patience for her and regarded her as a passing amusement. He preferred to spend his hours outside or playing tables with me. I could see it annoyed Barbara tremendously when he chose me over her.

Anonymous lives tallied our freedom, and as the autumn winds cooled the heat of summer, we waited for the death toll to decrease. Each week, Oliver or Will ventured to White Hall to read the broadsheets and return with the latest news. As autumn crept to winter, and I thought I would go mad with the diminishing daylight hours bringing further enclosure, we sank into brief days and endless nights.

At last, Will rode back with the news that the deaths had reduced to less than thirty souls within the city walls in a week and that the king had authorized a license to open the theaters again. Our Christmas celebration in 1603 was the quietest ever. As the year turned and the solstice marked the sun's dominance, we began to believe that the worst was behind us. Surely the new king would ascend with the coming year and bring us hope again.

3

My dearest Lucy,

Praise God you have survived the plague year unharmed, for I write to you with joy in my heart. Our brother John is to be married to Anne Leighton this July, and we are all to attend the wedding. Lord Zouche, a dear friend of Anne's father, will host from his mansion in Hackney, just a day's ride from Battersey. Now she is twelve years of age and achieved her maturity, Anne's father is eager for her to wed John immediately. This contagion has reaffirmed frail mortality to all men around. I believe Sir Thomas does not want John to slip through his fingers as did his other ward, our brother Walter.

John has told us that Anne is a very sweet and loving maiden, modest, kind, and fair of face. He fancies himself in love with her, and although she is two years younger than you, I believe she will be a welcome friend. Perhaps even Aunt Joan will be happy now that such an influential family joins with ours, for Anne's mother was a cousin of Queen Elizabeth. Make haste to prepare for our reunion, sweet Lucy, for although it has been many years since your sisters have seen you, I am sure we will come together as a family once more—even Barbara.

Your loving sister Eleanor
2ⁿᵈ May 1604

Will was commanded to accompany Barbara and me Lord Zouche's house in Hackney while Joan supervised the cart of chests and household belongings she deemed critical to bring with us. And there were was much to look to, for my uncle had been the first to bring the news to King James of the Irish defeat, and he was rewarded richly. Flush with coin, Barbara and Joan reveled in the stream of dressmakers that made their way to our door and the craftsmen who tidied the appearance of the old manor house.

"Our crumbling old home is like an elderly bride, Will," I whispered to him as he helped me mount my mare.

"How so, sweeting?"

"It's tricked in fancies, like mutton dressed as lamb. Just to distract the groom from looking beneath her skirts."

Will snorted with laughter and patted my horse's neck to cover his amusement. He looked especially fine this morning, his handsome figure enhanced by the Flemish lace at his throat and the close cut of his black leather travel jerkin.

"Your gown is almost becoming. For once, you might be mistaken as one who would uphold the pedigree of our family." Barbara's words, hissed under her breath, were intended for my ear alone, as they were so often.

"You should know, for our pedigree has bred many fine bitches." The prospect of leaving gave freedom to my tongue.

"And runts, dear sister. Do not forget your place in the litter." Barbara stepped away before I could answer.

"Two sisters, ready to explore the world. And a more beautiful sight I have yet to see. It is my privilege to escort both of you. My lady Barbara, let me help you . . ."

I watched as Barbara flirted with Will as he helped her mount her horse. She spent a good deal of time fussing over her riding habit and arranging her skirts while he stood holding her reins, his hand on his hip, foot tapping. Finally, she settled in her saddle, and as he turned to check my mare's girth, his eyes softened.

"Are you ready for your journey?" he asked, as if he knew the significance I placed on the day.

I drew myself up straighter in my new gown and hood.

"Yes. I shall be curious to see the city and to be reunited with my sisters."

Will placed his hand over mine and squeezed it softly.

"And they will not recognize the babe of the family grown into a beautiful young woman." His compliment warmed my heart. "I'm here if you need me," he continued softly. "Don't be hesitant to seek me out if the family and the festivities become too much for you."

Blessed Will. Since his arrival with Oliver, we had become close. He knew my limited tolerance for frivolities and that, on occasion, I just needed time alone with my book or in my gardens.

With a jingle of harnesses, we set off. As we left the manor house behind, I did not look back, only forward to the lane that led to the London highway.

Our route to Hackney could take us two ways: either be rowed downriver or make our way over the bridge. We begged Will to take us through the city from the bridge, for we wanted to experience London in all its fullness, and so that was our path. We traveled eastward through the lanes along the riverbank, under canopies of tall beech trees and brushing scented hedgerows of climbing roses and blackberry blossom.

We soon joined a noisy crowd of travelers streaming to the crossing. I had not seen such a variety of people together all at once, and I relished the clatter of shouting and laughing, cartwheels creaking and stray dogs yelping as they fought among the hooves of the horses and oxen. The road appeared chaotic, pulsing with life, and a spirit surged within me, suppressed for so long I did not know it existed. Barbara held her head high and ignored the commoners, but I looked into every weathered countryman's face and smiled, joyous to share their day.

As we skirted the Lambeth marshes, Westminster appeared across the river, spires gleaming in the rising sun, and Will pointed out the Palace of White Hall, sited as its own city. Buildings of all different complexions subsisted cheek by jowl on every inch of land. I feared they would tumble into the river such were they jostling for space. Jetties reached out into the river, where canopied barges flying heraldic flags were secured so closely that one might walk from boat to boat, so many were moored together.

"The palace." Barbara reined her horse, ignoring the people behind her on foot who were forced to stop. "Joan and I are to visit as soon as we are done with John's wedding."

"You have not mentioned this before, Barbara." Will's voice was questioning. "Oliver did not inform me of a change in our travel."

"It is not in your plans." Barbara turned her shoulder to Will and looked across the river. "But it is in mine."

"It is my responsibility to escort you, and I have no such orders from Oliver."

"You can take your orders from me, for I am informing you that after the wedding I will be at the palace with my aunt, and whether it is your business or not is up to you."

Will shrugged. "Have it your way."

"Oh, I always do." She spurred on her horse and rode forward.

"I should like to see the palace too, one day, Will. It appears as though from a fairy tale, and I hear the gardens are beautiful." I looked to the soaring spires, the colorful pennants fluttering in the breeze.

Will's frown subsided as he turned to smile at me, his eyes crinkling with amusement.

"Know what you wish for, Lucy, for all is not as it seems. I swear 'tis like the worst tenements in St. Dunstan's and a commotion to challenge Bedlam," he replied, nodding his head over the water. "Each one of those apartments houses a lord or the queen's maids of honor or an earl and his retinue—and each is so crowded and cramped they squabble like fishwives and disturb each other all the day long."

I laughed at the thought of the most important people in the country fighting like apprentices and looked again at the crowded buildings. Will turned his horse to keep pace with Barbara, and I fell in beside him.

"Oliver will take you there when the occasion is right," Will promised. "He spends much time at court now. Long ago, when the old queen was in her prime, your uncle was one of her favored courtiers, as were many others who fought with him in Ireland. Although their beards are now longer and grayer, they have not forgotten their courtly ways."

"Is that when he killed the man in a duel?"

"Yes. A poor outcome to a night's gambling. He had to flee the country then, for even the queen did not take lightly to her favorites fighting each other, and some were too quick with their rapiers when trawling the taverns." Will kicked his horse forward, for Barbara was not waiting for us. "He soldiered on the Continent for many years until Lord Essex helped him attain his pardon, and he returned to serve the queen again. It was said their reunion at White Hall was a touching one, for she never forgot a trusted courtier. She rewarded him with his commissions in Ireland."

I gazed back at the palace buildings, now softened by a glistening haze rising from the Thames. No longer did they appear a crowded tenement, but a promised city, swathed in silver and touched by gold, at the center of which beat the royal heart of England. Will said the gilding of beauty concealed the squalor of circumstance, but like so many others before me, I was entranced by the mystery of majesty.

"Keep your eyes down and look to the road in front of you," Will's sudden command was suggestive of a man leading an army, not escorting his cousins to a wedding. Startled, I glanced at Barbara, who shrugged her shoulders and ducked her head.

Obediently I did the same but was quickly distracted by the people around me, who were gesturing to the top of a large tower that formed the bridge gate. I followed their pointing fingers to a hodgepodge of pikes jutting from the ramparts, and a foul stench wafted to me, no doubt heightened by the warming sun. A tremor ran through me, and my stomach turned over, but I could not avert my eyes quickly enough from the rotting flesh and crow-pecked eye sockets, the gaping mouths and straggling hair. The pikes displayed heads of men, traitors executed and impaled to pay warning to those who dared to subvert the king.

"'Struth, Lucy, I told you to keep your eyes away," said Will, clearly exasperated I paid no heed to him. "This is not a sight to greet you to London."

He seized my mare's harness and pulled me closer to him while at the same time shouting at those in our way to clear our path. Such was his command that they quickly complied. I was not a stranger to death, and he did not need to protect me from the knowledge of our inevitable ends, but it was sobering to see the results of executions so near. I knew I would not soon forget the grisly welcome to the city.

We left the south side of the river, where the theaters, cock pits, and bull baiting were free from the laws of the City.

"This is the Southwark Gate," Will shouted, his voice lost over the clamor of the crowds as we were forced into a congested narrow passage at the foot of the bridge. "Stay close, for there are more than traitors' heads to unnerve you now. We are entering the streets of London, and you must keep your wits about you."

The avenue narrowed as we pushed our way onto the bridge with houses three or four floors tall crowded tighter than any village street I had ever seen. Level with my eyes were shops and services, oyster sellers and fishmongers with their catch dangling from poles over the water, while above were chambers. Over my head, ornate signs of all shapes and designs advertised the goods sold within, the buildings so densely packed that I scarce knew where the land ended and the bridge began. I could no longer hear Will's commands, for the noise of the river itself was a roar. Through a gap in the buildings, I glimpsed a churning waterwheel, and turbulent river currents swirled around the pontoons, frothing the brown water. This Thames was not my indolent companion that lapped the banks of Battersey.

"Stay close and do not stop," Will repeated over his shoulder, his mount clearing a path through the throng.

Barbara ignored him, letting her horse drop back as she peered into merchants' windows on either side of her.

"Barbara, come, we have to keep up with Will," I called to her, anxious that she should fall behind.

"He can wait." She allowed more people to come between us as she dallied, her horse now sidestepping as she pulled it on a tight rein.

"God's Blood, Barbara, do you want to end as the victim to a cutpurse or worse?" Will turned his horse tightly and grabbed her reins, yanking her horse to ride alongside him, his fine horsemanship challenged by Barbara's obstinacy and the crowds around us. She ignored him and continued to gaze at the vendors and their wares while I tagged along behind them.

Crossing through Nonsuch House, we clattered over the drawbridge and rode into the City of London. Will released Barbara's horse and led us again, shaking his head.

A piercing shriek made my mare shy, and I struggled to keep her steady. 'Twas naught but a woman selling milk, her cry a way of attracting attention to her wares. Next to her, another sold strawberries in little legged baskets to protect them from the street dust. She had a different cry. Blending with pealing church bells and the barking of stray dogs, the noises of London crashed over me like a summer thunderstorm. But it was exciting, and I embraced the chaos, ready to join the adventures that surrounded me.

As we rode through the narrow streets, we encountered grim memorials of the plague. Some doors were still daubed with a thick oil-painted red cross, and others boarded, no one left to pull the imprisoning wood away and release the ghosts inside. Yet even amidst the signs of death, London teemed with life. The noise reverberated as we drew close to Bishops Gate, where the hammering of the pewter-makers in their factories deafened us. Eventually, we passed through the city wall and rode across the Spital Fields, on the last part of our journey to Lord Zouche and our waiting family.

"How much farther, Will?" I asked, my throat dry with dust.

"Not far. We have just to reach the church tower ahead. Lord Zouche's house stands right by it. Are you feeling ill, Lucy?" Will's voice was soft, but Barbara heard him.

"She looks completely disarrayed." My sister stroked a few strands of hair loosened from her cap while smoothing a wrinkle in her fine leather riding gloves. I felt even more at a disadvantage than usual in her company.

"You look fine," Will assured me kindly. "Mind your tongue, Barbara, for you are so sharp you may cut yourself."

"And you are so tedious you would dull my wits," she retorted and again spurred her horse forward, leaving Will next to me, his face like thunder.

I sighed. The prospect of a reunion with my family was overshadowed by the unpredictability of Barbara's temperament and the havoc she always seemed to enjoy creating around her.

"But you're both so beautiful," blurted Jane, and we all laughed as she blushed and looked uncomfortable.

"You are too, Jane," responded Barbara graciously, although I knew her voice well enough to know that she was appraising our sister and found her wanting.

"We are all beautiful today, for the joy of reunion is illuminating all of us." This was Katherine, the oldest of us, and her reassurance earned a grateful smile from Jane.

As is my way, I stood a little aside from the circle of people in the hall of Lord Zouche's house. After the excitement of our journey, the rich wood paneling, tapestries, and beautifully carved furniture soothed my eyes. Tall windows let in the sunshine, and through the panes lay a glorious garden, colorful with summer flowers, and yet with hues and shapes that I could not easily identify.

I found the opulence overwhelming while also feeling a little shy encountering my newly reunited family. Barbara quickly became the center of attention, as is her gift, drawing all eyes upon her. My sisters surrounded her and hung on her words as she recounted our journey from Battersey.

"Of course, Lucy was terrified when we crossed into the City." Barbara was warming up to her usual theme. "But I knew I would simply steal Will's sword and cut off the hand of any cutpurse who threatened me!"

There was a gasp from my sisters until they realized Barbara's dramatics were in jest.

I shrugged, for to counter her words was a useless endeavor.

"Welcome, my sweet sister. I have prayed for you every day since we parted and have longed for this moment to arrive." Eleanor's soft whisper lay beneath Barbara's chatter but clear enough for me to hear the kindness in her voice.

Eleanor clasped my hand, drawing me into the circle, and my heart opened to these women whose soft arms embraced me and scented cheeks pressed to mine. I did not know how much I was starved of affection until embraced by their warm greeting, filling me with joy and gratitude. It was as though I had been in a desert and discovered a holy well of fresh water that sustained my soul and rejuvenated my spirit. I could scarce believe I belonged with them.

Eleanor's oval face had a stillness, a depth to it that entranced me, and her soft dark eyes were kind, looking deep into mine.

"I have longed so for this moment." I felt a lump in my throat and fought to control my childish emotions. A recognition passed between us. Although Barbara divided us in age, there existed no such amity with her as I felt with Eleanor.

She smiled. "My sweet little sister. How you have grown! It has been too long since we last met. You are no longer a youngling."

"My lady." Arriving at my side, Will swept a deep bow and stood tall, his soldier's bearing endowing him a silent strength. "I am honored to make your acquaintance. Will St.John, from Fonmon. I have heard much about my Wiltshire cousins, but I did not expect such a lovely gathering of beauty."

"Why, Will, such formality." I laughed at my friend and pinched his arm.

"Thank you, sir." Eleanor glanced down, her cheeks suddenly rosy. "You are most welcome here. I am Eleanor, Lucy's sister."

"Will, Eleanor saved me from going mad, I declare." I laughed and reached for both of their hands. "She has written to me every month since I can remember. Perhaps later we can play a game of backgammon together."

"Perhaps." Will let go of my hand and held out his arm. "Mistress Eleanor, may I ask you to show me the gardens? I am a little stiff from the ride, and I would welcome stretching my legs."

"You, Will? But you ride all the . . ." My words were already lost, for with a shy smile, Eleanor took his arm, and they walked away. A pang pierced my heart. As I turned, I bumped into Barbara.

"It appears you have lost your swain, dear Lucy," she whispered softly. "Not to worry, for I am sure we have plenty of other poor relations from which you could choose."

She strolled from my side and tucked her arm in Katherine's, saying something that caused them both to laugh aloud. I was left standing by myself, and I pretended to be busy looking at the gardens through the fine glazing. It didn't help that I saw Will and Eleanor walking slowly through the knot garden.

Presently, Katherine beckoned to a waiting woman standing a respectful distance away.

"Barbara, Lucy, you must rest, both of you, for tonight we celebrate with a banquet in John and Anne's honor. Lord Zouche is presently attending the funeral of the Earl of Oxford, who rather inconveniently chose to die here in Hackney several days ago."

Katherine sniffed her pomander as if the aroma of death still lingered. "We are just relieved that the burial is this evening and not in two days. It would not have been an auspicious beginning to their marriage to have that dissolute man lying in church for viewing hours before the ceremony. He has caused consternation enough to Anne's family without disturbing her wedding day too."

Katherine's frank words surprised me. I recognized in her tone a similar peevishness that tainted Aunt Joan's frequent observations about the careless selfishness of the aristocrats whose society she longed to enter.

"Who else attends the funeral?" Barbara's attention focused on Katherine upon hearing of the banquet.

"Others from Lord Zouche's circle of friends. As a Privy Counselor, he is intimate with many at court."

"It is a pity the Earl of Oxford did not live to attend our banquet," Barbara responded. "Perhaps others will come."

"His colleague, the Earl of Lincoln, remains here. I believe he may join us." I heard in Katherine's voice a kindred ambition to Aunt Joan's.

"Good." Barbara smoothed her gown as she was wont to do when planning her next move. "I shall dress accordingly."

"He is rather a disreputable and notorious man, Barbara. I would caution you—"

"I can manage myself, thank you." Barbara turned away, leaving Katherine in mid-sentence.

My good humor drained from me, overwhelmed by the noisy chatter of my sisters and Barbara's rudeness. Jane took my hand and led me up the grand staircase, wide enough for us to walk abreast, its balusters most curiously carved with glorious flowers and fruits.

"Lord Zouche has many influential friends, including the Earls of Oxford and Lincoln," she explained as we walked together to our shared chamber through a long gallery lined with portraits and tapestries.

Bowls of flowers stood on plinths along the way, and I listened with half an ear to Jane as I tried to identify colorful blooms which I had not seen before in any English garden.

"Although neither is a friend of Anne's father, for Oxford tried hard to supplant him at his post as Governor of Guernsey and created another enemy while so doing." She smiled as she watched me struggling to absorb more information about my family. "Now, to rest with you, and you'll be refreshed for the celebrations."

My head swam with all the new people that had suddenly joined my life. I gratefully allowed the maid to help me out of my traveling gown. After swabbing my face and hands with a lavender-scented napkin, I lay down to rest on the sumptuous bed.

4

I have been given this recipe by the maid who attends us, for here at Lord Zouche's, there is much attention given to the furtherance of beauty. The previous queen, my kinswoman, (as I have been told to refer to her), set a great fashion for white skin, and it is one I should copy.

To make the skin white . . .

Steep a manchett for two hours in milk, then boyle in an hour. Then boyle more with the following things—a quarter a pound of bitter almonds, white poppy seeds, half a dram of camphor, an ounce of spermaceti, one dram of alum. Beat with the yolk of a new layd egg and let it just boyle. Rub all in your hands and face with as much as a walnut of it very hard and well and wash them with a little water after and wipe them.

Lucy St.John
Her Recipe Book

As I cautiously descended the sweeping staircase, a little unsteady in the new turquoise silk heels that Oliver insisted Joan purchase for me, the tinkling of a harpsichord drifted from below. I strained to hear the beautiful music, rarely heard at Battersey, but conversation and laughter drowned the chords. I reached for Eleanor's hand, my heart racing a little faster. The new silver-threaded satin bodice squeezed my chest, and I could not take a deep breath. I fiddled with the lace at the neckline.

"Don't be anxious," she smiled as she squeezed my hand reassuringly. "You look beautiful, Lucy, a true court lady."

"I have not dressed like this nor conversed with courtiers." I swallowed. "I'm not sure what to say."

"Observe others, and remember from whence you come. When Queen Elizabeth visited us at Lydiard and knighted our father, recall she dandled you on her lap for the sake of our shared ancestry. You have more royal blood in your veins than most of these upstarts." Eleanor's sloe-dark eyes were merry, twinkling at me. "Besides, they are usually so impressed with themselves that you won't have to say much. Just nod and smile and ask the occasional question of them. Their favorite topics are either themselves or the king. They won't expect more."

Unlike the rooms of Battersey Manor, which were low ceilinged, blackened with the smoke of many generations, the hall at Lord Zouche's was substantial. Its ornate wooden beams were lost in the height of three floors, and the minstrel's gallery was packed with musicians. Finely woven tapestries and bright carpets, weaponry, and portraits crowded the walls, competing with ornately dressed people gathered on the black-and-white tiled floor. Jeweled hairpieces shone in the late afternoon sunlight, and gauzy ruffs adorned the necks of many of the women, each costume piece outdoing the other in fantastic height and width.

At first, I could not distinguish anyone, such was the assault on my senses of the numbers assembled, but soon I recognized Katherine and Jane. With Eleanor at my side, I summoned the courage to walk the length of the room and take a spot by the tall windows. Few turned to look at me, and even fewer spoke. Within a short while, I relaxed enough to view those around me, chattering and exclaiming in the way of a roomful of exotic birds. Between the colorful gardens and lavish gowns, my senses were alive as they had never been at Battersey.

"You are beautiful, Lucy." Will appeared beside us and bent over my hand, kissing it softly.

I almost laughed, for here was my friend dressed as a gallant, but I did not spoil the moment and happily played his game.

"My thanks, sir," I replied, admiring his burgundy velvet doublet and pristine white lawn shirt. His lace falling collar was embellished with black work, the quality of which I had not seen before now. "You look remarkably well put together."

He laughed. "Hush, I have a reputation to maintain." He turned to Eleanor and held out his arm. "Would you care to promenade?"

Eleanor blushed. "Thank you, Cousin, I would be—"

A ripple of exclamations across the room interrupted her, and we looked up. Barbara stood on the grand stairs, framed by the dark oak paneling and lit by the sun's rays. One by one, the guests turned to look at her. I knew she had planned this precisely, for her dress was magnificent, square cut low in the décolleté style. I had been banned from her fittings; now, seeing the ornate green silk gown, clustered with peach and navy rosettes and with a great farthingale, I could sense her allure. She paused, receiving the room's admiration, but not acknowledging one man over the other. A few closer to her bowed deeply, and after she descended the stairs, a cluster of courtiers surrounded her.

"Is she always like that?" whispered Eleanor. "I would say she cares little for the sumptuary laws."

"She hasn't had much opportunity to appear this way, but it does not surprise me." I was mixed 'tween annoyance and relief, believing that she would leave me alone now that she had a more important audience to tease.

"I would say she has made her point." Will's voice crackled with sarcasm, and Eleanor and I smiled at each other.

"This must be my little sister Lucy! How she has grown—quite a beauty, I would say!"

I turned swiftly at the sound of a man's voice, his tone prompting a memory long lost in solitude.

"John!" I flew into his arms and felt a welcome hug in return. We stood linked in each other's arms, the room around us fading into the background.

"How very touching. An embrace for me too, Brother?"

In the few moments we spent together, Barbara appeared at our side.

"Why, of course . . . if I can make my way through the thicket of suitors you appear to have conquered already."

Barbara laughed, her pitch low and musical.

"None as handsome as you, John, for I can see why Sir Thomas is so eager to marry you to his little daughter."

Her eyes swept across the room and lighted on Lord Zouche, who was with a group of people across the hall.

"Ah. It appears our host is speaking with her now. Introduce me, dear John, so I might make the acquaintance of my future sister and her family. I hear they have a similar connection to the queen as we do, only closer in blood and more recent. How very interesting."

She took his arm and guided him across the hall.

Presently, Lord Zouche led Anne into dinner, and we followed, joined by Anne's parents, Sir Thomas and Lady Elizabeth Leighton, and the remainder of the honored guests. Barbara found a way to seat herself next to the Earl of Lincoln, with Joan watching closely from next to me, across the board. Soon he was chuckling at Barbara's words and leaning closer to hear her, for he was an old man with a deafness in his ear. Her elaborate preparations and revealing dress were not wasted on her first court conquest.

The lingering July day brought a soft light to the faces around the table, and the golden sun rays through the paned windows illuminated the joy of those gathered. For me, the wedding signified more than a joining of two houses and a reconciliation; it also ended a sad time of separation and loneliness. Although we were strangers to each other, the blood bonds that tied us had remained strong in our isolation.

My handsome brother John sat at the head of the board, his doublet a dove-gray velvet, stitched with silver thread, and a fine lace collar framing his face. A jaunty gold-and-pearl earring gleamed in the setting sun, and his cheeks grew rosy as the night progressed and the wine flowed. Anne sat at his side, a composed young girl, dignified beyond her years. She presented such a sweet face and soft demeanor that I loved her already, my heart opening to my newly reunited family. And yet despite her quiet countenance, when she whispered a few words to John, I could see he paid attention and nodded his agreement.

Tapping his goblet, John called for silence around the table, and we gradually stopped our chattering.

"Anne and I have an announcement." His voice rose, his arm around Anne as he surveyed us. "I have decided that as soon as we are wed, we will reside at Lydiard. And all of my sisters shall return with us. You shall all be brought home."

There was a silence as we heard John's words and then an outbreak of excited talk. Joy constricted my heart, which beat so rapidly that I thought I would faint, and my hand clutched the stem of my glass, the decoration pressing into my fingers. I took a deep draught of the spiced wine to steady my racing heart. My Lydiard, my talisman. I would be home in my special place and no longer under the jealous confinement of Aunt Joan.

I lifted my eyes and met Anne's calm gaze across the table. She smiled sweetly at me and lifted her glass to me in a silent toast. I returned her smile and gesture.

"Thank you," I mouthed silently. She nodded, and then John distracted her attention, kissing her pale cheek and calling for more wine, his excitement evident in his first important decision as head of the household.

"Now we all rot in the country and become bumpkins as well as orphans?" Barbara's sulky voice, directed at Joan, could not be heard by John. The deaf old earl at her side mumbled over his beef. It did not surprise me that Barbara's thoughts would turn to herself and her future rather than the happiness of being reunited with her sisters.

"Do not fret, my dear, for I shall be sure that Oliver does not forget his duty in finding a fitting match for you. There is time; you are but sixteen."

I listened quietly. Joan continued in a fierce whisper.

"This is but the first step in a prosperous ascent for our family, and one that will pay handsomely in our future prospects. Oliver has the king's ear now, and I shall ensure he fills it with our requests. Anne's father has the connections at court. I fancy a knighthood for John and a title to follow. It will improve our standing and restore John to his rightful rank."

"And make me the sister of a more important man." The unconcealed ambition in Barbara's voice revealed no emotion.

"Of course. I will make sure that Oliver seeks the most advantageous matches for his nieces. And you, my dear, will be the jewel in the crown, for you know how to display your talents to their best."

I sickened to hear this and glowered at Joan and Barbara, who stared, not ashamed of their overt ambition.

"I will marry for love," I said clearly. "You will not force me to make an arrangement."

Barbara burst out laughing. "You think you will have a choice?"

"You will obey your uncle's wishes." Joan's eyes were narrowed, and her voice was low.

"I would rather never marry than not wed the man I love." The confidence of my new position in a larger family than just Joan and Barbara gave me courage to speak up.

"We shall see." Joan dismissed the conversation and leaned over to Barbara again, whispering something to her that prompted her to adjust the neckline of her bodice. In response, she leaned over and murmured to the earl, causing him to abruptly cease his conversation with Sir Thomas and turn his attention to her. I watched her charm at work, unobserved, for I was no more important to her than a moth to a candle.

I made Anne a wreath of rosemary and roses for her wedding day and found myself in the Garden of Eden as I walked through Lord Zouche's estate to find the perfect blooms. Lord Zouche had been to Constantinople in his youth, and so inspired was he by the healing properties of the gardens of those fruitful lands that he brought back ideas and plants that none in England had ever seen before.

I was surrounded by trees I could not recognize, and fragrant white lilies that grew in abundance amongst their shady roots. Exotic blooms rooted in the cool English soil and brought a fierce vivacity to the soft light, as though they remembered their blazing Moorish sun. I wished that Donna Anna could be with me, to explain the curious plants and tell me their uses. I stopped by one tree, its fruit a rosy red and weighing down the slender branches. I reached out and touched the glossy skin.

"Pomegranates, the Greek apple of love. They appear in the stories of Persephone and Aphrodite and have been revered through the ages." The old man appeared by my side while I gazed at the unknown tree. He spoke with a strong accent, brusque in his speech, but his clothes were those of a gentleman.

35

"I would lead thee, and bring thee into my mother's house, who would instruct me: I would cause thee to drink of spiced wine of the juice of my pomegranate." I responded with one of my favorite verses from the Song of Solomon. Perhaps not the most appropriate of quotations, but I felt he would understand the reference.

His eyebrows rose, and he peered deeply into my face. I stepped back slightly, his intense gaze a little unnerving.

"Now who are you? And why are you so interested in my garden?"

"I am Lucy, John's sister." He made me feel as though I was a child in trouble. I lifted my chin and spoke clearly, for I had committed no offense. "I love plants, and I wish I knew all that these could do, for I would bring them back to my garden and use them for my physicks."

"Hmm. And you wish to treat the sick with your crops?"

"I do. Donna Anna says I have a feel for the gifts of nature, and I helped with the plague potions this past winter. I believe it kept the infection away from our family."

"And what did you use in your infusions?" His questions came quickly, but I did not take offense at his abruptness, for his voice was melodious.

"The thistle, carduus, and Indian snakeweed, poppies and hartshorn."

"And why those?"

"They are all to clear the blood and the bile. I thought if I made a concentration of leaves that did the same but came from different families, they might work better in concert."

"Hmm."

He beckoned me to a knot garden that was a few feet away. Crouching down, he snared the rosemary between his fingers to closer examine the glossy foliage.

"Look intently at each plant, study the leaves, the stalk, the flower, the seed. Do not consider plants just for medical uses. Look where they originate in shape and form. Therein lies the knowledge of how to unlock their secrets and make your physicks. Observe the botany, and you will find the virtues."

With that, he gave a short bow and stumped off without a backward glance. He paused only to nip the head of a rose bloom that had passed its prime, shaking his head as he did so.

36

There are occasions in your life journey when you encounter a person who will have such a profound influence that they shape your thoughts and remain there to converse, even when miles apart or no longer of this earth. Matthias L'Obel became such an inspiration. . For the next week, I absorbed his fascination with plants and their origins, their species and their indications, following him from dawn to dusk as he strode Lord Zouche's gardens. I must confess that John and Anne's wedding was lovely, the feasts and entertainment were amusing, but they remain in memory to me now a distraction from my real joy of that week, for my eyes and my heart were absorbed in learning as much as I could from Dr. L'Obel.

For twenty years, he and Lord Zouche had created a garden the likes of which none had seen before. And when the new king came to the throne, he appointed Dr. L'Obel his physician because of his skills in medications and physicks.

During the precious daylight hours that he supervised Lord Zouche's army of gardeners, marching from tree to bush, I followed at his side, breathless with his energy, hot and flushed from the blazing summer sun. At first, he had little time for me and barely spoke as I trailed in his footsteps. I did not falter though, and over the next precious days, he became used to my shadow and tossed out pieces of learning as if scattering grain to a hen. His method was capricious, but I learned—how I learned—to know each plant, its virtues, and its origin. At the end of each day, before the night drew in, I scribbled my notes in my journal and kept record of all that he had told me so I would not forget the precious knowledge he had imparted to me. And while Barbara and my sisters played music and danced and flirted with the titled visitors that Lord Zouche invited to his home, I sat apart and filled my book with drawings and notes.

Sir Thomas, Anne's father, encouraged me, for he was a kind man and one who valued learning, whether in boys or girls. I found a quiet window seat in Lord Zouche's study and carefully read Dr. L'Obel's book on species of plants while Sir Thomas sat at his correspondence. Every so often, I would catch him looking at me.

"You have such an air of Walter about you," he said softly, his expression hard to read.

I put down the book and listened. I knew that he had loved my brother as his own son.

"When Walter drowned, I thought I would not survive the sorrow and the burden of his death." He continued, speaking almost to himself, as if I were a ghost. "For many, many nights, I could sleep but brokenly. His image visited me, and I relived his last moments. At any time of the day or night, he haunted my mind, and I grieved, wretched with the futility of the drowning, counting the lost moments I had to prevent his death." He took a shuddering breath, and I waited quietly for him to continue. "And yet, I know the decisions were those that any man would have made, and those things we say in the moment, we cannot predict the effect they have on the future. I agreed he could join our expedition, and I agreed he could swim in the sea with his tutor and the other boys. I cautioned that he should be careful of the currents, and then I rested in my tent, for I was tired." He dropped his head into his hands, his voice muffled. "My hour of sleep cost him his life, for I would have prevented his drowning if I had accompanied them."

I rose from the window seat and crossed to the desk, putting my arms around Sir Thomas and holding him.

"You must not blame yourself, for destiny led to his death, and the Lord wanted Walter at his side," I said. "And Walter himself would not wish you to carry this burden with you through your life. Remember the Lord's words—forgive yourself just as you have forgiven those who tried but failed to rescue him."

Sir Thomas smiled and stroked my hair.

"You are a kind soul, Lucy," he said. "I am glad you have befriended my Anne. She is quiet and needs a friend such as you. Walter would have loved you very much."

"And I him," I replied. "Now tell me of some of his tricks that he played on you and his tutors, for I have heard he was mischievous too."

Sitting back in his chair, his sadness put aside, Sir Thomas began to tell me of life in Castle Cornet, his home in Guernsey, and the larks that Walter and the other boys got up to while in Sir Thomas's care.

His stories were amusing and painted a vivid picture of my brother and the charming island, as much French as English, that the Leightons called their home. Our evening, which began in sorrow, ended in laughter, and I was happy that the power of memories could also bring comfort to Sir Thomas.

The next morning, our last with Lord Zouche, was a scramble of good-byes and promises to see each other in the coming months. Anne stood forlornly in the courtyard, the excitement of the previous weeks ebbing from her as we started to leave.

I ran over to her and clasped her hands in mine.

"I am dreading returning to court, Lucy. My mother will do nothing but criticize me while she plays her silly games of courtly love."

"But she's married, Anne."

"That does not deter this court. Sir Walter Raleigh secreted a love poem in her pocket, and now she thinks all the men are in love with her. I hate it."

Anne was leaving for White Hall, for at twelve years of age, she and John would not consummate their marriage nor live together as man and wife for several years. Her mother detested Guernsey as much as Anne loved it, and she refused to spend time there, preferring the pleasures of the royal court.

"Do not be sad, Sister, for we must see each other again soon."

Tears filled her eyes, and although she did not drop her composure, I could see it cost her great effort to speak.

"It has been as though I have discovered a new family, and yet I lose it again today and return to the unbearable court." A tear overflowed and glistened on her cheek.

"I too have longed for a family and found them again. And I found a new sister in you, Anne, for I feel our friendship is one that I shall hold dear for the rest of my life."

Anne smiled a little through her tears and squeezed my hands.

"We share much, Lucy, and I wish I could travel with you."

"I do too, my sweet Anne, but your mother would not permit you to stay at Lydiard without a chaperone."

She shrugged and smiled poignantly.

"I know. I must obey her, but it pains me to leave you." She held me close and kissed my cheek, and as we drew apart, I watched as she straightened her spine and held her head high. A lifetime of court etiquette protected her dignity as she gathered her composure and walked to be at John's side for a final farewell.

Excited to be returning to Lydiard, I could scarce wait to go to Battersey, pack my books and papers, and leave that sad house. I would depart without a backward glance.

"We shall be at Lydiard by September." Eleanor and I hugged each other good-bye. "It will not be long, and we'll all be together."

Will, who always seemed to be standing by us when we were together, bowed deeply. "It will be my pleasure to escort you. I hope I may see you again."

I turned away, for it was apparent in the way that Eleanor's cheeks colored that it was not me he was talking to. Though today, no jealous thought could dim my excitement, and in truth, I could feel no envy of Eleanor and Will, so evident their enjoyment of each other.

"It will be delightful to be together in our home, to live as a family once more." Katherine smiled as she kissed my cheek.

My heart was so full of anticipation of our future I had hardly noticed Barbara and Joan standing in the corner talking to John, but my eye was drawn to them in spite of the distractions of leaving. They were deep in discussion, and John nodded in agreement.

"It is decided, then," I heard him say.

I glanced quickly at Eleanor, and she shrugged.

Barbara and Joan walked toward us. Although they bore no resemblance physically, there was a shared look of complicity.

"Oliver remains at court, for he has much business to attend to," announced Joan as she drew near. "Barbara and I visit him now at White Hall while you, Lucy, return to Battersey. You have no use at court, and it would be a waste of money bring you." Her obvious pleasure in humiliating me underscored her words. "We have a new position and responsibilities, and it is only right that our home should reflect our stature. I will rebuild Battersey and must develop the plans with the appropriate London craftsmen."

I knew more vitriol had to come from her; I could tell by the way she savored her words. I waited to hear her next statement, her thin lips drawn over yellowing teeth in a triumphant smile. "However, once the construction is underway, I shall stay at Lydiard."

ʃ.

Dearest Anne

I discovered the lost garden at Lydiard today. The land has been sore neglected, for although the stewards have taken care of the farm and the cattle, and the house is in good repair, there has been no woman here to tend the flowers and harvest the herbs. I shall use all that Donna Anna and Dr. L'Obel taught me and bring the land to life. I shall plant medicines and herbs and create walkways and paths and ponds and quiet areas to rest. The gardens are terribly overgrown, but structure is here, blurred by time and forgetfulness. You will love to walk here with John when you take up your life at Lydiard.

The occasion of our return has been marked by much activity. All the county families are coming to call on us, for we are quite a conversation within the great houses of Wiltshire. Six daughters, all eligible, all with dowries, arrived from London, with family at court. We have caused a stir, and suitors are arriving, which Eleanor and I find very amusing. I even heard, when none knew I was in earshot, one visitor say to another that in living memory there were not so many beautiful women found in any family as ours. I also heard say that I was favored above all the rest, but that I do not believe, nor do I care, for these frivolous things do not interest me at all.

Lucy St.John
23rd September 1604
Lydiard Tregoze

Returning to Lydiard, I rediscovered a childhood friend, grown a little older perhaps, with a different perspective, but still familiar, welcoming, comfortable. There was the poignancy of missing my parents in their remembered places, but life's river had taken them away to their own destinies, and we arrived to reclaim Lydiard, our generation now making its mark upon the old house.

John proudly strode the buildings and grounds with the steward to draw his plans for improving the farms, to restore comfort and luxury to the house. Our father had carefully managed the family wealth, maintaining the estate in excellent condition for John to inherit and providing for his six daughters' dowries, to the sum of six hundred pounds each. This great amount was to be bestowed after we achieved the age of twenty-one, providing we married a man who met with Uncle Oliver's approval. He took that responsibility most seriously, and we teased him to look far and wide for suitable bridegrooms for all of us—handsome to fulfill our dreams and well established to meet his.

"Never have there been so many visitors to Lydiard in all its days," he would grumble as carriage, cart, and mount arrived and left, brimming with curious county gentry come to call on us. "I shall be sharpening my sword again to fend off these suitors."

Aunt Joan squatted as a greedy spider in the center of her glistening web, spinning daily with the intent of capturing prey, playing the grand dame and presenting us as tasty bait as she established herself at the center of county society. I found it most tiresome to be constantly paraded before the local gentry, but she preened and prated her way through the visits and became even more unbearable in her demands of my demeanor.

On just such an afternoon, I finally escaped her attention and explored the passageways in the attics of the house. Numerous little doors marked the warren of small rooms that housed the servants. The ancient bones of the old house were revealed in its attics. There were but small windows, set deep into the dormers of the roof. Through the old panes of translucent horn, I could faintly see the church tower, appearing so close I could almost touch it, with rooks alighting on the old stone walls, whirling in the wind as smuts from a bonfire. I shivered slightly—today there were storms, and there was a chill in the air.

Reaching a short flight of steps to another door, a draft of air whistling through the ill-fitting frame, I pushed hard and entered a low-ceilinged room, bare apart from several panels leaning against the wall.

As I walked toward them in the gloom, a portrait of my mother emerged, dressed in her best gown, girdle book at her waist. I knelt on the rough planks and tentatively drew my finger across the dusty frame. Memories flooded back, for this had been painted to celebrate the queen's progress to Lydiard.

An elusive memory returned, and I recalled standing by my mother as we welcomed the queen to Lydiard, watching her from my smallness, for I was not above four years of age. I remember how my mother distracted my fidgets with the girdle book, opening it to the treasures inside, the tiny writing, the minute illustrations. I could smell the tang of lavender captured in the folds of damask gowns—and other odors not so sweet—as the September sun warmed. My father, dignified and dressed in his best, my mother, flushed with pride—or was it the onset of fever, even then?—welcoming Her Gracious Majesty to Lydiard. I believe I remember all this, but perhaps it is all in the telling. For what is memory but the telling of stories, whether to oneself or aloud to another?

Later, I brought John to the garret.

"Lucy, this is a marvel! I am joyful you found the portrait, for I feared our steward had turned it into firewood, such is his zeal for the land and contempt for the finer things in life." John clasped my hand.

"This means much to you, doesn't it, John?"

"When I was with Sir Thomas in Guernsey after Walter died, I never felt so much despair. I had nothing to keep my memories alive. Walter was gone. My sisters were displaced. And Lydiard just a distant far away dream."

"But Sir Thomas was kind, wasn't he?"

"Aye. And fair. And fatherly. But he was not family." John's face tightened. "He cared not for Lydiard or our heritage. He was just ensuring his wardship money was not interrupted by anything happening to me."

"And nothing did happen. And now you're home."

John knelt down in front of the portrait and traced the outline of our mother's face.

"Yes, home. And so are my sisters."

"You should commission a painting of yourself too, John. To commemorate your wedding to Anne. Wear your silver doublet and pearl earring. And hang it next to that of our mother."

He smiled and carefully carried the portrait down from the attic, placing it in the great hall where all could see her watching over us.

I loved the portrait of her, for standing in front of it, I could secretly converse with her and share my joy at being back in our home. During these times, I missed Anne, for we had become great correspondents, and our letters included our shared sadness of losing our mothers—mine to fever, hers to court. We accepted each other as we found our similarities, for we had both brought ourselves up, solitary in an environment that was not of our choosing. An instinctive amity developed where we understood the loneliness and longing that can appear with no warning, adrift from a mother's comfort. Instead, we found each other.

With spring came my wish fulfilled to see Anne again, but not as I would have wanted. In March, her mother died of the sweat, and Sir Thomas decided that the family atmosphere at Lydiard would suit Anne more than isolated with him in the Castle Cornet garrison on Guernsey. Aunt Joan was appointed chaperone for his daughter, and with John away studying at Lincoln's Inn, Anne continued her upbringing with us at Lydiard.

We joyfully reunited. Our lives assumed a rhythm of days that ebbed and flowed with the seasons, marked by the festivals of church and country. Long days of summer turned into fire-lit winter evenings where we gathered each night to play music, sing, and dance with each other. These times were golden, for although Aunt Joan and Barbara continued to exhibit their dislike for me, Eleanor and Anne filled my days with laughter and joy.

"Now, a little cochineal on your lips . . . and a dab more on your cheeks. Kohl for your eyes . . ." Anne stood back and tilted her head. "Hmm. I think I have applied these with great skill and enhanced your natural parts exquisitely, madam."

I pursed my lips and peered into the glass. "A little ceruse for my complexion, perhaps?"

"Ah no, madam. Your skin is as white as a babe's bottom without need of further condiments."

We both burst out laughing, and as Anne stood behind me at the glass, she caught my loose hair and piled it above my head in a simple twist.

"You are beautiful, Lucy, and have matured much since we last met. You may not know it, but the women of White Hall would give much for your unblemished cheeks and sparkling eyes."

"Where did you get those cosmetics, Sister? You look absurd, for there is no skill in the application and no natural beauty to start with." Barbara stood in our chamber door, unheard by us in our game of make-believe.

"They are mine, Barbara, from the finest apothecaries in Cheapside. It is of no business to you what time I spend with your sister."

"It is if she decorates herself as a courtesan. I would counsel a little modesty, my dear, or you will gain quite a reputation."

"And I would counsel to look to yourself before criticizing those around you," Anne shot back. "Your gown is of a fashion that is at least two seasons old, nobody dresses their hair in that style any longer, and your dancing depends much on posturing and little on skill."

Barbara turned and slammed the door behind her. Anne and I held our breath for a moment, our eyes locked in the glass, before letting it out in a loud exhalation. Anne's mouth began to twitch with laughter, and soon we were doubled over with as much relief as joy.

The first of us to marry was, rightly so, Katherine. Her groom came not from Uncle Oliver's careful research, but an acquaintance of John's through his studies at Lincoln's Inn. He brought Giles home one Christmastide. Although his family lived in the county, he chose to stay with us.

"Giles Mompesson, I would have you meet my sisters—Lucy, Eleanor, Katherine, and my wife, Anne." John stepped into the hall at

Lydiard, shaking snow from his cloak. Next to him, a short, swarthy man stood staring at the walls, hung now with fine carpets and the family portraits John so lovingly restored.

"Welcome to Lydiard, Mr. Mompesson." Katherine stepped forward and held out her hand, and the man bent over it and kissed it soundly.

Eleanor and I exchanged swift glances, trying not to giggle.

"'Onored, I am sure, madam," he replied, his educated accent a veneer over a rougher burr.

"And will you be staying with us long, Mr Mompesson?" Eleanor ventured, eyeing his stout form and large traveling trunk.

"As long as John can stand me company." He cleared his throat loudly and looked as though he was about to spit but changed his mind."'E mentioned there was plenty of amusements at Lydiard, and I sees what 'e meant." He swallowed, causing Eleanor to flinch.

"Ah, John. Just what we needed for the festive season, jolly company and welcome guests to enjoy our hospitality!" Katherine threw her arms wide and beckoned both men closer to the roaring fire, her hands waving anxiously to the maid to serve wine.

During the past six months, male company increasingly agitated Katherine. She also spent a great deal of time sighing in front of her mirror, trying new ways to style her hair, pulling it back tightly from her face, thus erasing the fine lines that creased her high forehead.

"Suitor," mouthed Eleanor to me.

"Swain." I responded, causing Eleanor to stifle a laugh. Poor Katherine was feeling her age, and we thought it most funny that she should be inspecting each man who arrived at Lydiard as marriage material.

I found him disconcerting. I struggled to determine his character, for he waxed different with each of us, putting forth a persona to fit that which he appraised most advantageous. His flattery turned Katherine's head, she yet to be betrothed and we younger sisters receiving much attention. He appealed to her, for although they were mismatched physically, he presenting shorter than she and quite dark, they shared a similar character.

Of all my sisters, Katherine displayed the most covetousness, for although Barbara enjoyed the trappings of wealth, she did not interest herself in the money. Katherine counted every penny and always priced and commented on the cost of goods. When Giles returned from his tour of the estate with John, he totaled fully the value of the land and cattle and business opportunities. He made me most uncomfortable, for there were times I caught his eyes on me, as if appraising my worth, and with relief, I welcomed the announcement that he and Katherine were to be wed. I was happy for Katherine too, for I sensed in her a disquiet when I was in hers and Giles's company. She always endeavored to insert herself, as if to distract his calculating eyes from me. Our family did not know his family well, for they were not particularly distinguished, but Katherine wanted him, and Uncle Oliver seemed to consider his prospects fair.

After the excitement of Katherine's wedding, we expected our days would resume the same gentle country rhythm as before. They did for a while, until the invitation that Aunt Joan and Barbara had been waiting for finally arrived. The messenger took a measured pace and rode upon a very fine horse caparisoned in the Suffolk livery of murrey and sea blue.

"Get out of my way; you're blocking my view," Barbara hissed as she elbowed me from the window in her eagerness, adjusting the neckline of her gown and pinching her cheeks to add color.

"'Tis here, 'tis here," whispered Aunt Joan, her voice suppressed with excitement as she peered at the horseman approaching through the sun-dappled beech alley. No back door stable yard entrance for the Countess of Suffolk's messenger, and he rode with arrogance to the front of the house.

We arranged ourselves in the formal paneled parlor and waited to receive him.

"The Countess of Suffolk announces the opening of Charlton Park and the arrival of Lady Suffolk and her family to take up residence this summer." The messenger spoke in a high-pitched, nasal voice, and Anne and I tried not to giggle at his superior airs.

"Yes, yes, of course," burst in Aunt Joan, unable to contain her excitement. The messenger handed Aunt Joan a rolled parchment tied with murrey ribbon and bearing a seal. He bowed and left the room, his haughty shoulders set. Joan broke the seal and unfurled the message, frowning as she formed the words.

"The Lady Suffolk requests the presence of Dame Anne St.John to attend the celebration and wishes to extend to her the hospitality of Charlton Park by lodging with Lady Suffolk in the month of August. The Lady Suffolk," Anne and I looked at each other as Joan stumbled over the words, "furthermore extends this invitation to include Dame Anne St.John's close family and her chaperone."

Barbara snatched the document and perused the lines.

"Charlton Park. Finally, they have finished their construction, and we are invited." She spoke with satisfaction, as if she were granting the favor herself to the Earl and Countess of Suffolk. "It was most fortunate, Cousin Anne, that you are here with us this summer and that the invitation from your cousin extended to our family. You and I shall find much favor among the guests from court."

Anne nodded and smiled faintly at Barbara. Her hand reached for mine in the concealing folds of our dresses, and she squeezed it tightly. Shy Anne did not relish these occasions, and she preferred to be at home occupied with simple daily routines than surrounded by the stiff manners and ornate ceremonies of court.

"We shall all go together and enjoy their hospitality," I said firmly. "Charlton Park is one of the finest new buildings in Wiltshire, and Lady Suffolk spared no expense in the appointments of the structure and the planning of the gardens. I am sure we will be made much welcome."

"Of course, I suppose you have to come." Barbara's tone was icy. "Just be aware of your place, Lucy, and do not put yourself forward in your usual unbecoming way. The county's most influential families will be there along with visitors from court. Do not bring embarrassment to our family."

"I have no interest in being 'forward,' as you say." The heat rose in my cheeks. "I rebuff any attention that is brought upon me, for I have no truck with suitors or their ridiculous posturing."

"That is not how you appeared to Giles," she responded. "We saw how he looked at you to the exclusion of Katherine whenever you entered the room."

"I had no interest in him, none."

"Just mind your place. You are the youngest, and you should heed your elders." She turned to Joan and linked her arm through hers. "Now let us plan our dress, for there will be plentiful entertainments, and I need new gowns."

Later, I sat in the shelter of the warm brick surrounding the walled garden and reflected on Barbara's cruel words, struggling to understand the vehemence behind her tone. Giles's manners did not extend to hiding interest in me before Katherine, through no fault of mine. It saddened me that my sisters should suspect I vied to attract attention when I felt no desire to engage with him. I knew that Eleanor and Anne would not think that way, for they loved Will and John, but I was troubled at the envy of the others as suitors came to call.

I watched a bee, drowsy with nectar, dipping from one bloom to another, taking his fill before moving on to another blossom. Idly, I thought of how we too were as a garden of summer flowers, open to the attention of suitors who called, sampling one sister against another until a choice was made.

6

For the heart breaking . . . take burnt claret wherein put a little bag of saffron. And for a giddyness in the head, chew the dryed roots of gentian continually.

Recipes to protect the heart in love

Lucy St.John
August 1607

The Charlton Park festivities coincided with Lammas Day, the traditional August festival of harvest, where the first ripe crop of the land is celebrated with dancing and mummers. Although Uncle Oliver claimed this had fallen out of popularity in London, here in the deep country, old ways still prevailed, and it was not surprising that Lady Suffolk chose Lammas to commemorate the warming of her ancestral home. She had grown up in Charlton Park as a girl, but once married to the powerful Earl of Suffolk, Lady Suffolk left Wiltshire for White Hall.

As we rode through the lanes from Lydiard, the cow parsley frothed in the hedgerows, sweetening the air with its distinctive musty scent. Fields of ripe corn stretched as far as I could see, spread across softly undulating land like a cloth of gold and threading between deep, bosky woods. In the tranquil villages and comfortable farmhouses, the land appeared prosperous and at peace. Little evidence remained of the previous years of poor harvests, plague and deprivation.

The stone house-lined village street leading to the estate looked spruce and spotless. The parish church was neat and well-tended, with trimmed trees and freshly scythed grass. Lady Suffolk's benefice included the village and lands around her renovated home, and it showed. Entering through an ornate pair of pillars as the gate guards waved us on, we trotted to a graveled track. Felled trees created a vista across the parkland to the house.

"Aaaaahh." Joan's sigh of pleasure told all. "It is truly a marvel of design. Such height, the turrets, the windows . . "

"So much glass. And look at the stone carvings." Barbara, riding next to Joan, took up the theme. "The renovation must have cost a fortune, Aunt Joan."

"A fortune is what Lady Suffolk has, Niece. And she has invested well. I have no doubt this magnificent palace has the latest designs, the best of craftsmanship. I must see what I can recreate at Battersey."

Anne fell back and joined me as we rode up the long driveway.

"Rather vulgar, don't you think?" she remarked.

I smiled. "I would have preferred the old manor. This looks like an upstart."

"Much like the court," Anne replied. "New money, no taste. Ah, well, Joan and Barbara will find much to entertain themselves. I pity Uncle Oliver's purse!"

Even Barbara and Joan fell silent in their gossiping as we drew close, their tongues stilled by the wonder of the building, the scale of the walls, bronze cupolas dazzling in the afternoon sun, and an intricately worked stone-and-brick façade.

Gaily patterned tents dotted the parkland in front of the house, revealing a fete with all manner of players and musicians.

I caught Anne's eye.

"Counterfeit," I mouthed to her.

She looked at me inquiringly.

"Look at their shoes." I nodded down at the feet of the nearest gypsy. She was wearing a pair of silk heels that could only have been made in Cheapside and probably cost more than my entire wardrobe for this visit. We laughed at the deceit and enjoyed the theater as we suspended belief and entered Charlton's world of make-believe.

Elegant courtiers sauntered between the stalls. On a wooden stage erected in front of the house, a company of actors performed a play, and roars of laughter greeted us as we rode by. I must admit that I felt light-headed with excitement.

Aunt Joan turned almost purple with suppressed envy as she appraised every part of the new house. I could imagine many of its innovations would find their way to Battersey, albeit rough-copied by her cheap trades. I took a deep breath as we crossed the threshold into the world of the court.

After being shown to our chamber through opulent galleries that outshone even those of Lord Zouche, a deferential maid helped Anne and I dress for the evening's festivities. I caught Anne looking at me with a small smile on her face.

"What, Anne, what now?" I asked, unintentionally abrupt.

"Katherine had good cause to be jealous of you and question Mompesson's faithfulness," she responded, her smile warming her words. "You are beautiful, Lucy, and grow more so each day."

I shrugged aside her words, secretly a little pleased, but not really believing her.

"Be careful, for you will continue to attract suitors, and at Charlton, you are in a different world. Court manners are intricate. Do not trust those who profess adoration, for to them it is but a game. You are not encountering the likes of simple Giles Mompesson, and we are not playing make-believe in our rooms at Lydiard."

"I have no interest in games of love." I helped the maid finish attaching my sleeves and tugged my bodice into place. Our new gowns were stiff, fresh from the weavers, each intricately embroidered piece of cloth designed to flatter and enhance. "Let us join in the spirit of the warming and dwell in the fantasy that Charlton Park offers. But I am well aware that at the end of this visit, I shall return to digging in my garden at Lydiard, for I have my own harvest to gather before the weather changes."

Anne laughed. "You are right. But heed my warning, Lucy, for I know these people. Trickery and deceit is their common vocabulary. I do not want you to be hurt or to attract further envy from Joan and Barbara upon you."

The days passed as though in the Elysium Fields, where time was suspended and only the progression of the summer sun marked day and night. The sweet-scented dusk crept far into the evening, brightened by torches and candles, the like of which I had never seen before. At Battersey, Joan's parsimony limited our candlelight to only necessary tasks, and although well stocked at Lydiard, we conserved our light.

Flames burned long into the night at Charlton, illuminating the fresh paneling and vibrant tapestries, chasing shadows into the farthest corners. A forest of candles lit the long gallery, casting a golden glow. Bright ambers and ruby reds, glowing emeralds and sparkling diamonds spangled on the clothes and in the ornate hair of the countess's guests. Everywhere gleamed newly painted portraits, freshly woven tapestries, and curiously designed furniture. The walls were paneled in honey-colored oaks, newly sawn and still carrying the fragrance of the forest. Such brilliant colors and craftsmanship constantly astonished me, living mostly in a dim world of objects softly tarnished from the toll of decades of wood smoke.

As the week's end approached, our excitement heightened. The traditional Lammas Day of the first of August fell on Saturday, and Charlton's guests were invited to attend the fair in disguises provided by Lady Suffolk's household. Moreover, the evening featured a play by Mister Shakespeare, fittingly about a dream upon a midsummer's night. I heard rumored that the author himself performed in it, along with other players from the King's Men.

"It's because the rest of the family are arriving from their London estates," said Anne, reporting gossip from our maid that morning as she dressed her hair. "Frankly, I am dreading this, for the countess's daughter, Frances Howard, will join us. She hates my cousin Devereaux with a passion—and I'm sure that extends to all his family. She was contracted to marry him at a young age and grew to despise him. Her older brothers are quite mannered, but she is dreadful."

"I'll protect you." I hugged Anne. "She won't be able to be unpleasant to you if I'm there."

"She sounds like someone who knows her own mind." Barbara walked over to the glass and examined her face, smoothing the cochineal on her lips and smoothing her hair. "There is nothing amiss with expressing opinions. I am sure I will find her interesting. You will introduce me to her, Anne."

Anne said nothing. Barbara, encouraged by Joan, spent much of her time at Charlton with a set of courtiers we knew not. There were greater ambitions at play than simply enjoying the hospitality of Lady Suffolk.

The maids entered the chamber with our costumes, fitted for us by Lady Suffolk's seamstresses. Disguised as country fair people, Anne was a milkmaid, Barbara a fortune teller, and I a lavender seller. Although our disguises mimicked gypsies, charming touches of exquisite ribbons and French lace adorned the precious gowns.

As we wandered the booths, the day glowed with a dreamy quality. Beautiful women and handsome men strolled arm in arm in the golden August sun, and musicians played merry tunes to accompany us in our promenade. There settled a haunting sense of time suspended, for no worries, no sickness, nor poverty intruded upon this gilded setting. I recalled my impression of White Hall when we rode to London with Will and how the golden towers of the palace shimmered above the waters of the Thames. At Lydiard, I was part of the world around me, and we lived alongside bad harvests, difficult childbirths, disease, and death. These people knew nothing, and I thought it pitiable.

Pausing by an herbalist's stall, enchanted by baskets of petals displayed to select for the best rosewater, I experienced that uncanny awareness of someone staring at me from behind my back. I turned. He stood a good height, his auburn hair capturing beams from the sun, and his green eyes looked merrily at me. Disguised as a huntsman, dressed in forest green and chestnut, he carried a grace that belied his common costume.

I turned to seek Anne and found her gone. I paused, for I could not determine a way forward, and the surrounding crowds prevented me from retreating.

"May I assist you?" He bowed low, now in front of me. "I believe your friend the milkmaid was distracted by the musicians and remains to listen to their playing."

He reached out his hand, and it would have been discourteous of me to refuse it. I could not meet his eyes, for he was so beautiful in appearance. My cheeks colored as my hand touched his. His smooth fingers lightly held mine, and I could feel the warmth of him.

"Don't be concerned," he said softly. "The crowds here are not like those of St. Bartholomew's Fair. You will not find your purse stolen or your modesty affronted by a vagabond apprentice. Come, let us find your friend."

As he escorted me through the crowded paths between the stalls, I was conscious of his presence by my side. Merriment sparkled in his bright eyes and ready smile, but he also possessed a quiet courtesy, unlike so many of the prideful young men who attended the fete.

"The music is most pleasant, is it not? And such a charming setting. One could believe all of England lived in such a bucolic world." He steered me around a drunken baker who suddenly spewed on his shoes in our path. "And many do. Believe, that is."

"You do not?"

"I have seen enough to know the underbelly to this chimerical life."

"These people are deluded. They have no understanding of the true meaning of the old country ways."

"Ah . . . that is a strong opinion, my lady. And you do?"

"I have seen enough to know that even in this land of wealth and luxury, poverty and sickness lie waiting at its gates."

He stopped, paying no heed to the curious glances from a group of courtiers who had to step around us.

"Such a dire outlook from one so young." He tilted his head.

"It is just my experience. This world is alluring, but it is an illusion." I made to walk on, but his hand on my arm stilled me.

"But what if you had the means to maintain that illusion, with no cause to step outside the gates?"

"And would that shallow life satisfy you? One where all opinions were shared, all experience traded? Such a world does not appeal to me." I removed his hand and tried to sidestep him.

"You speak from experience?" His tone was eager. "What know you of a world outside of the court?"

I laughed. "I am no courtier's daughter. I am here as a country cousin. Do not look for me in White Hall."

"So you prefer the land to the city? Are you not dying to attend court? Most girls are."

"I would see for myself all that it is. And then return to the true world." I peered again into the crowd, searching for Anne.

"I share your thoughts. I love the land where I am from, and it is most dear to me."

I looked at his hands, elegant and yet with calluses on the palms.

"You enjoy the country too?"

"I do. And your name, country cousin? Can you tell me that?"

"Lucy. And yours?"

"Theo." He looked at me curiously. "Are you hungry? Come, let's share a plate of roast meat and cider. Even serfs must eat."

Giving up my thoughts of finding Anne, I walked with him to the shade of a sturdy oak and sat on a bench beneath while he fetched food.

As we rested and shared our meal, we observed the manners of the overdressed ladies and the posturing of the gallants. We laughed aloud as a portly shepherd in a highly embroidered smock lost control of his small flock of sheep. They scattered amongst the stalls, causing the women to shriek aloud as they were tripped and butted by the confused animals.

And we talked, of books and agriculture. He spoke of his home in Essex and his work in the gardens and countryside. I told him of my love of Lydiard and the joyful time spent in Hackney with Matthew L'Obel. We passionately discussed the crops of saffron that thrived so well in the chalky soils of the land in his part of the country. His stories of cultivation were especially fascinating, for saffron is well known to be the most efficacious cure for the plague. Its expense prevented all but the richest of patrons from acquiring it.

The afternoon lingered into twilight. As the sun set behind the woods and shadows lengthened, torches flared, and Charlton took on the guise of an enchanted castle. In every window candles glimmered, and great lanterns shone on the roofs and battlements. A silver crescent moon hung in the velvet sky as another expensive adornment.

"Come, country cousin, it is time to rejoin the others."

He held his hand to escort me, and as I took it, our afternoon friendship changed swiftly into something else. His hand dropped to my waist, and as I leaned forward, he bent his head closer to mine and touched my lips with his. I hesitated, but just for a fleeting moment, and as he pulled me closer, I yielded. I felt the rasp of his beard, the strength of his mouth, and as I stood beneath his kiss, a warm delight rushed through me.

Hidden in the shadow of the broad oak tree, he kissed me until my skin flushed and the dew settled around us. Drifting toward the house, my hand in his, we rejoined the crowds, who now settled onto stools and benches to enjoy Shakespeare's play. We chose to stand a little to the side, in the shadows of a planted grove. There could not have been a more appropriate performance than that of the fairies and wood sprites, dukes and star-crossed lovers in the play's fairy world. That night, Charlton transformed to the hidden land we knew lay just beyond our mortal eyes, inhabited by gentle ancient magic that still walked the earth.

"Lucy, finally, where have you been?" Anne rushed to my side accompanied by Aunt Joan and Barbara, neither of whom looked particularly happy to see me.

"We've been looking everywhere since you disappeared in the crowds this afternoon."

"I've been here." It was difficult to pull my thoughts back to the reality of Joan and Barbara's ire as they glared at me.

"I am so tired of your ridiculous behavior, creating such consternation and making a spectacle of yourself. We hunted for you high and low." Joan was clearly furious while Barbara looked with interest at the man standing beside me.

"But, my lady, who else but a huntsman could find your missing quarry and return her unharmed to her protectors?" He turned and gracefully bowed low over Joan's hand, and as he stood again, she looked at him suspiciously, flustered at his attention and yet obviously still angry at me.

"Theo!" Anne exclaimed, bursting into laughter. "How? What?"

"Anne?" he questioned, a surprised look crossing his face. "Is that truly you? You have grown so much since I saw you last at White Hall. You look charming, Cousin."

"And you are very handsome, Theo, as always. When did you arrive?"

"Late last evening. And imagine my joy upon finding such delightful company on my first day at Charlton." He drew me imperceptibly closer to his side, his hand resting lightly on my arm.

If there was one moment in my life so far to paint in a permanent record, it was Joan's expression when she recognized my huntsman escort as Lord Theophilus Howard, the heir to the Earl of Suffolk, and probably the most eligible young man in England. Of course, the discovery shocked me too, but I controlled my features and looked directly in her eyes, challenging her to speak ill to me now.

Lady Suffolk's guests stayed up well past the conclusion of Mr. Shakespeare's play, and as Anne and I lay in our bed, we heard giggles and whispers from beyond our door and footsteps back and forth throughout the night. Barbara stayed away until early in the morning, remaining with the courtiers and family. Anne and I were sequestered in our room—because of our age, according to Joan, but I knew it manifested her revenge on my afternoon adventure. Exhausting Anne with my questions of him, I lay staring into the single candle flame that burned by the side of our bed, my thoughts returning again and again to Theo.

When Barbara eventually came to our chamber, she was full of stories of dancing and card games, and music and entertainments, giddy with the excitement of the evening.

"I spent much of my time with Frances," she announced gleefully, kicking off her high-heeled slippers and sinking onto a bench. "She is delightful, and we found much in common. She is so fashionable and current with all the news. I do not know why you do not find her admirable, Anne."

"Perhaps because she shows little modesty or respect for her marriage to my cousin," replied Anne quietly. "She has been wed to Walter for more than two years, and yet she acts as though she has no husband. She attracts all manner of admirers, who fill her head with meaningless compliments."

"Bah, 'tis the ways of court." Barbara crossed the room and sat at the dressing table. "She is sophisticated, worldly, and has been brought up by her mother to appreciate the finer things in life. She had the same opportunities as you, Anne. It is just that she chose to take advantage of these things, whereas you . . ." She looked disdainfully at Anne as she ran a comb through her abundant hair.

"I honor John and all that he has given me. I would not tarnish his reputation or mine by disregarding the vows we made before God."

"Pshaw! Frances is having fun. She is young, she is beautiful, and she is a daughter of the wealthiest family in the kingdom. Why shouldn't she enjoy herself while her husband is on the Continent learning how to be a man? No matter I have heard that it would take more than learning swordplay from the French masters for him to know how to use his weapon!" Barbara laughed crudely.

Anne ignored her and blew out the candle by our bed, leaving Barbara to fumble her way in the darkness to climb under the covers with us.

As we gathered in front of the house to leave the next day, Barbara was subdued, and I suspected she was nursing a headache from the night before. Quietness overcame me, for Theo was absent all morning. I questioned my recollection of our time together and wondered if it was just part of the performance of Shakespeare's magical play. Though I knew that, unlike the dissolving insubstantiality of a dream that fades with daylight, my thoughts of Theo would not become as gossamer. My eyes searched for him among the bustle of people and servants. Many people were departing, leaving only the family and close friends to remain. Just as we were about to ride away, my horse whickered at a touch on her bridle. I looked down to see Theo's merry face smiling up at me.

"You did not think to leave without saying farewell?" His eyes twinkled, and his hair gleamed in the morning sun.

"You deceived me."

"And you have a secret." He touched his finger to his lips, and I flushed as the memory of yesterday's kisses warmed my skin.

"I did not think you would remember. I am just another courtier's amusement."

"I could not forget. Yesterday was more than a midsummer's dream, Lucy. You have enchanted my thoughts. And just as Oberon declared, the spell of the love-in-idleness flower has been laid upon my sleeping eyes. I beg you to allow me to see you again." He spoke urgently and directly, and I did not know how to reply to those words.

"I will be at home, at Lydiard."

A melodic voice interrupted us.

"We must call on you, Barbara, for I fear you will die of boredom! Theo, I command you to ride with me to Barbara's estate."

"Oh, Frances, please do come." Barbara perked up, her headache seemingly lifted. "It is ghastly, with so little amusement, and I should love your company." She fluttered her eyelashes at Theo, but he ignored her flirtation.

"Consider it a promise."

The girl who spoke turned and presented an alluring face, with dark eyes and pouting red lips, compelling attention. She was of my age but held herself in the manner of a sophisticated woman. Her dress billowed of exquisite fabric, cut daringly low across her bosom in the fashion of the court. Her hair, dressed with charming ribbons and jewels, rippled like gold thread. All eyes were drawn to her, and she knew it.

"Theo, please, let us go back inside, for I fear this bright sun is bringing me a freckle!"

Theo laughed and turned back to me.

"It sounds as though I am commanded. But I shall see you at Lydiard soon. For if Frances decides that is her pleasure, then none can stop her." He held out his arm to his sister, and they strolled together across the courtyard, perfectly in rhythm, two beautiful peacocks among a crowd of drab sparrows. As they walked away, he threw his head back in laughter, as comfortable in her world as he had been in mine.

7

My Lady of the Countryside,

My heart is lost without its love, for you are the light of my life, and in your absence, my heart has no torch to guide it. My time with you is measured in the miserliness of our moments together, and hence I live in "miseri." Oh, my beautiful lady, how I mourn for Charlton, for I will never forget our secret fairyland and the love potion with which you enchanted me. I sicken to think of the time I have lost while my father has commanded me in Essex, and I long for some poor excuse to see you at Lydiard, even though when I came with Frances your aunt welcomed me as a bitch greets a fresh marrowbone.

Your news that your brother is to be knighted at White Hall is welcome indeed. I shall arrange to be there too. Meet me in the promenade at the Stone Gallery on February 17th.

Ever your lord,
Sir Misery-in-Heart

As we rounded the river's bend, the imposing tower of St. Paul's East Minster dominated the skyline. This time, no cleansing flames from the plague fires reflected from the lowering cloud blanket, and the spires resembled an army of spears thrusting to the skies. No welcome extended to us from this bleak prospect. I recalled my excitement of first seeing the city as we rode with Will that summer's day to John's wedding, but I could not conjure up the same feelings this morn.

"Lucy, over there. Parliament's meeting place." Oliver pointed across the water to a collection of ramshackle buildings—a shambles, in my opinion.

"Is that where they found the explosives in the cellars?" People still celebrated the king's rescue from the Gunpowder Plot in November, even though four years had passed.

"A storeroom close by. Narrow escape that day, for the Catholics nearly succeeded had we not been warned to stay away." He spat into the water gliding by our barge. "God damn their souls. Martyrs, they call themselves. Murderers, I say."

"They were all captured?"

"Aye. After three days racking in the Tower, even Fawkes broke. Didn't take long for the rest to be rounded up."

I shivered and looked across the water at Westminster. I should have been thinking about the possible consequences of the acts of terror by the Gunpowder Plotters. All I could summon was Theo's face and the hope he waited somewhere in those buildings.

I shook my head and tried to lighten my heavy heart. Although but twenty years, I felt as dried as an old crone despite the excitement of the day ahead. Theo haunted my senses. His sweet attention to me when we were together fled before the tendrils of uncertainty when he returned to court. I had little else to occupy myself; a bitterly cold winter buried my garden beneath a frozen mourning veil. It provided no distraction except a worry that my flowers may have died a chilled death from which there was no resurrection.

Day after bleak winter's day, I could only imagine the worst. I wore ragged my precious few memories of him—the time he called with Frances after Lammas Day, a visit in the autumn with her again, a chance encounter at another's house at Michaelmas, and letters sent professing his great affection for me. And his kisses. The longing tugged at the very core of me, the yearning for his touch. And the deeper, darker moments, stolen in an arbor, behind a door, hidden from sight, where I dared to entertain him more. Scant encounters to build a life with, but enough to bind my heart.

His letter confirming our assignment was tucked into my bodice, the paper prickling against my breast. It was painful to be so entrapped and to hide these feelings from the envious eyes of my sisters and Joan. Only Eleanor and Anne were aware of the depth of my misery.

"You seem distracted, Sister. What occupies your thoughts?" Barbara's voice cut across my dreaming, her sharp tone causing the others to turn and look at me.

"Naught."

I turned from her and looked out across the gray water. My other fears converged on rumors of the court of King James. The old queen had ruled her courtiers with severe discipline, and her court had been one where a woman's virtue was still prized. The Scottish king and his vaporous Danish wife demonstrated no such morality. There persisted stories of great debauchery, drunkenness, fornication, and other vile practices.

As if catching my musings, Barbara persisted.

"There is much merriment at this court. Frances and Theo recently performed in a masque that won great favor with the king and his circle. No doubt there are many such diversions that would cause any man to stray."

"Merriment is not what is said on the streets."

I shifted on my cushioned stool and glared at Barbara. Servants' gossip related that the masque in which Frances Howard performed fell into great chaos because of the drunkenness of the players, who could no longer speak their parts or even stand up, and that many a maidenhead that night was lost. As children of the influential Howard dynasty, Theo and Frances lived in the center of the circle of courtiers who enjoyed the extravagances and immorality of the new age of James.

"Really? So now my sister listens to gossipmongers and broadsheet sellers? Why so anxious for news, Lucy? One would think you had reason to be so concerned of the ways of the court."

Joan looked at me sharply, and I turned away again, my cheeks flaming in the cold winter air. No matter what innocence I proclaimed, Barbara always found a way for me to feel guilty, tarnishing the love I felt for Theo.

Will's cautionary words from that long-ago summer journey echoed in my thoughts as we approached White Hall, and I knew he meant that the guise of gilding concealed a corrupt heart.

How different the palace looked as we approached it from the chilled river rather than glimpsed across the green Lambeth fields and sparkling water on a sunny summer's day. The buildings crumbled in sad repair—green waterweeds revealed by the ebbing tide coated the foundations, and much stinking rubbish bobbed against the pilings. I gazed up at the formidable heights of the apartments, the sheer walls and tiny windows more fitting a fortress than a palace.

We soon joined a procession of other elegant vessels arriving at the Privy Stairs, and I found distraction in watching the occupants of the other boats. Plenty of young men and their families were dressed in their finery, and the rented barges were hung with celebratory flags of crimson and gold. We moored alongside the pier, its imposing two-storied entry manned by yeoman guards. A surge of anticipation quickened my step as we disembarked, for the events ahead promised much for John and our family.

And Theo, always Theo, clouded my thoughts.

Walking through the narrow tower that guarded the entrance to the palace grounds and into an open courtyard, I entered a rarified world, leaving behind the common commerce of the river and its business. To the west stretched a garden laid out with formal walks and statues in every square, flanked by a row of tall buildings, hewn from honey-colored stone. Observing different faces, I tried guessing at their occupations and rank as they flowed around us, intent on their business, ignoring our gawking. Oliver confidently guided us through the crowds, and we soon arrived at the Great Hall for the investiture.

"Queen Bess loved to dance and watch the plays here," he mused as he stared around the smoke-blackened walls. The old building, obviously much used, had seen better days.

"Was it really so grand, Uncle?" I stared at the peeling plaster and sagging ceiling, for no amount of tapestries and carpets could conceal the dilapidation.

"Once, she filled the hall with trees, all at the peaks of their blossoming, just for a night. The roof was a canopy of branches. Songbirds filled the air. The musicians could scarce be heard for the caroling. Her ladies were masked as mystical birds. She appeared as a swan, all diamonds and white velvet." He sounded melancholy. "Those simple times are gone. For all her love of splendor, she bestowed the common touch. This throne puts many an interloper between majesty and man, more's the pity."

He guided us to a place in the middle of the hall with a view of the ceremony while John made his way to the dais where the other prospective knights sat.

"It was worth the money to be here today," Aunt Joan whispered coarsely as she craned her neck to see the assembled courtiers and nobles crowding the front of the great hall. "You brought John's name and status fortuitously in front of Carr so he could arrange for the king to add him to the list."

Oliver shrugged his shoulders. "'Tis the way of the court now," he murmured. "I had to approach Overbury. Carr is ruled by Overbury, and the king is ruled by Carr. Not so difficult to work the favor. Had to pay a little extra gilding for service. Selling knighthoods comes easy to this king."

I listened quietly. Although I knew that Oliver bought John's title, it saddened me to hear how it came about. I thought of our father, so humble when Queen Elizabeth traveled to Lydiard on her progress and knighted him in the ancient ceremony, bestowing honor on the family. It seemed a travesty that now this ancient rite could be bought and sold as thoughtlessly as a set of clothes.

"Shh, the king is coming." Joan and Barbara both stood on tiptoe to see more clearly.

There was a wave of rustling as the ladies in the room sank in deep curtseys and the men bowed. A crowned figure appeared, his body stiff from a thickly padded doublet, his arm flung around the shoulder of another man, handsome and magnificently attired, and they both made their way to the dais. The king shuffled hesitantly, his step lurching, and although he clung to the man next to him as if embracing a friend, it was apparent that he relied on the strong young back to support him.

"Carr. Lord Rochester," murmured Barbara. "Frankie considers him the most beautiful man at court. She is most preoccupied with thoughts of him."

I turned to look at her.

"Why would Frances Howard openly express her regard for the king's favorite? She is married to Essex."

"In name only. There is no marriage for all their cohabitation. Frances told me that Essex is not capable of being a true husband to her. She hates him with a passion and wishes only to be rid of him."

Even I was taken aback at Barbara's flippant way of expressing such dangerous statements.

"Barbara, you cannot say things like that. It is neither respectful nor wise to talk thus," I whispered back, concerned that others would hear. Joan turned, curious.

She shrugged. "I am only repeating what my friend confided in me. You are so naïve, Lucy. You take these words literally. I could say I hate you, but would you believe that as the honest truth?" She opened her eyes innocently wide, but I sensed the vitriol behind her light tone.

I sighed. Barbara embraced Frances as the model of her aspiring ambitions and emulated her clever, defiant tongue. I feared it would lead to trouble for all of us.

Turning back to the stage with a full heart I watched my brother kneel before the king and receive the honorary sword tap on his shoulder, signifying his elevation to knighthood. Although a purchased privilege, the occasion was momentous for our family, and one that I knew John had craved for many years. As I looked across the courtiers, an auburn head caught my eye, and my heart jumped as I recognized Theo by Frances's side. He stood here, in this same hall, and I could that moment break through the crowds and run to his side. Anne, standing next to me, sensed the change in my demeanor and followed my gaze.

"I see him," she whispered. "You will have a chance to meet him later. I'll help you find him."

She squeezed my hand, and I met her sparkling eyes with mine, knowing my excitement reflected in her face. She loved me so much and wanted only my happiness. She did not know I already had an assignment planned.

After the celebratory feast in the great hall, I begged Anne to take us to walk the Stone Gallery for our afternoon exercise, just as Theo instructed. The February weather closed in, and a fine snow drifted past the tall arched windows, flakes whirling from the gray sky and settling on the leaded panes. Through a colleague of Oliver's, our accommodation that night was an apartment in the south rooms around Scott's Yard. The time was ours to spend, with no urgency to hurry back to Battersey on the rising tide.

Led by Anne, who knew the rambling palace of old, we walked briskly across the courtyard, where snow lightly covered the gravel, and turned to enter the long gallery overlooking the privy garden. Here were the apartments of some of the most noble of the king's men. Elegantly furnished, with high windows placed so that exquisite tapestries could be hung below them, the gallery appeared endless.

"There are so many people, Anne." I hesitated at the threshold, no longer buoyed by the confidence of my subterfuge.

"Come, they will not eat you."

She guided me to join the promenade, stepping delicately in front of a group of young women who giggled and linked arms as they walked. By their similarity in dress, gold thread embroidered on red damask gowns, I thought they might belong to the queen's household.

"Just follow the pace, and you will find yourself moving with the crowd."

An intent purpose guided the courtiers' walk, measured, and all followed the same pace, their rhythm only slightly punctuated by bowing and greeting. For those not exercising, many convenient resting nooks were interspersed between the tapestries, and ladies receiving the attentions of gallants filled the window seats.

With Anne's encouragement, I started walking and soon forgot my own nervousness. At frequent intervals, young men strolled past us in the opposite direction as they turned about the gallery in the flow of the promenade.

"My lady bountiful."

"Mistress of my heart's desire."

"Keeper of my passion, my life."

"Anne . . . that whispering . . . what should I do?"

My palms were moist, and I could not tell if the anxiety was driven by the speech of the men or my planned assignation.

"Oh, for heaven's sake, Lucy, must you be always the innocent?"

Barbara had caught up with us, glancing from left to right under her eyelashes and fluttering her ostrich feather fan. "They are paying us compliments, and it is up to us to receive them."

I must admit that Barbara looked beautiful and drew many an admiring eye to our little group. As I walked by her side, my confidence grew. I could enjoy the fantasy of being within the gilded palace and living a life of which most can only dream.

Theo approached us. As he walked toward me, no other existed in the room, for his eyes locked into mine, and his gaze made a backdrop of the rest of the world. Other young men surrounded him, laughing and flirting with the ladies in front of us. Only his serious eyes told me he wished to be with me rather than them.

"Mistress Lucy," he acknowledged. "Barbara, Eleanor, Cousin Anne." He bowed to all of us, and we paused in the ceaseless promenade. "I am so glad you were able to attend today. Frances is entertaining in our apartments later this evening. Please come, all of you."

He bowed again, without waiting for our response, and moved forward in the tide of people, his friends throwing backward glances at us.

"Well. That was fortuitous," said Barbara. "I was hoping to receive such an invitation from Frances. I wonder why Theo would want to invite you when it is just Anne and I who are really known to them." She smoothed the skirts of her gown and adjusted the lace at her wrists. "However, I suppose he was simply being courteous. This will be a great opportunity to meet Frances's friends, and perhaps even Lord Rochester. They say he calls on her frequently."

8

For those that are near distraction with vapors and cannot sleep. Boyle as much hempseed bruised as oatmeal in water gruel. Take it at night, it causeth sleep.

For the palpitations of the heart, take an ounce and a half of juniper wood, angelica roots and galingale root each two drams, and a half citron and orange peel each three drams, juniper berries an ounce and a half, St.John's wort flowers two scruples, corinths bruised two ounces and a half. Put these into a cup of white wine and let them infuse some time. Then drink a wine glass every morning and an hour after dinner and supper the same quantity.

Recipes for the miserable heart.
Lucy St.John

Our borrowed apartment was a shabby one, forced into existence by two adjoining chambers inexpertly cobbled together. As we prepared for our evening with Frances, Will's words returned to me, reiterating his description of the inhabitants of White Hall. Now I found the truth in his observation. It presented an unsettling world, so much a veneer concealing an underbelly of baseness. Overhearing the extravagant compliments in the long gallery this afternoon, I was amazed that women would pay heed to the empty words. Yet it provoked a game they responded to with their own lies, and it appeared no one spoke from their heart.

"Barbara!" Eleanor's shocked voice roused me from my daydream "You cannot intend to go abroad dressed that way?"

"Not without my cloak," my sister replied arrogantly.

Barbara held out her arm, and the maid stepped forward and hesitantly offered her cloak.

"Is there something you wish to say, Lucy?" She turned to me, and I took a step back, startled into silence by her appearance.

Barbara's black velvet dress cut deep beneath her breasts, squared below so that her bosom displayed completely. Only the sheerest silver gauze inset draped her with any modesty, and rather than conceal, it only drew attention more, shimmering in the candlelight. A silver-threaded ruff extending beyond her shoulders and to the crown of her head framed her pale skin. An embroidered stomacher, ornately stitched with the design of our family crest of a falcon, accentuated her breasts by its tight lacing. It was a subtle reminder that we shared the same emblem with the old Queen.

"Do you not think the fashion becoming now, Eleanor? Do you not wish to dress in the court style?" Barbara tilted her head, as much as the oversized ruff would permit.

"Not at the cost of my virtue," replied Eleanor, her tone flustered, her cheeks red.

"Oh, by my troth, Eleanor, don't be such a hypocrite. I see you lust after your cousin, insignificant Will. At least I'm honest in my pursuits."

"That's enough, Barbara." Although she was the youngest, Anne's position as John's wife gave her authority over all of us. "You will apologize to Eleanor, and you should cover yourself."

"I can say I'm sorry her infatuation prevents her from having fun." Barbara paused. "And yes, I can cover myself."

She snapped her fingers at the maid, beckoning her forward and grabbing the marten cloak. Flinging it around her shoulders, she walked out of the apartment. We had no choice but to follow, and although Anne should have had precedence, we trailed in Barbara's wake as obedient children.

The fresh snow squeaked under our pattens as we traversed the shadowy alleys and courtyards to Frances's rooms, flaring torches throwing an orange glow over rough walls, creating light pools between the darkness. Our shadows stretched long over the buildings and pavement. The night bit cold, and a hard frost descended.

"The Thames freezes over as far as Putney." Eleanor's breath flew in a white cloud as she hugged at my arm to stop from slipping.

71

"It would be fun to walk across the river again," added Anne, who held my other arm.

"And enjoy the ice fair," I responded, determined to be as normal as possible. Barbara just snorted and walked faster. Slipping and sliding, we arrived at the buildings where the court elite were housed.

Entering Frances's apartment, a fug of warm air and aromatic oils enveloped us. Priceless jewels and gold ornaments reflecting in a thousand candles dazzled our eyes, accustomed to dark passageways and dimly lit stairs. The babble of conversation, merry musicians, and bursts of laughter washed over us, and for a moment we stood in the doorway, uncertain of our welcome as the maids took our cloaks and outer shoes. Surrounded by a group of women, Frances looked up at our arrival and languidly waved us to her side. No longer unique in her court dress, Barbara blended with the fashionable company. Many ladies looked at her and whispered behind their hands as we walked through the crowded chamber.

"My lady." Barbara curtsied, and Eleanor and I awkwardly bobbed behind her while Anne swept an exquisite court-polished curtsy.

"Barbara, just in time for a curious amusement." Frances gestured to a stool by her side at the small table. "And your sisters?" She had never really bothered to learn our names, and it was apparent she wasn't about to do so now. "Come, let us see what Mistress Turner predicts for you."

I stood close behind Barbara as she took her seat next to Frances. Opposite sat a heavily painted woman with her hair dressed in the fashionable court style of frizzed curls surrounding a small jeweled cap. Even the kind candlelight failed to soften the deep lines weathered in her face that betrayed her country pedigree. Her claw-like hands were marred with prominent veins.

"Anne Turner is able to tell of the future, especially in matters of love."

The woman drew Barbara's hand across the table and turned the palm upward. Her eyes narrowed.

"You ain't content, my dear, with your position. You scheme to advance, to make an advantageous marriage. And you 'ave already started to walk that path, ain't you, poppet? You must love it 'ere tonight."

Barbara stiffened in front of me and tried to draw her hand away, but the soothsayer gripped it tightly.

"My Lady Frances, this is more than a friend; she could be your sister of sorts." Anne Turner lifted her eyes from Barbara's palm and, ignoring her, looked into mine. "Or is there some other who joins with the 'Oward name, one we don't have knowledge of yet, who 'ides her true desires?"

My cheeks burned, but I refused to drop my gaze.

She returned to Barbara.

"I see ambition, my dear, and I see you by the throne. Your fate lies with those who are close to the king, a favorite perhaps, and a man he loves." She glanced at Frances. "I don't think 'e is the 'cur' you call 'im for his reluctance to obey, for I see 'is affection to you, Frances, as loyal as a dog."

The crone's veiled reference to Robert Carr created a tension, and then Frances broke into laughter. She threw a bag of coins across the table, and Mistress Turner quickly snatched it up.

"Old woman, you always have an eye for seeing what is concealed, whether in the room or in the future. I am glad to hear my life is entwined with Barbara's. I enjoy her company very much."

Anne Turner stood and curtsied to us. "Take 'eed that the bonds of friendship do not become the bars of confinement, my lady. I see you is a prisoner of love, and these threads will weave all your lives together."

She left an uneasy air behind her.

"Sometimes she goes too far in her magic." Frances dismissed the incident. "Come, Barbara, sit by me while I play a hand of Maw. The king insists we learn his favorite cards. I predict you will bring me much luck tonight, and the fortune I need is one to pay my debts, not foretell my future."

I was left alone with my thoughts. It unnerved me that the sorceress stared so directly at me when she foretold of our family joined with the Howards. I hardly dared to dream that this could be anything other than a greedy woman's attempt to exhort additional coins from her audience.

As I relived the words of the old hag's predictions, a hand grabbed my arm, drawing me into an alcove concealed by a thick tapestry. It was Theo, and as I protested, he held my head and kissed me deeply, taking my breath and will together, leaving me no choice but to kiss him hungrily in return. We stood entwined until the entire world was within that small dark space and the sounds on the other side of the tapestry faded into the background.

"Dear God, Lucy, I needed to hold you, beyond all measure," he whispered fervently, "for when you appeared this afternoon in the gallery, I swear I don't know how I restrained from kissing you then."

I embraced him joyfully as I met his passion with my own and led him to greater intensity. He groaned, and my body strained toward his, so alive, so joined to him. He broke free and took a small step back.

"Leave me, please," he implored, half laughing. "For if you kiss me more, I swear I shall have you here, and there will be no stopping." He brushed my cheek with his thumb and wrapped a lock of hair around his finger. "You have entranced your Oberon, fair Titania, and I am willingly your prisoner. I beg you to be kind, for you hold my heart and soul in your hands, and my destiny in your words."

My spirit kindled and flared after the months cooped in the dark winter, trapped with Aunt Joan and Barbara fussing and gossiping about courtiers they did not know.

"I have a powerful passion for you. My heart follows yours, for it guides mine, and I pledge my destiny to yours, for I have reason to believe fate joins our lives." I spoke confidently, echoing Anne Turner's prophecy. "Come, court me and pay me attention as you would a princess, for tonight I am in royal White Hall."

"Then travel with me, Lucy. I desire nothing more in this life than to be yours and to declare myself your love."

Theo drew me farther behind the tapestry, and I heard a click as a hidden door in the alcove opened. We entered a small chamber lit only by a glowing fire and the icy light reflecting from beyond the arched windows. In the velvet darkness, his breath was warm on my face, his hands urgent on my bare shoulders. I tasted sweet wine on his lips and wanted more, wanted to drink deeply of him, wanted to pull him into me. The noise of Frances's chamber was but a distant murmur.

As Theo's lips brushed my neck and he pulled me down onto the cushions before the fireplace, I felt the urgency of his desire. While he kissed me deeply, his hands gently gathered my skirts and pushed them around my thighs. I could not break away, my heart humor ruling my head.

"Theo, I cannot . . . I cannot lie with you this way." I sounded like a young girl and cursed my own innocence, thinking for once of what Barbara would do in the arms of her lover. I pushed back on his chest with both my hands, breathless with desire and apprehension.

He stopped kissing me for a moment and pulled back slightly, eyes shining in the shadowy room. His auburn hair and beard captured glimmers from the fire as if the very embers burned within him.

"I would not compromise your virtue, Lucy," he said softly, slowly. "But let me show you ways to love. Let me take you on a journey of discovery, make you mine. Fear not for your chastity, nor shall I put a child upon you, but I will show you how to love and be loved. You will not forget this night, I promise you."

"Do not speak of this to any other, Theo." My heart was pulsing with desire, and yet my head still sought reassurance.

"I would rather die than betray you, Lucy. Your trust is safe with me."

His lips closed upon mine, and as I felt the touch of his fingers between my legs, his seduction of me began. I could not but entertain him.

A lifetime later, we slipped back into the noisy chamber, flushed and loved, and found Frances and Barbara shrieking with laughter at the antics of a small monkey on a silver chain. I welcomed the distraction, for in truth, I emerged forever changed. I was no longer the only person who knew my body; another had tutored me to take and teach pleasure.

Half a dozen extravagantly dressed gentlemen joined the women, one of whom held the end of the chain and called instructions to the creature.

"Carr." One word from Theo and I knew that he was not impressed with the new arrivals. "And Overbury, his lapdog. I wish that Frances did not enjoy Lord Rochester's company. I fear he distracts her much from her wifely duties, and her enemies know this."

I looked at the king's favorite, recognizing the courtier who served as his crutch during the ceremony that morning. He was surrounded by sycophants who hung on his words and laughed frequently. Frances's preoccupation with them was suddenly distracted, and she looked searchingly at Theo and me, her eyes narrowing. She leaned over to Barbara and whispered something in her ear, at which Barbara frowned and her mouth tightened. Frances laughed and blew a kiss to Theo, who pretended to catch it and press it to his heart.

Barbara got up from Frances's side and walked across the room to me. Under the pretense of an embrace, she whispered clearly.

"'Struth, Lucy, if you intend to pursue this road with Theo, judge your odds and be prepared to wager the stakes, for those who aim high can also fall far. Do not look to me for aid, for you choose your own path, and if ruin is the outcome, I shall publicly disown you."

I stepped back involuntarily.

"What have I ever done to make you hate me so much?" I asked. "I don't understand why you are this way to me."

"Not hate. Indifference. I do not see what others see in you. And my plans will not be compromised by your foolishness. Straighten your gown — you reveal too much." She pulled the soft muslin across my reddened skin, kissed my cheek as though she were Judas, and left.

"Theo . . ."

I turned to him for reassurance, but he was gone. Drawn into Carr's circle, he was loudly joking and drinking steadily from a goblet of wine. As I stared at him, trying to reconcile this frivolous courtier with the man I loved, he shrugged, laughing at his situation, and turned back to his friends. The musicians, who sounded so glorious when I first arrived, now rang discordant. I sickened of the entire confusing visit to White Hall and wished myself back in the peace of Lydiard.

"But you know this is the way of the court."

The night lay between us, and we met at the Stone Gallery again during the afternoon promenade. The pavement reflected a cold light; falling snow continued to swathe the palace in gauze, softening the angles of the roofs and chimneys, and settling on charcoal-etched branches. A woman in a crimson cloak hurried across the privy garden, a daub of color in a black-and-white landscape. I wondered whose arms she was seeking, so swiftly, in such inclement weather. All my thoughts turned first to lovers now.

I touched Theo's arm to bridge the distance.

"I know, I am not stupid. Anne has told me of her years at court where she witnessed firsthand the deceptions and lies, the flattery and untruths. It just does not sit right with me to see you in that world."

"Ah, Lucy, it's just a game. Seize the opportunity to know us better, and you will find this amusing. As long as you do not take yourself seriously, there is no harm in playing these subtleties."

"Is that what last night was?"

"No, that was no game, for you have captured my heart and enchanted my soul, Titania." He pulled me to him, ignoring the glances of those around us. "Learn the ways of White Hall, and enjoy courtly love."

"Until we no longer discern between truth and falsehood?" I wriggled from his grasp.

"Come, sit with Frances and me for a while and converse. And then, I promise you, we'll explore the king's library and discover faithful friends. Along with his fondness for drinking and hunting, he is a learned man and has a marvelous collection of rare books and maps." Theo intertwined his fingers with mine and pulling my hand to his mouth kissed each finger delicately, softly, and yet with such a lingering tongue that every fiber of my body yearned for more. "And perhaps later, we can find ourselves alone again. There are many secret places here at White Hall."

I shivered and allowed myself to be tempted with the thought of being with Theo again, sharing his desire, snatching a secret love. With him at my side, I went to sit with Frances in a large bay-windowed alcove. Across the gallery, Carr attended on Barbara in a paneled chamber, where he was teaching her the complicated dance steps of a French gavotte.

Frances looked up as we approached and smiled faintly. The cool, translucent snow-light illuminated her face and reflected her perfect unblemished complexion. She held her hand out, and I curtsied and sat next to her while Theo leaned against the sill, his long legs casually crossed.

"So my brother tells me I should acquaint myself with you, for he is of the mind to learn more of you, and he trusts my intuition." She laughed softly. "Now we will begin the lesson of Lucy, so I may judge this paragon my Theo says intrigues him."

I took a deep breath and smiled back.

"I am no paragon, my lady. Just someone who believes that truth is more effective than flattery in developing character."

"Hmm. A girl in White Hall who speaks of character and not charm is already a rare find." She looked up at her brother. "Theo, I believe you have challenged me here. Leave us that I might explore uninterrupted."

He pulled a face at her and gracefully sauntered across the gallery, where he stood in the entry to the chamber and watched Carr and Barbara. A servant appeared with a flask of wine, and he drank deeply.

"So you value character over charm and fear not truth. Tell me more of your virtues, Lucy, and how you acquired them. What is your education?"

"Humble, my lady, but I speak fair Greek and French, and I write a reasonable hand in Latin."

"How surprising, for one so humble." The sarcasm in her words was not lost on me. "And what tempted you to enter that scholarly world?"

"To better understand the nature of the plants and their purposes in physick and medicine."

"Charming. A country wench well-versed in her stillroom recipes. And what else have you learned, Mistress Lucy?"

"To study the word of God and discuss the meanings of the scriptures."

"Oh, what a delightfully distracting conversation partner that must make you. And what do you do for pleasure, dear girl?"

"I read and tend my gardens. I devise my medicines. And I like to ride and spend my days with the company of my family."

"Charming. A simple country maid, untouched by the corruption of society. And why is my brother smitten with you?" She gazed directly at me, appraising my face, my hair, my person.

I had no answer for her and sat in silence, her scrutiny causing a blush to wash over me.

"I'll tell you why. Because you are as a fresh breeze in this stale environ. You do not seek to be a part of this world, although you have the brains and the beauty to conquer it. There is an intriguing air about you that is incorruptible. It is not often our circle finds a fresh amusement."

I sat silent, hoping this uncomfortable interview would end shortly.

"Your sister, Barbara, is different. She too has the beauty, but she also has ambition and a desire to go far in life. I understand her. I am not sure what steers your heart and destiny."

"A wish to live a peaceful life in harmony with my husband, where I can help others who are less fortunate that myself. There are many influenced by a melancholy humor, and I wish to practice medicinal cures."

Even as I spoke, my words sounded somehow inadequate to express my true passion, and they sounded trite and sanctimonious uttered aloud in this palace. Frances stifled a yawn and stood up.

"Charming and innocent, for now. I shall tell Barbara I find her sister quite amusing. And Theo should continue his exploration of your virtuous mind, Mistress Lucy."

The interview ended, and I still was confused by the conversation, disadvantaged by her clever court manners and slippery words. My dear Anne approached, and knowing that she would not wish to talk to Frances, I curtsied and withdrew.

"How was the she-wolf?" Anne did not conceal her contempt for the woman who had married her cousin and made such a laughingstock of him.

"I don't know, Anne. She feigned interest, and yet I sense that she was playing with me too."

We watched Frances and Theo, now dancing together with Barbara and Carr, their steps weaving a pattern between them, their laughter uniting them. Barbara approached Theo in the dance and took his hand, murmuring something that caused him to lean his head to hers. His auburn hair mingled with her chestnut strands, and as he listened to her whispered words, she looked across the chamber at me with a small triumphant smile on her face.

"It's time to leave," Anne said abruptly, taking my arm and leading me away. "Let us return to Lydiard."

9

Mistress, my Lucy, my light,

Farewell. Although I take my leave, my desire will never depart you. I write in haste from Harwich, for Thomas and I sail for Amsterdam on the morning tide. My brother has a passion to fight, and we join the Netherlands war to defend the Dutch Protestants from the Catholic suppressors. Do not be alarmed, for we are well equipped. We have a troop of fifteen hundred liveried men raised from our lands, and are well stocked with more than five-and-thirty wagons of supplies, including our tents, bedsteads, and dining needs. We will not starve, to be sure, for we bring with us my father's chefs and servers, for an army marches best on its stomach. We are safe in the Lord's work to relieve the oppressed citizens of our allies, and I think this will be a marvelous adventure. Keep this letter close to your heart, and tell none other yet of us, for I would bring you to Audley when I return and introduce you to those who matter to me.

Your affection has engendered an awakening in me that pierces as the first sun in a spring morn and brings the warmth to the dormant bud. This posie ring enclosed will reveal all, and I have ordered the words "I live in hope" inscribed secretly within. I may be removed from your eyes, but you are ever in my thoughts, for I carry with me that which you pledged to me that night at White Hall.

Theophilus Howard
Harwich
6th May 1609

I knew something was terribly amiss immediately upon returning to the chamber Anne and I shared. I was in a joyful humor, for while clipping fresh herbs, my thoughts had returned to Mathew L'Obel's tutoring, and I became engrossed in studying the needle leaves and tiny blue flowers of the rosemary planted against a sunny southern brick wall. My thoughts remained with my recipe book when I entered the room to change my smock.

Joan, Barbara, and Anne stood there, Anne in tears, the others holding open my writing casket, Theo's letters in their hands. My heart slammed against my ribs, and I ran to grab the papers.

"What are you doing? What right have you to pry into my privacy?" I shouted.

"Do not dare to question my right when such immodest and wanton behavior is occurring beneath my roof," retorted Joan, red-faced, waving the letters out of my reach. "You bring disgrace on our family by entertaining this man and his entreaties to you."

"It is nothing, nothing; he is an honorable man. There is no disgrace."

"That is not what I have heard from Frances." Barbara's demeanor grew taut. "She seemed to have it on very good account that her brother was highly entertained by you. And not just by your conversation, dear sister."

"It is not true, whatever you're saying, it is not true, it is not, it is not…"

"What?" demanded Joan. "What are you defending, Lucy? The fact that you spent time alone with this man, that you entertained him privately at the palace in White Hall while others watched you disappear with him, and yet more gossiped of his infatuation with you. And now I find these."

She shook Theo's precious letters at me, a little drop of spittle trembling on her lip.

"Barbara came to me because she was concerned about your behavior. She thought your head was being turned by flattery and falsehood at the court. You intentionally disregarded any conventions to behave modestly and played me for a fool."

"Lucy stayed with me," Anne spoke bravely, her little face streaked with tears as she tried to intervene. "I can vouch for her integrity and her modesty."

"At all times, Anne, you were with her? I think not. I heard that the Lord Howard presented plenty of occasions upon which he was able to secure Lucy's unchaperoned company. She is ruined, for as Barbara says, the gossip at court is such that he has already had her."

"You aimed high, dear sister, and now you tumble to the earth, for no man will want you now." Barbara's words hung in the air between us. "You think your absence was not observed that night in Frances's apartments? If you are to play those kind of games, you must learn to do so with more skill." A rush of anger flooded over me.

"My absence with Theo was only for him to declare his love."

Barbara laughed aloud. "You little fool, the only declaration he makes is with his lust, not his heart." She took Theo's last letter and read it aloud in a dramatic voice.

"'Your affection has engendered an awakening in me that pierces as the first sun in a spring morn and brings the warmth to the dormant bud . . .' That doesn't sound like a marriage proposal to me."

"You are not going to continue to ruin my life," I shouted. "You have no right to read my private letters, no right to tell me how to govern myself. Theo told me he loves me. He has spoken to Frances, and she thinks I am a good prospect. You wait until he returns, and then we will see who is ruined."

Joan held her hand up to stop Barbara's retort.

"He returns to you Lucy? And what then?"

"He takes me to his family; he promised."

"And what then, Lucy? Can we use this to our advantage? Do you really think he will propose to you?" Joan looked at me with interest.

"If you could but see his love for me, you would know that he is true. As soon as—"

"She's lying, Aunt Joan," Barbara interrupted me, her voice trembling with anger. "Frances told me that he should aim higher than this . . . this . . . country cousin."

Her emphasis on the last words, an echo of Theo's endearment when we first met, shocked me.

Barbara took advantage of my silence.

"She is lying, Aunt. I tell you, Frances said—"

"You are a jealous, envious, miserable wretch, Barbara." My words burst forth; no longer did I care what I said. "And you too, Aunt. You cannot conceive of love, for all is anger and hate in your hearts. And when Theo returns and takes me to meet his father at Audley End, then you will see who is truly prized in this family."

Joan raised her hand and slapped me across my face. The room went deathly silent.

"Do not threaten me, for you will never win that battle, you whore," she hissed. "Come, Barbara. Leave this wanton girl to contemplate the place in hell the devil has reserved for her."

She threw the casket on the floor, snapping the hinge, and with the remainder of Theo's letters clenched in her hand, left the room. Barbara swept out behind her. The chamber reverberated with the intensity of the spent emotion, my beloved room tainted by the anger and envy that had engendered this encounter. I drew a deep, shuddering breath, my hand on my breast, feeling the posie ring concealed beneath.

"I can't bear it, Anne. I can't live this way any longer." I slumped into a chair, such a paralyzing emptiness overwhelming me that my tears were frozen. Although the afternoon sun warmed my chamber, my hands were icy cold. I had hidden my emotions for so long that only hollowness remained, and the loss of Theo's letters slammed the door shut on my soul. I hated the thought of Joan and Barbara reading his precious words, spitefully laughing over his declarations of love and his promises for our future. I did not care of their opinions of me, for I did not respect their morality, but to consider their envious suppositions tainted his writings disturbed me beyond words.

"Lucy, they are so terribly jealous of your happiness. It is horrible. I tried to stop them from forcing the lock on your box. I tried to prevent them from removing Theo's letters. I am so sorry I could not intervene." Anne's white face was pinched, her cheeks streaked with tears.

"It's not your fault, Anne. Don't distress yourself more. I do not know what I have ever done to deserve this treatment from them, but it has been this way since I was a child, and it appears it will never cease."

I looked around the familiar room, my sanctuary at Lydiard. The polished chestnut paneling glowed in the afternoon sun, and the vase of yellow roses on the chest emanated a heady fragrance that promised the long summer days ahead. Through the diamond-paned window shimmered the green parkland, where an ancient cypress tree marked the boundary of the bowling green and offered a shady resting place. All were loved by me with a passion that had sustained me during my exile at Battersey, and they became my refuge when I returned. Now they taunted me with an oppressive familiarity. I longed to be stripped of all the layers of family and emotions binding me to this place and to be free of the jealous web threatening now to strangle me.

"Anne, I need your help."

She lifted her head eagerly, her sweet expression expectant.

"Of course, Lucy, of course. I will tell John of Joan's cruel accusations. He will not believe her."

"No, leave John from this for now. He will not understand the woman's jealous heart that steers these resentful actions. No, it is something different that I ask of you."

"Anything, for I cannot bear to see you be the object of your sister's envy this way."

"You leave for Guernsey to visit your father next week. I would come with you."

There. I set in motion a whisper of an idea that I barely knew existed, but as it was spoken begot life and became my survival. Anne gasped and knelt by my side, clasping my hands in hers. A tentative smile brightened her face, the sun appearing after the rain.

"And Theo? What if he returns and finds you gone?"

"He will hear that I am with you, visiting Sir Thomas. Besides, he is not likely to come to Charlton, for his life is in White Hall."

"My father would welcome you joyfully to Castle Cornet. I shall write to him this moment and tell him that you will be coming with me. But Lydiard, your garden, it's your favorite time to be here. How can you bear to leave?"

"I cannot bear to stay, Anne. Theo haunts me at every turn. And I am stifled; I cannot breathe. My refuge has become my prison. Now that Joan and Barbara have decided I chose to ruin my virtue, they will delight in commanding me beyond all measure. And with Katherine and her dreadful husband arriving to stay this summer, my life will be one of complete misery."

"I believe to remove yourself from your sisters' envy would be the right choice. Guernsey is very different from Lydiard, and my father would welcome you with great affection. I would love to share the island with you, for it's a place I hold most dear."

I looked again at my peaceful room, but now with a detached eye that no longer found comfort in the familiar treasured things. In the depth of my hollow heart, a small ember of hope glowed. If I could be with Anne and Sir Thomas in Guernsey until Theo returned, then all would be well.

"Your request is sudden, Lucy." John glanced from me to Anne as we stood before his large battered desk in the library. "And I am curious as to why you feel the urge to travel now?" He kept his eyes on his desk and shuffled the documents that were littering it.

"I am sad to leave my family at Lydiard and travel alone, Husband. I would welcome Lucy's company."

"It never seemed to trouble you before. You have traveled to Guernsey every summer since you were an infant."

"I have grown so close to Lucy. I want to share my love of the island with her."

"Or take her away from Barbara and Joan's ire." John held up his hand to stop me from speaking. "Joan has already been to see me with some story that paints a poor portrait of you Lucy. And yet—"

"John, you must believe me. Lucy is the innocent party in this tangle." Anne's inherent court breeding added authority to her statement. "They are simply envious that she has attracted more admirers than Barbara."

John gathered his papers in a pile and placed them hurriedly in his strong box.

"Do what you wish, madam; there is much work here on the estate. I have little time to investigate these petty sisterly squabbles." He paused as he shrugged on his doublet, ready to step outside. "But do not let me regret my leniency this time, Lucy."

After we received John's permission, there came the slightest lifting of my spirit, as the first stirrings of a breeze flutter the very highest leaves. I still grieved the loss of Theo's letters, for Barbara took delight in telling me that she and Joan burned them all, ostensibly to preserve my reputation. I knew it was her envy that destroyed them, not a charitable effort to protect me.

A soft lake mist drifted across the park the morning we left Lydiard. The drizzle was not heavy enough to dampen our spirits, for we were most excited that John had arranged for us to travel to Portsmouth in his new coach. Anne and I thought it very grand to be traveling in such style, for not many families had this luxury in all the county.

I had left detailed instructions with the gardeners for all my plantings. Although I was disappointed not to see the garden's progress this summer, the thought of our adventure ahead compensated for the loss. Besides, I would be returning in September in time for the harvest and the gathering of apples and pears to put up for the winter.

We would take three days to travel to Portsmouth, lodging in Devizes on the first night, and Salisbury the second before making the long final leg of our journey to Portsmouth harbor. Our ship was to sail early the morning following our arrival. For Anne, this was a familiar route, for she had traveled many times to Portsmouth to take the ship to St. Peter Port in Guernsey. For me, this was a new adventure, and I was particularly interested to see the great plains of Salisbury and the mystical Druid temple of standing stones. John's manservant traveled with us to see us safely on the ship, and two footmen rode with us to protect us from outlaws.

In the darkness of the coach, the jolting and shaking did little to distract me, and I fell into my thoughts.

"Lucy, I must ask you this." Anne's voice was quiet, barely audible above the clatter of the wheels. I dragged my gaze from the countryside and looked at her, sitting across from me in the gloom.

"What are Theo's intentions, and how have you answered him?"

I could see it pained her to ask, for she was not someone who would pry into another's heart.

Sighing, I leaned across and took her small hand.

"Theo has declared that he wishes to introduce me to his family when he returns and to show me his estates at Saffron Walden. He tells me that he lives in hope that we might be together."

"Together?"

"Married."

And did you give yourself to him? Is the court gossip true?" Anne's voice was a whisper.

"I pledged my love to him, Anne, but I did not surrender my maidenhead."

Discouraging any further questioning from Anne, I looked from the window again, reliving as I had so many times that night before the fire with the snow falling softly beyond the panes. I may not have put myself at risk of conceiving, but I had felt the passion and deep pleasure of being loved by a man who knew intimately how to please a woman. I ignored the small voice in my mind which questioned if my initiation into courtly love was too high a price to pay. After my conversation with Frances the next day, I did not see Theo alone again.

As we left Devizes, the small country lanes and leafy tracks gradually broadened until we sighted the Salisbury plains, and a barren and treeless landscape emerged, which suited my melancholy mood. Anne had removed me from my sisters' envy, but I still carried a heavy heart from leaving Lydiard, and with it a worry that Theo's messenger might not know how to find me.

The Druid's circle could be seen a distance away on the empty moor, a desolate reminder of a people gone before. As a fine drizzle wetted the gray stones, I recalled the stories told at the inn the previous night. Some thought that this ring was the final resting place of King Arthur, while others feared the devil's altar and warded off evil spells by counting the stones. The monument had the redolent sadness of a cemetery, for spirits slept among the stones and were given voice by the hawks that circled above. I was not sad to leave this lonely place.

Portsmouth was a wretched town, beggarly and cramped. We arrived late in the day and found lodging at the Dragon, one of the small inns that straddled the High Street. It was dubiously clean and very simple, but Anne had known it from previous stays on her way to Guernsey and considered it safe. The landlord welcomed us to his front chamber, which we shared with another woman and her daughter, who were also traveling to St. Peter Port. I did not sleep well, between the fleas and the excitement of boarding a sailing ship the next day, but toward dawn, I fell into a restless doze where Theo wavered through my dreams.

The cutter to take us to Guernsey was moored at the old harbor, and walking through the mean streets distressed me. In London, I saw much poverty alongside great wealth. Here coexisted despair and decay, with many destitute men lying in doorways or grouped around meager fires.

"This town's fortunes rest in war," Anne explained. "Since the last Armada, there has been little need to muster fighting men or provision them from here, and so there remains only the poorest men who have nowhere else to travel. They hope to be put to work, or even to be pressed again, for it is better to serve on board a provisioned ship than to starve on the land."

It was a heartbreaking sight, and I wished I could help these men, for somewhere a woman worried and waited for them, not knowing if they were alive or dead.

Portsmouth was the main departure point for people from the west who wished to travel to France or the Channel Islands, and the harbor bustled with people preparing to embark on several sailing ships. The fortified walls around the harbor were intimidating, and I could see how the town could transform into a military fortress rapidly. Anne pointed out the immense chain that was stretched across the mouth of the harbor, now submerged, which could be winched high across the water to protect the town against invading warships. I could easily imagine the forest of masts when the defending flotilla was assembled.

Stepping carefully on board, we found ourselves a quiet spot out of the way of the rigging and perched on a rough-hewn bench. The morning dawned softly, a pearly sunrise reflecting on the rippling waters of the harbor.

"They are unfurling the sails, Lucy. Say farewell to England. Soon we will be in Guernsey. How I have missed these ocean breezes." Anne breathed deeply.

"Thank you with all my heart, Anne. I could not bear to be at Lydiard any longer. You have given me the chance to sort out my thoughts—and have removed me from Barbara's envy."

Anne linked arms with me and smiled.

"Leave thoughts of her behind. She cannot harm you here."

As we sailed south from the harbor and left the shelter of the Isle of Wight, our ship's sails billowed and flapped as the wind filled the canvases.

"Hold steady, Lucy. You will soon find your sea legs. Feel the motion of the waves beneath you." Anne held my hand firmly and bade me keep my eyes on the horizon.

After the first moments of apprehension, joy and freedom grew in the breezes blowing us forth. I imagined great Aeolus, the God of Winds, his cheeks filled as he steered us on our course. Vicar Ridley would be proud of my recollection of his classical teachings. The flapping of the sails subdued as the wind stretched them taut, and the spray of cold sea water whipped color into our cheeks.

The ship shuddered and picked up speed, leaping forth into the darker waters.

"Anne, look, I'm balancing. I must be a natural sailor!"

Anne laughed. "Lucy, there is not a white horse in sight," she teased. "But I warrant you will ride those with equal ease."

"Did you ever see the Barbary pirates Anne?"

"No, nor sea monsters or mermaids. But I have traveled where the ship has plunged into troughs deeper than the height of the crow's nest." She crossed herself in the old way. "I cannot imagine how fearful those storms were when the Spanish Armada sailed."

Later, as the light faded, the ship's captain offered to escort us below decks to rest within his cabin, but after seeing the cramped and noxious quarters, I decided to stay on our sheltered bench. Anne recommended this to prevent the sickness, and we pressed against each other, wrapped in warm rugs, and dozed through the clear night.

The dawn blanketed itself in a sea fog, and until the sun came above the horizon, our world was swathed in gray. Gradually, the rising sun melted the fog away. An island appeared to our left, Alderney, its barren cliffs tumbling to the sea, gleaming white from the chalk exposed by the west winds. Flocks of seagulls swirled around the headlands, and large birds that the sailors called cormorants fished in the waters churned by our wake. Moments later, a larger landmass appeared on the horizon and our ship adjusted course and steered toward it.

"Lucy, there it is! There's Castle Cornet!" Anne pointed out the hulk of her father's home, its tall keep piercing the morning sky and a long jetty stretching into the water. Occupying every inch of its own outcrop, the castle was an ancient structure, built for defense and withstanding long sieges. Soft green hills formed a backdrop and a small town perched at the water's edge, its buildings colorfully painted in pastel hues.

The sails were furled, and as we navigated into the crowded harbor, we encountered small rowboats carrying passengers to and from the sailing ships, fishing boats, and even a warship. St. Peter Port was bustling.

"There is Jacques, my father's steward, come to meet us!" Anne was excitedly hanging over the side of the boat's railing, waving enthusiastically at a tall man standing on the quay. "He's brought the sedans, so we shall have a comfortable ride home."

The harbor appeared even more hazardous from the small rowboat that ferried us from the ship to the jetty, and I was glad to arrive safely and be greeted with a deep bow from Jacques. Anne and he immediately broke into an excited discussion in French, which I had difficulty following, the language not being high on the list of Vicar Ridley's classical instruction.

I looked around and thought how immaculate the town appeared, a vast contrast to the decaying streets of Portsmouth. Evidently, Sir Thomas governed with a firm hand and did not countenance beggars or vagabonds on his streets. A mild and sweetly scented breeze, also unusual for a town, gently caressed my face, soothing and welcoming me to Anne's island home. My spirit was the calmest it had been in many weeks.

10

For melancholy—the medicine which cured My Lady Bernard

    Take of the juyces of the herb mercury 8 pound juyce of borage and buglos each 2 pound. You must beat the herbs three times over and squeez then in an almon cress, the last straining is the best clarified honey 12 pound. Boyle them a little then let them runn through a flannel bag.

    You must have 48 hours in a close pot or tankard. 3 pints of white wine 6 ounces of orrace rootes beaten, 3 ounces of gentian rootes sliced thinn. Strain this through the same bag without pressing. Put the white wine so strained into the honey and juices boyle them to a syrup. Take a spoonful or two in ale or any liquor and the same in the morning and afternoon. If the person can bear it, the first must be taken fasting. This must be done at least 2 months.

Recipes gathered while on ye Isle of Guernsey
Lucy St.John
Summer 1609

"My dear girls, welcome, welcome. I have missed your company, Anne, and my heart is joyful to see you both once more."

Sir Thomas opened his arms wide and enveloped us both in a warm embrace as we crossed the drawbridge and arrived in the ancient castle yard. Anne and her father showed their love to each other with a heartwarming simplicity. Although he had aged in the five years since we met at Lord Zouche's, Sir Thomas appeared hearty and full of plans for our visit.

"Lucy, you need a tonic, for you are pale," he said. "Our island air and sea breezes will return the roses to your cheeks. And I have a special undertaking for you if you are interested."

He was excited to tell me something, and as a typical military man, he did not hesitate to come straight to the point, his familiar tone reminding me of Uncle Oliver. I smiled, appreciative of his interest.

"What is that, Sir Thomas? Of course I would love to be of help to you."

"I have a mind to cultivate a garden here at Castle Cornet. We grow some salads for our garrison, and a little fruit, but we are sorely lacking an experienced eye to guide our efforts. Would you be willing to help?"

He exchanged a sideways glance and a wink with Anne and burst out laughing.

"You have plotted this, for I know my darling Anne was worried about my sadness at leaving Lydiard's gardens. I thank you both and gladly accept."

Sir Thomas gazed down at his shoes and cleared his throat before continuing.

"I thought as much. Labor can do wonders to heal the heart and help the mind grow stronger."

I looked at him and Anne more closely. "What else has Anne been telling you?" I asked sharply.

He lifted his eyes. I sensed a powerful personality under his benign countenance.

"Do not feel compelled to hide your feelings here, my dear. Anne has a sister's love for you and wishes only to help you find your way. You are among those who love you. You can be honest with us and trust that your wishes and your heart-secrets will be honored."

My eyes filled with tears of gratitude as Sir Thomas spoke with such kindness. In so many ways, Anne was the family I pined for. I reflected, not for the first time, that one does not have the opportunity to choose family as one does friends. Sometimes friends can be closer than blood.

"Now come and rest after your journey, and we will have a simple family supper before you retire. Tomorrow, you have work to start."

He guided us across the broad yard, where the sheer ancient walls rose around us, casting deep shadows across the cropped grass. The keep tower stood stark against the brilliant azure sky, its purpose plain and unrelenting. It was not a fear of entering a prison and a place of warfare, but more a sense of protection that enveloped me. There was peace within these walls that had guarded many from the turbulent outside, protecting the castle dwellers from all that assailed them. I had found my shelter from the storm.

Our time at Castle Cornet flowed from one idyllic moment to another, the soft spring days blending into early summer, the light in this southerly island translucent in the mornings and gold and tawny in the evenings. I grew quickly to love Guernsey, and on the days that I did not supervise Sir Thomas's navy recruits to plant the castle's new garden, Anne and I explored the island and its ancient villages. There were no roads, and we guided our horses through the old high paths that wended between ancient hedgerows full of primroses and harebells and twisted round bends to deliver breathtaking views of an expanse of sparkling blue ocean.

When we hungered, we stopped by the low stone cottages of the parishioners and always found welcome from them in a fresh pitcher of milk and cake. Anne had been a summer visitor since she was a small child, and the islanders loved her. Sir Thomas had a reputation of being a firm and fierce governor. As a result, the island was free of much crime and dissolution, and although the islanders might grumble at his restrictive governance, they understood that their well-being benefited from his strict rule.

"Each parish in Guernsey has its own symbol, one that describes their pride in their community." Anne loved to recite legends of the ancient isles.

"What do our neighbors call themselves?" I asked. We were riding along the wharf of St. Peter Port, heading to the high hills again, one of my favorite tracks.

"Donkeys, of course!" Anne laughed. "Without those creatures, the goods would never make it up the steep streets to sustain the townsfolk. They are cared for as family."

Pausing by the harbor, we watched the fishermen hauling their boats onto the pebbly beach, the women of the town already gathered to select their catch.

"Bonjour Madame Montrachet. Comment te sens-tu aujourd'hui?" Anne's French was exquisite as she greeted a woman on the quay.

"Très bien, madame. Il est un bon jour quand nos hommes sont sûrs et nos enfants heureux." The woman straightened from the basket of fish she was sorting through and grinned at Anne.

"It is a good day when your children are happy and your men are safe." Anne smiled.

The language was musical, the words flowing like a song. "Do you think you could teach me to speak French as you do?" I asked.

Anne turned from her conversation. "I could, Lucy, but that is not the best way to learn a language. You should stay with a family that speaks only French, for it would force you to converse at all times."

"Could you help me find such a household?"

"I could . . . but what about your work in the castle?"

I looked down at my hands, my fingernails chipped and a little grimy.

"My garden is almost done. And if truth were told, Anne, I would learn an accomplishment that would serve me well at court."

"For Theo?" The morning sun was behind Anne. I could not read her shadowed face.

"Yes. For Theo."

I looked around the small harbor and watched as a ship left its mooring, bound for England.

"I love the time I have here, Anne, but my thoughts return to White Hall. I would use my mind wisely . . ." I stopped. Lately I sensed myself falling into a gray world of suspended time, waiting for word from a messenger that Theo had returned safely from his adventure on the Continent.

"Of course." She turned again to the young woman and rapidly asked her a series of questions. The woman responded just as rapidly, curtsied, and left to purchase her fish.

"Done." Anne was triumphant. "Madam Montrachet has both the inclination and the room to house you, and she would be honored to do so. Her family are recent refugees from the persecutions in France, and her husband, as a minister, has much learning he could teach you."

"They live here in the town?"

"In a godly household by the parish church. My father knows them well."

Anne's swift decision left me little time to think. After discussing this with Sir Thomas and receiving his approval, I departed Castle Cornet for the town, where I would temporarily stay and be taught the language.

St. Peter Port tumbled down the hill to the harbor, its streets so narrow that the houses almost touched each other on their second floors. If two people were to lean across from the upper windows, I was sure they could have shaken hands. The alleys were precipitously steep. Each day, patient donkeys toiled hard, delivering fish from the harbor and goods from the ships through the cobbled streets, taking fire ashes and packages down again.

The town was full of French immigrants. Many fled the bloody persecutions and sought safety in Guernsey, finding a welcome air of tolerance in these islands. Monsieur Montrachet was a refugee, a minister versed in the Geneva doctrine, and with his wife, Simone, lived in a small house by the harbor.

I was shy to begin with, for I knew not their language. But with their patience and kindness, I quickly grew to understand simple words, and their little girl, who was five years of age, delighted in teaching me from her hornbook. Anne suggested that I speak nothing but French while I was at their home, and although it made my head ache, soon the words became familiar.

Simone was a devout woman, dedicated to her family and to establishing a new life for them in St. Peter Port. Their experiences in France were horrific, and Simone's father was one of those slaughtered by the Catholic mob in the massacre in Paris on St. Bartholomew's Day. As I understood more, she told of her escape through the French countryside and how she had settled in Normandy, where she met Monsieur Montrachet. They believed that they could live a quiet life in devotion to God safely there, but the persecution continued, and it was with great sadness that they left their country to begin anew.

"*Temps pour votre leçon, Maîtresse Lucy.*" Each morning after his own meditation, Monsieur Montrachet and I discussed the Calvinist doctrine that guided his life.

"*Merci, Monsieur Montrachet. Je suis prêt,*" I replied.

He smiled and nodded his head at my response.

"Now let us discuss Calvin's doctrines." He spoke slowly and carefully so I could follow his words. "How would you summarize the central theme to his writings?"

"That the sum of human wisdom consists of two parts. Knowledge of God and knowledge of ourselves."

"Very good. And why was that such a dangerous statement?"

"Because the Catholic Church did not want us to think of ourselves as separate from God and its priests."

"Why not?"

"The power would then be moved from the priests to the people."

"And the pope?"

"The true Church places Christ at the head, and there is but one Church."

"And what was Calvin's political viewpoint, Mistress Lucy?"

"To safeguard the rights of the people. He believed in democracy and the separation of powers." I paused, looking to Monsieur Montrachet for approval of my language and my interpretation of our readings.

"Very good. You will be debating the finer points of the Geneva doctrine with me in no time." He took a bite of one of the pastries that Madam Montrachet had kindly provided to sustain us during our lesson. "What think you of his position? Many of our citizens in France have died for these beliefs. Would the same happen in England?"

I thought for a moment.

"I do not know who would lead such a struggle, in truth, for the aristocracy is well established, and there is no one to challenge the king."

"What of these Puritans who are speaking up for the freedoms they wish for? Freedom of speech, the practice of their religion without harassment?" He paused his munching and looked sharply at me. "These winds of change that are blowing across Europe may sow seeds of discontent in England too, Mistress Lucy."

"It would not be a bad thing to engender a voice for the people."

He nodded. In the quiet pause, I could hear the ticking of his clock, a precious object that he brought with him from France.

"Now what color is this?" Changing the subject, he pointed to a brown leather book cover. "Madam Montrachet will be most disturbed with me if I only teach you religious doctrines and neglect your practical knowledge."

I laughed and followed his pointing finger around the room as he called out objects and asked me to name them. But in my mind, my thoughts remained with those brave Huguenots whose courage affirmed that all men should have a voice in how their lives were determined.

As the days shortened and autumn began to make its presence known even on these balmy shores, my thoughts turned frequently to Theo. During the summer months, my work in the castle grounds and my education with the Montrachet family distracted me, but with the garden completed and my French studies diminished, there arrived room in my contemplations for my heart's voice to be heard again. Theo became an insistent companion.

"I am most anxious for news of his travels and his return," I confided to Anne as we sat stitching smocks by a north-facing window in the castle house. Our charitable sewing work was tedious and required little concentration, allowing other thoughts to intrude. "I thought I might stay here with the Montrachet family after you leave for Lydiard, but I have a powerful feeling in my heart to return, and I must travel back with you."

I allowed myself to wonder if, in some foreign castle, he too was gazing from a window, westward this time, imagining me at Lydiard, waiting for him.

Anne looked at me anxiously. "He has not written since you have been here. You know not if he has returned from the war. Do you wish to encounter Joan and Barbara's envy again, and are you strong enough to withstand them?"

"I am. I have found my voice." I spoke with a newfound confidence that Monsieur Montrachet's teachings had bestowed upon me. "Anne, I must remind you that Theo pledged himself to me at White Hall, and we will find a way to be together. It is our destiny." I touched the ring, which I now wore outside of my gown, confident in displaying the love that was mine.

"It seems you have learned more than the French language during your stay in Guernsey," replied Anne, smiling. "You have embraced the doctrines of Calvin and use them for your own."

"I had hoped that this visit would help me see my life more clearly, and it has. I believe in my love for Theo, and I will not let the petty jealousies of others tarnish our future. I must be brave and fight for my future and not be cowed by envy."

"Then let us make plans to return." Anne put her sewing down and walked to the window. "I long to see John again, and although I am torn between worlds, my place is at John's side. My father will understand."

Sir Thomas accompanied us to the quay to bid us farewell, and with poignancy, we left. As Anne held her father in her embrace, I knew she was very mindful that each voyage she made from Guernsey might be the last, for Sir Thomas was aging, and this winter he had decided to stay quietly at Castle Cornet rather than return to England. The Montrachet family stood with him, and as we prepared to embark, Monsieur Montrachet pressed a small book into my hands. It was his own precious volume of Calvin's teachings, and I protested at his generosity. He smiled and shook his head, insistent that I accept the gift.

"I have these words learned, and they are all here." He tapped his head in a very Gallic way, his eyes twinkling. "You continue your studies, and may these words guide your life. And remember, all men deserve a voice."

It was the closest to a blessing our reformed religion permitted, and I accepted his gift in the spirit in which it was presented. As Anne and I stood on the cutter's deck, focused on our family and friends remaining on the quay, I left a piece of my heart in Guernsey. . I knew I would always find a home on that welcoming island. It was my turn to comfort Anne as she waved good-bye to her father, and we stood together for a long time, our arms around each other, until the ship weighed anchor and we slowly pulled away from the land and set sail for England.

11

Lucy

You will attend us at Battersey, to join the family here. I have requested the same of Anne, so you should travel together. Please bring my warm cloak, the one with the fur trim, for the winter has turned bitter. Also, Joan requests that you pack a cart of venison and pheasant, for the supplies here dwindle, and we long for Lydiard's bounty. I hope you have recovered your senses, for Barbara informed me of your foolishness and fancy for Lord Howard. Your sister Anne is to marry Sir George Ayliffe, and you should consider your prospects, for you do not grow younger.

Make haste, for I would see my wife, and you shall not hold her back from me as you have done in Guernsey.

John
Battersey,
February 1610

I threw John's letter into the fire, watching it flare up before turning black and vanishing into the blazing logs.

"Barbara has poisoned John against me, I swear. I should never have left Lydiard, for now she has put John in the mindset that my love for Theo is—Anne, what's the matter?" I ran to her as she broke into a loud sob, the letter she was reading fluttering to the floor.

"My father . . . he has passed away. It must have been days after we left. Oh, Lucy, I'll never see him again." Her sobs were heartrending. My own troubles forgotten, I held her tightly, rocking her as I would a babe.

The news of Sir Thomas's death following on our heels as we returned to Lydiard was a shock to us. It was with bitter sadness that we held each other and wept, our thoughts and tears mingling as we mourned the loss of so kind a man.

"Here, another letter is in the pouch. From Monsieur Montrachet."
I quickly broke the seal and read through the fine penmanship.

"He was with your father at the end, Anne. He saw that he had his testament and that he left nothing unsaid. His last words were those of love for you. And the islanders attended his funeral with great respect."

Anne's sobbing quietened a little at these soothing words, but the sorrow of Sir Thomas's death weighed heavily on her. I too wore black mourning, and oft times it was as though we were two of the dark ravens perched on the Tower parapets. My independent nature chafed at the conventions of observing the mourning time. It delayed our departure for Battersey, but only by a few days. Anne's letter from John echoed the sentiments in mine, and she was eager to reunite with him.

Battersey was quiet, for Barbara had persuaded Oliver to arrange for her to board at White Hall with our relations from Bedfordshire, who had found influence there on the rising tide of King James's patronage. No doubt she enjoyed much attention from the vapid courtiers who hung about the palace chambers wasting their days in idle pleasures. Joan occupied herself weighing Barbara's marriage opportunities. Eleanor was my only sister left at home, and we grew close as the days drifted from one to another. Still, I was restless.

My relief was time with Vicar Ridley, and I enjoyed many a lively discussion with him on my newfound education in the Geneva doctrine. Although he was firmly Protestant, he was a little alarmed by my forthright views on predestination and my Calvinist learnings from Monsieur Montrachet, which I had now committed to heart.

"It is the way of youth to embrace and amplify the radical doctrines preached by their elders," he remarked after one particularly heated debate. "There is a long road between education and experience, Lucy, and do not confuse the two."

I laughed at his rueful tone, delighted that I could match his intellect with my own.

"I am just happy that I can discuss these ideas with you," I replied. "It is a house of women next door, and I swear I shall go mad if I have to look at one more set of bride laces or stitch one more smock today."

We were sitting in the study of the vicarage next to the manor house, and I loved the musty, book-filled atmosphere. Donna Anna was forbidden from entering Vicar Ridley's private room in case she disturbed his papers, and there was a pleasing muddle of books and objects that had not lost their fascination for me. I picked up one large volume and idly looked through the pages until a particular illustration caught my eye.

"What is this?" I asked, fascinated.

"The alchemy of turning iron to gold. There is discussion through the centuries that men have been able to contain the elements and manipulate them to their own devices. The secret has been lost over time, and I join the quest of many who have searched for the formula in order to regain the knowledge."

"And you believe you can really change base metal to precious?" I was intrigued with the thought, and his childhood teachings of King Midas came to mind. "Why would you pursue such a mission?"

He smiled. "I could do good if I had money to help my parish," he said. "There is much suffering for want of just a little comfort that an ounce of gold could bring. Many have tried to find this source for enriching themselves. I hope to one day benefit others."

He crossed the room and took the heavy, well-worn volume from my hands.

"These secrets are best left to old men who dream, Lucy. Do not become intrigued with these thoughts, for they suck time from you in ways that you cannot imagine. One day, you will find yourself old, just a hollowed husk, with still the vision unfulfilled."

In the reflective river light, I realized my old friend had aged, his curved back now even more hunched, his face deeply lined, his eyes rheumy. I shivered as though the goose had walked over my grave.

"Time to go outside." He shooed me from the room, his familiar voice now echoing our school days. "Go and run through the long meadow grass, Lucy, and find yourself some wildflowers. Today is a day for youth, and you should be out enjoying yourself."

I walked through the orchard, wishing I could run and roll in the grass again as I had done with the Ridley boys in our youth. The last of the apple blossoms was drifting from the trees, and as I paused and sat on a bench that overlooked the river, my thoughts drifted with the

103

ebbing tide. Fragments of petals speckled the black velvet of my skirts, and as I mused idly that they were as snow, sprinkling across a cinder path, my thoughts returned to White Hall. I daydreamed so deeply I could hear Theo's voice again calling my name, feel his touch on my skin. My eyes brimmed with longing, and the watery scene in front of me shimmered with unshed tears. I resolved I must find him rather than wait for him to return to me.

I would go to court and seek news of him.

My opportunity came sooner than I expected, for Oliver was delighted to report that John's application for a baronetcy had been ratified by the king. He was to be bestowed this honor in May at the court of White Hall. We shed our mourning gowns and prepared to go to court.

"What occupies your mind?" asked Anne, sensing a difference in me.

"I am going to find news of Theo," I replied firmly. "While we are at court, I shall seek Frances out and ask for her help. Perhaps she can send a letter for me, for I know not where he resides now. His last note said he was moving on to Angers, but I have heard nothing since."

"She will help you?"

"I do not see why not. When we spoke before, she said she would know me more, to discover Theo's attraction."

"Be on your guard, Lucy, for you know the ways of the court are different than ours. Not all is as it seems, and no one seeks alliances without a motive."

"Her motive will be to see her brother happy, for they are very close. She will be generous with her news of him."

Anne lifted her eyebrows and shrugged. "I do not trust Frances Howard with anyone's well-being except her own. Heed my words."

John's ceremony was even more elaborate than his knighting, although there were moments that echoed the former. There were many titles and honors being conferred, and John appeared last in a long line of men who had won or paid for the king's favor. During the ceremony, Carr still supported the shuffling king, although it seemed that often he was exasperated with James's lavish attention and several times shrugged off the royal arm when it was draped around his shoulders.

Spring sunshine poured through the tall arched windows, catching specks of dust and pollen in the air so the very atmosphere glistened with a golden haze. I found myself searching for Theo's distinctive auburn hair and, of course, did not find him, for he was abroad. I saw Frances and noted that Barbara was standing with her in the middle of a group of nobles, looking very grand and quite at ease in her silks and spangled piccadilly.

When she caught sight of us, she walked across the hall, a tight smile on her face.

"It has been long since we have seen you." She turned to me and Anne. "And you have returned from your exile in Guernsey, I see. Much has happened since you left, but I am sure you have heard."

"No, I have not troubled to catch up on court gossip." The memory of Barbara's betrayal with Theo's letters burned in my heart.

"Ha. Well, it seems Theo neglects to catch up with you. Has he not sent you a message, Sister?"

"And what of you, Barbara?" Anne interrupted. "Are you betrothed, or are you still a maid in waiting?"

"I do not care to marry the first man who asks me."

"Oh, so more than one has? Certainly, I am delighted you have such prospects. It must make your life so busy. After all, you have very little else to occupy your mind."

"What do you mean, has he sent me a message?" I demanded of Barbara.

She shrugged and pushed her way back to Frances.

Anne placed her hand on my arm and nodded toward John as he knelt before the king and arose a baronet.

"John has lived for this moment," she whispered. "I hope this will fill the emptiness in his heart."

I put Barbara's curious words to one side and swept Anne the best curtsy possible in our confined space, deferring to her elevated position within our family. She giggled, and I joined her laughter, happy to see a smile return to her face. As I did so, a strong arm embraced me, and I turned quickly, surprised at the response my body gave to a familiar touch.

"Will!" I quickly covered my thought that it was Theo. "I have not seen you for so long! Where have you been?"

He grinned and kissed my lips so sweetly.

"I have been commanding the king's ship Advantage, Cousin." He looked wonderful, bronzed and healthy and full of life. "There are still many prizes to be found at sea, and after the torture of Oliver's bog campaigns in Ireland, I had to return to my preferred occupation."

Oliver, standing a few feet away with Joan, guffawed. "So, Will, you escaped from the little problem you had with the Spanish?"

We all looked at Will, who scratched his head and shrugged.

"It was fair game. The ship did not resist. In the name of our king, I simply helped remove its very heavy cargo."

"You pirated a Spanish ship?"

This time, it was Eleanor who asked the question, her eyes wide.

"All for the good of my country. We need to pay for John's honors, and a little Spanish gold in our treasury wouldn't come amiss." He laughed at his own joke, Eleanor's attention causing him to preen with pride.

"Where did this happen, Will, and when?" Eleanor touched his shoulder, her face tilted up to his.

"Last year, off the Cork Coast of Ireland. Fortunately, I had friends in town who smoothed over the Spaniard's misunderstanding over the ownership of the gold, so no harm done."

Eleanor and Will continued their conversation, oblivious to others around them. A pang diced my heart, not of jealousy, but of emptiness and longing, and I resolved to find Frances before I left White Hall.

12.

A restorative for any faintness

    Three drops of oyl of cinnamon, a spoonful of syrop of July Flowers, as much cinamon as water.

Recipes
Lucy
Summer 1610

I dressed in my finest blue silk gown with the slashed silver sleeves and a delicate lace collar, glad to now have reason in John's celebration to discard my mourning. I needed to once more wear color that would become me and make me feel lighthearted again. Anne, Eleanor, and I had been invited to attend supper with our relatives, and it was with impatience I sat through the tedious evening, knowing I had to find Frances and create the opportunity to speak with her that evening.

For much of the meal I sat in silence, crumbling my bread and picking at the delicacies that had been prepared. Finally, supper was over and the table pushed to one side to make room for dancing. A small group of musicians arrived, and the room became crowded and warm.

"Anne, I have a terrible headache," I murmured to her under the babble. "I am just going to our chamber to rest a little."

"Oh, Lucy, I am so sorry." She turned her attention from John's story. "In my purse, you will find a cordial that will help. Can I come with you?"

"No, thank you. I mean, thank you for the cordial. I will be fine."

"Rest, my sweet. I know not what time we will retire tonight." She absently kissed me, her attention already distracted by John taking her hand to dance.

I slipped from the rooms, my heart beating a little faster. I checked my pocket to ensure my letter to Theo was still safely tucked away. Flaring torches mounted on the walls illuminated the alleys between shadowy tall buildings. As I crossed the yard toward Frances's chambers, many people were abroad in the warm spring evening, calling on others within the maze of the old palace.

A group of young men walked by, singing loudly and laughingly shoving each other. I pressed against the rough brick wall of an entryway to avoid their attention. It was exciting to join the courtiers who were enjoying the evening, and my spirits soared as I mingled with the White Hall milieu. I congratulated myself that I was able to blend in so well and become part of palace life.

I recognized the Stone Gallery ahead, where we had promenaded that distant winter, and knew that Frances's apartments were close by. Asking a guard to direct me, I was pointed toward the river and the tallest of the buildings that lined the bank. Soon I found myself standing outside imposing double doors, hearing the noise and laughter echoing from within. Taking a deep breath, I waited for a moment in the antechamber to get my bearings, not wanting to appear confused or at a disadvantage. The hubbub from the inner chamber grew louder and more confused, and I stood at a loss, uncertain how to move forward.

"Lucy!"

Barbara stood behind me, surprise on her face.

"What are you doing here?" She neglected to kiss my cheek in greeting. She was painted and perfumed and wearing a yellow starched ruff, a fashion made popular by Frances. Her dress revealed her breasts. Nothing much had changed about her or her attitude.

"And who is this charming creature?" A sumptuously dressed man accompanying Barbara looked at me searchingly, his eyes flickering between us. He was in full court fashion, his small beard carefully groomed to a point, his hair a shining chestnut and falling carelessly over his forehead. "I see a resemblance here. Could this be a relative, Babs?"

"My sister Lucy," she said dismissively.

He raised his eyebrows and affected a bow, this time taking my hand. He kissed it lingeringly, his full red lips moist upon my skin.

"Edward Villiers," he introduced himself. "I have heard much of you, Lucy."

"What would you have heard, sir, and from whom?" His intimacy caused me discomfort.

Before he could answer, a burst of cheering and applause interrupted us from the adjacent chamber. Frances stood on a small dais, posed in a tableau of classically dressed girls, all in similar flowing white robes and ornamented with spring flowers. There were five of them, and as the group of courtiers applauded, they came to life and joined each other in a lively dance, accompanied by pipes and drums. I watched, fascinated. Without saying more to Barbara and her friend, I squeezed through the audience and found a place near the front of the room.

As the women danced, celebrating the arrival of spring, a horn sounded, and a group of masked men rushed on stage, dressed as hunters. They proceeded to chase the nymphs, to loud cheers from the audience. I enjoyed the chaos that ensued and laughed with the crowd as the masque deteriorated into a raucous kiss-chase. There was an unmistakable familiarity about one of the huntsmen. I caught a glimmer of auburn hair under his hat.

I could not move, for the crowd pressed forward to better see the performance. I was trapped into watching Theo kiss one maiden after another in his role as hunter, an echo of our midsummer evening at Charlton Park. As the dance ended with a flourish and the audience broke into renewed applause, the huntsmen and the nymphs bowed from the stage, and the men removed their masks.

It was Theo, and my heart leaped with sweet recognition as his flushed face and joyful grin illuminated the stage. He was back. He was safe.

"Good people, the huntsmen have earned their ale tonight," announced Frances as she stepped forward, the foot-candles illuminating her beautiful face. "And I would like to welcome home one who has traveled far to sample good English brew."

She turned to Theo and held out her hand, and he caught it, laughing.

"My brother recently arrived from France, and we are most glad to receive him back in England. He has much to account for leaving me for so long." She pulled a sad face, and the audience voiced a collective groan in sympathy. I laughed along with them at her charming speech.

"But good news, my friends!" She paused. "Theo returns not just to me. He has a more important purpose to be back in England to assume his position at court. A reason to remain and not leave us again."

I was so happy to hear that he was to stay at court, full of the delight of seeing him again, the long and lonely year of absence already a memory. I thought of the joyful times we would have ahead of us and his plan to show me his land in Essex, and how I could persuade Oliver to let me spend time at White Hall so I could be close to him. I would even swallow Barbara's unpleasantness to stay with her.

Frances took the hand of one of the nymphs standing at her side. She was lovely, surely no more than fourteen years of age.

"My Lady Elizabeth Hume," introduced Frances, smiling at the crowd. "Daughter of the Earl of Dunbar, and now my sister, for we have completed the bride contract. Welcome, Theo's wife."

I wondered at first if words had been spoken, for my mind refused to comprehend what my ears had heard. Around me, there were loud cheers again and much applause with calling out of wishes and raucous comments.

There pooled a depth of stillness inside me that blurred all around to a jumble of colors and noise. All I could see was Theo and the maiden standing on the stage, their hands joined now by Frances, smiles on their faces and a blush staining the cheeks of the girl.

I could not move for the press of crowd around me. I could not speak; my words would not come. I could not take my eyes from the scene before me. Theo was laughing and bantering with his friends, parrying their jokes in his good-natured way. He was still laughing when his eyes caught mine. For a moment, his laugh and smile were just for me until he recognized me and took a startled step forward.

"Lucy," he mouthed the word, breaking his hand free from Elizabeth's grip, his other held tightly by Frances.

I stared at him, unreachable, already part of a world that was no longer his and mine. A wave of anger and shock gave me the strength to turn and fight my way through the press of courtiers and run from the room.

I know not how I found my way to the river, but with a single purpose I followed the scent of water. The damp air swathed me, but still I could not breathe. An anxiety rose in me that threatened to bring me to collapse.

I dropped to my knees, feeling only the stone path under me, conscious of the blackness that surrounded me at this late hour, the ripple of the water reflecting distant lantern lights. Fumbling for the ribbon, I tore the posie ring from my neck and threw it as far as I could, the gold spinning and weighting the ribbon as it curved into the Thames and slowly sank.

"Die in hope, for you have murdered my heart." I stuffed my fists in my mouth to muffle the scream that rose raw in my throat.

I breathed so shallowly that I barely moved, for I could not allow even the smallest movement to interrupt the pictures of my thoughts. I had no words except why, which echoed and reechoed in my mind. I greedily searched for any clue foretelling this dreadful betrayal.

All I could find was the laughter we shared, the intimate talks, the touch of his hand in mine, that night at White Hall, all torn from me in a single moment in a crowded room. Repeatedly, I ransacked my memories for the answer, angry with the world for tricking me into this belief of love's lies.

The persistent thin cry of a night bird penetrated my consciousness. Other small noises emerged, the lapping of the Thames as it slid by, unconcerned, a frog on the bank. Out on the river, a few wherries bobbed by the jetty, their lanterns swaying with the tide, casting broken paths of light upon the water. The night was clear, and starlight illuminated the heavens, a great bowl over the land. I searched deep into the night sky to find meaning.

I could not look behind me, to the palace walls that rose sheer, the gilded city now shrouded in darkness. It was as when I turned a pretty stone in my garden, only to find all manner of night creatures wriggling beneath it, revealing a world of dank and gloom, a realm I knew not.

Even my prayers were silenced, for as I called out to God, only questions arose.

A chill seeped through me as deep as a crypt, but I had no mind to leave this place of frozen time, no need to meet the coming day. Eventually, the firmament betrayed me, and although I was as still as the grave, the world moved through its hours regardless. A gleam appeared downriver, faintly at first, but then more resolute as the sun ascended.

A soft touch across my shoulders disturbed my musing, and as I turned my head, I found Will by me, down on the ground with me, holding me.

"Barbara eventually told us she met you in Frances's rooms," he said softly. "After some time, I extracted from Villiers a recounting of the pageant. Lucy, I am so sorry, for if I could take this sword thrust for you, I would absorb it with all my heart and soul."

I said nothing, for along with my prayers, my words had deserted me.

Picking up a pebble and rolling it in his palm, Will spoke, almost to himself, his calm and steady words washing over me, his soft Welsh accent ebbing and flowing. In truth, I did not hear much, but in my misery, I clung to the providence that brought Will to my side in my dark hour.

He spoke of the plight of those who did not have shelter, whose land had been ravaged by war or plague or famine. He talked of children who were forced to eat the very earth where no crops would grow and mothers whose babies died at their breast, suckling an empty teat, exhausted from starvation. Will opened my world beyond my own immediate sorrow and pushed me to travel beyond the misery that trapped me. He showed me through his stories to have faith in survival.

The sun rose over the river, illuminating the distant shore and bringing light to the darkness. I resolved to lock my thoughts of Theo away with the dress I had worn to Charlton Park, my hidden bride coffer slammed shut. As the sun gilded the turrets of the palace, now it appeared a theater, Theo and Frances players on its stage, proclaiming the words and deeds of parts scripted by their birth and destiny.

A great shudder ran through me. My dry eyes suddenly filled, and the unshed tears flowed. I wept for my lost love, my youth, and the agony of a love betrayed.

In Will's arms, I could cry and be safe.

13

If I am not to have a love of my own, I can record that of others. And maybe that is my destiny, to record life but not to truly live in it. Here are the events of those whom I know, but none of mine, for there is no change in my life.

Barbara m. Edward Villiers, 14th March 1611

Eleanor m. Will St.John of Fonmon, 10th Feb., 1612, at Battersey

Theophilus Howard m. Lady Elizabeth Hume, 14th March, 1612

Huw, son of Eleanor & Will, bapt. 3rd Dec., 1612, at Battersey

Frances Howard married Robert Carr, 26th Dec., 1612

Oliver, son of Anne and John, born 9th Feb., 1613, at Battersey

Anne, d. of Eleanor & Will, baptized at Battersey 15th Feb., 1614

Anne, d. of Eleanor &Will, died, bd. Battersey 12th Aug., 1614

William, son of Barbara and Edward, born 6th Sept., 1614

Lucy, spinster, twenty-five years of age

Lydiard Tregoze,

November 1614

"Why must you constantly be with her? Am I not good enough company for you? Do you wish only to hear again and again of her broken heart and lost love?" John's raised voice penetrated the wall of his study into the chamber where I was quietly reading, the weather being too inclement to venture out.

"I am tired, Anne, tired of the time you spend with her, encouraging her mooning over Lord Howard. Jesu, Anne, it has been two years since he married. Two years. She refuses to consider a marriage prospect here who is willing to overlook her indiscretion. Was it not enough that you allowed her to become disgraced, and you too could be tainted by her reputation? It is not good for you nor our family to be so immersed in this."

"It is not like that, John, I promise you. We have a sisterly love for each other and enjoy our days together. She was not disgraced—it is merely jealous rumor. Let her be. She is doing no harm. This cut her deeply, and the heart knows no calendar for healing."

I could hear the anguish in Anne's voice as she defended me.

"You enjoy your days with her overmuch, Anne, to the neglect of time with me. I have it on good authority that you pine for your old life at White Hall and plan ways to return."

"That's not true. I hated court, and I do not want to be there."

"It is not what I heard. I know that you secretly long to be away from the country. Well, I tell you, I will not go, I will not let you go, and you will never leave our home, your children unattended, your nights spent away from me." John's voice rose again, and he spoke over Anne's softer voice.

"Why do you not believe me, why are you attending to the envy of others?"

"I am listening to those who have my best interests at heart, and it seems you are not one of them. What do you wish for next? To return to court and play the adulteress now that you have borne me a son and heir? Would you too want a Howard lover, Anne? I hear it's quite the fashion. Is that the next step in your life?"

I could not bear to hear John's relentless anger and the deep untruths with which he was punishing Anne. I opened the study door and crossed the room to stand between them. I was as close to John as I dared, challenging him to push me away.

"You are wrong, John, completely wrong. Anne is a most virtuous and loyal wife, and she would never betray you or go against your will."

"You!" John was white with anger, tense, his hands clenched at his sides. "You dare to talk of betrayal. I know of your secret meetings with Howard. I know you brought shame on this family with your lust and wantonness. And now you wish to corrupt my wife to your court manners."

"It's Barbara, isn't it? It's Barbara who has poisoned you against me."

"You did this to yourself, madam. And now you refuse to consider marriage to a good man who will overlook your indiscretions."

"A good man?" I laughed bitterly. "Some ancient clodpole who doesn't know one end of book from another and breeds pigs?"

"His land stretches from here to Swindon." John took a step toward me, his face white with anger. "And he's the only one who will have tarnished goods. Let me tell you, if you don't accept him, you can leave here. I am done with your disruption in my family."

"And I am done with your hypocrisy and distrust. I would rather die than marry your pig farmer. Or anyone."

After a silence that echoed with the words that lay between us, I turned aside.

"Go, please, Lucy. I will talk with John." Anne spoke softly, her eyes imploring me to leave, to allow her to manage her husband's jealous rage.

Reluctantly, I left the room. Pulling my cloak from the peg by the door, I stepped out into the damp November afternoon.

This was not the first time that John had exploded with anger over my living at Lydiard and distracting Anne from her devotion to his needs. John always demanded attention from those around him and was a man of contradictions. For all the times he poured scorn on the court and its lavish behaviors, he loved to pose for his portrait dressed in fine clothes and purchased many beautiful objects with which to furnish Lydiard.

But lately his rages worsened, and I could not continue to be such an obvious contention between them.

I walked slowly across the muddy bowling green and sat on the bench under my beloved cypress tree, its needled branches offering some respite from the steady drizzle. Still, a cold damp steeped into me. A gardener had lit a bonfire of leaves earlier in the day. Although the rain tamped it to a mere smolder, the mournful smell of autumnal smoke lingered in the air, a reminder that the year was drawing to a close, and ahead lay winter's long, dark nights. I huddled deeper into my woolen cloak and gazed at Lydiard. A sense of detachment gave me strength to make the decision that had been haunting my thoughts for months.

A gust of wind blew a shower of raindrops from the cypress branches across my face. The spray of water recalled a time when I trembled full of excitement of the adventure that lay ahead of me, and the heady power of following my own destiny as I sailed with Anne on the ship to Guernsey. I allowed myself to feel again the swaying of the boat beneath me and hear the calls of the wild seabirds as they followed our ship.

When the gray light darkened to indigo, candles started to glimmer in Lydiard's windows, casting hospitable pools of light within the rooms, welcoming travelers to the warmth inside. I softly said adieu to my talisman. In my heart, I knew I would not live here again.

"Carr's star has waned, and there is a place for another to rise in his stead. One that is even closer to me." Barbara said confidently as she and I stood together for the artist to paint our likeness. As the closest in age, we were to appear next to each other in the massive family portrait John had commissioned, our arms linked, shoulders touching. The irony was not lost on me.

It meant a day in each other's company, the first time we had seen each other since her wedding to Edward Villiers. I was fortunate all I needed to do on that occasion was to wish her happiness in her marriage, for she had no interest in talking to me, nor I to her. There existed a great chasm between us, for although I knew she had witnessed my flight from White Hall, we did not ever speak of it.

"And what of your friend Frances? Does she not wane with Carr's decline?"

Barbara shrugged. "She shines less brightly now, and I hear that her family is finding other ways to remain high in the king's favor."

"And so now the Howards set their sights on a Villiers?"

"Edward has gathered funding from a number of gentlemen, including the Howard brothers, to contribute money for his brother George's wardrobe. They will be expecting him to catch the king's eye at every opportunity this Christmas."

"Does he wish to be paraded so?" I asked curiously. "It seems as though he has no say in the matter."

"George will do what his family tells him to. This has been a long time in the planning, and many people have an interest in his successful entry into society."

"And Edward is helping him?"

"Edward has been directing his education and accomplishments. George was taught all the fine skills of swordplay, dance, conversation, and manners when he was in France. He attended the same school as Edward in Ang—" She bit off her sentence and looked quickly at me.

I nodded slowly, knowledge dawning on me. I had no occasion but to exchange small conversation with Barbara since I left White Hall after Theo's marriage announcement, and it had always puzzled me why Edward said that he had heard of me when I met him at Frances's chambers.

"Angers. So Edward studied with Theo in Angers? He knew him well?"

"Oh yes. All the young men were lodging together."

"He knew of his marriage contract?"

Barbara stared ahead, immobile for the artist. Her voice was low, emotionless.

"It was well known in his circle that Theo was contracted to Elizabeth Hume. The negotiations had been in place for a while. When Edward met Theo in Angers, they became good friends and talked of Theo's marriage plans and his conflictions."

"Conflictions?"

She took a deep breath and sighed impatiently. "Theo loved you, Lucy, and wanted to find a way to marry you. His mother and Frances refused, for your rank is far below his. He threatened to break his marriage contract."

She smoothed the skirts of her gown, still looking at the painter and not at me.

"Finally, they told him they would find a way. By continuing the contract to the young Elizabeth, they considered her pliable enough that she would not protest if her husband continued his relationship with you." She tried to look at me, and the painter tut-tutted his annoyance. "They planned to marry you to a titled friend of Theo's, so you would be brought to court."

I was aghast. "And Theo agreed?"

Barbara shrugged. "'Tis is a common enough solution. Much is done for convenience to facilitate desire. In truth, Theo wanted to explain this to you himself, but when you attended Frances's performance at White Hall, the betrothal announcement was made, unbeknownst to him that you were there, and you ran away."

"And who was this friend I was supposed to marry?"

"'Tis of no account. It was someone Theo trusted, who would look the other way when his wife showed preference for his best friend. Besides, once you had provided your husband with an heir, as a married woman you would be free to choose your companions."

I fell silent, revolted at the scheming swirling around me, at these unprincipled people who played with lives and emotions and desires, plotting infidelity campaigns as though a military strategy.

Barbara continued, her arm tucked in my mine as we posed for the portrait painter, commemorated in false affection as I was forced to listen to her poisonous words.

"It is an excellent solution, Lucy, and one that is still available. He's married the heiress the family needs. Sired a child on her. It's been time enough to start his dynasty and prove his commitment to his lineage. His young bride will look the other way when he returns to court. This is my message to you."

"And why did Theo never reach out to me, write to me, tell me what was happening?"

"He had a young wife to impregnate. And he is not always comfortable confronting moral decisions. He has friends who would help him take care of the more unpleasant duties in his life. That is why I am talking to you now."

"Who thinks of my feelings or my desires? Did not Frances consider once what she was doing with his life or mine? And what about love and decency and honesty?"

Barbara laughed. "Not words that you would find within five miles of White Hall, Sister. You've spent enough time there and in Anne's company to know that."

The painter worked at our images, the quietness in the room broken only by his brushstrokes dabbing on the wooden panel and Barbara's sighs as she fidgeted with impatience.

"So what is your response to Theo, Lucy? Has enough time passed to change your mind? You could return to court with me, and we would have much stature, especially with you as a favorite of the Howard heir. Edward thinks it would help George's cause immensely too."

"Are you asking me to become Theo's mistress to further your own ambitions? Do you take me for a whore?"

"You have that reputation already, Lucy. Theo has not been discreet in his tales of your entertaining him while we were at White Hall. However, Edward knows of several young men who would find you marriageable and would happily facilitate Theo's desires. Why not take advantage of the situation? I would."

"You would because you are a bawd, Barbara." So many years of her cruelties to me gave speech to words long suppressed. "I despise you and the world you have chosen. Go to Theo and tell him to keep his whores in White Hall, for I would have nothing to do with him."

I ran from the room, ignoring the painter's protests, for I cared not for the ridiculous portrait, the subterfuge of a family of sisters united in love.

As the afternoon closed in around me, I vowed to control my own future, a simple future in Guernsey filled with the pleasures I loved, dedicated to God and serving my fellow citizens. It would be a peaceful life, undisturbed by the ambitions and schemes of others, with no promises, and no betrayals.

14

The virtues of Gilberts water:

It is bad for nothing. It cures wind and the collick, restoreth decayed nature, good for a consumption, expels poison and all infection from the heart. Helps digestion, purifies the blood, gives motion to the spirits, drives out the smallpox, for the grippes in young children, women in labor, bringeth the afterbirth, stops bloods for sounding and fainting.

Lucy St.John
Lydiard Tregoze
Twelfth Night 1615

Eleanor arrived last for the portrait sitting. She brought with her the sorrowful news of the death of her little baby, Anne, of the sweating sickness at just six months old. A deep shadow veiled her face, and many times I found her in quiet contemplation. I knew that her arms ached from emptiness.

"Lucy, stay with me for a while in Wales?" She held my hands tightly, the longing apparent in her eyes. "Will wants to see you, and I would love your ideas in making Fonmon hospitable for the time we are there. It is an ancient fortress, and not one designed for comfort. Will is waiting there for me now with my precious Huw, and I long to see them."

I could only begin to imagine how deeply she must want to hold her remaining child and be in Will's arms again.

"I am departing from Lydiard right after Twelfth Night." I hesitated. "I thought I might visit friends, stay with Uncle Oliver in Battersey, travel for a while." I quickly made my decision, for in truth, I dreaded leaving Eleanor the most. "I could come to Fonmon first since it is not likely that I would be back in the West Country for a while. A month in your company would be a memory I would treasure to take with me."

Eleanor looked at me inquiringly, but I did not elucidate further.

"Settled. Come back with me now when I travel at week's end. There is no reason to remain here."

"No reason to remain," I repeated.

"Will's men will arrive soon to escort me to Fonmon. It will be good for you to travel with us then." Eleanor grasped my hands, tears glistening on her cheeks. She had her own sorrows, and I had not been a good sister in understanding the depth of her grief. I smiled back and hugged her, remorseful that I had been selfish in my own desires, uplifted at the thought of seeing Will and their little boy, Huw, before I left for my new life.

Time for me to tell her of my plans later, for I would not pile more sorrow on her.

"Anne."

She raised her head from the sewing where she was seated by the window, catching the last of the afternoon light.

"I'm leaving Lydiard." I continued swiftly, stemming the denial that rose to her lips. "I would return to St. Peter Port and resume my life with Monsieur Montrachet and his family, serving the French refugees."

Anne stood up, not noticing that her sewing had dropped to the floor.

"Lucy, why? John's anger is only passing. You know this of old."

"It is deep-rooted and festers, Anne. You may be able to soothe him, but it is not my place to constantly stir arguments between you both."

I walked to her side and put my arms around her small frame, which trembled with the unshed tears she was suppressing.

"In John's view, the gossip would always follow me. Now that I've refused his suggested husband, no man would marry me." Even to me, my voice sounded bitter. "Barbara has seen to that."

"How will you live? Who will take care of you?"

"I don't need a husband to take care of me, Anne. I shall persuade Uncle Oliver to give me my dowry to pay for my keep. Lord knows he would prefer to give it to me than some clodpole. Or worse, an arrangement with one of Theo's companions." I grabbed her elbows, pushing her away slightly so I could read her face. "I could teach English to the new immigrants from France, for they need the language as they embark on their new lives. I could grow my own food and medicines to support myself while being no trouble to others."

As I spoke the words aloud, my plans took shape, became real. My heart lifted at the prospect.

"How long, Lucy? How long will you be gone?"

"Long enough to let time heal, Anne."

She nodded slowly, the strength that I had always loved about her supporting her now. She had her own life with John and her babies, and I could see that the prospect of a cessation of conflict within her home was a relief to her.

"You will always have a home here, Lucy," she said. "John has a hot temper, but he loves you. He's finding his way too. As he grows older, he will discover there is tolerance for all kinds of love in his heart and that it is not exclusive between husband and wife. A little distance between the two of you will give you both the time to reconcile."

"Thank you, my sweet sister." I let her go. "Please, no word to anyone, especially Eleanor. I would tell this news in my own time."

She took a deep breath and nodded.

"I am glad my island holds such a place in your heart, Lucy. I will be familiar with your life as I think of you, and I will not worry about the unknown."

Saying good-bye to Anne was very difficult, for her affection was as kind as a mother's to me, and we had grown so close that it was as if we shared one soul. But she inhabited a world I did not know, with her husband and her children. I knew that our love would bind each other close and that as the years passed, we would always kindle the companionship we held so dear. It was hard to keep from her that I was not returning, but I knew she would be horrified and blame herself for my decision. It was best to veil my plans and let them emerge gradually as the years went by.

I carefully packed my medicinals, my recipes, my precious stores, so that when I arrived in Guernsey, I would have the basis of my apothecary. If I could not immediately find occupation teaching, I could at least bring relief to those refugees who arrived in such sad condition after escaping the persecutions in France.

As for Lydiard, the parting was bittersweet, for as I walked the familiar paths and brushed my fingers across tree trunks and old stone walls, I said my good-byes silently, from my heart, one inanimate object to another. Although I would not be there to observe the turning of the seasons, I could take with me memories of the blossoms, the small green shoots, the summer roses, and the golden autumn leaves and know that Lydiard endured.

15.

For convulsion fits

A stone growing the gall of an old oxe and the same quantity of a dead mans scul that come to an untimely end. Mix an equal quantity and give as much as will lye on a 2 pence a little before the fit comes. The hair that grows between the hinder legs of a hee bear, boyle in brandy til the brandy be consumed, lay it warm to the soles of the feet.

As told to me by Donna Ana at Battersey
Lucy St.John
My recipes

At week's end, Eleanor and I set out on our journey to Fonmon Castle, the fortress in Wales owned by our cousins and leased by Will for a year when he returned from his latest expedition.

"I do not know why Will would choose to live in such a remote place." Eleanor was resigned to the travel, but I know it pained her to put such distance between herself and our family.

"I think it is his pride," I said quietly. "It's important to him that he provide well for you, Eleanor. Barbara is not the only one who has called him a poor relation."

Will was born in a small village just a few miles from Fonmon Castle and grew to embrace the restless life of a soldier and an adventurer. He dwelled on the fringe of the St.John wealth and prosperity. I believed when the opportunity of leasing the castle coincided with a particularly prosperous trade transaction, he was ready to return to his birthplace and claim a higher status in society.

I imagined him as a little boy, playing privateer under the shadow of the fortress walls, aspiring one day to return home with means to live in the castle.

"He always imagined himself living at Fonmon." Eleanor caught my thoughts.

"So perhaps this is his way of proving himself to you, Eleanor." I was quite looking forward to seeing Fonmon Castle, for Eleanor had described its wild beauty and isolated situation. It suited my present mood.

The weather was most dreadful when we set out, dark clouds rain-swollen from east to west. Across country to Wales, there were little more than carters' tracks in many places. Impassable by coach, we rode on horseback, which made better time but resulted in miserable traveling conditions. The rain waterlogged our heavy woolen cloaks, so we never really dried out, and the damp penetrated to the depths of our bones, so we were never warm. Daylight was brief, limiting our progress. As we left Wiltshire's cultivated fields behind and headed to the western forests, our little party fell silent, traveling in single file for many hours with only our thoughts to keep us company.

The days passed in a blur, one roadside inn indistinguishable from the next. The comfort was basic, although the welcome warm, for there were few travelers abroad in the midst of winter, and the landlady always eager for news. We obliged with our talk of court and the stories we had heard. On everyone's lips was the rumor that the recently married Robert Carr and Frances Howard had by great bribery arranged for the poisoning death of Thomas Overbury as he lay detained in the Tower of London.

I lived two lives on that journey, for as we shared tales, hearing from the innkeepers their version of the news and repeating the snippets and scraps we had gleaned by firesides the night before, a story emerged that I could scarcely believe in the telling but which rang true with the knowledge I had of the characters. It was most strange to speak of people I knew, who had themselves impacted my life and yet fallen by the wayside as I relinquished my former being and embraced my new.

"Do you believe it's true?" asked Eleanor of me one night as we sat by a smoky hearth in a hospitable inn outside Chepstow. Our clothes steamed from the damp as we tried to warm through. We had traveled the old ferry crossing from Aust to Beachley earlier and were within two days of Fonmon. A hearty stew warmed our stomachs, and with a tankard of good brewed ale, a sense of well-being settled over us.

"Would Frances really have bribed someone to poison Overbury? Did she detest him that much?"

"She and Carr were desperate to be together," I replied, remembering them at White Hall, intertwined with each other, their infatuation evident. "After the scandal of her divorce hearings, and her success in defaming Essex, she thought she was invincible. Overbury despised Frances and thought her a great distraction to Carr and ultimately his own ambitions. He did all that he could to prevent Carr from spending time with her."

"Is that why the king commanded Overbury to the Tower?"

"It had to be. Overbury had no friends at court, for in truth, he was a most arrogant man. I suspect Carr told the king to imprison him to teach him a lesson, to curb his manners, for he was trying to possess Carr as Carr possessed the king. And that was dangerous."

Eleanor stretched her feet toward the fire, wriggling her stiff toes wrapped in heavy woolen stockings, her boots standing to the side, drying out.

"And Frances was not content with mere imprisonment in the Tower of London?" Her tone was sarcastic.

"It seems not. She must have been fearful of Overbury's influence on Carr. I'm not surprised; it was said that Carr did not have one idea of his own that was not thought of by Overbury first."

"They say he could not stand, nor sit, so great were the convulsion fits that came upon him."

"And every medicine that Frances sent to cure him only made him worse." I shuddered. "It would not surprise me if the witch Anne Turner did not have a role in this."

"White Hall appears a world where much can turn on a whim or perception, and there is little recourse for innocence." Eleanor snuggled deeper into the blanket draped over her shoulders. "If arrogance warrants incarceration, there would be few men left to run the country, for it is not a rare trait, and Overbury possessed much of it. But it is far from a crime that justifies prison."

"Nor death," I replied somberly, my thoughts turning again to Frances and the sycophants that surrounded her, the fortune tellers and wizards, the lackeys who were eager to do as she bid, the hangers-on who encouraged her willful behavior by carrying out her outrageous requests. It was not beyond the bounds of reason that she would demand the death of someone who obstructed her desire. After all, she had killed my heart without a second thought.

Our final miles to Fonmon followed an ancient holloway that plunged through deep forests and forded rushing streams. We traversed an old land, full of mysteries and legends, and the woods kept their secrets close as we guided our horses westerly. A sense of watchfulness, but not malice, followed us. I refused to be frightened of the wood spirits, for I did not feel their presence to be evil. I welcomed the embrace of the old forest and mused of those who had traveled these paths before me, heading to Fonmon for shelter and protection.

As the trees ahead thinned, a stone tower appeared through the bare winter branches. At the moment we rode into the clearing, the rain stopped and a shaft of pale sunlight pierced the clouds, causing the castle walls to shimmer. It was dazzling, and after days of gloom and darkness, we could not but break into delighted laughter at the glorious sight before us.

"'Tis nature's way of welcoming you home," I called to Eleanor. "After eight days on the road, for the rain to cease at this very moment is surely a sign that you are blessed."

"And you too, Lucy, for your journey with me has already soothed my troubled heart. I was dreading returning here alone, and you have eased my burden with your company." Eleanor waved vigorously. "Look, look, it's my darlings!"

She scrambled from her horse, not waiting for assistance, and ran across to the castle entry. Will had emerged, a broad smile on his face, carrying a little dark-haired boy who was dressed in breeches and shirt similar to his father's. They embraced Eleanor, Huw clinging to her neck and Will's arms encircling both of them as they stood together in the silvery winter sunlight. Will looked up from Eleanor's embrace, and his face broke into a wide smile.

"Lucy, it is so good to see you. It's time you paid us a visit, and I hope you can stay a while with us. Eleanor is lonely for women's talk in Fonmon, and I know she would welcome your company."

I dismounted stiffly with the help of a groom who had come to take our horses, a military man by his bearing.

"Thank you, it is so good to be here with you. But I would not overstay my welcome, Will. This is yours and Eleanor's time to spend together, and it is not for me to be in your way. I have other plans . . ."

"Ah, don't trouble with that," Will interrupted. "Since living here, I have had a stream of visitors from my days in Ireland. They find it a convenient place to stop on their arrival in Britain. Unfortunately, all have been army men that are looking for peacetime occupation now that the wars are over. Eleanor's patience is wearing thin if one more soldier puts his dirty boots on her hearth."

I laughed, knowing that Will was teasing us. Eleanor was the most hospitable and welcoming of people and would never turn away a man seeking shelter.

"Then I will stay, for I would not want Eleanor to suffer alone. But I must tell you . . ."

"'Tis settled, then. You will stay, for I want my wife to be happy, and happy she is when you are with her. Come along, come, and let us show you Fonmon Castle."

I gave up trying to tell Will that I was not planning on staying for long, for those disclosures could be saved for later. At this moment, I wanted to share his excitement in showing me his castle and enjoy his pride in providing such a significant home for his new family.

I took a deep breath and looked around me, the soft Welsh air fragrant, a distant tang of the ocean blending with the sharpness of damp pine. The keep was not large, but rooted in the land, covered all over with the bare tendrils of vines, a dark forest nudging its walls. It suited my nature, for it dwelt as remote as any could wish for, stark and with no village sheltering at its feet.

As Will escorted me through the gatehouse, the ancient fortress encircled me. It reminded me of Castle Cornet and sheltering within its walls, the same sense of safety overcoming me. Once again, a building intended for defense came to my rescue.

16

My dearest Anne,

It has been a while since I had inclination to record my thoughts, but here at Fonmon, for the first time in many months, I feel alive again. My moments of joy have arrived in the smallest of incidents, when little Huw has climbed onto my lap or brought me a posy of the first snowdrops from the wintry woods.

Huw has other playmates, children of the castle steward, and the groom, and I much enjoy their games of pretense as they tumble among the castle walls and ramparts. Today I was their captive princess, locked away in the Tower by her wicked sister, a story I told them of our own Queen Elizabeth. They took great delight in escorting me to Fonmon's dungeon, and my angry protestations and loud cries were very satisfactory to my little gaolers. In truth, I found the dank walls and gloomy prison quite disturbing, although no prisoners had dwelled there for many years, and it did not require a great deal of pretense for my screams to sound real.

On the matter of which we spoke before I left, I intend to put my plans into action within the month. Eleanor fares well, and the crossing should be calmer by April.

Lucy
Fonmon
1st March 1615

My breath panted in ragged gasps, harsh to my ears. My cheeks were whipped with the cold wind blowing through the bare woods, carrying the saltiness of the wild sea that pounded the rocky castle boundaries. I plunged through the forest, my boots kicking up the damp leaves. My legs flew free from inhibiting skirts, enclothed as they were in a pair of Will's old breeches, buckled tight at the waist with a large leather belt. My long velvet jacket flapped burdensome, catching brambles and twigs in its overlong sleeves, but I was most pleased with my large-brimmed hat that stayed firmly on my head as I raced through the trees. With Will's purloined Spanish cutlass in my hand, I appeared suitably terrifying as Lucifera, the Lady Pirate, intent on capturing Huw and his little friends.

It was a game we played since the March winds had chased away the storms of winter. I must confess I escaped into happiness in the children's excitement and the marvelous stories they concocted each day for us to act. To be so far from the conventions of society was liberating. Will and Eleanor told me often they were relieved to witness my spirit recover and come alive.

I burst through the last copse that bordered the castle entryway. Waving my sword above my head, I chased my little band of pirates across the wet grass, all of us sliding and whooping with delight and uttering blood-curdling screeches.

Huw was the first to stop in his tracks, and we collided with each other. More visitors had arrived at Fonmon, and they were staring at us with concerned curiosity. A boy and girl, aged about twelve and ten years of age, I would guess, were standing quietly by the great iron portcullis, as if washed up on the shore, alone and orphaned. Their hands reached for each other's. The older one, the boy, took a step in front of his sister as if to protect her from our noisy gaggle. Their faces were pinched with tiredness, and they looked chilled to the bone.

Sending Huw and his gang around to the side door to beg refreshments from the kitchen, I swiftly walked to the children, who huddled closer together when I approached them. I dropped the cutlass on the ground, calling to them that I meant no harm. As I drew close, a small smile tentatively appeared on the boy's face.

"My name is Mistress St.John. I welcome you to Fonmon and wish you well, travelers."

The boy bowed and the girl curtsied, their manners fine and well executed.

"I am Peter, and this is my sister, Jocasta. It is an honor to meet you, mistress."

"Are you here alone? Where is your escort, your nurse?'

"Our father brought us. He has gone to find his friend who lives here. Our nurse died of the sweat three days ago. Are you a pirate?"

I looked down at my boots and britches and carefully picked a bramble from my velvet cuff.

"Not really, although there have been times in my life when I had wished to run away and join the privateers on the Spanish Main. And I have sailed a ship across the Narrow Sea and consider myself most fortunate that I did not encounter the enemy corsairs, although I may have seen his sails billowing on the horizon."

"My father recently sailed too. He had to take a ship to come and get us. He was a long time gone." The girl spoke quietly, her voice subdued.

"I am so sorry to hear that. Was it an arduous voyage? Has he returned?" I was curious, for these children were not French refugees.

"From Ireland. Just these past days."

"Come inside—you both are exhausted. Come on." I clasped their cold hands in mine and escorted them through the portcullis and across the yard into the kitchens. As we walked, I sensed their tiredness and something more. They carried a heaviness of spirit, not just induced by exhaustion, but by something much deeper. I wondered who their nurse had been and if she had been ill for long.

"Martha, our cook, will warm you by her fire and give you some food. I shall go to the stillroom and find a potion that will soothe your aches and help you rest. Then to bed with you, for you both need to sleep."

The boy smiled gratefully at me, but the girl appeared lost in her own world. Her brow was hot when I placed my hand on it. I suspected the onset of a fever. I pushed open the door to the kitchens, and the warm air engulfed us, scented by the day's bread and a hunter stew that was bubbling in a cauldron on the hearth. The kitchen was the heart of the old fortress, and the cavernous fireplace built to roast enough meat to feed the army that had originally occupied Fonmon. Now it was more a welcome place to warm. As the children perched on the bench before it, the fire lit their tired faces, and I could see their tension begin to ease.

"Martha, we have guests. Please give them some of your fine stew while I find something to ease their fatigue." I spoke quickly to the cook, who nodded and filled two wooden bowls and handed them to Peter and Jocasta. Peter gratefully cupped the warm vessel and began to eat, but Jocasta just sat with hers untouched, her eyes glassy.

In the castle stillroom, one of the first improvements I had made at Eleanor's insistence was to organize the potions and medicines. Now the room was immaculate, ready for the first crop of herbs and plants to gather and dry in the spring. I had convinced Will that we needed to spend money in purchasing the basic medicinal compounds, and on his last trip to Bristol, he had returned with a quantity of physics that I had requested, enabling me to stock a simple apothecary for the castle and its tenants. Because our little community on the Welsh coast was isolated, we were the only source of medicine for many miles, and it quickly became known that we could offer help to those in need.

When I returned to the kitchen, the children were leaning against each other on the bench, barely awake. I gave them both a dose of my chamomile posset to ease their aches, with a little extra mint for Jocasta to quieten her sickness, and led them out of the kitchen and across the yard to the main hall.

I could not see Eleanor or Will, and so I took Peter and Jocasta to my room and helped them lay down on the large bed, covering them with a warm fur mantle. Their eyes closed before I had even left the room, and their breathing was quiet, a little color returned to their cheeks. I stood and looked at them, so young and vulnerable in their sleep, and was satisfied they were resting at last.

In the great hall, Eleanor and Will were standing in front of the fire with a tall man who had his back to the room, deep in talk. A flash of anger rose in me as I guessed this was the children's father. I marched up to the little group.

"Your children were exhausted. I have fed them and put them to bed. You can attend to them when they wake up—if you have the time and interest to do so."

He turned swiftly and bowed.

"Madam, I am thankful for your concern. I—"

"You showed no concern by leaving those poor children out in the cold while you stand by the fire and trade stories with my cousin. Save your concern for them, not me."

He was visibly startled and opened his mouth to say more.

"And it is no thanks to you that they were starving and tired and that Jocasta is sick from her travels. I hear their nurse died, and yet you still put them through this journey. What kind of father are you that would push these children to the limits of their endurance?"

"A devoted one, Lucy, and one that has traveled far to seek our hospitality." Will laid his hand on my arm to quiet me. "As soon as Allen found me in the guardhouse, we saw you taking the children to Martha. We knew they were in good hands." His mouth twitched at the corners. "You are a fearsome foe, Lucifera."

My anger was stilled mid-sentence, for I had forgotten I was still dressed in the makeshift pirate's costume from my morning adventures with Huw. As I looked down at my britches and boots, Eleanor stifled a giggle, and the stranger cleared his throat several times.

"Thank you, madam, again, for your kindness and concern," he said carefully. "The children have traveled far from their home and lost all they hold familiar these past few days. I am very grateful for the welcome they have received from Will and his family." He rubbed his face tiredly. "How fares my daughter? Is her fever high?"

His voice was low and with a slight accent that lilted the words. I could see the shadow of exhaustion across his blue eyes. A similar sense of heaviness weighted his spirit as did his children's. Although his hair was graying, there was a stamina in his bearing that told of a strong physique, and his dress was that of a gentleman officer.

"She needs rest and care. I have her in bed, sleeping in my chamber now. I am sorry I was angry. I was concerned for them."

He smiled wryly.

"As am I. If you will excuse me." He turned to Will. "Let us finish our business where we do not tire the ladies, and then I wish to see Jocasta."

Will smiled and nodded as they left us.

"Eleanor, we'll be in my study. Perhaps we could dine early this evening so Allen can rest tonight."

I was curious about the little family that had arrived at Fonmon. Although it was not unusual for Will and Eleanor to receive visitors, and especially not rare for soldiers such as he to arrive, we had not had children come before.

Eleanor and I discovered a small chamber nestled over the castle gate and furnished it with a thick carpet, tapestry, and carved chairs to add a domestic comfort to the cold stone. In some places, Fonmon's walls were six feet thick, and although they kept the weather at bay, there was a deep chill that lingered. Outside, the fickle March winds blew western rain squalls in from the sea again. Showers chased across the skies, casting distracting shadows over our sewing and encouraging gossip rather than labor. As we sat that afternoon and stitched charity shirts, Eleanor talked more of how Will had served with the man in the Irish wars.

"Sir Allen was a captain in the Queen's Guard in Ireland," said Eleanor, biting a thread and poking it through her needle. "His family is all from Devon, and he received his knighthood around the time John acquired his."

"Bought or earned?" I asked. It would be a long time before I thought of John's acquisition without rancor.

"Definitely earned. He fought long and hard in Ireland. Uncle Oliver served with him, along with Will."

I paused in my sewing for a moment and thought of Peter and Jocasta.

"Why should he bring the children here, Eleanor? It seems that they were ill prepared to travel."

"Their mother died of the sweating sickness a few weeks ago," she replied. "Sir Allen just returned from Ireland and secured his position as Victualler of the Navy. The children and he are removing to London now that he is assigned to his duties there."

"It seems harsh for the children to travel with him. They appear exhausted."

"His wife's family is from the West Country, and I believe that's where the children were living. He has to bring them with him to London now that their mother has died." She paused, her face soft. "Those poor children must be in deep grief, for I hear that they looked after her in her dying but could not save her. And then, just as they were to set out, their nurse passed as well. He had no choice but to journey forward."

"I must watch the girl closely. Do not go into my room, Eleanor, for if she has the sweat, we may all succumb. I think these are not the symptoms she presents, but the next days will tell for sure."

I continued stitching, the watery sun casting a fleeting light upon the shirt that allowed for me to see the pattern again. It was sad to think of those two young children witnessing the dying woman, their father far away in Ireland. "Is Will engaged in commerce with him?"

"Sir Allen has many connections throughout London and Ireland, and he has suggestions for Will's next venture." Eleanor put down her sewing and studied the raindrops chasing each other down the wavy glass pane as another squall spattered the castle. "I hope this will bring Will back to land again and persuade him that the life of an adventurer is not one that compliments being a husband and father."

"He'll always have that wild streak, Eleanor. That's what makes him so appealing." I smiled at her, knowing that she heard no envy in my voice, just a love for a cousin who was as a brother to me.

Our talk drifted to Will's expeditions and tales of his exploits, or at least of those that we knew. Eleanor was so captivated by him that she could talk for hours about the distant voyages and rough adventurers who shared his journeys, and I let her voice flow over and around me, not needing to do much more than occasionally agree with her.

As she spoke of those travels, Theo came to mind, but as I recalled the meager words of his few letters and the secret times we shared, I realized something had changed, for I could now recall him without the piercing pain that had characterized my previous musings. I half smiled to myself, acknowledging that my head had overruled my heart at last and that I was no longer tormented by the heartbreak that had defined so many of my days. However, the numbness that often blanketed me was in some ways more disturbing than the anguish.

What would it take for me to feel again?

17

A posset drink for a fevour. 9 spoonfuls of treacle water, 3 more of white wine a quarter a pint of ale, the juyce of two oranges, put all these into a quart of milk, give this as often as you please. It is good for all malignant fevours.

Recipe from Sybil ap Morgan
Fonmon

"They sleep soundly." Sir Allen leaned over his children, gently brushing a strand of Jocasta's hair from her closed eyes. "Your posset was effective."

"A simple recipe. Sleep is the best medicine for young bodies." I had taken Sir Allen to his children and found them fast asleep in my bed, curled up together like two puppies.

"Would it indispose you if they stayed?" He tucked Peter's hand under the fur mantle. "They have not rested this well in a while."

"Of course not. The trundle is being made. I'll sleep here with them tonight."

"You would do that for a stranger's children?" He straightened, the moment of tenderness over. "You can arrange for a maid to stay."

"What an odd remark. I would do that for anyone's children." I brushed past him, close in the confined chamber. "Jocasta should not be left to a maid's ministrations tonight, whatever you think."

Sir Allen and Will continued their discussions over dinner, their talk turning to the plight of Sir Walter Raleigh, a good friend of Will and a distant cousin of Sir Allen, and his long imprisonment in London's Tower.

"Why should a man be punished for having a free spirit and a desire to explore the unknown?" I asked. "For is our world not one that is open for us to seek God's wonders?"

Sir Allen appeared surprised that I joined the men's conversation.

"You think it is right and just to finance those who make war upon others on the open seas?"

"Sir Walter may have encountered the Spanish, our declared enemy, on his voyages and fought against them. But he also has done much to further our knowledge of botany and biology."

"So you have read his works? Your knowledge of medicines is more than that of an idle interest?"

"I am far from idle."

"My pardon. I did not intend to—"

"I have some learning, at my Lord Zouche's. And I have studied with Dr. L'Obel, the king's physician, who cultivates seeds from Sir Walter's voyages."

Sir Allen looked at me quizzically and returned to his discussion.

"Will, if we can free Walter, I firmly believe he will find the El Dorado gold on his next voyage. He has come so close before. He just needs one more chance. With age has come a wisdom, and I feel he will steer a smooth course this time."

"We must create this chance, Allen." Will stood and paced just as Huw did when he was full of excitement. "This is the time to raise the idea, to gather men to support the voyage, to obtain royal approval."

"The king will require convincing that this is not another excuse to war with the Spanish."

"And God knows Walter would find some reason to fire if a Spanish ship came within range of his guns."

Sir Allen laughed heartily.

"'Twould not be the first time Walter has been distracted from a mission to by the chance of a good fight."

There was a pause in the conversation.

"Barbara has returned to court with her husband," I said. "She mentioned that his brother, George, was one they were hoping would catch the king's attention. Perhaps she could help find a willing patron for Walter."

Will turned and looked at me. "Is the Villiers plan really coming to fruition?" He sounded surprised. "When Oliver told me of this on our last visit, I forecast that none could remove Carr from the king's affection, no matter how fine a leg or beautiful face could tempt him."

Sir Allen laughed again. "Did Oliver beg funds from you too, to support the Villiers cause?"

Will smiled mischievously. "I contributed enough to buy George a new hat and told Oliver to remember me as someone who helped him get a head. Maybe I did bet on the right horse."

We all laughed at Will's jest, and the talk turned to their recollections of Raleigh and his travels. In truth, he was a man of legend, and the stories of his exploits, as told by Will and Sir Allen, were most entertaining. I could see, however, that Will was distracted, and I suspected he was still planning ways to could help his old friend.

The fire cast a warm glow over our little party. We dined in the small antechamber at the end of the great hall, nestled deep from the storms that had again risen from the ocean and were battering the thick castle walls. Every so often, a heavier shower would patter against the shutters. The fire hissed as rain found its way into the chimney, but the interruptions of these outside elements served only to emphasize the warmth and peacefulness within the chamber.

"'Tis good to be here, Will. I am most grateful for your hospitality." Sir Allen leaned back in his chair and stretched appreciatively, his hand finding its way to the large head of one of Will's Irish wolfhounds. "And this good fellow seems to have made a friend of me." He scratched the dog's ear, and I caught again a tenderness in his face that belied his gravity.

"He welcomes a fellow countryman, Allen, and appreciates your affection too." Eleanor spoke kindly, her eyes soft on the soldier.

He laughed. "I am no Irishman, but it will take me a time to return to English ways after so many years away. In truth, I feel I have a foot in each land. As for this fine fellow, 'tis easy to find affection from one so steadfast, for he wants of nothing but a head scratch and a scrap from my plate. Those are simple rewards I can give him."

"Have you been away long, Allen?" Eleanor inquired.

"It feels so," he replied. "Between my service abroad in the Queen's Guard and my appointments in Ireland, it has been twenty years since I was here in Britain for any time. I must confess I feel trepidation upon settling. But Peter and Jocasta deserve a hearth better than the latest garrison to which I am appointed."

He continued to fondle the dog's head, his voice soft as he spoke, looking down at the hound. A lock of his thick gray hair cast a shadow over his face

"And so you return to a permanent home in London?"

"I have now a home in East Smithfield, a house of the king's that is given to the Surveyor of the Marine Victuals, hard by the storehouses and warehouses of the docks. It will be a different life for all of us, but one that I believe will be more conducive to family than the hardships of military life." He looked up from scratching the dog's head, as if realizing there were others in the room, for his words had been said almost to reassure himself.

"And what of you, Lady Lucy?" he asked, his tone polite as he changed the course of the conversation. "Do you forecast any more privateering in your future?"

I half smiled at his reference to my costume game with Huw of that morning.

"No, my life is modest and one that I see with little opportunity for adventure. I am but visiting here for a while and plan to continue my travels and then retire in peace and study the word of God."

Sir Allen raised an eyebrow and looked at me directly. His eyes narrowed, assessing my face, questioning my words, as though I were a prisoner under interrogation.

"Retire in peace?" he repeated. "That sounds a singular existence. Will you not miss your family and friends?"

Will interrupted. "We are holding Lucy captive here at Fonmon, Allen, as I do not wish to see her pursue that path. She is needed here. Huw would be heartbroken if his pirate lady left him now, and Eleanor would miss her sister beyond all measure."

"Thank you, Will, you flatter me." I looked down at my plate, not wanting to meet the gaze of my family and new acquaintance. "We shall see, for it will soon be time for me to move on. I cannot impose on your generosity for much longer. Besides, I am eager to see my other sisters. Now that Barbara has recently delivered of a son, I would visit her. And perhaps I should see Katherine too, for I hear that she has a fine new home."

My voice drifted to a halt, and I was aware of how unconvincing I sounded, even to my own ears. I did not meet Eleanor's eyes, who knew that I would not choose to visit Barbara of my own volition. It was time to leave the pretense alone and to tell the truth of my plans.

"For someone who has such strong opinions on how others manage their lives, it seems you have clouds concealing your own future," observed Sir Allen, his voice neutral, although his words cut.

"I have given my own destiny plenty of thought," I retorted. "There is little I can do except to chart my course and hope that I will find refuge in one home or another. Our world does not allow for women to have much independence. I have some small means upon which to exist and a mind to teach others."

He shrugged slightly, as if dismissing my words. Will and Eleanor were silent, watching our exchange.

"There are many ways to declare independence, some more apparent than others," he replied. "Having the freedom to think, to act, to manage, and to decide the course of your family, your education, your aspect in life . . . those are all ways to express your own individual choices."

"That is not a role that is easy to come by. Too often our lives are shaped by decisions that others make and are not in our best interests." I scratched the dog's head too, looking for distraction. "I prefer to withdraw from any situation wherein others decide my fate. I would rather manage my own destiny, lonely as that might be, than to be at the mercy of those who would decide it for me."

"No middle ground, Lucy? No partnership of a life together with someone who thinks women have a voice—no give and take, better or worse?"

My fingers accidentally brushed Sir Allen's and I quickly drew my hand away from the hound.

"Such a someone does not exist. Excuse me."

I left the room and returned to my chamber. My room did not welcome me with the solitary comfort I sought, however. His children were still sleeping peacefully, their sweet faces lit by a flickering candle, relaxed in the deep slumber of youth, their hands clasped. I lay on the trundle bed, my emotions churning between a mixture of disquiet at his impertinence and gratitude at seeing Peter and Jocasta sheltered in the warmth and safety of my bed.

My discomfort with Sir Allen continued, for in truth, his eyes observed more than his words revealed. Jocasta's fever did not abate quickly. While I was not concerned that she was in danger, it was important that she rest and partake of the medicines I made for her.

During her convalescence, I avoided Allen as best as I could. In my heart of hearts, I did not welcome conversation that would reveal the weaknesses in my logic. In many ways, Sir Allen reminded me of Uncle Oliver. I did not trust his plain speaking would serve me well in my carefully constructed plans.

In the ensuing weeks, my attention was on the children. I spent time with them, reading aloud and talking, encouraging them to rest. Peter seemed to recover his spirits quickly, and it wasn't long before he was up and about, followed everywhere by little Huw, who trailed as a puppy on his heels. It was delightful to see them both together; Peter was very kind to the little boy and had much patience in joining in his games. I encouraged this, for it was healthy for Peter to be as a child again. I sensed he had assumed many adult burdens caring for his mother in his father's absence.

Jocasta was still quite subdued, and although I guessed it to be her nature to be quiet, there was still a melancholy that hung around her. I knew she felt desperately the loss of her mother. Here was something I could understand. Although she did not wish to speak much, I was able to share with her my story and the comfort that comes of making those dear female friends that can deepen into a lifetime sisterhood.

In truth, I was sorry for the child. She was lost in her own world. It seemed she had no relatives with whom she could spend time, and although Sir Allen and Peter were looking forward to their new life in London, I sensed Jocasta was greatly nervous of the change and longed for the old ways.

After they had been at Fonmon for several weeks, I came to the castle yard in the morning on my way to the stillroom and found much commotion. There was frenzied bustling of the servants, and in the stable block, the horses were saddled; Will's groom was checking the harnesses and girths on the animals while others were lading packs on the dray ponies. I caught sight of Eleanor by the hall doors and walked swiftly to her side.

"What has happened, Eleanor? Is everything all right?"

"A messenger arrived from Oliver late last night, summoning Will to Battersey. It appears that their plans for George Villiers are coming to fruition, and Oliver has sent urgently for Will to help support the cause and witness the succession."

"The cause? The succession?" It sounded revolutionary.

"So they call it. It seems that the rumors surrounding Carr's role in Overbury's death have grown beyond control and that in his panic he has made intolerable demands on the king. Oliver and Edward join others in seeing this as the opportunity to topple him."

"And replace him with George?"

"That is the plan. There are many in his faction that have spent excessive money and time waiting for this moment and would not be turned from this course."

"And Will is part of this?" My heart dreaded to hear that my cousin was caught in this intrigue.

"Oliver encourages him so, with Edward's friends. And he sees the prospect of rewards to those who have picked the right horse to back."

"Oh, Eleanor, I wish this were not happening. Will does not belong in this plotting. It is a dangerous game and one that I feel Will has neither the temperament nor the guile to play."

Eleanor looked at me with eyes bright with tears but smiled still the same.

"It is his nature to take on a challenge, Lucy. He is bored with being a gentleman farmer. He longs to be on the move again, where he can live by his wits and take advantage of opportunities that come his way. Now that he has proven his success here in Wales, he is ready to return to the heart of the action. And that is now in White Hall, where the gains are greatest."

"Lucy! You heard the news?"

Will's voice interrupted our discussion as he strode across the yard, alight with excitement. By his side was Sir Allen, similarly dressed for

143

travel, and they cut imposing figures in their great cloaks and high boots, swords at their sides. I glimpsed the child in the man, directing their fate. Neither of them were much different from Huw and his band of friends, searching for the next adventure.

"I did. I will not tell you to take care, Will, for I know that you are not in physical danger. But I will tell you to take heed. The game you play is as dangerous as that of an Irish war, with enemies hiding in secret places waiting to ambush. It is not a familiar landscape to you."

He laughed. No warnings would dampen his spirits that morning.

I turned to Sir Allen.

"And what of you, sir, do you engage in this cause too?"

He was more somber in spirit, although a restless vigor flared in his bright blue eyes.

"I ride with Will to London and assume my new home and responsibilities. I am late already, for I had only planned a few nights at Fonmon on my way to the city. I am urgently required to meet with the Privy Council."

"'Tis a pity your sick child delayed your plans." I sounded sharp, even to my own ears.

"It has been a joy to see them recover their health and spirits, and time that I consider worth any business delay. I owe you my thanks, Mistress Lucy. I leave them here in good hands while I ready their new home."

"They are staying?"

"Yes, Eleanor has offered shelter until I send for them. I thank you again for your kindness. I hope it is not an imposition on your time if you could continue your healing for a few weeks more."

He turned to Eleanor and held her hands as he kissed her cheek.

"My heartfelt gratitude, Eleanor, for coming to my aid. You have been merciful in repairing my spirit and my thoughts. I will always remember your wise words."

Eleanor laid her hand on his shoulder and spoke softly. "Trust your heart over your head, Allen, and listen to your inner voice. Do not always look for life's map that cannot be rewritten, for sometimes an interrupted journey can bring a new choice in routes." She stood on tiptoe and kissed him. "It is up to the traveler to be open to change and to trust there is a purpose in all things, even though we may not see His road for us clearly."

He turned to me and made as though to kiss my cheek too, but then drew back.

"Mistress Lucy. I am forever in your debt." He bowed abruptly and walked rapidly across the yard.

"What was that supposed to mean, Eleanor?" I asked. "Your words implied a lot more than they said."

"Allen had some private matters that benefited from a woman's advice. 'Twas nothing." She turned and shaded her eyes from the rising sun, which pierced the ancient courtyard through the portcullis.

Will had already mounted his horse, and Sir Allen swung onto his with the ease of a commander. Clattering on the cobblestones, the party departed, Will and Sir Allen leading the line, their horses eager to have their heads. There was a sudden silence as the last of the pack ponies left the yard, and in the quietness, an unexpected emptiness. It was not sorrow, but it was disturbing all the same, for I did not want to feel anything. It crept upon me unawares and uninvited.

18

Sir,

May this find you in good health and your plans in London progressing.

I have devised a simple routine for Peter and Jocasta, whereby I established a small schoolroom in the castle tower, and it is with pleasure that I spend each morning with them. They have been given the rudiments of an education, but there is much opportunity for more, and although Fonmon's library is small, there are the necessary volumes to make some impression. In the afternoons, we exercise in the castle grounds or work in the physick garden. The children's cheeks are rosy, and they are grown strong and active. Jocasta has flourished, and though she is still quiet, I hear her laugh now, which was not the case before. Although this interlude with the children has delayed my plans to leave for Guernsey, the island will wait for me.

God keep you in safety
Lucy St.John
5th April 1615

"I am with child." Eleanor stood by the scrubbed table in the kitchen, her face alight with joy.

"Eleanor—I'm so happy for you!" I dropped the pestle into the bowl of fragrant spring herbs and hugged her. "When? How long?"

"Just newly. I think no more than two months." She broke into another smile and laid her hand possessively over her flat stomach. "A girl for Will, I hope and pray."

"The morning sickness?"

She nodded.

"Terribly so, much more than with Huw. More as it was with Anne." A shadow chased across her face. "A girl, they say, if the mother sickens in the early days."

"A girl it will be. And I shall sprinkle salt on you while you sleep tonight, and we'll see what name you say when you first awake." I loved the old stories and collected all of them for my recipe book.

"I must be careful, Lucy. Huw's was a difficult carrying time, and Anne was a frail child."

"Do not worry, my darling. We will make sure this baby is healthy and hearty." I sat Eleanor down at the table and poured some hot water from the kettle onto crushed rosehips. "And we'll start with some nourishment that will also settle your stomach."

The door flew open, and a gust of wind blew into the warm kitchen.

"Mistress Lucy! Mistress Lucy, there are guards and a messenger from my father." Jocasta burst into the kitchen, hair flying and her gown disheveled.

"Now what more news is coming this morning?" I wiped my hands on a rag and, leaving Jocasta with Eleanor, walked out to the courtyard.

"I have a letter for Mistress St.John." The messenger dismounted, and the half dozen guards that accompanied him clattered from their mounts. Our stable boys ran to take the reins, looking curiously at the armed men.

"I can take that." I held out my hand, and the messenger pulled a document from his saddlebag, folded and sealed. "Please wait here while I make arrangements for your refreshment. You will be staying with us? And the guards?"

"Yes. The information is all in the letter."

Walking back into the kitchen, I broke the seal and unfurled the parchment. It was written in a clear, strong hand.

"What is it, Lucy?"

"A letter from Sir Allen." I hurriedly read through, his words dropping like stones in a well, rippling through my mind. "He requests his children be sent to London. He has ordered an armed guard to escort them. Will has asked that you accompany them, for he has secured a house in Blackfriars. They expect to see you within the fortnight."

"Oh, Lucy."

"There's more. Will includes me too. It seems there is much going on in White Hall. He wants the family there."

"Lucy, I can't. I can't endanger this baby. I can't go."

"What do you mean, Eleanor? You have to go." I turned to Jocasta. "Sweetheart, go and find Peter. He's probably with Huw at the butts. Bring him here."

She scampered away, leaving a silence hanging between Eleanor and me.

"Lucy, if I travel now and lose this baby, I will surely die too. I cannot risk this."

"Eleanor, Will and Allen both command the children be returned and you accompany them."

She looked down into her lap.

"You go."

"What?"

"You go. You could leave tomorrow and be back by month's end. You take the children to Allen."

I sat down on the chair next to her.

"Eleanor, I should leave for Guernsey. I cannot be taking Sir Allen's children across the country back to London."

"Then who else will?"

"God's truth, Eleanor. Why are my wishes always the last on the list? Does no one take my dreams seriously?"

"Don't be so selfish, Lucy. All that is being asked of you is to take two children to London to be safely handed to their father. Is that so much?"

"I think so."

"Then think again. Think of how it was when you were orphaned and delivered to Aunt Joan's. Recall how lonely you felt, how bewildered, how sorrowful for the loss of your mother. Bring yourself out of your own thoughts, and consider others for a change."

"Oh, leave me be," I shouted at Eleanor, jumping up and running from the room, brushing past Jocasta and Peter. "Leave me be."

I walked furiously the mile toward the shore, my temper cooled with the bracing wind that chased in from the Bristol Channel. By the time I reached the sea, I was calm again, and as I sat on Will's bench, I became mortified at my behavior.

Fear. That's what prompted me to lash out at Eleanor. Fear of returning to London and all that came with it.

We were eight days on the roads to White Hall, and although Sir Allen's guards made sure our way was safe and kept clear of bandits, we could not travel more than about twenty miles a day. As much time as possible, the children and I rode on horseback, for the carriage was uncomfortable beyond measure, its rough-hewn wheels not smoothed much by the bands of iron that encircled them. Only when the weather was at its most inclement did I insist we sit inside, and we were fortunate that for the most part April's showers were brief and passed quickly.

Our approach to White Hall was north of the river, and I was happy to avoid both Lydiard and Battersey on our journey. Much as I wanted to see Anne, I was not ready for John's questions or Joan's prying into why I was escorting another man's children on the long journey from Fonmon. Fortunately, I found that Sir Allen had provided a purse sufficient for us to stay at the most comfortable of inns along the route, and I made full use of his funds to ensure we purchased the best hospitality.

"Look! Mistress Lucy, look at the spires ahead." Peter was riding with the front guard, as was his choice, and Jocasta and I followed behind. It was one of those times where we were free from the wretched coach, and I was grateful for the fresh air.

"We approach the village of Chelsea," I replied. "Soon you will see the start of the city, for London continues to spread westerly, and we will be upon it in no time."

"Do you know it well, Mistress Lucy?"

"No. I was brought up across the river." I was more abrupt than I intended with Jocasta. "Come, just a few more hours and you will be back with your father. You must be excited to see him."

She smiled.

"I am. But sad to leave you."

I didn't know what to reply, so I kept my peace.

White Hall. The last I was there, I vowed not to return, tossing Theo's posie ring in the river and locking my dreams away. It took every part of my faith to believe I was returning for a reason, that destiny had steered me here for a purpose. And then, looking at the children's faces, I knew that it was important that I help them with the transition to their new lives. We had become so close, and more than anything I wanted to be sure they were safe and happy.

It was not a hard thing to do. Ride into White Hall, find Sir Allen, explain to him why Eleanor had not accompanied me, and leave.

"Whoa! Make way! Make way!"

The guards closed formation around us as we approached the Holbein Gate. An imposing four-story edifice with checkered flint work and lodgings on its upper floors, the gate itself was keeper to the entrance of the palace, its narrow arched entry funneling traffic to almost a standstill. Our horses whickered and pranced impatiently as we queued to enter, but our guards knew their way of old and were not intimidated by the imposing height and dominance of the building. It was a very different welcome to White Hall than the fluidity of the river and its colorful barges.

As we passed through the gloom of the gate into the broad openness of the sanded and cobbled yard beyond, the children gasped at the size of the buildings and gardens. We were immediately surrounded by citizens, horses, and carts, a clattering riot of noise and motion echoing between the ancient walls. My stomach was fluttering, but I kept a calm demeanor.

"Is this where we are going to live?" Jocasta whispered, worry shaping her words.

"No, sweeting. We are just meeting your father here in his temporary lodging. You will have a beautiful home well away from here."

She looked relieved. Peter was twisting in his saddle, looking around him at the crowds, his attention next caught by a unit of soldiers that were marching across the yard.

"I wish we were staying here," he said wistfully. "I want to be where the men are."

"Time enough for that later. We need to find your father."

The guards halted opposite the enormous banquet hall, just by the walls to the tiltyard, which were low enough to see over from horseback.

"Look," shouted Peter. "Look at the maneuvers!"

A troop of a dozen horsemen were riding in close formation across the tiltyard, their war horses tightly reined and packed together as the unit moved as one. Led by a broad-shouldered man who sat tall in the saddle, they trotted diagonally in a pack, their disciplined mounts kicking up small puffs of dust. At an unseen command from the leader, they burst into a full gallop, thundering toward us, and just as suddenly came to an immediate halt without breaking formation. It was an impressive display of horsemanship.

I glanced at Peter, whose face was a picture of joy. He turned and grinned at me.

"I believe we have found him, Mistress Lucy."

I looked again at the tiltyard as the commander swung himself down from his black charger, threw the reins over its head, and strode toward us. His horse remained motionless, and the cavalry stayed in silent formation.

"My loves," he called, opening his arms wide.

The children scrambled down from their horses and ran to the tiltyard gate. Sir Allen swung it open and caught them both up in a strong embrace. A lump in my throat prevented me from swallowing, and sudden tears filled my eyes. I blinked rapidly.

"Lucy?" Sir Allen looked up at me and, disengaging Peter, held a hand out to help me dismount. "You came? Where is Eleanor?"

"She is with child. All is fine," I continued hastily as a question rose to his lips. "We just considered it prudent for her not to make the journey."

"And so you came in her stead? "

"I was not going to let the children travel on their own."

He still held my hand as I stood by my horse. Around us, the cacophony of people and soldiers created a ring of noise.

"Once again, I owe you thanks for your kindness to my children."

"And once again, I would say that it is of no consequence." I extracted my hand and brushed my skirts, suddenly conscious of how disheveled I must have appeared. "I would freshen myself and then be on my way. There is no need for me to remain here. The sooner I leave, the sooner I can be back with Eleanor."

"You must rest. I insist. Although it would not be seemly for you to stay in my lodgings."

I looked up sharply at his words.

"Will has rented rooms close by. Come." He signaled to an officer in the courtyard, who grasped the reins of Allen's horse and dismissed the men. Putting his hand under my elbow, Allen led me toward the palace buildings. Our whole encounter had not taken more than a few minutes, but I felt I had passed into a new age.

"Are you sure she is going to be all right?"

"Will, that must be the seventeenth time you have asked me that since I have arrived." I hugged his dear, familiar form. "Eleanor will be fine. She is just being precautionary."

"Thank you, Lucy. I know returning to White Hall must have been hard for you."

I shrugged.

"'Tis of little consequence. My thoughts are with the future, not the past."

"You will dine with us tonight? We have reason to celebrate."

"Why? What has happened?"

"The queen intervened. On Villiers's behalf."

"What? What do you mean?"

"The queen." A broad grin appeared on his face. "Her archbishops counseled her that George Villiers is a fine young man to advance with the king. And that he would most certainly be favored over her enemy, Carr."

"So it's happened? Your plans have come about?"

Will took my hands and swept a deep bow.

"Today. St. George's Day. The king loved the pun. And he loved to knight his favorite and appoint him Groom of the Bedchamber."

"Barbara must be joyful."

"We all are. Our kinsman is now the most favored man at court, Lucy. Many new opportunities will present themselves."

"Oh, Will." I reached out and touched his cheek. "Take heed. Along with favorites come enemies, and you have certainly made some today."

For me, the grim satisfaction was not in hearing that Barbara's brother-in-law was now firmly in the king's embrace, filling a need that had long been unmet by Carr, in a position to influence and grant perquisites to all those who helped him ascend. Yes, there were rewards ahead for Edward and Oliver and their syndicate.

My thoughts turned instead to a certain familiar chamber just close by, where behind two large carved doors, a woman raged and consulted her soothsayers, fortune tellers, and seers. A woman who now, for the first time in her life, knew how it felt to be cast away and rejected, to have her hopes and dreams for the future dashed by the actions of others. A woman who thought she had a life ahead of her assured, only to find it slipping away through her fingers.

It was not Robert Carr that I had any compunction for, and it was certainly not for his wife, Frances Howard.

Will's rooms in Scot's Yard were not far from those where we stayed during my last visit, and the familiar low-ceilinged chambers tucked within a hidden square evoked emotions that I had long buried. This time, though, with Will and Allen's brotherly camaraderie and the absence of Barbara, I could relax and enjoy a familiarity that echoed our many evenings around the fire at Fonmon. With the children bade good-bye and safely tucked in bed in Allen's adjoining rooms, and one of his loyal guards standing watch, we were free to speak.

"So, now begins the age of Villiers," mused Allen, a silver strand in his dark hair catching a gleam from the fire, his booted legs stretched out in front of him. "Where do your plans lead you now, Will?"

"To commerce and opportunity," responded Will. He leaned forward eagerly, and I caught the excitement in his face. "If we can now obtain the ear of the king and set in motion Walter's freedom, there is much that he could do to raise our worth . . ."

". . . or squander it," interrupted Allen. "Have a care, Will. You know that Walter's weakness is his arrogance, and his enemy is ambition. I love him as dearly as a brother, but I cannot always agree with his motives."

"You are so conservative. For a man who has won so much in war, you speak with a cautious heart."

Allen smiled. "War is not always won by bravado, and Ireland is no theater for players. There are many kinds of valor—and imposters of the same."

A sudden banging on the door and a burst of laughter outside interrupted our peaceful room. The door was flung open and crashed loudly against the wall. Two men staggered in, arms over each other's shoulders, singing loudly and waving wine flagons in their free hands.

Allen leapt to his feet and drew his sword more quickly than I could blink, Will a moment behind him.

"Stand down!" Will grabbed Allen's sword arm as the intruders burst into another gale of laughter. "Jesu, Edward, you idiot. Allen could have run you through. How much have you drunk, fellow?"

Edward Villiers waved his flagon in Allen's direction and gazed blearily at him.

"J-j-j-ust celebrating the raise in family fortune, Will."

He turned to the man who was hanging on his shoulder, hat askew.

"Isn't that right, my friend?" He belched loudly and pushed the man's head back. "We have much to celebrate with our beautiful George's promotion today. We stand to gain riches beyond our wildest imagination!"

The man next to him shook his head as to clear it and took a long draught from his wine.

"We certainly do, my friend," he slurred. "As one star falls, another ascends. We are now all celestial beings in the royal firmament."

It was Theo. Theo, drunk, leaning against the doorway of Will's apartments.

"Holy Virgin, Mother of God,"

Theo's oath flew from his lips as he swayed forward and peered at me.

"What ghostly spirit delivers this magic to my bewitched eyes?"

Will grabbed his arm and turned him quickly aside. Theo stumbled and struggled, trying to push by Will toward me.

"Is it Titania, Queen of the Fairies, come back to claim her Oberon?"

Allen stepped in front of me, sword raised. His body filled my vision, blocking Theo from my sight.

"'Struth man, you are drunk. Get ye both gone and back to your carousing. We'll talk on the morrow, when your heads are clear." Will had the advantage of sobriety over both Edward and Theo and shoved them from the room, slamming the door and bolting it.

"Titania," wailed Theo, banging on the door until I could hear Edward shushing him and dragging him away.

The room was hushed, with only the crackling of the fire to disturb the quiet. Will ran his hands through his hair, shaking his head.

"Edward was never one to hold his drink well."

I remained silent, the emotion of the incident still coursing through my blood.

"Nor, it appears, is Lord Howard." Allen sheathed his sword and turned to me. "Are you all right? That was not a pleasant interlude."

I drew myself up and squared my shoulders.

"I am fine, thank you, Sir Allen. Those are not the first drunks I have seen here at White Hall."

"I have no patience for these shallow courtiers, who think only of their own pleasure. And ambition. And pay no heed to the outcomes of their deeds." He laid his hand on my arm, and I felt a powerful strength flow from him to me. "Keep your heart true, and do not be seduced by these charlatans of fortune that are now joined to your family."

Will stood, watching us, not speaking.

I took a deep breath and tucked a loosened strand of hair behind my ear.

"Thank you again, Sir Allen. For both your protection and your advice. I am grateful for both. Now, if you will excuse me, I have to start early in the morning for Fonmon, and I am tired."

Allen nodded, and this time took my hand and kissed it, lingering perhaps a heartbeat longer than was protocol. The imprint of his mouth stayed with me as I tossed and turned through the short night before dawn sent me back alone to Wales, with only his guard for company.

19

To make a woman have an easy labour:

Oyle of Almons and spirmacitty. Anoynt the bottom of the back and belly therewith every night.

Lady Craft's recipe from Bristol
Lucy St.John Recipes

Fonmon's grounds stretched all the way to the Bristol Channel, that sliver of water separating Wales from England. My favorite path led south from the ancient fortress, skirting a ravine and winding through deep woods before emerging through the dunes onto the shoreline. I loved the constant surprise of seeing the mantle of ocean framed by the tallest of pine trees, and today was no different.

A healthy girl, praise God. It had been a long night and a difficult time for Eleanor. But this child was healthy, full term. A girl for Will.

A strong wind sprang up, carrying the tang of brine, and I breathed deeply, cooling my mind and my senses.

Time to leave for Guernsey now. There was nothing left for me here. Will had his family. Jocasta and Peter were with their father, who was set in his new position in London. I would not see them again. And Theo? That brief encounter in White Hall left me cold.

I sat on Will's bench, my eyes on the ocean, seeking the rhythm of the swells to order my thoughts. A wind-tossed flock of seagulls hovered close by, their intent to reach the water thwarted by the strong westerly breeze that blew them sideways. And yet they still remained aloft, off course, their eyes focused on their destination, knowing the wind would eventually drop so they could fly forward again.

As I looked to the horizon, hoping to spot the distant cliffs of Devon across the Channel, the sea mist rolled in, and the line where the sea met the sky became indiscernible—all was the same color and substance. I took these as God's signs of my own life and thought carefully of their meaning, the birds trusting the invisible power of the wind, the horizon unseen, shrouding the land I knew lay beyond the fog.

"You are pensive, Lucy."

I froze, not knowing if the wind had conjured his voice or if it was real.

"You look sad. This is not the woman I saw at White Hall, laughing with my children."

I shrugged. I had no voice.

"I am sorry if my plain speaking disturbs you."

I remained silent.

"You see, I am someone who has to speak the truth when I see it."

"You disturb me. And I have no need of your version of truth." I refused to look his way. "What are you doing here? Traveling to Ireland again, leaving your children alone with another nurse?"

Allen ignored my questions. "I thought you would appreciate honesty when so much harm has been done to you by deception."

"How do you know of my life?" I turned angrily and stood. "What gives you the right to assume you know the deeds behind my feelings?"

"I know only what your sister has told me, in her concern for you." He held his hands out in a gesture that indicated puzzlement. "I do not mean to offend you."

"Eleanor. How dare she reveal my secrets to a stranger?"

"I have known Will for many years, fought by his side, lived in fear with him, watched men die with him, and yes, saved him from peril more than once. Eleanor knows she can trust me with her worries. I am no stranger to them."

"Worries? Why should she be worried for me? I have done nothing to ask for help from her."

"Exactly. Lucy, you have set a course for yourself which is a difficult one. You wish to isolate yourself on a foreign shore, far from friends and family, with no one to turn to for comfort except a minister and his wife that you spent a summer with once. That is not choosing a course, it is running away."

"How dare you speak to me in this manner. You do not know my thoughts, my dreams. And why are you here? What are you seeking?"

"I know that your family here is concerned for you, that they fear your dream is just an escape from past hurts, that it has no substance, no thought for the future."

"I shall be with Monsieur Montrachet. He will become my family."

"He is a kind man, with a loving family, by account. But he has his own life too, his mission, his purpose, his congregation. He may not have the time or the capability to look after you." His argument was relentless.

"I do not need looking after." I was almost in tears, for with his words, he methodically shredded my dreams, his ruthless logic and his voice of truth undercutting my plans.

"Lucy, accept this destiny written for you and cease avoidance. You have revealed to yourself with Peter and Jocasta where your talents lie. It is in soothing and comforting, in healing and playing, and in laughter and in a family, not as a hermit on a distant island."

His words brought into focus the disparate paths that he had drawn for me, and my dream of an independent, quiet life in Guernsey suddenly appeared the choice of a coward.

"Marry me."

The words were so shocking that I did not know at first if they were said or thought, and I stood stone still, as if not to spill them from my mind, the world paused around me.

"Marry me and become a mother to Peter and Jocasta." Allen stood before me, sheltering me from the wind, his words tumbling as if a torrent released. "When I first saw you, there was something that drew me to you. I left, but a powerful passion in my heart made me return. My curiosity wanted to see you again, to see how you were faring. The woman who brought my children to White Hall shone brighter than you do today. What ails you?"

"You don't know me. You know nothing of me."

"I know someone who knows how to love and has buried that deep within her heart. I know someone who knows how to teach and has used that skill to bring out the best in others. But you have not answered my question."

"I did not consider you asked that of me. You simply stated it."

"Please marry me. I dare not question for fear you will refuse. But listen to my statement and dwell deeply on my words." He held his arms wide to embrace the dunes, the ocean, the sky around us. "Marry me, and I will provide you a home to call your own. I will provide you an income to do with what you please. I will support your love of learning, and I would not quench that spirit I see with demands of obedience where your will is lost."

His voice lowered.

"Lucy, I will respect your dreams, and I share your love of God. I share your belief women have a mind equal to that of a man, and I would not suppress your voice. And I will bring you Peter and Jocasta to raise as your own, to educate and to nurture."

"And children of our own, and our life as husband and wife?" I wanted to hear all his plans since he appeared to have thought this through so carefully.

"That will be as God wishes," he replied. "I will trust to time and the healing power of His love, and mine, to bring those elements to fruition."

"You say you trust time, and yet you rush to marry with no courtship, little discourse."

He stared at the fog-bound channel, pausing to find words.

"My friends would have me marry a wealthy widow. They have already spoken to her. She has land, income. Her children are grown. She is amenable. It would be a comfortable life, convenient. She could be a fit stepmother to Jocasta and Peter." He turned to me. "But for the first time in my existence, Lucy, I have found someone who inhabits my same soul. You awaken in me an ardor that I did not know existed."

"You talk of love, and yet you hardly know me. You tease me with a life that could be mine, and yet you are a stranger to me."

"Lucy, I am older by far than you. I have had my share of love and loss and seek only to find a path in life where I can devote myself to my family, serve my God and king, and prosper in my business. My head tells me that you share many of my ideals and would be a worthy wife. My heart tells me that if I did not express my love and ask you to marry me, I would regret it for the rest of my life."

At those words, I looked up at him, into the transparent honesty in his blue eyes, and realized the seriousness of his purpose. I also caught something more; a vulnerability around his mouth that

160

reminded me of Peter, bravely stepping in front of his sister, ready to defend, summoning courage. That, more than anything, broke through to my soul.

"You risk much, returning to Fonmon with your heart on your sleeve. Let me think on your words, for I am surprised beyond all measure." I reached out my hand and touched his cheek, as if to confirm his substance and validate his offer, and he made a small gesture of his head, nudging my palm for a second before stepping back.

"Tarry not long, for I leave for London tomorrow, and I will not return." His abrupt words startled me again.

"You give me but little notice, sir, to decide for a lifetime."

"Look only into your heart, Lucy, for it will not lie to you. Wait not long on your decision, for your first instinct will be your truth." He strode away, the wind catching the last of his words and tossing them to fate.

So life presented two paths, and God placed in front of me a choice, in jest, perhaps, for He knew my destiny as clearly as He knew the land that lay behind the fog. I thought of all the small reasons I delayed traveling to Guernsey over the past months and wondered if it was His way of making me hesitate so Allen would cross my path and divert my course. Running through my thoughts like a constant, clear stream sang the challenge that Allen had tossed to me. I could live my life's purpose within the embrace of my own family rather than as a recluse on a distant island. And yet still I wrestled, not convinced that I could make the choice today, but knowing that Allen would not wait beyond tomorrow.

A wealthy widow. She could be a fit stepmother to Jocasta and Peter.

Just as Joan was a stepmother to me. My heart cried in protest.

The runt of the litter. No one else would take you.

As I stood alone with the ocean and only the cry of the seabirds for company, I looked again to the hidden horizon across the silver sea. In that moment, the fog drifted apart, and a ray of sun shone through, illuminating the cliffs of England, from which a path rippled across the calm waters to me. To my right, where the Celtic Sea and Guernsey waited at the end of the Bristol Channel, the fog bank closed in, a wall preventing sight of any passage. There could be no clearer sign my journey lay on the land, on England, and a life with Allen and his children.

It would require more courage and more fortitude than ever I needed to slip away to Guernsey and live in solitude, but perhaps the rewards would be greater and my life's purpose would be fulfilled in a different way. I had a chance to begin again, to conceal all that had gone before, to start afresh with a man who would not consciously betray me. He had not asked directly of Theo, and I had no desire to tell.

I made the choice. I would marry. And as the fog drifted in again and the fleeting sunburst became shrouded in gray, I carefully and knowingly drew a line through my past and placed my future in destiny and Allen's hands.

As I returned to the castle, Allen appeared in the doorway and looked across at me, his head tilted in a question. I slowly nodded. His face broke into a wide smile, and he strode across the yard and knelt before me, kissing my fingers.

Later, I climbed the stairs to Eleanor's chamber and shared the news with her.

"You made your choice, Lucy?" she asked, her eyes searching mine.

"How did you know I had one to make?" I looked at her glowing face, her child nuzzling her breast, and shook my head in disbelief. It seems there were abundant conversations concerning my well-being occurring without my knowledge.

"Allen took me into his confidence and asked about you when he was here previously. He told me of his growing feelings for you and asked if I thought you would consider his proposal."

"And what did you tell him?"

Eleanor's reply was simple.

"I told him that you were in great melancholy, which directed your thoughts to a life of solitude. If he were to present an alternative, your spirit might have the courage to look at another aspect, a life with a man whose conversation and maturity would embolden your confidence."

There was a moment of silence as I digested Eleanor's words and thought of how far I had come from the carefree girl at Lydiard or the young woman riding the country lanes in Guernsey. To be described as melancholy made me sad, for I had suppressed much of my natural joy in mourning the betrayal of Theo, and my faith made me serious. It was a revelation to me, for solemnity did not come naturally to me, and gravity was a recent mantle.

Leaving her with her newborn, I returned to Allen. He smiled as I entered the hall and placed a cup of wine in my hands.

"To your health, Lucy. And to happiness. For I think you have not had much in your life."

I took a deep breath. My life had changed so much in just a few moments. I may as well continue.

"I am not all that I appear to be."

Allen looked at me curiously.

"You have also agreed to marry another."

His face creased into a frown, his mouth opening in protest.

"Lucifera, the Lady Pirate."

Allen's seriousness lifted, and he laughed aloud.

"That will be most useful when I have to argue before the Privy Council at Westminster next month to release more funding for victualling the king's fleet. You can brandish your sword and frighten them into submission."

Allen's words sank in and the world rearranged itself again. That moment earlier, before I crossed the yard, I existed still a single woman, with no responsibilities other than her own, her destiny that of a solitary life in a distant place. Now, after these brief words had been uttered, I became a wife, a mother, with a household and a mature husband who carried many business concerns and a full life that I should adopt as my own. And his life was based in London, and the court, and the politics and manipulations that accompanied it. By marrying Allen, I reentered the world I had rejected and sought to expunge from my life.

Fate beckoned, and I followed.

20

Dearest Anne,

I have some surprising news for you. I am to marry. His name is Sir Allen Apsley, and he is a friend to Will and served with Uncle Oliver in Ireland. He is recently appointed Victualler of the Navy. God knows I place my trust in Him to guide me on this journey I have chosen. The time to our wedding is brief. Our difference in age is mitigated by our similarities in perspective.

Eleanor and I will be at Lydiard in a few days, as we travel back to London together. I am happy, Anne, for he is a good man, and he says he loves me, and I see in him a kindred soul. I am cautious to dream too much of what my life will be, for I know not what I am really entering into. I know only what I am leaving behind.

Your loving sister Lucie St.John
17ᵗʰ July 1615

Our summer is blistering hot even here in Wales, where usually every rain cloud which crosses Britain is compelled to drop its contents on our land. Instead, the lanes have filled six inches with soft, dry earth, and any trotting horse kicks up a cloud around its heels. The nettles and cow parsley are coated in fine gray powder, and there is a visible line along the hedgerows where the dust is settling on the dark green leaves.

The path to Fonmon has become well worn, for as the months passed since Will and Allen left, messengers have traveled back and forth with increased frequency, and many visitors have stayed for a night before moving on to their next destination, their pigskins filled with cool Fonmon well water for the parched ride.

Eleanor came to me one morning, the heat already shimmering across the castle ward.

"I have heard from Will again," she said abruptly, papers clasped in her hands. "Now that our daughter is born, he commands us to join him in London. He does not intend to return to Fonmon, for he engages with Edward Villiers in a venture at court that requires his full attention. He asks I remove there as quickly as possible."

Eleanor walked over to the deep window enclave and gazed at the castle woods, shimmering under the fierce sun. "It seems our time here is over, Lucy, for Will finds another adventure." She turned and looked at me with a wry smile on her face, halfway between laughter and tears, and I knew that she held back her dismay at the change ahead.

"I will come with you," I said decisively. "I am intended to be in London in autumn anyway, when Allen has completed the repair of the house at East Smithfield. I can stay with you."

"You are sure?" she asked. "Will made no mention of Allen asking for you to join us. It might be more comfortable for you to return to Lydiard until your marriage."

"I am positive. All things have a season, and our time here at Fonmon has come to an end. I am eager to start on the next stage of our journey." My words sounded strong, and I thought I did an excellent job of concealing my anxiety. Fonmon no longer offered me a haven, and my return to London would bring my life full circle.

A few days later, we left Fonmon Castle and headed east, accompanied by a convoy of several carts of household items. We traveled well-guarded by Will's small company of soldiers he had left at the castle for the purpose of escorting us to London. This journey, more than anything, reinforced the changes wrought in my life, for as we retraced my path from Lydiard that I had traveled just a few months earlier, I could not but reflect on the difference. Then, I was a bereft woman intent on leaving the world behind, and now I rode to marriage, with two children and a future husband waiting for me in London. Life's shifts can happen with any chance encounter, but the memories warned me again that our fate lies in God's hands, for only He knows the journey ahead that He plans for us.

After several days of pleasant riding through high summer's ripening countryside, we rested at Lydiard, and with great joy, I reunited with Anne. She expressed her happiness to see me along with her relief at my news to marry Allen and forgo my plans for solitude. As a home-loving creature, she wanted her life choice to be mine too.

John approached me cautiously, but he appeared interested to hear of Allen and questioned me closely as to his character and history. In some ways, although I could not answer many of his questions, it surprised me to hear John taking an interest in my well-being. In truth, our quarrels and his jealous anger had placed a wedge between us that could not be removed easily.

Taking us to the church, where he had embarked on a project of grand decoration, John proudly showed Eleanor and me the memorial painting of our family. It amused me to see that he had instructed the painter to place the coats of arms of all my sisters' husbands at their feet, even Jane, who was betrothed to our neighbor Charles Pleydell, but not yet married. My lozenge still appeared blank, and John told me that he would complete this upon the confirmation of my marriage.

"It is an intricate piece, John," I said, although I thought it most ostentatious. "You have obviously gone to a great deal of trouble to learn our family history and transmit it to this monument."

"Our uncle helped me design the tree of our forebears," replied John. "As the king's herald, there is no truer source for the accuracy of our lineage."

I could not resist.

"And, of course, you paid him well for his research?"

"Of course. His work entailed tracing us back to the Conqueror. There was much to be researched, much to be sanctioned."

"And will you be adding Allen's arms to my image?"

"If you do marry. I have not yet met this man, and since you agreed to marry him without telling me, I can wait until you've told me the wedding has occurred before I order more work done on the painting."

"I do not need your permission to marry, John, nor your approval of whom I choose. Uncle Oliver has granted me both approval and my dowry. Leave it blank for all I care, for I do not need a painting to ratify my decision or reassure me of my standing in this world."

Anne stepped between us as she had so many times. It was apparent that although John and I could be courteous to each other, there was still much unresolved below the surface.

Eleanor and I stayed at Lydiard for just one night, and it was a bittersweet interlude. I had returned as a guest, and although I knew Anne would always welcome me, and John would be courteous, it was no longer my home to come and go as I wished.

It gave me joy to see that the walled garden flourished and that John's stewardship improved the fabric of the house and church. My talisman was in good hands. Still, my heart wrenched when we departed through the long drive of elms, and I looked back over my shoulder to the view of the house in its summer beauty. The dew-strewn bowling lawn glistened as the sun warmed the honey-colored stone walls while my beloved cypress tree cast its deep green shadow across the shorn summer grass. I locked Lydiard with me in my heart.

I took a deep breath and turned and faced the road ahead, resolved to no longer question where I traveled to or look back for where I had been. My journey continued.

And so to London, where I returned to life's theater, for Blackfriars hosted the greatest players, Burbage's King's Men, and all considered this ward one of the most fashionable areas of the City in which to live. I might have known that Will would choose such a place from which to enter London society, for the old liberty was a touchstone for all manner of people. Its narrow streets teemed with life and color.

When King Henry and Cromwell purloined the spoils of the monasteries to line their pockets, Blackfriars was a ripe fruit for picking. Its expansive riverside collection of cloisters, orchards, and a wealthy abbey provided much riches and building material for magnificent new homes. Now, a hundred years later, some of the wealthiest and fashionable courtiers lived within. Many French reformer refugees settled there too, even in the same streets as recusants who openly practiced their own Catholic religion.

It brought me much joy to hear French spoken in the streets, and I happily joined the Huguenot community that worshipped at St.

Anne's Church by the city wall. Cheek by jowl also dwelled apothecaries and physicians, book printers and sellers. Blackfriars thrived as a community of tolerance, all manner of people living peaceably side by side.

Dominating all was the marvelously designed indoor theater and those that it drew to its surrounds. Not only actors and writers lived within its benefice, but all manner of players, musicians, fight instructors, wardrobe masters, seamstresses, prop makers, scenery painters, and many other diverse artisans dwelt within its precincts. Hard by the theater was Will and Eleanor's new home.

"Mistress Lucy!"

"Madam."

"Mother . . ."

Three voices greeted me simultaneously as I stepped into the house, for Allen and the children were waiting for me in the parlor. I held out my arms, and Peter and Jocasta ran to me.

"You are truly going to be our mother?" Jocasta's little face turned up to me, as pretty as a morning daisy.

"The pirate lady! We've a pirate lady in our family!" Peter jumped up and down, bumping my chin with the top of his head, for he was almost as tall as me.

"Careful, children. Be too boisterous and my lady may change her mind." Allen hung back slightly, as if uncertain of his reception.

"Never," I said firmly. "I am certain of my decision, and nothing you can do or say will dissuade me."

My words were as much for him as they were for the children. Or perhaps for me. Once said aloud, they could not be taken back.

In July, when we arrived, the players had moved to their summer home over the river at the Globe, but Will promised to take us to performances at Blackfriars when winter brought the theater indoors to the old abbey hall. I heard that even Master Shakespeare had recently purchased a home by the old gate in Playhouse Yard, and I wondered if I would see him again after so many years had passed since the Midsummer Night's Dream I watched with Theo by my side.

While Allen busied himself with his new position and Will reacquainted himself with his courtier friends, my days were spent exploring the maze of small streets that meandered around the ancient monastery. The children, cautious at first at being in such a crowded and noisy environ, soon gained confidence. The river lay to our south and great Saint Paul's to the north, and they served as boundaries for where they could walk.

As for me, I embraced my new surroundings. A weight lifted from me as I left Lydiard and my old dreams behind. I came alive again and drew such joy from the humanity that surrounded me, connecting with all manner of people and their lives.

Each day, after helping Eleanor with her domestic duties, I roamed freely, and I walked and walked the alleys and pathways of this old city. This was when I truly fell in love with London and its indomitable spirit. I took great joy in every incident I encountered, each person who made up this great hive of life that seethed within its ancient walls.

Apothecary's Row, where I struck up a friendship with many of the shopkeepers, was one of my favorite streets within the liberty, and I spent an hour or two most afternoons in the narrow alley. The houses were stacked high; the second and third stories jutted out to the extent that they blocked almost all sunlight from penetrating the streets below, casting a perpetual deep shadow. In the cramped stores on the ground floor, all manner of herbs, potions, plasters, and precious powders could be purchased. I was delighted to renew my acquaintance with the curatives that I had learned from Mathew L'Obel and modestly pleased that I could display my knowledge to gain the confidence of the apothecaries.

After one particularly intense discussion with a Genevan doctor, who was curious to hear more of my alchemy learnings with Vicar Ridley, I left with my head full of new findings and returned to Will's house, eager to transcribe my newest recipe. Magnificently caparisoned horses were tethered outside, surrounded by admiring stable boys and several apprentices who should have been at work. There was no doubt that someone of import called on Will, and I headed for the back stair to avoid having to speak to anyone.

"Lucy!"

There was no mistaking the voice, and I turned reluctantly to meet Barbara as she appeared in the doorway.

"You have nothing to say after all these months apart? Come, Sister, embrace me and tell how you are faring. I hear you have news for us." She was dressed fashionably, her clothes speaking of a station that I did not think she was entitled to assume. Seeing me eye her gown, she smoothed the gold-threaded fabric of her slashed sleeve with all the satisfaction of a cat grooming itself in the sun.

"Edward is fortunate to have the king's attention," she remarked. "It has paid off well for him."

"So your marriage to Villiers is a successful arrangement?" I could not help but put it in terms of a business transaction, for I did not consider that Barbara married for love.

"Eminently so. We are delighted with George's ascension and his ability to charm the king. And I hear you have made a match too. Your plans for solitude were short-lived."

I should have known that Barbara would have a retort.

"Allen is a good man, and his children are in need of a mother. We have a respectful understanding of each other." I tried not to sound defensive.

"So you learned to think with your head, not your heart. I hope you feel the same way when you next encounter Theo."

"I have no desire to see him, nor any prospect of doing so." I thought of his disheveled appearance at Will's apartments and dreaded the thought of encountering him again.

"Really? Edward and I spend many pleasant evenings at his apartments at court, and Elizabeth, his wife, is most charming. You and Allen must join us when you can. Edward has marvelous opportunities for our family, and you wouldn't want to stifle Allen's career because of old wounds, would you?" Barbara pulled her self-satisfied cat smile, and I longed to slap her. "Of course, none want to be seen with Frances anymore. Theo and Thomas are quite ashamed of their sister, much as they plead with her to recant her ways." She shrugged. "It is of no consequence to me. I refuse to see her anyway."

I didn't know which gossip to respond to first. I chose to speak of the news less painful. "Frances is falling from favor too?"

"You have heard the suspicions surrounding Overbury's death. It will not be long before the investigations prove there were more than idle words in her role in his demise. And, of course, where she goes, so goes her husband, Carr." She smiled again, but there was no warmth in her face.

"They were your friends, I thought?"

"Edward provided a much more interesting proposition with his brother, George. Frances tired me anyway, and once you were no longer Theo's, I could think of little reason to associate with her. Besides, Edward's friendship with Theo has advanced us more than any fortune telling with Frances."

Many would have been surprised at Barbara's callousness, but a lifetime of experience made me numb to her statements. It was reinforcement, however, of how little I trusted Barbara. She was a beautiful facade, so empty that if the conversation did not center on matters that influenced her, she did not care. What concerned me more was Edward's conversations with Will, for I feared for his impulsiveness.

"So we find you here, Barbara . . . and with Lucy." Will strode into the room, Edward following. "I do not think I have ever seen you both so amicable to each other."

"Fortunes change and make strange bedfellows," replied Barbara, tucking her arm in mine. Her perfume was sensual, musky. "Lucy and I were gossiping of the court and George's successes."

I tried to withdraw, but she only gripped me tighter.

"She was just agreeing that her new position as Sir Allen's wife will give her excellent access to the court. He spends most of his time at White Hall requesting funding for the navy—it will be good for her to support him."

"I do not intend—"

"There is much you could do, Lucy." Edward interrupted me, speaking over me as if I had not even opened my mouth. "Your intimate knowledge would be very helpful in our planning."

"And what knowledge could Lucy have that would help you, Edward?" Allen's low voice, softened by his Irish lilt, cut across the conversation. He entered without me hearing, so bothered was I by Barbara's proximity and Edward's insinuations.

"Ah, Allen. How good to see you." Edward clapped him on his shoulder. Allen just looked at him, silent now. "Will and I were just discussing Walter's release from the Tower. If we can persuade the king to grant him permission for one last voyage, he will sail to El Dorado and bring back the gold he has proof exists."

"We have it all planned, Allen," Will broke in eagerly, his face alight with enthusiasm. "We just need to raise the funds to pay George to seek the king's ear, and Walter will be a free man."

"So your own brother charges you a fee to speak to the king? Seems as though that should come free for kin." Allen moved away from Edward and stood in front of the window, contemplating the busy street outside.

"What knowledge, Edward?" he repeated, his back to the room. "Who would Lucy know that could help our plan to free Walter?"

"Howard, of course."

My heart began to race at the mention of his name.

"She knows the earl of old. She could air our scheme. Perhaps invite Theo to join our syndicate. A few more contributions and Walter will be sailing for El Dorado." Edward looked from Allen to Will, his face eager.

A small smile played on Barbara's rouged lips. In the moments of silence that followed, I held my breath, for I knew not what would come next.

"We'll find partners to fund your brother's bribe, Edward, for as much as the next man, I want Walter free." Allen turned back. "But there will be no going to Howard for money to support our cause. Lucy has no truck with him, now or ever again. I will not be in his debt."

His face was inscrutable, and Edward subsided into silence.

"Come, all of you, come eat. We have a table set for you, and food at the ready," Eleanor spoke as she entered, oblivious to the conversation that had just occurred. She ushered us toward the dining chamber, her sweetness breaking the tension that filled the room. Will hugged her and offered her his arm, and Edward and Barbara followed us, where I could not see them but could hear their whispers. As we walked, Allen took my hand and squeezed it softly, but I could do no more than return his gesture, my mind was so full of what had just taken place.

It would take all the influence that Edward could muster to persuade his brother to plead with the king. It was a delicate matter, for the Spanish despised Raleigh. James battled long to keep his new allies satisfied that the Tower was punishment enough for him when they were demanding his head. George was taking a mighty risk as the new favorite, asking the king to release Walter. I wondered how he could consider Walter's freedom worth confronting the king, and then I learned the price. Will and Edward were amassing fifteen hundred pounds with which to persuade George to talk to the king. I could not believe that so huge a sum could be raised by my brothers-in-law, and it greatly frightened me to contemplate the debts they owed to the various men who were prepared to back Walter's last voyage. In truth, the tales of the lost city of El Dorado would tempt the most prudent of merchants to throw their lot in with Raleigh, who would be sailing with the winds of fate and the blessing of the king.

Allen did not mention the conversation or Theo's name again, and his silence was one that could not be broached. Sometimes I caught him looking at me with a contemplative expression, but when our eyes met, he would smile or look away.

For all my talk of finding my voice, I lacked the courage to raise this conversation, and I hoped that by letting it lie, it would sleep. This moment lay between us as one where he had come to my defense, but I could not measure at what cost.

21

For a tertian ague, use oyle of scorpions, anoynt the soles of the feet and the palmes of the hands and the forehead and the backbone before the fitt comes.

For an effective clyster, crush mushrooms and boyle in water in a pipkin. Mix in camphor. Beware to pick only those mushrooms that are not death cap.

Blackfriars
September 1615

As summer heightened, so did the tension in our house. The men argued, short-tempered, anxious to hear news from George, impatient to know when he would pick the right moment to whisper his desire into James's ear. They taught him how to speak longingly of a need to bring earned gold to his pocket, to feel his own worth.

London sweltered under an oppressive heat that incited the body's humors to rage fiercely, causing dreadful sweating. I made sage infusions to cool the blood, and it helped for temporary relief, especially for those who perspired excessively. We were fortunate that there was no plague in the city this summer, but the prospect lurked. Each day, I diligently examined the children and Eleanor for signs.

As life has its way of doing, all things came to a head in September, as if the humors that swirled around me could no longer be contained within the confines of their mortal environ. I received word from Allen in Portsmouth that he thought the house in East Smithfield would be ready in October. He suggested that the 23rd of that month might be an auspicious day for our wedding. He had no loyalty to any parish, and since I had registered within Blackfriars, it seemed that St. Anne's Church could witness our marriage, and so I should speak to the cleric there and arrange for the banns to be read. I had a small twist in my heart, for I thought that perhaps we would be wed at Battersey, with

Oliver to give me away and my family around me. But that dream had taken a different path. My destiny lay with Allen and his practical, soldierly ways. So be it, and I planned my wedding day.

Shortly thereafter, my sister Katherine and her husband, Giles Mompesson, paid us a visit. It seemed they also availed themselves of Edward Villiers's useful connections at court. I did not wish to spend time with them, for Giles still made me feel very uncomfortable, and they had grown arrogant as their fortunes increased. Now Giles added boastfulness to his avarice, and to hear him speak so intimately of the king and the court as if he were the best friend of the monarch made me roll my eyes at Eleanor as she politely listened to his declaiming.

"And so it appears that the king agrees with my concern that the standards of inns around our country are sadly lacking. The hospitality of our fair English taverns is being debased by unmannered rogues who set themselves as innkeepers but are indeed scoundrels wishing to relieve innocent travelers of their hard-earned monies, for they run but simple alehouses with no license to provide a bed for a night." He stood in front of us in Eleanor's small parlor, legs planted, arms akimbo. Despite his arrogance, he still appeared like a weasel to me.

Katherine sat by and nodded complacently. She had grown plump and obviously enjoyed the fruits of Giles's labor.

"What is he talking about?" I whispered to Eleanor.

"Money," she replied succinctly.

"His Majesty agrees that action must be taken to . . . shall we say . . . encourage . . . these inns to apply for a license to meet our standards of hospitality." He stroked his sparse beard, an irritating habit I noted he repeated constantly. "Those who don't buy the license are closed down."

"And, Giles, how do they purchase the license?" I asked, knowing full well the answer.

"Why, from me, of course." His fingers moved more feverishly on his beard, and Katherine gave a fat chuckle, rocking in her chair. "I will be spending my time surveying the inns. Although the justices of assize are responsible, they have insufficient time to inspect these hostelries, so I have outlined a plan for how I can do this for them."

"That's an undertaking," I remarked. "You will need quite an organization to travel the country and carry out these inspections."

Giles glared at me.

"My proposal to the king," he began arrogantly, "works on the simple premise that three knowledgeable men on swift horses, traveling disguised, can efficiently inspect and fine accordingly those rogue alehouses and inns that do not meet our standards. The fewer inspectors involved, the quicker we assess and impose our fines, and the more revenue that can be generated for the Privy Purse."

"And his pocket," murmured Eleanor.

"Edward believes this is an efficacious idea, and one he is encouraging his brother to put before the king. He feels that the rewards will be such to all concerned that I will deserve a monopoly on this scheme and that it will be in place within a year."

It seemed that Edward was the source of much wealth within our family. Although I knew it was the sign of our times that the fortunes of our family increased along with the fortunes of George Villiers, it made me uneasy to realize how tenuous a link it was. I thought of the rise and fall of Robert Carr and all those who were scrambling even now to find their place in the new favorite's sphere. I prayed our family would not suffer similarly.

With a week left until my wedding, I spent my time collecting the necessary medicines, herbs, spices, and other apothecaries for our stillroom in my new home. I did not know how much provisions came with the East Smithfield house. Since Allen had embarked on such a major rebuilding, I thought it best to bring our necessary physicks with me and so made good use of the friendships I had in the Friars. As I hurried through the narrow streets, it struck me how few people there were in these normally busy thoroughfares. Clusters of guards were stationed at various street corners where normally apprentices loitered.

To avoid their watchful presence, which made me uneasy, I cut through the old abbey yard and under the stone arch. As I walked from its shade into the bright yard beyond, I stopped and drew back into the shadows. A unit of soldiers stood across the gravel outside Lord D'Aubigny's fine house. A coach, its windows concealed by heavy black leather blinds, drew up in the yard, more guards on either side.

People jostled the coach, subdued by the presence of the soldiers but pressing forward to get a glimpse of whatever was about to happen.

And then, from the coach alighted a black-clad courtier with Frances Howard by his side. The crowd drew a collective breath, a hiss that echoed around the courtyard as she walked to the house under guard. Heavily pregnant, white-faced and with tears on her cheeks, I had never thought to see such a sight as this. The once proud face was blotched with fear. Although she held a fan to shield her visage from prying eyes, she did not hold it steady, and I gazed upon her ravaged face above the trembling of her hand.

"You got what you deserved, madam!" A shrill cry from the crowd broke the silence, and it released a torrent of shouts, from which I could discern the words poison, witchcraft, and guilty.

"Thomas Overbury was a martyr to your wickedness, God bless his soul," shouted another, causing Frances to stumble a little and shrink against the man as he briskly walked her to the house stairs and helped her inside.

A clod of earth was thrown at the door, followed quickly by more, and the crowd jeered loudly. The guards quickly stepped forward and broke up the good citizens, pushing them away from the building and dispersing them across the yard.

I grabbed the arm of an apprentice who ran by me toward the crowd, eager to join the melee.

"What's happening?" I asked him urgently. "Quick, boy, tell me."

"They got 'er!" he announced gleefully. "It's the end for them! They've arrested Lady Muck Howard for Overbury's murder. She's under 'ouse arrest, 'ere at Lord D'Aubigny's. Ain't long afore she's in the Tower!"

He broke free from my grasp and picked up a stone, hurling it at the departing coach as it clattered through the street, slicing through the mob, who were now banging on the sides of it. If they could not touch her, they would take out their hatred on the conveyance that transported her to Blackfriars and imprisoned her here.

"What charges?" I turned to the woman at my side, a Huguenot silk weaver I recognized vaguely from my attendance at sermons at St. Anne's. "And where is Carr?"

"Foul witchcraft, poison, and keeping company with the devil," she replied. "Carr avoids arrest, for the king cannot bear to think his favorite has been corrupted by his family. But those who put him high now drag him down. It won't be long before he joins his whore wife." She turned to me, the entertainment of Frances's arrest no longer holding her attention. "Not to fear for our king's pleasure. I hear there is another catamite prepared to take Carr's place—until his favor is lost. I would not be in their shoes for all the gold thread in Flanders."

The crowd around us melted away, and I was left standing alone outside D'Aubigny's house. The square restored to its quiet summer zenith, but the heat did not warm me. Her words smote a fear that pierced me through. I offered a desperate prayer that this course Will and Edward were steering would not wreck our family too.

22.

For the beating of the heart:

Of the powder of nutmegs and borage and wheaten flower, of whites amber and of the bone in a stag's heart and of cinomon each alike quantitie, Mingle them well and let the patient take as much as will lye twice on an English shilling. Drink it in wine, ale, or beer every morning and at night. This will cure in short time.

Blackfriars
October 1615
Lucy St. John
Soon to be Apsley

A few days later, I visited with the clergyman at St. Anne's, putting into place the final details for my wedding, for the banns had been cried and our ceremony confirmed. After seeing all was in order, I spent the rest of the morning in deep discussion with the playwright Mr. Jonson, who was at my favorite alchemist's workroom. I must confess I found great fascination in this art, for although it had been decreed that it was not a true science, I still found the search for knowledge compelling. I enjoyed sharing my thoughts with Mr. Jonson, whose recent comedy so accurately portrayed these local streets and their trove of practicing alchemists.

Now I was late for Eleanor, who wanted to me to try my wedding dress on again. I was hurrying home, the day's heat having reached its meridian and a late storm gathering over the city. Saint Martin's summer had brought its sudden October heat to the city, the air heavy and oppressive. The thunder rumbles which had been rolling around the ochre sky since daybreak were growing more frequent, so even in our sheltered alleys, the storm was intruding. A laden vegetable cart tipped over, blocking my usual path home. I took what I thought was a deviation around the back of the old abbey and found myself in the courtyard of D'Aubigny's house.

I could not look at the door through which Frances had been escorted just a few days ago, for her deeds disturbed me greatly. The harm she caused was too severe to be in such a congenial prison. I wondered if she sat at her window, regretting the terrible actions she had taken and bribed others to do, and if the tears on her cheeks had been real or simply more artifice.

In the open yard, the thunder crashed louder, echoing from the stone walls. Other walkers sheltered as fat raindrops began to pelt the dusty ground, raising the pungent aroma that precedes a downpour. Just one man stood under the arch to the river path. As I hurried out of the rain, there grew such a sense of familiarity about his stance and his physique that I knew inevitably it was Theo.

Our playwright neighbor, Will Shakespeare, would have summoned the spirits of heaven and earth to declaim some significance between the advent of the storm and two lost lovers reuniting in its bosom. In truth, his drama was unnecessary, for we could write the lines of this play ourselves. The first flash of lightning drove me to the archway; the second stayed me in front of him.

The rain was now drumming the ground and racing in channels, the thunder reverberating around us, lightning illuminating our shadowed faces. In retrospect, our meeting could not have been better staged, for nature's tempest reflected my heart's turmoil.

"Is it really you, or are you a sprite sent by the storm to pile more agony upon me?" His familiar voice loosed a torrent of memories. This time, no Rhenish wine tainted his speech.

"It is I. You are here to see Frances?" I surprised myself to hear how calm I sounded. "It appears her past has ensnared her, in more ways than one. You were not the only fool she convinced to act against their better judgment. Your sister has quite the power of persuasion. Now excuse me." I stepped to one side, intending to escape from him, but he stood in my path.

"I was tricked." He spoke softly, his voice pitched low, so I strained to catch the words snatched from his mouth by the elements and tossed to the gusty wind. "I was tricked by those near to me into devastating those dear to me. When I came to my senses, I found myself the victim of a terrible concealment. The wedding contract was a device. My marriage is a mockery. And now I have nothing, for I abhor Elizabeth, and I have lost you."

I had no response. It was not my story.

"I would have died that night at White Hall," he continued, his hair now rain damp, drops on his cheeks like tears. "I severed my heart in half in that moment, and I have yet to rejoin the two parts, and I fear I never will. For the heart that stayed with the body still fills a function and keeps this man alive. The heart that flew with you from the room that night has yet to return. I dread it is lost forever."

I looked at this man who had once been mine, still so beautiful, now in his prime, older, carrying that same easy grace. Clothed in white velvet and slashed green satin, he was as careless of the stains imposed by the inclement weather as only one of his station could be.

"I am to be married tomorrow." There was naught to say, for in truth, what else was left? "He is a good man, a loyal man, a man who would not be led astray by those who promise what cannot be had." I listened to my words slicing through the heavy air and marveled at my levelness. "Wish me well, Theo, for although this is not the life I dreamed I would have, it is my destiny, and one that I accept with gratitude."

His green eyes shone in the shadows, bright as emeralds.

"Apsley? Edward mentioned as much. You are wasted on him." He gripped my arms with fingers that curled into my flesh. "You could still be mine. We could meet. Establish a life together . . . many do in this city. I have friends here, away from court eyes, who could help us to be together, in secret, without others knowing, just as we did before."

I knocked his hands away, not caring who saw us tussle.

"You insult me with such base suggestions . . ."

"I felt you respond. You still tremble under my touch."

". . . and tarnish what we had when you pledged to me your love. You disgust me."

He threw his head back, his laugh echoing from the stones around us.

"Ah. So you call what we had love. Well, perhaps 'twas so. Courtly love. Did you not learn a lot from the game?"

I leaned against the wall, pressing my hands behind me into the sharp flints.

"You dismiss our love? I trusted you with my heart, Theo, and pledged my future to yours."

A shutter closed across his face, his eyes empty, his expression the bland mask of a polished courtier. And yet, he was still so very beautiful. A hundred moments spent with him flooded me with emotion, for still my body was loyal to the memories, the sanguinity within me ready to pulse alive again.

"That was your choice." He glanced down at me and quickly looked to the square, where a finger of lightning flared.

"You professed your love for me! You plighted a trust. You sent me the ring." I took a shuddering breath. "And just now. You swore that your heart was ripped asunder when you saw me at White Hall."

"The little posie ring. A lovely touch. As are our speeches and declarations. Did Barbara not tell you of the games we play at court? Did Anne not warn you of our ways?"

"Your words, your letters . . ."

"Ah, what an amusement amongst us to compose those speeches, those ardent missives. Edward was a great help, for word-smithing is not my strongest talent. And yet, you were more than a passing pleasure, that is true. I too hoped we had a future. We still can, if you will play the game."

"Why are you doing this, Theo? Why are you debasing all that we had?"

"The consequence of courtly love, Lucy. Why separate reality from delusion? What is truth? What is lie?" He stepped closer to me and softly drew his finger across my lips. I shivered, his touch still jolting me. "But carry our truth with you when you bed your husband. Conceal it well, for soon you will play the games with him that you learned from me."

He gazed across the courtyard to where Frances was imprisoned.

"Your marriage may release you too, Lucy, and give you a guise of respectability that you had not as a maiden. That was always Frances's intent, you know. You just chose to marry the wrong man." Adjusting his lace cuffs, Theo glanced at the sky. "The rain has ceased. I shall see you again, for no doubt Barbara will engender some occasion. When next we meet, sweeting, think of what could be should you tire of that old man you are to wed."

He suddenly turned and kissed my lips, forcing my mouth open under his, clasping my head between his hands while he drank deeply from me.

"You will not forget me soon, Lucy. You know where to find me. I am not so easily dismissed."

I had no strength to run home and no urgency to rejoin my family. Now I needed the storm's solitude as I fled from the last remnant of my old life and into my future with Allen.

The old melancholy fell upon me as a mourning veil. I observed myself walking the streets of London as if I had stepped outside of my body. Only this afternoon would be mine to decide if I could go forward, or if I would allow Theo's threat to send me running back to my sorrowful plans for a life of seclusion. There was no choice, for all was arranged, all was in place. If ever I needed the strength of my convictions, it was now, when I could still taste the sweetness of Theo's kiss on my tongue. I was destined to marry Allen and put my affair with Theo behind me.

God knows what wounds I concealed within this hasty marriage.

23

My beloved cousin,

It seems so long ago that we were at Battersey, and you promised me one day you would show me White Hall, and you cautioned me about those who dwelt there. Now I am at the eve of my wedding to a man who serves the king through and through, and you have secured your place at court with Raleigh's search for gold.

You saved my life twice now, Will, once by the river that night of Theo's betrayal and then when I took shelter with you at Fonmon. I am sentimental this night, for I will miss you beyond all measure if you truly do take up command of the king's ships again. But I know Allen is a good man, and he has assured me that I am to be my own mistress and not live at the whims of court intrigue. I am so happy to move to the house at East Smithfield and create a home for us and the children. Will, in truth, I have my doubts, for you hold my secrets in your heart, but I will trust in God that I have made the right decision and that my past haunts me no more.

Your loving cousin
Lucy (Apsley)
22 October, 1615

Allen arrived at the house early in the morning, bringing with him a great surprise: my sweet Anne and my brother John. As Anne tucked rosemary into my bodice and wound bride lace into my hair, we reminisced of her wedding and our lives since.

"You look content, Lucy," she said softly as she pulled on and tied my sleeves of fine blue silk, embroidered with forget-me-nots and lilies. "Blue for fidelity and everlasting love." She smiled. Although she looked searchingly into my eyes, I was sure she found no clouds of doubt there, for I hid myself well.

"And purity," I said. "Don't forget purity."

I adjusted the bride lace at my breast and, taking a deep breath, walked across the threshold to where Allen was waiting for me.

Before noon, when our luck was strongest, my wedding procession wound through the alleys of Blackfriars toward St. Anne's, escorted by my family and friends, old and new. Musicians played as we strolled through the streets, bringing people to their doors to heap good wishes on us and call out cheerful blessings.

I held Peter's and Jocasta's hands as they walked by my side, Allen and Will following us, and then Eleanor, Anne, John, and others. Of course, I had asked Oliver and Joan to attend, and I welcomed them both. Joan responded with suspicion to my welcome kiss, but found no duplicity in my face, such was my skill at dissembling this day.

Edward and Barbara declined to participate in the procession. They were waiting for us at the church, their coach drawn up in front in such a way that we all carefully picked our way around it, it was so large. Eleanor and I stifled our smiles at this display of ostentation, and I composed myself as I entered the church, now with Allen at my side. All others stood behind me as we presented ourselves.

Allen was dressed in fine gray-and-green satin, his ruff beautifully starched and pleated, his sword at his side. His hair and beard were neatly trimmed, and he smelled fresh, of sandalwood. I detected a slight nervousness under his splendid apparel and knew that he had dressed with great care, wanting to present the best possible appearance for me and my family. My heart tore at the effort he had made.

As we stood together and the minister spoke the words that bound me to Allen for life, I went through the ceremony as if watching another there, such a detachment I felt. And as Allen placed a ring of wrought silver with a pure blue sapphire stone on my heart finger still I remembered a posie ring, with the words "I live in hope" inscribed within. I hated myself at that moment and swore to God that I would honor this man who stood by my side and make amends for the deceiving thoughts that haunted me.

Edward and Will, determined to celebrate in the new style to which our family aspired, had rented a room in the Blackfriars theater for our wedding luncheon. It was there we walked after our ceremony, through the streets so familiar to me. I was relieved we would not be in the street by D'Aubigny's house. I would have considered it a bad omen to venture close to where Frances was under arrest.

The room was filled with laughter and talk, and the wedding brought us together, my family united around the table, our differences forgotten. Even Joan entered into the spirit of the occasion and became quite merry as she drank the wine that Allen provided from his best cellars. She had grown plump in the years since I had seen her, satisfied now that her station in life was secure. Oliver was attentive to her, and she hung on every word of Edward and Barbara to a degree that I found to be obnoxious, so full of fakery was it. However, I was happy that her attention was drawn away from me and that she was occupied with them rather than criticizing my being. She had not lost her uncanny knack for making me feel as though I were still nine years old. Today of all days, I did not need to return to my childhood.

Allen reached for my hand and squeezed it.

"This is truly a happy day for me," he said softly. "I hope for you too, Lucy."

I smiled at him, touched at his quiet admission. He was such a kind man, and in spite of his long career as a soldier and a mercenary, his was a soft heart that cared for people's well-being. I appreciated that he took a moment from his talks of the Irish with Oliver and Will to see that I was comfortable.

"It is, Allen. I never dreamed I would ever be in this position, and I am grateful to God and to you for providing me with this new life and family." I looked across the table at Jocasta and Peter, sitting with Anne, behaving with great dignity and manners. Taking a breath, I lowered my eyes. "I hope perhaps my love may engender the gift of children too." With each word, I grafted myself to my new life.

"All in good time," replied Allen, his hand still holding mine. "I have no doubt of the love I feel for you, Lucy, and that we will be rewarded by the joy God can bring to us."

At that moment, I could vision my life ahead of me and saw what may come to be. I wanted to raise Jocasta and Peter, bring them happiness and security in a loving home. I wished for my own children to fill my house, my garden, my life with Allen. In that moment, I sent such a fervent prayer heavenward that this be granted, for it was so simple and nothing that would require favors or bribes, intrigues or political maneuvering. I prayed for this with all my heart. I wanted nothing more at that moment than to seek the secure haven of Allen's wisdom, experience, and orderly life.

From all I heard tell, this man would be reliable and predictable, give me security and stability, and would appreciate me as his partner in life. I gave further thanks for his kind character that would grant me independence in my thoughts and deeds.

Where my doubts came were not in Allen's ability to fulfill this wish, but in my worthiness to receive it.

The voyage to my new home along the Thames was a brief one. Unlike Walter in his sailing ships to a new world, my boat was a wherry, and the time was counted in hours, not months. But it may have been as strange and unique a journey for all the turmoil inside as we departed the Blackfriars steps and were rowed downriver. As we waited to steer under the bridge, I was a lone explorer, for my family remained at Blackfriars when Allen and I departed for his house at the Yard.

"The Tower, and there is Walter's gaol." Allen pointed out where Walter dwelt, and I looked gravely at his prison.

"How did a man of his adventurous spirit fare when his horizon was stone walls and iron bars?"

"He had his books, visitors, and liberty to walk around the precinct some of the time." Allen paused. "But 'twas not easy. There were occasions where he fell into such a dark humor his life was despaired of."

The Tower loomed high. Anchoring the crowded city, protecting it from the foreign marauders who threatened invasion from the Essex estuaries, the ancient fortress guarded access to London's wealth. It served as a royal palace and a prison, oft times both. I thought of Queen Elizabeth and her royal mother, Anne, both of whom had tasted the Tower's hospitality, one to escape, the other to die.

"St. Katherine's Steps." Allen pointed to a wharf by the Tower where a flotilla of trading ships were moored. "This is where we alight."

"I did not realize we were so close to the Tower."

"In its shadow, but not in its liberty. Our home is within the Royal Navy Yard." He pointed to the riverbank, where behind the thicket of masts I glimpsed a stone wall enclosing a collection of buildings and pastures.

"There is much going on and none of it palace traffic."

"It is a very different world here, Lucy. One where commerce rules."

As the ferryman steered between the sailing vessels and barges toward the stairs, a new world entered my sensibility, one I had never considered or seen before. There were tall sailing ships, laden with all manner of cargo and materials, some unloading, others being provisioned. There were massive timbers and crates, bundles and urns, all concealing their contents but moving swiftly from ship to shore and back to ship.

As we moored, my senses were assailed by the cries of the porters loading and unloading, the screech of gulls attracted by scraps from a broken case, a tang of spices, and the aroma of tar from the barrels lined up on the wharf.

"Come, we are nearly home." Allen helped me from the rocking wherry.

We walked the brief distance up the hill from the dock to the Yard, Allen pausing every so often to greet a merchant or inspect a cart of goods, so what should have taken us a short time took nearly an hour. I was dropping with exhaustion, for the day was long, but Allen appeared invigorated by all that surrounded him, and I discovered another side to the man I married.

It was apparent he was well known in the area, and although treated with respect, there was a worldliness to his person which made me realize he did more than sit at his desk and make lists of victuals. He was intimate with all aspects of his duties, including the acceptance and loading of supplies as well as the ordering.

We approached the stone wall marking the southern boundary of the Yard. As we continued to walk up the long hill and finally entered through the black iron gates, I was struck by the size of the property and the industry that it obviously contained. In front of me was a small town of every kind of provisioning facilities. Allen pointed out to me the bakehouses and oven houses, the slaughterhouse, salt houses, cooperage, and numerous pens, yards, and dwellings.

There were ancient orchards, where the last of the autumn russet apples were still on the branches, and orderly gardens, the earth neatly turned and ready for winter planting. It was easy to see how the original abbey and manor house were expanded and remodeled over the years to form the Yard. There was a delicious aroma of bread baking, and I looked at Allen with joy as he introduced me to our new home.

"It's a wonderful sight," I exclaimed, so surprised by the extent and orderliness of the compound. "I had no idea of the size of this facility."

He smiled. "'Tis not a small thing to provision the Royal Navy," he remarked. "This is just one of many of our yards. But it is an important one, being located so close to the king. He takes a great interest in the welfare of his men, and he has personally asked me to be responsible for providing the very best provisions available for them." He paused, a small frown on his brow. "Of course, quality does not come without a price, but I have many eager tradesmen who are only too happy to extend to me their credit to serve the king."

He took my hand and led me toward the manor house built into the walls of the old abbey, the ancient stone forming the skeleton on which the body of the Yard now settled. Opening wide the door, he led me into the hall, dimly lit but sweet smelling, with fresh rushes on the floor, the tang of lavender and rosemary rising as our feet crushed the dried herbs. There was little light from the small, high windows, for the room was as ancient as the abbey walls it rested on, but the thick walls encouraged a quiet calm from the hustle and bustle outside in the Yard.

"It is to your liking?" I heard an anxiety in Allen's voice and understood how hard he had tried to make this hospitable for me.

"More than to my liking, Allen. I feel so cherished." I embraced him, and we stood quietly together for a while.

"To bed, to bed!" Will roared through the entrance hall, his arrival closely followed by Edward, Oliver, John, and other male relatives and friends. It was apparent they had continued toasting our happiness after we left and had visited the Cheapside taverns on their ride to the Yard. As we jumped apart, laughing, Allen was quickly surrounded by the men, and a brimming tankard of ale was pressed into his hand.

"Come, Lucy, let us prepare you." Eleanor and Anne were at my side while Joan and Barbara stood behind them as they led me to the staircase. "It is not a true wedding until you are bedded, and although Allen has been this way before, it is your first, and you must be so honored."

"Some may say not."

I turned, hardly believing I heard Barbara's words, so softly were they said under her breath, the general tumult of the room drowning them to all but myself. I took a step toward her, my anger swift.

She looked at me, and mouthed, "knowledge," turning before I could do more.

Eleanor hurried me forward.

"Come," she repeated. "Allen is waiting for his bride."

I allowed myself to be steered away from Barbara, but her words cut deep, and the threat behind them was not lost on me.

We climbed the staircase to the chamber above, where the crowd of men awaited us, laughing and joking crudely. Allen was already sitting in bed, his doublet removed, a fine white gown covering him. Eleanor and Anne took me to a small wardrobe and carefully removed my wedding dress, slipping an embroidered lawn shift over my head and loosening my hair. Tying the satin ribbons around my bosom, Anne whispered her blessing, and together they escorted me to the bed where Allen was waiting. A cheer arose as we lay side by side, and Allen reached for my hand, his clasp warm and steady.

"All of you, leave now," commanded Anne. She shooed the men in front of her. In truth, it was a funny sight to see my sweet friend scattering the raucous men like mice before a cat. She turned and smiled before pulling the door shut behind her.

Our first night as man and wife was of exploration and tenderness, and I was grateful for Allen's kindness. I knew it was my duty to follow my husband's desires, and I did imagine this would be as it was with Theo, when he led me to a place of ecstasy, albeit hastily and with his own pleasure first.

But just as Allen pledged his love to me and declared that I would be his equal in our household, so he taught me to be his equal in love. Further than I ever ventured with Theo, I discovered the ancient ways as Allen's eager pupil and became the master to his satisfaction. I delicately explored his body and delighted in tracing his battle scars with my fingers and lips, touching his muscled limbs, tempered by years of physical labor and warfare. His was a good body, strong and well formed, and one that I could see had fulfilled the purpose for which God designed it, fighting for his monarch and country.

Only once did I feel a hesitation, a pause as he smoothly entered me, when he ceased his rhythm for a moment before continuing. My body responded to his, and after, as we lay together in the light of the fire, he smoothed my hair from my face and gazed deeply into my eyes. I willed myself to look back with the same intensity.

"I did not hurt you, Lucy?"

"No, you did not."

Although he searched my face wordlessly, as if waiting for me to speak more, I remained dumb. The moment passed, and he turned from me to sleep. The next morning, at first light, he pulled the covers back and saw the blood on my gown, and softly made love to me again, gently, masterfully.

I settled into life at the Yard with its packed storehouses, bread ovens that burned day and night, and perpetual movement of provisions and supplies. All of the fleet's victuals were reckoned from here and much made and stored. Allen employed an army of clerks to track all the orders and payments that changed hands daily in London and at the yards in our ports and depots in Bristol, Portsmouth, Plymouth, Southampton, Ipswich, and other strategic towns.

In these times of plenty, many merchants were eager to supply the king with his needs in the anticipation there would come immediate profits and future recognition of their services.

When Allen was home—which was not often—he sat late into the night reviewing papers and bills of fare, and the times that I did sit with him, I was amazed at the considerable sums of money passing through the Yard, both on credit and in actual coin. On many occasions Allen paid for these supplies himself and charged the king's accounts later. Although this seemed a precarious business, Allen assured me the king's purse was generous. Allen's earnings for lending the money were in the significant difference he paid the merchants and charged the king.

I was proud of Allen, for to provision the Royal Navy was no small task even in these times of peace. My mind often returned to the scenes I had witnessed with Anne in Portsmouth, where the unemployed sailors had to shift for themselves, begging on the streets and seeking shelter in doorways. I saw another side to my husband, for in his career as victualler, he had befriended many seafaring captains and their families. He considered it an honor to continue to care for them in peace years as he had in war.

A calm had descended upon our nation, and our navy was no longer on war readiness to battle the Spanish fleet. The effect was of a two-edged sword, for the women were glad to have their husbands at home, but their employ had ceased, and there were no wages or vittles to support them in these times. Allen continued to look after so many of the men he fought with during Elizabeth's reign, redeeming those who had been imprisoned for vagrancy through no fault of theirs, taking care of the widows and children of the men who died in poverty, seeking wages on the land.

All men to him were equal, and he was liberal with his generosity to so many that were in need. I wondered often at the depth of his coffer. Each day, many men waited at the Yard gates for sustenance, but it seemed that his resources were great, for none were ever turned away.

"Allen, there is much you give to these men from your own purse," I ventured one morning after watching him again distribute coin to more than fifty men who spent the night lined along the Yard walls.

192

"It will be returned to me a thousandfold in blessings." He smiled and took my hand. "And as we speak of money, Lucy, I wanted to tell you that I am making over your wedding portion to you for your own governance."

I was shocked, for although as a spinster, I might have some say in how my portion was distributed, as Allen's wife, all my inheritance belonged to him. I opened my mouth to protest, and he softly put a finger on my lips.

"I am also giving you an allowance of three hundred pounds a year to do with as you wish." He traced his finger across my mouth, his eyes soft. "I remember, one day in the wild Welsh countryside, promising a young woman that her freedom to choose within a family could offer equal independence as running away to a remote island."

Tears filled my eyes, and he gently brushed one away as it slipped onto my cheek.

"Trust me, Lucy, as I trust you. You will be a formidable custodian of this money, for I know your heart to be true and your intentions Godly. It is just coin, to be spent where you see fit. I would remind you not to hoard your treasures on earth where rust corrodes, but use it wisely to store treasures in heaven."

I honored his generosity with prudent spending—except for one great extravagance. Our marriage bed was one of utility and not comfort, and it must have been the years of military life that permitted Allen to sleep anywhere and in any circumstances. I secretly ordered a new marriage bed, velvet hangings gloriously worked in orange, tawny, and silver velvet. When he arrived home from one of his numerous provincial inspections, he laughed aloud to see the beautifully worked wood, luxurious hangings, and heap of pillows arranged in the center of the plain chamber of our home.

The bed must have blessed us with its benefits, for within a few months of our marriage, I suspected that I was with child. My transition to my new life was surely complete, and I could leave the past behind.

24

Dearest Anne,

News from court—the king has made George a Knight of the Garter, and his benefice extends to his family. Edward, Oliver, and Will continue to receive and anticipate much reward in their ventures. I hear that Giles's scheme for licensing inns has received approval from the king, and Katherine visits Barbara's dressmakers daily.

As my belly swells, I grow placid, and just as spring is coming to our Yard, so today appeared the first stirrings of the new life of the child within me. Allen is much excited but makes a great fuss of me, concerned that I not overtire myself, while Peter and Jocasta vie for my attention, each hoping for a younger brother or sister. I walk down by the river, I feel as an island, and the water flows around me, bringing me news and providing me sustenance, but not interrupting much the rhythm of my daily life. The Yard's larders are thriving under my supervision, for Allen knows how dearly I love the land, and charges me with growing as much provision as I can from the old monastic gardens.

Your loving sister, Lucy
East Smithfield
Spring 1616

In April, we received news that George Villiers approached the king and presented the plans for Walter's release and expedition. Freedom cost dearly, for not only did Will and Edward pay fifteen hundred pounds for the king's ear, but they forfeited one fifth of all the gold that Walter would bring back from El Dorado, to directly line the privy purse.

Sir Walter arrived at our house late one evening, after curfew, released from the Tower at night to avoid the City crowds. The king knew that the Londoners would either celebrate or condemn his release, so greatly did he divide men, and did not want the public spectacle to incite the Spanish more. Instead, accompanied only by his servant and a Yeoman Warder, Walter was released unto Allen's care as his dear friend, relative and, more than any other priority, the king's trusted guard. Our home became Raleigh's refuge on his first night of freedom in more than eleven years.

His arrival was foretold by a sudden and loud banging on our door, and as Allen went to answer, I stood in the dim hall, my thoughts flying to the children, and their safety. I heard a shout of greeting, quickly stifled, and Allen returned, accompanied by an elderly man, grizzled and grey, stoop shouldered and walking carefully.

"My dear, I would introduce you to Sir Walter Raleigh," Allen said with great suppressed emotion in his voice.

I held my hand out to the old man who stood in our hall, his suit worn, with hair unkempt, and beard straggled. I could not fathom how this frail elder could be the famous adventurer. What a travesty we were caught up in, paying this huge sum of money for the release of a broken bodied man who appeared on the verge of collapse.

Then, he took my hand, and kissed it softly, and stood straight and looked into my eyes with a piercing gaze. Such beautiful eyes he had, with such strong charisma I felt the only woman in the world that existed for him. His bow was still graceful, and his smile tantalizing. For a moment, there was a glimpse of the exquisite young courtier, Elizabeth's favorite, the adventurer, the pirate king, the dancer, the lover.

I know not how all this happened in a heart's beat, for I had never encountered such an influence before. In a flash of lucidity, I knew why men followed him and how he could persuade queens and kings to throw their lot in with him. In truth, in that moment, I would have followed him to the ends of the earth, such was his compelling attraction.

Long into the night, he sat before our fire and wove his stories of adventure and exploration, tales of endless horizons, distant lands and Ethiopians, mysterious rivers and impenetrable jungles that challenged a man to find his path. I could understand Will's fascination with Walter and his longing to be part of this man's voyages. Raleigh's conviction that he was close to discovering gold in El Dorado was compelling, and he made mention several times of a map that he had secreted away which would provide the passage along the Orinoco River and lead him to the treasure.

It was hard for me to discern the difference between fantasy and truth, and I believe that was at the heart of his charm and why people either loved or hated him. So tall were his tales, so incredible his stories, men despised themselves for being swept away by the magic his words wove only to find he had feet of clay. And then he would loot a Spanish galleon or sack a town in the Caribe and bring back such a wealth of treasures that those who still believed in him and invested their money along with their dreams were rich beyond compare.

Walter's knowledge was extensive and his interests broad. With tongues loosed by freedom, we talked by the guttering candles, touching subjects as wide as the oceans he sailed.

I did have a sense of wonder of all this man had witnessed and his extraordinary courage, for he knew no fear in his exploration and spoke as though it was his destiny to rove the seas and lands we could only imagine or touch in the map books. His deep interest in medicines and alchemy I found fascinating. He promised me when he returned from El Dorado and recovered his beloved home of Sherborne, he would take me to the gardens and workshops he had built, all in the pursuit of the curatives and transformations he sought to find the mystery within.

In a fit of spite, the king had leased Sherborne to Robert Carr while Walter was in the Tower, but with Carr's arrest and disgrace, Walter knew he could win back his property and live there with his beloved Bess, content in his retirement. I believed he would do so, and so eventually I went to my bed, my head filled with his precious recollections of the gardens of Sherborne.

"They've summoned the peers of the realm to Westminster." Eleanor looked closely at me as she gave me the news one morning while she was visiting me. The weather was warm at the end of April, and she came to stay for a few days, bringing young Huw, who much loved exploring in the Yard. We were sitting in a sheltered spot of the monastery garden, where the mild spring sunshine warmed the old stone walls and daffodils danced around us, their golden trumpets nodding in the soft breeze drifting from the river. The orchards were in full bloom, and I delighted in the beauty surrounding me and reflecting my own fertility.

"All are gathering for the trial of the Somersets. They say it is going to be hard to find a fair judge, for many despise them, and Theo is distraught that Frances will be found guilty and sentenced to death for her part in Overbury's murder."

As she spoke, I gazed at the Tower, its presence always dominating our perspective, the walls higher than any other building around us. Today it presented a benevolent face, the cupolas piercing the robin's egg blue sky, small puffy spring clouds trailing in from the east. I thought of how deceptive its appearance was and if Frances Howard, now lodged within and awaiting trial, was walking on the Tower leads, looking eastward, wondering at the gardens and orchards of the Yard and who lived in such an idyllic enclave.

"Who told you this?"

"Barbara. She and Edward took apartments again at White Hall. They are constantly in the company of George and the new circle of courtiers around the king."

"She must be in her element." I thought of the girl I grew up with at Battersey, how far she had come and how she always seemed so sure of her destiny. "Joan too, for she aspired to so much."

"Joan is almost impossible now that Oliver is appointed Lord Deputy of Ireland. You would think she was the queen the way she is carrying on."

I smiled. "Edward's influence again?"

Eleanor nodded.

I turned to my sewing and thought of how rapidly all these rewards and perquisites were landing on my family. Our rise seemed as a shooting star blazing across the firmament. Even Allen had a queue of merchants outside his office every morning, eager to lend credit so he could acquire the best possible goods and prices and sell them on to the navy. They whispered of his wife's connections and gossiped of

Villiers ascending, speculating so too would rise those near to them. Our comet trailed many in its tail.

"So what of Frances Howard?" I admitted to a curious fascination with the woman who caused me such pain in her trickery and the damage she wrought Theo. "And is Theo so distraught that his wicked sister is to be on trial for her life?"

"Barbara says he is. He visits her often at the Tower to comfort her, and now that they are assembling at Westminster, he has reestablished his residency at White Hall."

I shrugged.

"I despise their corrupt hearts and sorcery. They thought themselves above the law, above man's morals, and above God's rules. I would like to see how their Catholic ways and secret superstitions will save them now."

"Remember Mistress Turner's prophecy?" asked Eleanor idly, her eyes on her stitching. "At White Hall, she foretold someone standing close would be linked to Frances. I wonder what it meant."

"Probably nothing. She was a witch, and they found proof before they hanged her at Tyburn. There were dolls pierced with pins in her possession and numerous magical potions. She was proven in her trial of being a papist and a bawd." I crossed my fingers in the old way, protecting against the evil eye. "But she couldn't foretell her own death, dangling from a gibbet, watched by the very women of fashion she played for the fools they are. Frances's biggest mistake was placing her trust in the coven of sorcerers and sycophants that gorged on her insecurities."

Presently, we fell to talking of other things, laughing at how exhausted Will was every night, taking Walter around London and showing him all the sights and amusements that had been built during his eleven years of captivity. It seemed that Walter exhibited the boundless energy of a child. Along with his curiosity to see the attractions was his desire to be seen himself amongst the citizens of London, and Will was challenged in keeping up with the old man.

"Will has been given command of the king's ship." Eleanor looked down at her hands, clasped tightly in her lap. "He sails this summer."

"With Raleigh?" I asked abruptly, for certain that would be a voyage where many left and few returned.

She shook her head. "Faith, no. He wishes it were so, but instead he has been charged with monitoring the Narrow Sea. Edward found him this position through George."

"Are you sad, Eleanor?"

"I wish that he did not play so easily into Edward's influence. He does not have the natural cunning that is required to succeed at court. I fear he will find himself beholden to these people because of his eagerness to associate with their ambitions. I know not the terms of the bargain he struck with George Villiers to release Walter from the Tower, but I fear he has pledged far beyond his judgment."

I was concerned to hear the worry in her voice. "Has Will promised more than he can give? What could he have committed?"

"All I know is that all rests on this voyage to El Dorado and his investment in its success. It's a venture that I wish I never heard of. I wish we had stayed in Fonmon, where life was so simple."

Eleanor's tears marked the depth of her despair, for I had not seen her cry before but once, at the death of her baby. I drew her close and held her, murmuring reassurance as I would to a child, for I could feel the fear trembling within her. Inside, I was seething with anger that Will would jeopardize his family for this venture, and I despised Walter for weaving his dreams around this family. Now I understood the other side of Raleigh and how his fantasies could wreck a man as well as reward him. I wished for nothing other than his departure and for our lives to be restored to our normal routines.

A cloud crossed the spring sun, casting gray shadows over the Tower's white stone walls, and it changed, as did a chameleon, from a palace to a prison.

Early one morning in the sweet month of May, when the hawthorn trees showered the footpaths along the river with flurries of decaying petals, Frances Howard was rowed to her trial from the Tower to Westminster. I traveled the river often enough to accompany her in my mind, and I followed her voyage to the unknown with all the trepidation that anyone left standing at the shore feels for the departing explorer.

In truth, it was not sympathy in my heart, but more awe in God's justice and how the plans He laid out for her took this long and circuitous route to damnation. I wondered at what time in her life she realized—for she must have—that she could not continue her wickedness and debauchery. I considered if she now was contrite or if she still stood contemptuous of authority and morals, challenging all with her famous beauty.

For our family, this stamped the final seal on the demise of the Carrs, and the succession was complete, for George was there to offer comfort to the king through all his distress at the fate of his former favorite and his beautiful wife.

Allen and I were at Blackfriars the day of the trial, for Will had business with Allen to discuss, and I did not want to miss an opportunity to visit Eleanor. Although my body was thickening with my child, I felt healthy and did not want to remain at home. As we sat quietly within the chamber, our conversation was broken by shouting outside. Moments later, there was a loud rumbling, and as we looked from the windows on the upper floor, we saw Edward and Barbara's coach pull up outside.

"She admitted her guilt without a pause," Barbara announced as she walked into the room, pulling her fine cream leather gloves from her hands. I focused on the intricate tooling, the beautiful cut, as she spoke.

"Even in her state of guilt, she still is beautiful." Edward was not far behind Barbara and was similarly ostentatiously dressed. "Seems so odd to see her in the dock, pleading for her life in front of her peers."

"Bah. She was always the best actress of all. Those tears were not real, her pleas well-rehearsed." Barbara clicked her finger at Eleanor's servant, who had brought ale to the room. Taking a sip and pulling a wry face, she switched her gaze to me. "Theo was there, Lucy. He looked very upset."

My cheeks flamed, although I had done no wrong. How I despised her.

"I am sure he is. It is his favorite sister who has been brought to trial."

"And no doubt the penalty will be death," replied Barbara triumphantly. "Surely Carr will follow. There will be no one left in George's path now."

"You have taken care of that well," I replied. "I wish all had friends such as you, for who needs enemies?"

"Come, Lucy, we should depart before the crowds become too large." Allen put his hand on my arm and drew me toward the door. "It appears there is much rejoicing in the streets, and the mobs will be celebrating the demise of the Carrs."

"And celebrating the elevation of the Villiers," crowed Edward, his beard frothed with ale foam from the brimming tankard he was clutching.

"That remains to be seen," replied Allen as he drew me from their company. "We may know the difference between Carr and George, but does the country?"

We sat in the covered coach silently, side by side, as the noise of the London crowds surrounded us. Allen pulled down the leather shades until there was just a sliver of daylight peeking through, the light refracting and enclosing us in a soft glow.

"Why does Barbara insist on bringing up Lord Howard when we are with her, Lucy?"

His voice was even, soft, his Irish lilt tinting the words.

I was silent, my usual defense. I did not know what to say, for whatever speech came, I felt I was defending a crime.

"Lucy, what exactly was Lord Howard to you?"

The coach clattered through the streets, heading east to the Yard, the roads clear ahead, where behind us the alleys and courtyards were filling with people. I smelled bonfires and knew this night was going to be a long one.

"He . . . professed his love for me, once."

"And did you return it?"

I could not tell his mood from his tone. He remained silent, waiting for my response.

"I thought, at the time, I was in love with him."

201

"And did you return that declaration of love, Lucy?" It was disconcerting that he should keep calling my name, for with each word he spoke, I felt more guilt and confusion.

"His attention to me was so discreet I could not but entertain him."

The words hung between us, the air within the coach thick with emotion.

"And yet you came to me a maid. What court games did he teach you, Lucy?"

My tears flowed then, for all the humiliation I felt and the kindness of this man, who still did not raise his voice to me. I felt the heat of my deceit, the false declarations I had given that I was truly his, in body and mind. The old shadow crept over me, and my voice was silenced, imprisoned by my conscience.

I tentatively held my hand to touch his, but he gently put my hand back in my lap and edged away. It was only an inch, but for the wall that was between us, it could have been a kingdom apart.

Frances's sentence was death, for justice must be done lest the mob would riot. We heard the countess took it with great calmness, unlike her arrest, when she vomited and shat in her fright. Of course, the king granted a reprieve for her and her husband, and their sweet necks would not be kissed by the executioner's axe. James may have enjoyed the hunt, but he did not relish the kill.

Back to the Tower she journeyed. As I walked in the Yard's gardens that long hot August, I mused again what was in her mind as she sat in her prison, and if the ghosts of Overbury and Anne Turner haunted and taunted her, keeping sleep at bay through those white summer nights.

Now we were truly neighbors, captives of our deeds, she in her prison, me in one of my own construction. Although this real-life masque was a long way from the banqueting rooms of White Hall, Frances's fantasy still wove its tendrils around us, keeping us tangled in an invisible web.

To bring pains in labour and bring away the afterbirth. Three pints of the smallest aquae vitae, a dram of hiera picra, put them into a stone bottle, close it and set it by the fire or in a warm place, shake it and give it for 8 days.

To bring away that which is left, take some of the woman's own hairs burnt, and give her half a spoonful of the ashes in some mugwort water.

Recipe from Midwife Wesley
The Victualler's Yard
October 1617

My attention turned inward as my baby grew and I prepared for the birth. I remembered the women in the villages around Lydiard when Anne and I visited. I knew from my discussions with them and the midwives that those who worked on the land until the final days of their birthing fared the best. I would not let Allen cosset me into retiring into a birthing chamber a month before and insisted I still walk in the Yard and tend the gardens daily, feeling strong and healthy as I did so. I pointed out that in our little world, there were none to frown on the eccentricities of the victualler's wife. I carefully cleaned the staining London clay from my fingernails when visitors called.

My birth gossips were Eleanor and a renowned midwife, Mistress Wesley, for I considered Jocasta too young to assist.

Late one evening, long after Allen had retired to our bed, I sat by the dying fire in our chamber, shadows chasing over the rough stone walls. Sleep eluded me, and I felt an energy humming through my body, a vibration that kept me alert. A little mouse scampered across the floor, and I smiled, welcoming her, for she was likely seeking a home for her young too. The first cramp came suddenly, as Eleanor said it would. I sat still for a moment, counting, anticipating not only the birth of my child, but the change he would bring to my life.

"Allen . . . Allen." I whispered, crossing to our bed and touching him lightly on the shoulder. He was alert immediately. "The baby is coming."

"I'll waken Eleanor. And send for Goodwife Wesley." He held me tight, and I felt his heart pounding through his lawn shirt. "You are in good hands."

I winced as another pain washed over me, this one heavier, more insistent.

"Walk, Lucy. Walk through the pain." He kissed me and moments later returned with Eleanor, who quickly moved the birthing chair close to the fireplace.

"Go, Allen. This is no place for you. Have Goodwife Wesley attend us as soon as she arrives."

She pushed Allen from the room and pulled the heavy hangings across the window to keep out the night humors.

"How frequent are your pains, Lucy?" She rapidly built up the fire until it blazed.

"Every few minutes . . ." I was interrupted by another cramp and groped for the birthing chair as the room darkened around me. I heard the door open and close with a click.

"Mistress Wesley, she fares well, I have given her the aqua vitae . . ." Eleanor's voice was dimmed by another wave of pain.

"The baby comes, Lady Apsley. Grip tightly the handles, squeeze with each pain, and keep silent. We do not want the sound of your cries to be the first your babe hears."

I felt the midwife's sharp fingernail inside me, ready to pierce the sac. Grasping the wooden handles of the chair, I bit my cheeks hard to prevent the scream that sat in my throat.

"The baby is coming right. You can give her some of Dr. Coradon's powder for the pain, Lady St.John."

I turned my head toward Eleanor, gratefully sipping the small cordial glass filled with burnt wine and the powders to hasten the birth.

"You are sure he lies straight?" I clenched my teeth as the pains became rapid. "The powders can't be given if the baby is breached."

"His crown comes. Push, my lady, for your child enters the world." Midwife Wesley was crouched by the stool. As I pushed, I felt a gushing and a final pain that would split me in two.

"A fine boy, my lady." A drawing of breath and a wail filled my ears.

"He is healthy?"

"He is healthy." Eleanor took a damp cloth to my face and smiled softly. "You have birthed a fine boy, Lucy"

"I told Allen I would do so. For all of our sakes."

We called him Allen, and when he was a few days old, he was taken to All Hallows by the Tower and duly christened. I chafed at home, wishing to come too, but knowing even I could not flout convention, which insisted I remain in my chamber so soon after the birthing. I was eager for all the details when Allen, Peter, and Jocasta returned home with him. As I sat with him on my lap, swaddled like a little chrysalis, I could not have been more content. I looked around at my family with such a sense of belonging and wonder that this child now bound us all together.

"You are a boon to this family, for you bring us much joy and happiness," I whispered to him as I rocked him in my arms.

"What is a boon?" asked Jocasta, standing by my side and playing with Allen's tiny hand as he grasped her little finger.

"A blessing," I replied.

"I like that. I shall call him Boon."

I laughed. "You just stood witness at his christening. His name is Allen."

"That will be most confusing for you. When he is hiding in the Yard and you call Allen, who is to say that my father will not come running instead of him?"

I could not disagree with her logic, and just as she insisted on calling him Boon, so next did Peter. The name stayed with my son, for who was I to take a name away from one who had earned it at such a young age? For Peter, it was much needed to dispel any burgeoning jealousy. Although he had been named in honor of his mother's uncle, who did confer much on his niece's family, I did not want Peter to feel slighted as Allen's firstborn that he did not take his father's name. And so our new child who bound us all together became Boon, and Boon he stayed.

Just as the September sun gilded our lives at the Yard, so the honors from George Villiers continued to heap treasure on our family. Edward was next to receive advancement, and as elder brother of George, his rewards were significant. Although he already earned much in farming and business transactions that lined his purse in their home county, now came the knighthood, bestowed with the usual ceremony at White Hall.

I declined to attend, for I was still nursing Boon and did not want to leave him. Only Allen knew of my secret, for any other woman of my status would have employed a wet nurse. I was convinced of the importance of feeding him from my own breast, and Allen supported me in my certainty.

Barbara was delighted with this appointment, for it certified that Edward was no longer the ambitious sheep farmer from Leicestershire that she married, but now a gentleman of London. His past was checkered with numerous dubious incidents related to his farming and regimental careers, and I warrant she kicked the last of the country dirt behind her and settled into her place in London society, her gamble paying her dividends.

Next on the honors' list was Giles, who satisfactorily proved to the king and Villiers his inns licensing scheme had lucrative potential. A knighthood was also granted to him, and I heard from Eleanor that he and Katherine grew even more self-satisfied with their position and acquisitions. Eleanor told me they were frequently seen driving the streets of London in their new coach with four runners ahead of them, causing much commotion and contempt from the citizens.

I was grateful both Will and Allen had earned their knighthoods in true fashion for bravery in war and success on the battlefield, and not at the cost of lining a sycophant's purse. That was the road to corruption and degradation. These new titles brought the beholders little honor and much value. It was disturbing to watch the advent of greed over posterity and the discordance this brought to men's lives.

At the same time, I should not judge, for in her own way, Barbara seemed most content with Edward and her life. Not only was she dressed in finery daily, she also bred well and was bearing Edward healthy sons.

"Like this, children . . . cup your hand so . . . take a deep breath . . . aahhhhhh . . . and blow it out." Allen exhaled into the chilly morning, puffing out a cloud of white as he waved an imaginary pipe in his hand.

"Look at me, Father, look!" Jocasta's breath mingled with Allen's.

"See! You are now all the fashion, smoking Walter's tobacco."

It was a glorious day of bright blue skies and sparkling frost, and our breath hung in the still morning air as we glided across the smooth Thames. The children laughed so hard I thought Peter would fall in the water. I held Boon close, and his little face, pink with cold, peeked out at me. I stared into his eyes as they gazed up at me, asking him silently who he was and who he would be, and he chortled and smiled back at me.

"Look—we are here!"

I was broken from my musings by the children's calling, for we had already reached the jetty for Battersey House. As we were rowed close to the pier, the new house came into view through the orchard. It was a marvel of design, and I could immediately see that Joan had used Charlton Park as her inspiration for the rebuilding of Battersey, for the windows, turrets, and weathervanes all boasted a similar architecture.

"That is quite a statement." Allen looked at me.

"Not what it was, that is certain." I shrugged. "Joan has used Oliver's wealth to improve much."

"May I escort you, my lady?" He held out his arm as I stepped from the barge. "You look very beautiful, Lucy. I am honored to be your husband."

"Thank you." I smiled gratefully. My heart was beating a little faster as I walked the old cinder path from the jetty and approached the house, memories tumbling upon me. Now I returned with a handsome husband, a family, and a new baby.

"You appear well, Lucy." Joan waited for us at the top of the steps, Oliver standing behind her. She wore a ruff almost as wide as her shoulders, and although the fashion for yellow starch had died with the witch Anne Turner, Joan's ornately designed costume and intricate embroidery would have more suited a lavish dinner than greeting her grand-nieces and nephews on a winter's morn.

"Thank you, Aunt Joan." I kissed her cheek, smelling the acrid lead in her cosmetics. "And so do you." I turned to my uncle. "We are happy to be celebrating Christmas with you. It is good to have our family all together."

He smiled and, putting his arm around Allen's shoulders in his old familiar way, escorted us into the house.

At dinner, the talk quickly fell to the advances of the family. I watched the eager faces lit now by Joan's lavish candles that burned on every mantel, chest, and table in the hall. Katherine and Giles, Barbara, pregnant again with Edward doting on her, Eleanor and Will, Oliver and Joan, and even my Allen, their faces animated by the talk of great advancement and acquisitions. It was not that I disapproved, for I was no custodian of another's dreams, but it seemed to me a pursuit of insubstantial fleeting wealth on earth at the cost of much personal capital. I sensed a reticence in Eleanor too. We were not comfortable with all this talk of riches and money.

"Raleigh left Plymouth and is sailing for Orinoco and the Dorado goldmine." Will's face was full of excitement, and I caught sight again of the boy who played pirates in his borrowed castle. "By this time next year, my prediction is we will be celebrating at court, and you, Joan, will be planning a new palace in the City on which to spend Oliver's purse!"

The family laughed as Oliver groaned in mock agony and raised his hands to his head as if suffering from a megrim.

"We shall live side by side," announced Giles as he joined the discussion. "The City may be a little cramped for me. I prefer perhaps a water palace near White Hall, where the new homes are constructed. Not for me is the remodeling of a wretched old monastery or abbey. I will build to my own design and start fresh and new."

"There is much land to be had around Westminster," added Edward, his groomed hands daintily navigating with the new-fangled

208

fork that Joan had provided. "And it is perfectly located to take advantage of all happenings at court."

"I had thought that the king had prohibited any new building in London for fear that the countryside will empty and all will want to live in the city?" Allen's comment stilled the talk around the table for a moment.

"That edict is for those who know not how to bend rules." Barbara's voice was her usual self-satisfied confidence. "His announcements do not apply to us. We have certain connections that invalidate the laws of the common man." She smiled around the table and lifted her wine to Edward, who nodded obligingly.

All laughed and the talk continued, growing more and more raucous as homes were planned, acquisitions discussed, and a sense of entitlement pervaded the room. I was silent, thinking of my satisfaction with my one extravagance in our marriage bed.

"You are so quiet, Lucy, what ails you?" Allen murmured his concern under the cover of the conversation. He and I were in accord, mostly, and I sensed his watchfulness where Barbara was concerned. "Do you miss your life at court? We could purchase a house by Edward and Barbara."

"I would rather die," I said, more vehemently than I expected, but his words caught me unprepared. "I long only for the simplicity of my garden, where nature has provided all the jewels and gem colors to satisfy man without the extra trappings of indulgence and vanity."

"Spoken like a true Puritan, dear sister," Barbara called across the table. I did not know she had heard my words. "Perhaps that's why your company was no longer so entertaining in courtly circles."

"What do you mean, Barbara?" Allen spoke before I could, his tone quiet but his words penetrating.

"Oh, nothing, dear brother," laughed Barbara. "Now, Will, tell me what you will buy first with your share of Walter's gold."

"A castle, of course!" Will's face was rosy, evidence of his fondness for Giles's fine malmsey that he brought to the table. No doubt it was a bribe from some wretched landlord he had threatened to close.

"Leave her be, Allen." I put my hand on his arm, and this time he did not remove it. "I don't belong here, and she only wishes to torment me as she always has."

"I will leave it for this time," he replied, "for I do not wish to be the cause of anger tonight. But she should watch her words with you."

"These perquisites are raining on the family, and I hope only my sisters have married men who have the wisdom to manage them prudently." I turned to Allen and spontaneously kissed his cheek. "As I have."

He smiled quickly. "It is enough to turn a man's head, the access to the power and the availability of funding. In truth, I am uncertain of how young Will is going to manage his fortunes when Walter returns, and I do not trust Giles with his licensing scheme of the inns. There is much temptation when abundant money is in the hands of the inexperienced and unscrupulous."

"Rather than the experienced and benevolent?" I teased him, for his seriousness sometimes made him seem so aged.

"I have seen many a man's head turned by the insubstantial trappings of court and king. I seek my advancement through honest work, not through favors bestowed because of a bloodline." He straightened in his chair and lifted his chin proudly. "Our investments in the Yard will continue to support us through the years ahead and provide a steady income, well calculated to keep us in good stead. I have no need of gold mines in foreign shores or schemes to rob men of their livelihood through illicit license."

He pushed his chair from the board and stood.

"Come, let us retire to our chamber, for I grow weary of this world."

I remembered how long he had served at court, back to the days of the old queen. I recalled the stories of his youth, when his blood had run hot and his purse had been emptied by the gaming and expenses of that glittering court. I could understand his weariness. I was grateful my encounters with Theo and Frances had inured me to the seductive charms of privilege and power. We were now within the inner circle of the throne, and there was much to be gained, and even more to be lost.

26

My Sweet Anne,

There is much dissatisfaction within the City for the dissolute ways of the courtiers, for not only do the publishers write of the fall of the Howards in the verses, they are now scribbling of the rise of the Villiers with equal contempt. Both families are hated, and I am relieved we are not in the forefront of this world of venomous gossip and envy. Barbara just shrugs, for even she has had a verse written of her, and it bothers her not. These political seas are more difficult to navigate than any waters that Walter has voyaged upon. I am thankful that my quiet life in the Yard behind the sheltering walls gives me a seclusion and a peace that is not disturbed by actions of others. Boon is growing fast, and I look forward to the approaching summer, when his little legs will carry him through his first steps in the orchards and gardens of our home.

Lucy

2ⁿᵈ March, 1617

When the Gods of fate decree a change, they act swiftly. As the new moon of March proclaimed the ides, I first heard of Allen's purchase. By the full moon, not twenty days later, my life was disrupted beyond all measure by the stars which guide our destiny. In truth, I experienced such a crisis of faith that I questioned from my deepest soul the teachings of Calvin and the belief of a preordained life.

I consulted with the astrologers in Blackfriars, desperate to know why Jupiter, who brought good fortune to all in this new year of March, should be in such retrograde for me. I sought the old ways to find answers and the new faith to discover a path forward.

The day of revelation dawned in innocence and joy. As I played in the hall with Boon, the fleeting March clouds dappled the mellow oak floors with shadows chasing the shimmering spring sun, and he was giggling as he tried to catch them. I was so proud he was sitting by himself, and as we laughed and attempted pat-a-cake, I became aware of Allen standing in the doorway

"See how strong he is?" I held my fingers out, and Boon clasped them tightly, his face red with exertion.

Allen smiled and came and sat on the bench beside me. He was wearing a fine starched piccadilly and his black velvet court doublet, one he usually reserved for formal meetings, rather than his usual sensible cloth that he donned for the Yard. He had left our bed at night when the darkness was at its deepest, and I did not see him dress.

"'Tis a powerful grasp he has for his sword arm. He will do well as he grows to learn the moves of thrust and parry."

I gathered Boon close to me. "That's a long time hence. For now, let him grasp his rattle and be fierce with that." I turned to Allen. "What brings you here in the day, my love?"

"I have some important news. I wanted to be the first to tell you."

"I am excited to hear. You look as if you had just been given a great gift."

"I have. We have. A marvelous opportunity for advancement, and one I know will bring much reward to our family."

A tremor started in my heart at hearing those familiar words echoed by others close to me. They did not bode well, for I cared not for advancements and rewards, the price of entry being more than I was prepared to pay.

"The time was opportune, and because of your connection with Villiers, the purchase was offered to me first."

I listened carefully, hoping the opportunity was one which required minimal investment on Allen's part, both financially and in obligation. I watched the cloud shadows scud across the floor with great intent and cleared my throat of the words that were lodged there.

"Are you sure this is something you want, Allen?"

"I am. It is the culmination of my career, a position which will bring me much satisfaction as well as the opportunity to further our wealth."

"A position—have you already accepted this?" I was startled into looking up at him, for in the past, he had turned down a baronetcy, not wishing to join the ranks of the upstart peers who purchased their vanity titles.

"I have. Many men were seeking it, and I was first to receive news it could be mine. I acted quickly in order to secure it."

"I am glad, for I trust your judgment. Was it a high price?"

"Three thousand and five hundred pounds."

I gasped at the huge amount of money. How he could have acquired such a massive sum was beyond my comprehension.

"But it can be paid over time, through installments, and the income will more than compensate for the investment." He sounded sure, and still I trusted his judgment.

"I hope for our sakes that it will." I looked closely at him, for he had not told me all, I could see in his eyes. "What more?"

He had the grace to look down for a moment before meeting my gaze again.

"We move, not far away, but soon, within the fortnight."

My heart dropped, but still I smiled at him, determined to be loyal to his ambition.

"Did the grand new position come with one of Giles's desirable bankside palaces? Am I to be first in our family who will live in a mansion with gardens stretching to the water?"

At this, his face creased, and I could not tell if it was a smile or a frown.

"Of sorts. You will be living in the Queen's House, in a palace on the banks of the Thames."

I couldn't quite grasp what he was saying, for it was riddles to me. There was only one Queen's House that I knew of close by, the mansion within the prison King Henry built for his Anne Boleyn. She never lived there, he having beheaded her on the green before, maddened by his love and her betrayal. I searched Allen's face, willing him to speak clearly. But the words that he spoke next brought a dreadful perspective to my thoughts.

"I purchased the position of Lord Lieutenant of the Tower. We remove to our new lodgings on the 23rd of March."

There was such a hush that I could hear all the noises of the Yard outside the deep monastery walls, the creak of the carts, the calls of the men, the stray dogs barking, the gulls squabbling; the everyday sounds that composed the fabric of my life here, which reassured all was well in my world.

Even Boon stilled, his eyes searching mine, his sweet rosebud lips trembling.

Allen reached out a hand to touch my arm.

"Lucy?"

"Oh, Allen, what does it mean?" I could not find words, for the images crowding before my eyes were too desolate to speak of. The bone-white walls of the Tower. The Yard's gardens. "What is it that you are doing? Why would you want more than we have, why would you change our lives beyond all measure? Why, Allen, why?" I turned from him then to hide my anger, scalding tears starting from my eyes.

"It is a great honor and a great opportunity for us. You should be thankful we are in a position to receive such rewards. It is your connections, not mine, which delivered this to our hands." His voice was suddenly tired, weary, aged.

"You sold our happiness for the sake of advancement, Allen. You, of all men, who did not wish to play these games of perquisites and favors. You are just as the others. I despise what you have done, for you have—"

"Enough, Lucy, you speak out of turn." A flash of anger sparked. Never had his rage been turned to me.

"I did not ask for this," I cried. "I would be content if we lived in a humble farmhouse in the deepest countryside, if we were together and left alone. I do not want to chase this world of glittering sham, where a price is put on every friendship and a man's worth is measured in gold rather than character. I thought you despised all that."

"It takes a great deal of money and resources to victual the Royal Navy," he replied. "In truth, I see opportunity to grow our estate here on earth, to leave my children more than my father left me."

I turned back and looked at him sharply. I could hear more disguised behind his words.

"A great deal of money? Whose money? Is your credit not to be trusted? Have you extended beyond our means?"

"Nay, hush, do not question my capabilities. It is just there are times when the king is slow to pay his debts. Other sources of income would supplement the flow of cash that is needed to maintain the navy stores."

"And so you paid three thousand pounds and more for the privilege of guarding the Tower's prisoners and moving your family behind those walls, to live as prisoners themselves?" My voice was rising in horror as the full picture of our future was emerging.

"There is much to be gained by serving within the Tower. There is lively commerce in the management of its inhabitants and much opportunity to generate income. My entitlements far exceed the inconveniences. I receive rents from herring fishermen; the ships sailing upstream must moor at my wharf and give me portions of their cargo. I can collect all the cattle that fall from the bridge, the carts that land in the moat, the crops on Tower Hill—"

"Hush with your list of perquisites! Is that all to you that matters? Money? I'm so shocked, Allen." I shouted then, even heavier thoughts piling onto my head. "Jesu, we will be the guardians of all prisoners. That includes Frances Howard. You expect me to be her gaoler?"

Allen smiled wryly. "Such a turn of events, eh, Lucy? I did not reckon with that condition when I applied, but now that you bring it up, fate has a strange way of returning, does it not?"

I do not know if he meant to sound so callous, but I took his speech that way. It could have been his plain speaking, but it was, for me, catastrophic.

I pushed Boon into his arms and left the room, no longer trusting myself to say more, and ran into the yard, where I could take a deep breath and try to arrange my thoughts. But there was no solace in the familiar scene that faced me. I took no comfort from the neatly maintained bakehouses, or the well-stocked pigpens. Instead, the orchard branches reached stick-stark against the pale March sky. Everywhere I looked, I was reminded that this was not to be my home anymore. Boon would not play hide-and-seek among these old gnarled trees or roll in the sweet young grass which thrived in the shelter of the monks' walls. Now all was emptiness, and again the unknown lay before me.

I had no one to turn to in those difficult days, for Eleanor had left for Lydiard to stay with Anne and John shortly after Will put to sea, and neither Katherine nor Barbara would consider my fate warranted sympathy. They no doubt would consider me most fortunate to have achieved a position of such prominence, for indeed the Tower was as its own country, and to be head of the liberty was as if to rule a kingdom unto itself.

The City of London had no jurisdiction over its boundaries, and only the king himself could dictate the fate of the Tower and its residents, both prisoners and keepers. As the enormity of our new position and the responsibilities that accompanied it began to settle on me, oppression and weariness threatened to drown me. I did not know how I could continue to live or bring up Boon, Peter, and Jocasta within those terrible walls, and it took every stretched nerve in my body to go through the motions of preparing for our move.

I had just a few days to pack our possessions and make ready to depart. Allen was already spending his days in the Tower, meeting with his lieutenants and acquainting himself with the challenges and duties he would be undertaking. I was on my own as I readied the children and myself.

I thought it best for them to join us after we had moved to the Tower, for I had no idea what I would be encountering behind those walls, and I wanted to prepare their new home as best I could. I did not know how children would live within, for in truth, the times I passed by, it did not seem a place where an innocent child could thrive. Before I made that judgment, I needed see for myself what I could create for them.

I took the children to Battersey—no other option being open to me—and placed them in the custody of Joan and Oliver for the days before our move. If it were not for Mary, my nurse, I could not have left them, but she had now been with me for the six months since Boon's birth. Her warm, sensible way would give my children consistency in my absence. Besides, I knew she would not let Joan interfere with my dictates of child rearing, which were most important to me.

Having left the children and promising to return for them as soon as we were settled, I departed Battersey by barge on the rainy morning of the 23rd day of March and was rowed to the Tower.

"Escort my lady to her lodging." Allen's voice became harsh. "Ensure my steward is there to greet her and introduces her to her household. I shall be at the armory."

He strode off, leaving me lonely on the wharf, my skirts heavy with the weight of the rain water, thoughts swirling.

Flanked by yeoman warders, I trod carefully across the wet stones, my heart beating rapidly as I was escorted toward the Bulwark Gate. Although Allen met me at the wharf, he did no more than welcome me with a story of the Princess Elizabeth and then left to the armory. The motley shops and hovels that lined the path were teeming with the most unsavory people, as though the Tower rejected these vermin. They settled at the base of its walls, eager to gobble the crumbs of patronage that visitors bestowed on them.

There were sundry goods displayed to entice those whose emotions steered their purses, hurrying to visit their loved ones inside the Tower, and who may stop to purchase a trinket of comfort. I was shocked to see mean apothecaries trading in salves and charms which were obviously full of superstition and fakery.

The narrow paths between the buildings were dark and cramped. The stench of the stagnant moat water mingled with that of the tenements, making me wish I had thought to bring my pomander with me. The rain now turned steady and did nothing to settle the smells, only turning the paths into mud mires. I walked the elevated planks that were strewn across the filth. As we paused before the Tower entrance, I sensed those who trod before me, queens and commoners alike. I was bowed by the weight of their fear, which languished in the fabric of these prison walls.

The gatehouse itself was an intricately worked red-brick structure, surrounded by cannons and well-guarded. Although there were many that morning who traveled through the gate's arch, none were there to stay, and I faltered in my steps as the warders escorted me forward.

The guards stood to attention as I drew near, their pikes tall by their sides, their eyes straight ahead. Their respect signified I was to them their new mistress, for inside the Tower, I would be as their lady. The responsibility was formidable. I hoped that Allen's years of command in Ireland would teach me the protocols of managing these men. I carefully inclined my head slightly, without appearing too eager or aloof, as I entered their rows.

Passing through the thick defensive walls, I was reminded of Castle Cornet. Tears threatened to spill as I compared that safe fortress that had welcomed me with balmy air and sweet Anne by my side to this hideous place of captivity. I wished with all my heart to have Sir Thomas walk forward to greet me. I suffered that those days were lost to me. I was singularly on my own here, for even Allen had not seen the need to accompany me, he being too concerned of the protocols of his position.

Ahead stretched a lane teeming with people of all sorts. I could now see the immensity of the inner-ward walls to my left, broken only by the curve of towers and the occasional archer's hole cleft in the stone. On my right lay Traders' Gate, and there was much activity as a steady stream of goods was brought in from the river through the raised portcullis. Of recent times, the name had slipped to Traitors' Gate, and this served to remind me of the multiple purposes of this citadel. All within served different masters, whether gaoler or minter, palace guard or keeper.

As I hesitated again, a cacophony like none other reverberated around the bricks and echoed from the stone walls. It resounded again and again and was joined by other screeches and bellowing. I was beset from all sides with such noise that I could not hear my own trembling voice. A warder looked at me and broke rank to guide me to the side path.

"'Tis only the Barbaries, my lady."

"What are they?" The noise had no description, no similarity to anything I had heard before.

"The lions, my lady. 'Tis their roaring you hear, and it upsets the others in the menagerie."

I drew myself together and recovered what I could of my dignity. I had forgotten the Tower also housed lions and other exotic creatures given to the kings and queens for many centuries, and that the tradition continued strong with James. Now that I knew what the noise was, it was less fearsome but still chilled my very marrow.

A shout went up ahead. My warders pressed closer as a cavalcade of riders clattered on the stone cobbles, the horses' hooves striking and sliding over the wet stones. The creatures were magnificent. As the dozen or so riders cut a swathe through the crowd of pedestrians, people cowed, unwilling to get trampled by the force of men. The guards surrounded me to prevent me from being pressed by the people or injured by the horses, and I was assaulted by a further wave of noise, shouts, and clatter.

"His Lord the Earl of Suffolk," shouted the guard on my right, flinging an arm out to shield me from the plunging hooves. "Visits 'is sister, 'e does, regular-like."

I didn't need the explanation. One look at Theo's face, blanched with shock as he found me surrounded by warders on my way to the fortress, was enough to twist my heart. He turned in his saddle, his eyes fixed on mine, and made as though to rein back. And then I lost sight of him. The guards escorted me through a small archway cut into the stone, and the walls closed around us.

The Tower was now my home, and in that brief encounter, it was also proven my penance.

27

To prevent miscarrying:

Take neare half an ounce of cloves bruised, put them in half a pint of red rosewater, let them boyle till the water be very red, then strain out the cloves and make a syrup of the water with double refined sugar. Take hereof a spoonful morning and afternoon and at night in a little sage posset. Doe the like at any time when any fright or disorder happens to you. This made Mrs. Sands go through her term.

Lucy Apsley
Tower of London

I awoke suddenly and could not bear to move, for heaving waves of nausea swept over me, and I thought I would vomit if I stirred. I lay prone in my marriage bed, staring at the canopy and the tawny velvet, concentrating on the embroidered birds that were picked in gold thread and wishing the sickness would pass. My treasured bed had been set in the best chamber on the top floor of the Queen's House. On my first night, I climbed in with trepidation, worried I could not rest with all the images that crowded around me, clamoring for my mind time, but eventually sleep stole upon me.

Now the realization that I awoke within the Tower and not in the Yard brought bile to my throat, and I sat up in great distress. As I did so, my shift brushed my breasts, and there was a tenderness which was familiar, and the realization came to me that I was sick from carrying a new babe. I steeled myself, for if I was to capitulate to the fear, my children would never discover their strength. In that moment of early gray dawn, I resolved I would face fear head on and peel its bony fingers from my throat. My trust was in the path planned for me, and with every part of my being, I prayed so hard for Him to guide me to be the best mother and wife I could be, to accept my allotted fate, and that He would not desert me.

A strong aroma of roasting meat permeated my chamber. As I pulled on a robe, I heard the rattles and clashes of dishes and pots. There was a significant kitchen somewhere below me within the building.

Crossing the room, I peered through the paned window and from this viewpoint discovered the maze of red brick walls I saw last night protected two large gardens. Within those enclosures, I could now see paths and beds. A straggled orchard was overrun with daffodils, their golden trumpets gleaming in the soft gray dawn. I leaned forward to see more, my breath fogging the green glass pane, my spirits lifting to see this patch of life within these prison walls.

Beyond the gardens was the chapel of St. Peter, huddled in the corner of the great walls, and behind that, a series of rooftops and buildings. The White Tower glimmered to the east, and a mass of smaller towers, walls, and fortifications appeared to join together to form an inner keep. Straining to see to the farthest boundary, I could glimpse the red-tile roofs of the Queen's Palace, and beyond, more walls and towers.

I sat for a moment within the window enclosure, huddled in my warm gown and watching the March dawn creep across the yard, gradually bringing color to the surrounds and hinting at a promising spring day ahead. Two children ran by the fence in front of the house, their hair tousled by the brisk March wind that had sprung up with the fresh dawn. I watched them skip and flap their arms as if they were trying to fly on the breeze. The sight of these two innocents in this palace prison gave me hope that perhaps there was a possibility of home here too. I offered a prayer of thanks that children and gardens could thrive within these walls. I pressed my hand to my belly, sending love to my new child, and proceeded to dress.

Of course, the first person who called on me was Barbara, oblivious to any discomfort her company bestowed, her curiosity outweighing any consideration of my feelings.

"What an interesting place you have found yourself in." She stood in the hall, aware of the stares of the staff around her as she removed her cloak, revealing an extravagantly worked red velvet gown and a fine dropped lace ruff. She held out her cloak, and someone scurried forth to take it, which amused me, for I am not sure I would have had the same service.

"Edward and George thought it time you left the grocery yard and put your talents to work in a more suitable environment for our family. It was a waste of resources to hide your light under a bushel." She laughed at her own joke, and her charm was so infectious I found my mouth twitching too, for she was beguiling no matter how much I distrusted her.

"Come, Lucy, let us be allies. We suffered much together in our childhood, for although you thought you were the odd one, I did not enjoy my time at Battersey any more than you. I just concealed my feelings better." She tucked her arm in mine, her fragrance clinging and heady, floral mingled with musk. I responded reluctantly, but she did not release me.

"Aunt Joan favored you and had nothing but hatred for me," I replied. "Your time could not have been so terrible."

"You really think living in that decrepit farmhouse with little prospects and no money was my choice? I could not wait to leave." She hugged my arm closer.

"But all those words with which you professed your love for Aunt Joan, the time you spent with her."

Barbara shrugged. "Everyone has to put in an apprenticeship of some kind, Lucy. I just happened to be indentured to a snob who believed I could be her way out of poverty as much as I did too. She had her uses."

"Then why me? Why were you so cruel to me?"

"Indifferent, Lucy, until you caught Theo's eye. Then I needed to act, for it would not do for you to better yourself above me. After all, you are the youngest, and I have more to offer than you."

"You wanted Theo, didn't you?"

"Of course. Who would not? Frances thought I should have him. And if I could not, why should you?" She shook her arm free of me, her mouth pursed. "And look where you landed—you are hardly a tatterdemalion, Lucy. You rewrote your story too. Now, at George's command, it is time we put aside our differences and strengthen our family by working together."

Drawing me to the window, she turned me to look out across the bustling green. The day had started in earnest. There was much activity, which I had not been aware of previously, looking at the high Tower walls outside from the Victualling Yard.

"There is a world of opportunity within the liberty, Lucy. Embrace this new course presented to you. We feel you have the means to make a very successful life here."

I stood by her side and watched, realizing there were hundreds of people who lived within the Tower Liberty, and Allen and I were now responsible for their well-being. It seemed a daunting burden, one I did not feel qualified to carry.

"How much were you involved in arranging this position?' I was suspicious, wondering, as always, her motive. "Why me, why Allen?"

"George wants to be sure he can count on loyal supporters where it is important to him. Allen has done him a great service in organizing the victualling of the navy, and he values the benefit of a trusted retainer."

She drew her arm from mine and turned to face me, her expression intense.

"Frances Howard and Robert Carr must be watched, Lucy, and they are now under yours and Allen's scrutiny. George does not want any opportunity for them to regain power. Although he persuaded the king into sparing their lives, he did so from a desire to appear munificent, not out of kindness. Sometimes it is better to keep your enemy alive and under your power than dead and a martyr to memory. It is up to you and Allen to keep them powerless within the Tower and not allow their family and allies to instigate a renewed influence."

"So that's the reason Allen was given the position. Not through his own merits." I was disgusted again, for we had been as pawns, and Allen's excitement at securing this important position was misplaced. He had not done this under his own endeavor, but was simply a convenient player who could be inserted into the game.

Barbara shrugged in her charming way.

"Read it as you will, Lucy. Allen obviously has some use since George surmised he could keep the Somersets under watch. He knew when he bid for the job one of his prime responsibilities would be to report on all their visitors and activities."

"So we become spies for the Earl of Buckingham now." I didn't even pose this as a question, for once again it seemed as if my life had been preordained by another.

"No, simply loyal family members who can be trusted by those who have given you much advantage. It seems like a fair exchange. Allen will meet regularly with George to present his reports on the Somersets' activities. I am sure you will be most helpful in compiling those. As the wife of the Lieutenant, you have access to all places within the Tower. Keep a close watch, Lucy, for George's security is vital to all our well-being, and we do not want anything to threaten it."

We both looked to the door as it opened, and Allen walked in, a gust of March wind on his heels stirring the wall hangings. He did not falter as he greeted Barbara, nor did his expression change, and so he was not surprised by her presence.

"Good day to you, Sister." He kissed her warmly. "I am glad to see you have called so soon. Lucy will welcome her family here, for I fear she is a little apprehensive of our new move."

"Do not speak of me as if I am a child." His words stung, and the retort sprang quickly to my lips.

"I speak out of concern, no other reason. You make no pretense this move has not been hard for you. Barbara will help you acclimatize to your new position."

"And I cannot do this on my own merit?"

"It is always good to have the support of family when life's path brings changes. Barbara is used to the ways of the court and knows what is needed to maintain the confidential responsibilities of our position."

"You mean be a spymaster." Even to my ears, my response sounded peevish, and I became even angrier, now with myself as well as with Allen.

He looked at me steadily without answering and turned away.

"Come, Barbara. Edward joins us for dinner, and we can talk more of his plans. Let us see if our kitchens are as cultured as those in the Yard in the preparation of dishes." They walked together in front of me, toward a doorway to the rear of the hall, and I trailed miserably, feeling out of sorts and resentful.

28

A precious drink for any weakness.

A gallon of milk of a red cow, put in a clean pann. Put to it an ounce of acorns, the same of nutmegs, slide. Boyle it from a galon to a bottle. Strain it and put into it a pint of rosewater wherein almonds have been strained. Sweeten it and drink no other drink. This brought a man that was carried on men's shoulders to carry a vessel of ale on his back in 6 weeks.

Lucy Apsley
The Tower
November 1617

My ill humor stemmed from self-pity, for in reality, there was nothing I could do to change our new situation. I was peeved I had not been consulted. However, since my family could anticipate I would conscientiously object to the demands of Allen's position, they simply ignored me and continued with their ambitions.

I had nothing more to say about the business, for I could not challenge either Allen or George Villiers, and so accepted my lot, as women do, and prayed I could make a life for myself within the confines of the walls, both material and invisible.

To that purpose, I set about learning life's routines within the Tower, preparing to receive my children, for I missed them most desperately. In spite of the hidden financial motives that drove Allen to manage his prisoners, I found much to occupy me those first few days as I came to terms with the demands made of me. As the wife of the lieutenant, the well-being of the prisoners was assumed to be under my command.

We were not as the Fleet Prison, where miserable conditions caused men to die unobserved in hidden cells. In the Tower were kept only those noblemen and women whom the king and the Privy Council deemed treasonous or guilty of crimes which carried a sentence of death yet to be acted upon.

As such, these high-ranking prisoners were watched at all times and not forgotten, and their entitlements continued, albeit within prison walls. The Tower was the king's personal gaol, for it was those close to him who had caused great grief or intended harm who lodged within. For those who remained captive without a sentence of death, it was an ironic shadow of their former lives.

A warder attended me on my second morning, bringing with him a detailed plan of the Tower Liberty on a large parchment he unrolled on Allen's table.

"Mr. Gascoyne devised this twenty years ago on command of the queen," he announced as he weighed the corners with thick ledgers and an inkwell. "He surveyed all of the Tower and mapped it as you see it today."

It was a most fascinating document, for the vicinity appeared as if spied upon by a bird flying over, and it was a perspective I had not seen before.

"Where on this map are we?"

He pointed to the bottom corner of the parchment, where roofs and a small garden were laid out.

"Here."

The Queen's House, which seemed so large, shrank into a little square on the corner of the illumination, and I realized the enormity of the environments we were within.

"There is much commerce with the Liberty, for the Mint, the munitions, the royal treasure are all stored within. The Chapel, of course, the menagerie, the storehouses . . ." From his description, we were within a bustling town dedicated to maintaining the king's well-being.

"And the gaols? Where are the prisoners held?" I wanted to know where my children should avoid encounter with those who were captive. "The Howards? The Earl of Northumberland?"

He drew his finger around the perimeter of the survey, jabbing at points along the way.

"Bell, Beauchamp, Devereaux, Martin, Broad Arrow, Salt, Wakefield, and the Bloody Tower . . ."

The entire fortress was ringed with prisons.

Upon the command of Allen, who thought it time I learn my environs outside of the Queen's House, I was first introduced to the hidden entrance to the Bell Tower, which was accessed from my own home. It was a shock to measure the proximity with which a prisoner could be kept. We simply walked ten paces along a passage from Allen's office and came to a stout door. When this was opened by the Yeoman Warder, we stepped from the warm house down into a cold, cavernous room of ancient stone blocks with fortified narrow window embrasures and rough-hewn walls. I was overwhelmed with a sense of sadness and despair and turned to the Yeoman.

"Who is kept here, and why?" I shivered, as much from the desolation as from the cold.

"Those who must have an extra guard on their activities or who should be kept in solitude," he replied somberly. "The Princess Elizabeth was held captive here by her sister, Mary. It has not been used recently. Some say they still feel the prayers of Thomas More within its stones, for he was held here before his trial and execution."

I looked sharply at the warder, for his voice softened as he spoke of More, King Henry's beloved minister and the first recusant in his Great Matter. It was treasonous to sympathize with More's refusal to take the Oath, and I wondered what secrets were hidden within the warders and what they were really guarding.

Later, I discovered a small shrine in the crypt of St. Peter's Chapel, where a tiny votive burned and a set of rosary beads lay on a simple wooden chest. It was symbolic of old ways. When I cautiously asked further of Allen, he told me it was a sanctuary the warders established, where they could find peace in the midst of their days. It was dedicated to Sir Thomas More, and they kept the candle burning for him to honor his memory.

It was not the first time I had encountered the old religion alive within our new beliefs. Just as I had embraced diversity in the streets of Blackfriars, where all sects lived together in harmony, I respected the warders and their loyal remembrance of More, although I could not agree with their papist trappings.

I did not approach the Bell Tower door again; there was a deep-rooted sadness emanating from the chamber, and a sense of despair. Perhaps it was also the old walls the Romans had built that embedded themselves within the plaster of our new home, a reminder they had been a witness to man's terror for centuries. I did not approach it, but it lingered in my mind, and I was always conscious of its role in the fabric of my home.

I retreated to the Queen's House, and after several days, Allen announced the following night's dinner would entertain not only Frances and Robert Carr, but also Henry Percy, Ninth Earl of Northumberland, who was captive in Martin Tower. I had familiarized myself with the expectations that we served food and cooked for all the tower residents, which is why we had such huge kitchens and sculleries within our house, but I did not anticipate we fed prisoners within our own home.

"It is an important part of our duties to ensure our privileged guests are entertained at our board, and we will invite them to meet you tomorrow." Allen did not seem in the least troubled by the paradox of my now hosting the Somersets and Northumberland to dinner, and I have to confess the thought was so ridiculous I had a great desire to laugh with hysteria.

"Guests?" My voice rose. "These are political prisoners who have been condemned for murder and plotting the king's death. Percy is a conjurer who was directly indicted in Guido Fawkes's plot to blow up Parliament and the king with it, and you know of the Somersets' darkness. Why are we hosting these criminals?"

"It is the way of the Tower. You will see dinner is suitable." Allen said no more, and for him, the subject was closed. My husband was taking his new role very seriously. I had to challenge his way with me, for although I pledged obedience and honor at our wedding, I did not like the tone with which he spoke to me.

"I am not one of your captains to be commanded that way, Allen."

"You are the wife of the Lieutenant of the Tower, and as such, you have a role which is extremely important to the security of this prison and the security of our country. Any conversations we have with our residents must be carefully transcribed, for I am committed to George Villiers to relay all information to him." He relented a little, and his tone softened. "By entertaining our guests at dinner, we will have the opportunity to speak to them more freely than when they are in their rooms."

He reached his hand out to me, and I took it, responding to his gesture of compromise.

"I am a fair man, Lucy, and I do not wish to command you. I wish to always work with you in partnership. I have not perhaps given you the time to explain all expected of us, but I ask you trust me now, as you did when you agreed to marry me."

"I do trust you. I just wish we lived a simpler life not bound by the dictates of others."

"Lucy, there is little I can do to change our circumstances now. You have a choice, to live this life fully, embrace your situation, and make what you can of it. Or you can resist and live a shadow life in sadness, always wishing for what you don't have, or hoping for a future time which may not exist, where life is what you imagine you want. I have witnessed too many sudden deaths, too many expired lives to believe the future holds the key to happiness. You must embrace your present and trust God will take care of your future."

He held me tightly then, and I relaxed for a moment against him, feeling his solid strength beneath his stiffly padded court clothes.

"Are there days you would rather be somewhere else, Allen?"

He held me at arm's length and looked deep into my eyes. I absorbed again his gray temples, his creased skin from years of weathering on battlefields and oceans.

"Many times, Lucy. I am at my best outside, where I am free to walk and unconstrained by my desk and papers. But I also know this time is opportune for me to gather wealth, and I can embrace this, knowing it is for you and my children that I do this work."

I took his hand and laid it on my belly, flat still but carrying a small seed of life.

"We are going to have another child, Allen."

His face lit with happiness, and I knew in that moment I had married such a good man, who only wanted the best for his family.

"We are fortunate, my love, for all you see as struggle is naught compared with so many. We have been given a multitude of blessings." He kissed me then and held me once more before leaving. "I must return to my office, Lucy. I shall see you later tonight."

His words stayed with me through the rest of the day, warning me I had retreated into my old ways of wishing for a time in my future without enjoying those days that are with me now. I did not want to return to a life of lost dreams.

29

My Lady Joan,

Please prepare Mary and the children for their departure to the Tower on Thursday next. I would ask that you ensure that Boon is wrapped warmly, for the river can be chill. Please ensure that Peter pays heed to Mary, and I would ask that you send your steward to accompany them for discipline. I will send a barge to arrive at the Battersey steps that morning to catch the return tide. My husband and I thank you for your kindness in providing for them while we arranged our new circumstances.

Lucy Apsley
17th May, 1618

I found the prisoners' dinner an excuse to explore the gardens in the hope perhaps some young plants may be used for a salad to impress, or a fresh vegetable to bring a new taste to a palate jaded with a winter of preserves and salted meats. It would be daring, for many still regarded vegetables the food of the poor with little value. However, my time with Matthew L'Obel and cultivating Sir Thomas's allotments of land at Castle Cornet taught me a carefully prepared dish of greens could be delicious.

Along with the formal gardens laid out between the Queen's House and St. Peter's Chapel, there was a smaller garden to the east of the house, crammed between the Bloody Tower and my side door. After directing the cook in the preparation of courses of meat, fowl, and fish for our dinner, I slipped outside to survey the allotment. In truth, it should have been the housemaid's task, but I was restless and wanted the air. Hidden as it was, this patch appeared sorely neglected. Apparently, no one had claimed ownership of this land, and it had been left to its own devices for many years. As a consequence, much had overgrown and rambled across path and fence.

In a corner, someone had heaped a pile of dead branches, adding to the air of neglect. Walking toward a crumbling structure that appeared to be a henhouse, I pushed through brambles that snagged my skirts and trod the slippery mulch of many leaf-falls, intrigued by searching for the original bones of the design. It reminded me of Lydiard's walled garden, my steadfast companion in my early years. As I walked and the aroma of young spring grass mingled with crushed wild herbs under my feet, my excitement grew. Maybe I had found my salvation again in restoring life where death and decay long ruled.

There appeared small signs that this area of the garden was cultivated recently. As I approached the shed, I came upon a neat, well-tilled area where small mounds of earth were pushed into hilled rows, and plants carefully placed on the rise were flourishing. Right under the shadow of the Bloody Tower, someone tended a garden. As I dropped to my knees in front of the dirt, disregarding the dampness seeping through my skirts, I pushed my fingers into the base of the plants, feeling between the roots to see if what I suspected lay beneath the surface. I laughed aloud as my fingers touched the smooth curved objects under the soil, and scrabbling deeper with my dirty hands, I pulled to the surface the concealed tubers.

I had found Virginia potatoes, which I recall reading about in Matthew L'Obel's notes. Rummaging for more, I soon built a small heap, a variety of jeweled colors and sizes, but most not bigger than my thumb. As I questioned who could have done this, I looked toward the Bloody Tower. The words of Wat Raleigh as he spoke to me of his beloved Sherborne gardens rang in my mind again. While captive in the Tower for these past ten years, he freed his spirit from its bounds by planting a garden with treasures brought back from the new world.

I rejoiced in this allotment Walter created, for what a delightful story I would have to tell him when he returned from El Dorado. His Virginia potatoes saved my dinner party, for none would doubt that we were not the most sophisticated of hosts, serving such a new and intriguing dish.

An adjacent stone basin overran with mint, and I picked a fresh bunch and added a handful of cresses that were thoughtfully planted in a boggy corner of the garden. I credited all to Walter, for he knew the value of greens on long sea voyages, where the scurvy was as much an enemy of the men as the Spanish.

The path to the henhouse was tidily graveled and led straight from a small arched door at the base of the Bloody Tower. I wondered if Walter had taken up husbandry too and kept chickens for company, for God knew that ten years of imprisonment would take its toll on anyone's desire for distraction. I trod the well-worn path, where no weeds appeared between the stones, and approached the shed. Its door was solid and surprisingly locked, with a shiny new padlock.

Brushing against the old splintered wood, I found a boarded window. Pulling the rotted wood apart, I could just make out the dim interior and sucked in my breath at the workbenches, shelves, and an array of instruments, pestles, mortars, and scales. An assortment of heating limbecks arranged on a shelf confirmed my thoughts. All were shadowy in the gloom of the small hut, but it was obvious that this was no henhouse, and I was surveying the instruments of alchemy and magic, not garden tools.

"Do you find m-much to interest you, m-mistress?"

I jumped. The voice from behind me was imperious, although high-pitched and halted by an impediment. I fancied there may be some deafness, which tempered his speech. Whirling around, I dropped a curtsy to the tall, thin man with a long and straggled beard who stood before me, wrapped against the chill day in a long black velvet cloak lined with sables. He was stooped and presented an air of elegant weariness about him that was belied by his sharp eyes.

"The Wizard Earl—" I caught myself before I said more.

He raised his eyebrows.

I stood still in front of him, with my apron full of potatoes and mint and the damaged window board behind me.

"I am Lady Apsley," I stated, awkward with deferring to his title and yet establishing I was the wife of his gaoler. "I wish you good morrow."

He stood silent, his high forehead gleaming in the morning sun, his elegance and breeding giving him an advantage in our confrontation. I took a deep breath and continued.

"I see that Walter set himself a fine workshop. It appears fairly well stocked. I particularly liked the arrangement of limbecks, and the

Hessian crucible seems to be one of the better designed." I thought of Vicar Ridley's library and visits to my alchemist friends in Blackfriars. "However, I feel he may have been taking a little bit of a risk with such a large athanor in such a small wooden shed. He may have burned the place down."

There was a pause as his scrutiny of me continued.

"I told him the very same, Lady Apsley. But he p-paid no heed to me, as always. He wanted the b-b-biggest furnace he could fit, to produce the m-m-most gold. Walter never does anything by halves."

A shared fondness for Walter bridged the distance between us.

"If he couldn't alchemize gold, he could always use it for boiling his potatoes," I started laughing helplessly, my apron full of Raleigh's New World treasures.

The earl chuckled heartily. He produced a key from the depths of his long velvet cloak.

"Come," he commanded. "Your familiarity with alchemy is intriguing. Let me show you our w-w-workshop. It may appear to be a henhouse, but there are m-m-more foul deeds than eggs hatched here." He laughed at his own joke and smoothly turned the key in the well-oiled lock. He paused and gestured for me to cross the threshold first, and I entered the secret world of alchemy and magic that existed in the shadow of the Bloody Tower, just a stone's throw from my back door.

Dinner that night was served in the upper chamber in the Queen's House, a room which witnessed much in our recent history. It was here that Guido Fawkes and his fellow Catholics had been interrogated and found guilty for their part in the Powder Plot. It struck me as ironic that I was now to entertain more accomplices. The Wizard Earl, accused of being a conspirator in the Plot, was only spared because he had announced he was to be in Parliament on the day of the crime. He pleaded no knowledge. Now he languished in the Tower along with others who offended the king.

The Chamber was an elegant room, completely paneled with good English oak and with a curiously carved stone fireplace that I ordered lit on this occasion. I stood in the entry as Allen brought the prisoners to my board for dinner. What a strange circumstance I found myself in.

It eased my nerves to call them prisoners, and as Frances entered the room, I hid my hands in the folds of my dress, pressing my fingernails into my palms. The candlelight, which previously flattered her with its mellow tones, served only to cast shadows upon her gaunt cheeks. Her eyes, which held such beauty before, were now marred by a fierce tic that twitched at the lid and caused a droop, marring her once-perfect features. More than anything, her spirit was beaten to a flicker, suppressed by the weight of trial, humiliation, and confinement.

Beside her, Carr strutted with his same vain demeanor. It was interesting to see that he carried himself apart from her. They presented as strangers, such was the distance that lay between them. He had weathered the storms better than she, at first appearances, yet it was soon apparent that his posturing was of old habit and well-worn mannerisms, and the vulnerability revealed by a trembling hand begged compassion.

As she entered the room, Frances looked straight at me, and a flare of recognition passed between us.

"You choose to join me tonight?" Disbelief clouded her face, her eyelid twitching. The candles burned behind me, placing me in a half shadow while illuminating her worn face, years of tribulation lying deep in its creases. "I heard a rumor you were lodged in the Tower. And now you may wait on me this evening."

I listened quietly, my hands still at my sides, although I longed to slap her sly face.

"I am married to Sir Allen Apsley. George Villiers appointed us to this position. I do not wait on you. We guard you now, Lady Somerset."

There was a satisfaction in the paucity of my words that fell like stones on her, and she took a step back, leaning for a moment against the narrow door frame. Her dull eyes, as blank as a garden snake's, appraised me once more. She lifted her skirts to one side and swept into the room. She might have been found guilty of murder, stripped of her belongings, and imprisoned in the kingdom's greatest fortress, but she was still a countess. She mustered all of her breeding to attempt a precedence that no longer existed within these prison walls.

Their tattered dignity put into perspective our shifted roles, for the road on which the Somersets had traveled by their own wickedness was one which emptied their souls. Captivity had indeed broken them, although the damage they caused through their meddling and plotting also brought me the blessings in my life with Allen and my children. Recalling Barbara's instructions that Allen and I were to report our conversations and observations of the Somersets to George, I thought that our dispatches would be quite brief. It would take some conniving for Frances to share her confidences with me.

When the earl arrived, the atmosphere lightened, for Henry Percy and Frances enjoyed much in common, both marrying a Devereaux, brother and sister, and both despising the arrangement. Frances plotted her way to a divorce, accusing her first husband of failing in his duties to consummate his marriage, whereas Percy remained married to Penelope, albeit estranged from her. They made twisted company, chained to each other through imprisonment and family.

I wondered at life's turns that brought these two great nobles to now sit as prisoners at my board, freed from the captivity of their lodging for a few hours to act as though they were at dinner in some White Hall chamber. Their talk was frivolous, full of court gossip and sly innuendoes, and I sat quietly as they chattered.

Percy ignored me, and I found his manner quite eccentric in that he did not even attempt to converse, a far cry from our encounter in the garden just that afternoon. I concluded that his great arrogance hid an insecure person and thought that perhaps his speech impediment affected his character more than he knew

"You recall those days too, Lucy, don't you?"

I started as Frances's throaty voice cut through my thoughts. "You were there at White Hall, weren't you? You, Barbara, Theo . . ." Her voice trailed off, leaving Theo's name hanging in the air.

"For a brief time, yes, I was there."

"You enjoyed your time at court, the feasting, the masques, the celebrations in my apartments."

"For a while. And then I tired of them."

Allen sat very still beside me, intently watching.

"You seemed to enjoy yourself very much when you were with the Howards."

"It was not a life I had seen before. All was new to me."

"Yes, I believe you enjoyed many new experiences." Frances's smile in the candlelight was all innocence. Only her eyes belied the mild words, for they were blank, unreadable.

Under the table, my fingers were curled tightly. I pressed my hands together to prevent a tremble.

"As they continue, Lady Somerset. It is a great new honor the Earl of Buckingham has bestowed on our family, appointing my husband as chief gaoler. As his wife, I intend to carry out my duty with great dedication."

"Yes, you always were dedicated, Lucy—forgive me, Lady Apsley. I always admired that about you. I thought it would carry you far. A long way. All the way . . ."

I had no response. I was no courtier parrying compliments and insults in the same breath. Beside me, Allen shifted in his seat, the creak of his chair filling the silence that lingered a beat too long. The conversation continued, but in my mind, all I could do was repeat Frances's veiled comments and try to anticipate from whence the next dagger thrust would come.

30

My sweet Anne,

Within the Tower is a shadow world. Here time is measured not by man's calendar but by a season's shifting sky. The blazing autumn beeches or a spring rainbow glimpsed through iron bars represent a seeping life's span. I know now why Walter created his garden. Along with his writing of history, he found solace in observing germination when threatened by death's reaper, and hope in autumn pruning promising spring growth.

I have returned his allotment to health. I avoid the shed within the gardens that is the place where the executions occur, its air hideous. I traced the names scratched into the stone of Beauchamp Tower, immortal long after their noble masons were executed. And I walk wide around the White Tower to escape the dungeons where darkness breeds torture and men's cries are lost within the thick walls. I believe a year has passed since we arrived. I lose myself in the sameness of our days, serving my sentence with the rest of them. Allen named our young son William, and already the boy thrives. I hear Will waits eagerly for news of Raleigh and the gold, for he and my sisters' husbands continue to acquire significant positions at court, the maintenance of which requires resources well beyond their means.

Your loving sister, Lucy Apsley
Tower, 1618

Each morning, I assessed which of the prisoners needed my ministration, for the conditions were such that many would die if neglected. I considered it my duty to alleviate the suffering under which they lived. Although these men had been found guilty of treachery, they were not condemned to the executioner's axe, instead waiting out a sentence of time. If they had cheated death by the blade, it was not moral they die of neglect. If I could ease them with my recipes and physicks, I would do so.

Here in the Tower, despair eats a man's spirit and devours his health. I did not want these helpless people and their families to be at the mercy of the quacks and tricksters who lodged at the Byward Gate and sold false potions and charms.

I created a stillroom below the kitchens of the house, a chamber that opened to Walter's garden where I worked undisturbed. It was an ancient hollowed room, set deep within the walls with an east-facing window that captured the rising sun and gave me morning light. I rose early those summer months. As the gray dawn light hued pink, I crushed and distilled healing herbs, the pungent aromas overpowering those of dank stone. I kept the back door ajar and watched as birds hopped around the garden, about their business and ignoring the prison walls. If I could encourage men to look beyond the mortal boundaries by bringing them comfort, perhaps their minds would take flight and find a freedom for their souls.

Allen's days were spent at the Tower and at the Yard, for he kept both positions and was now consumed by work. A feverish humor drove him to provide for me and the children, for he was conscious more so than me of the differences in our age. Realizing he was fast approaching fifty years draped the mantle of mortality upon his shoulders. He was determined to secure a good dowry for Jocasta and to provide the best education for his sons. He still paid to me an allowance of three hundred pounds a year. But it did not compensate for his time and his love.

There were many days when I wished for the simplicity of our lives at the Yard, where we shared our dinners, and our marriage bed called us early to our chamber. He left now at four of the morning and often did not return until past curfew, after I had dined alone with Peter and Jocasta, blessed Boon with a dream wish, and rocked the baby to sleep. I longed for his attention, for I married him with the need for loving company foremost in my mind, having been deprived of it for so much of my life. It was a sad reckoning that he no longer regarded his time with me as important as his appointments.

The purse he gave me was mine to spend as I wished within the Tower, and although his time was rationed with us, in truth, he was as a father to his prisoners. He took pains to see all were treated with respect and received reasonable nourishment.

Some of the money I spent in plantings, for I retrieved the herbal that I wrote when with Mathew L'Obel and was determined to grow a thriving physick garden. Other sums I gave to Mr. Ruthven, who was imprisoned on account of his plot against the king and who made use of Walter's workroom when the Wizard wasn't occupying it. It made me smile to hear the muffled explosions that shook the old shed, but when he was not playing alchemist, he did create curatives that were efficacious. I valued the knowledge of these chemists when they put their minds to healing rather than fool's gold.

It was in the stillroom that Eleanor found me on a June morning that promised a return of the heat that had settled on the city since May Day. She hastily shoved open the heavy door, startling me, for I was not used to visitors this early.

"Lucy, he's back—Raleigh's ship has moored in Plymouth harbor. The messengers just arrived at our home; they rode day and night to London—"

"What news? What news?" I tipped the bowl with a clatter, spilling precious saffron.

"We know not. We cannot get information; it is for the king's ear only."

"George Villiers, you mean. Have you spoken to Barbara?"

"Will sends a man there now. He is on his way to White Hall to seek Edward." She was breathing quickly and had high color in her cheeks. I grasped her hand.

"Come, let's find Allen and see if he may find out more. It is a day to rejoice in Walter's safe return."

"It is a day to rejoice in our successes, for Walter's return means the investment in El Dorado is secure for all of us." Echoes of Will sounded in Eleanor's words, and I sensed the relief that she did not express aloud.

The known was so much worse than the unknown. When word from Walter finally came, the messenger was Will, in all his disheveled charm. He stood before us, his travel-stained clothes reeking of the road, his hair damp with sweat, his face burnt from the hot June sun. My parlor was too small to contain the heat of his emotion, and we walked outside in the walled gardens, pacing and turning along the twisting paths.

"We are lost, Allen, lost." His voice was hoarse from the dusty journey; emotion cracked the words. "There is no gold. There is no treasure. And the king has ordered his arrest."

Allen stood still, his eyes drawn to the Bloody Tower looming above the garden walls. A small tic twitched in his cheek above his beard, and even the birds were hushed.

"You are sure?"

"There is no gold." Will's repetition enforced his own disbelief. "Our money has been spent. All is gone."

"What is left to us?"

"Nothing, Allen, nothing." Will's voice was harsh in its impatience. "We have nothing left."

"Does George know?"

"It was he who ordered Wat's arrest. I leave now, Allen, for I have heard from one of my captains that he flees to France. My orders are to intercept him and escort him to London."

"You? Why you?"

"George trusts me to see that his request is done. I have no choice."

"God's Mercy. You are now Walter's gaoler."

"As are you. I am ordered to bring him to the Tower."

As Will rode with the devil to capture Raleigh, my family gathered at the Queen's House, meeting as councils did before within the prison walls. Edward was the head investor in Walter's voyage, and along with the lost funds, his reputation was at stake. Giles had also invested significant sums. As they spoke with Allen in the upper chamber, I sat with my sisters in the parlor below, frustrated that we knew so little.

"We put all our wealth into Wat's voyage." Eleanor's voice was little more than a whisper. Her head was bowed, and she plucked at the fabric of her dress.

"I told Giles to be judicious with his investment. This will not impact his business. The licensing is going well, and this is a small price to pay for George's favor. We will be fine, and I care not what happens to Raleigh."

"Katherine, do you ever see beyond your own circumstance?" Barbara crossed the room and stood in front of our oldest sister, who continued to sit and help herself to the sweetmeats I had set out.

"No. My loyalties are with Giles, and as long as he is satisfied that we continue to grow rich, I am satisfied too."

"You stupid cow. You have no idea how this could affect all of us, do you?" I had not heard Barbara so angry for a long time. She turned from Katherine and spoke to all of us.

"It's not just the lost treasure. A ship under Raleigh's command burned a Spanish galleon, and men died. This is exactly what Gondomar, the Spanish Ambassador, has been waiting for—an act of war. The king has no choice but to execute Wat. And for those who supported him, their loyalty is deeply questioned. The king is a suspicious man at heart and does not trust anyone. And George's enemies rejoice he is the cause of this debacle, for he is the one who persuaded the king to release Wat."

"But the king wanted the gold. He was an investor too." I struggled to keep up with Barbara's inside knowledge of the politics swirling around our family "He would not question George, would he?"

"George's enemies will do anything to discredit him and precipitate his fall. Unless George can prove he is completely on the side of Gondomar and the Spanish, we are lost."

I crossed to the window and looked to the garden, but my eyes were drawn to the towers and turrets that surrounded them. This time, I could not distract myself by dreaming of plants and flowers when prison walls and iron bars dominated my vision.

"What is to be done?" I thought of the men upstairs having the same discussion and prayed in my heart that they could find a way through this political labyrinth.

243

"Edward says there is only one choice, and that is why he sent Will to arrest Walter. If we do not show complete alignment with the king at this point, we will be as guilty as Raleigh."

"But Wat is his dear friend. And Allen's too. You require them to betray one who is as a brother to them?"

"And if they don't, we will lose all. Money, position, family. It is one life sacrificed for many."

Barbara's tone was as ice, and even in the heat of the room, a cold sweat crept across my neck.

"There's more." Barbara continued her pacing, and even Katherine stopped stuffing sweets into her plump mouth.

"By heaven, what more can there be?" Eleanor lifted her head, revealing her tear-stained cheeks.

"Walter has a map to the location of the gold in El Dorado. We must find it. Edward believes it is the key to keeping our patronage secure, for if George acquires the map, then he will find a way to finance another voyage to secure the gold."

At this, Katherine sat up and paid more attention.

"There is still an opportunity to retrieve the gold?"

I could not stand this talk any longer.

"A friend is sacrificing his life because of the gold. Is that not enough? Is there no thought of the man behind the corrosive dream of treasure? His family, his love, his life?" I thought of those evenings when Wat had sat by our fire and told of Sherborne and his poignant love of his home and his son. "He has lost all too. He has nothing left. Can you not respect this for just a moment and give us respite from this talk of money?"

"No." Katherine shrugged. "It was his voyage, his idea. He deserves what he gets. As long as we find a way out, I have no care for Raleigh's end."

We heard the heavy footsteps of the men overhead as they pushed their chairs from the table and came downstairs. Katherine stood and brushed the sticky crumbs from her skirts as Giles slipped into the room, his swarthy face shiny with perspiration. They left together, without saying good-bye to Eleanor and myself. I knew they had chosen their way and that it did not include human decency or compassion, for it was the corrupting path of power and money.

Will's shame in arresting his old friend was matched only by that of my husband, who subsequently became Walter's gaoler. The tragedy of choosing between their closest comrade and the survival of their family was a decision that none should have to make. For these military men whose fellow soldiers were truly their brothers, the choice was agonizing. The day Wat returned to the Tower was one of immense sadness. He was broken, betrayed by those who he trusted the most, and grieving most sorrowfully the death of his son, who had accompanied him on his voyage. It was a pathetic inventory that Allen wrote when he admitted him to his cell, describing the few jewels which he locked away in a strongbox, and the sorrow of it all stole sleep from him as he relived the great downfall of his dear friend.

The Somersets refused to leave Raleigh's old lodgings in the Bloody Tower. For his first nights of captivity, he rested under guard by the yeomen in our house, where I made it my duty to give him as much medicine and sustenance as I could prevail on him to take before he was incarcerated in the Wardrobe Tower.

He returned in terrible shape, sore-encrusted and exhausted. When his emotional turmoil overruled his physical ruin, all he could do was turn his face to the wall. He slipped between consciousness and unconsciousness for several days, and I feared a total collapse of his mind and body. Given his circumstances, that may not have been so dreadful, for surely even King James would not execute a madman.

While I sat next to his bed and watched over him, Allen was endeavoring to muster compassionate support for Wat, entreating even Queen Anne to intervene for the love of the man who had been her dead child's favorite. It was all to no avail, for the king was so in the hands of Gondomar that he would not step into the political fray and resist the Spanish demands.

Meanwhile, George was too immersed in saving his own skin to guide his master on the course of fairness and integrity. He took the king hunting and continued to spend vast amounts of money that summer in amusements and masques, all to distract the king from the little pang of conscience he may have had. We waited in the Tower for the date of Wat's trial, hoping to the end that some justice might be granted.

"Lucy, I need to talk to you." Allen beckoned me from my place by Walter's side, where I was sitting sewing. He had stirred some this third morning, and I was hopeful he might venture from his bed today.

I looked up. "Can it wait, Allen? I believe he is about to—"

"No."

I left Walter and went to Allen, who drew me out of our captive's hearing and into a narrow alcove on the circular stone stairwell.

"Lucy, Walter attempted to take his life the last time he was in the Tower. We must keep a very close watch on him now if he leaves his bed."

"Dear God," I whispered, glancing back at his form, still with his back to the room. "What a terrible situation. The honor of his family. How could he consider such an illegal act?"

"He was out of his mind with sadness. I fear the same when he awakes." Allen ran his fingers through his hair. "You must remove all physics and medications from his reach, my dear. And do not let him out of your sight."

I nodded miserably. Another burden for Walter—and for Allen. To be harboring or assisting a suicide was a severe crime.

Now my watch was twofold: both to encourage this broken man back to life and to prevent him from snuffing it out.

One time I returned to his chamber to find him gone, and with a blood-rush of shock, I frantically ran to the window to see if he had leaped from the leads to end his poor life. In those seconds, I feared the worst, and only when I found him sitting quietly on the bench in the garden below did I know that he was beyond thoughts of self-destruction, for the violence that drove that act had fled his soul.

As much as I could, I tried to bring light to his days, for now he was denied visitors, and his beloved Bess was forbidden to see him. We became as his family, and through the burnished September days, I sat with him, bringing the children to play around him so that their sweet laughter and antics might brighten his life. He did lift his eyes to follow their games, for they brought him some small joys.

The Earl of Northumberland and Mr. Ruthven continued their experiments through that waiting time. Although Wat's health did not permit him to stay long in the shed, there were days when he did participate, standing on the threshold of my henhouse and watching their actions. Out of respect of his doomed voyage for gold, they limited their activities to physicks and medications and stored away the alchemy tools. Even they, in their intensity, acknowledged the fruitless search for gold was the downfall of any man.

During the days, Walter often accompanied me in the kitchens as I made my medicines for the prisoners, and I showed him my diaries from Mathew L'Obel, those childish recordings of the great gardens and mysterious plants. He spent many hours leafing through my collection of recipes and observations of the plants. Asking for pen and parchment, he added to my library, writing his own pages of curatives and restoratives, diagrams and drawings of plants he had observed and collected on his voyages to the New World. He also scribed pages of tightly written notes and instructions.

I had seen naught of Barbara nor Katherine, and it was most obvious that they now distanced themselves for fear of guilt by association, and my only companion on those interminable days was Eleanor. The circumstances of Wat's voyage had bankrupted Will, and from his glory days of leasing Fonmon Castle and playing manor lord, he was now reduced to a ship's captain's pay. This was little to begin with, and in these days of the king's penury, the wages were never paid. They came to live with us, for they had nowhere else to shelter, and Allen, in his generosity, gave them a chamber adjacent to ours within the Queen's House, where their poverty would be ameliorated by our charity.

The day came in October when the light of autumn equinox bronzed the spires of the city churches. The Thames slipped with sweet calmness through the city, reflecting cobalt and azure from the sky, emblazoned in royal hues as it lapped against the old walls. Today I wished the Tower to be not a prison, but a royal fortress, and one that celebrated man's accession to greatness, not his ghastly end.

I found a spot where I would sit, tucked into the leads Princess Elizabeth had walked. The peaceful river views provided an aspect all the way east toward royal Greenwich and the verdant Essex marshes. There I was sufficiently detached from the prison that was my life. The air was fresh and hopeful, carrying the promise of other places, the sweet scent of an easterly breeze bearing farmland and brine. I let this wash me clean before I started my day, for the stale night air trapped within the Tower walls made me queasy. I was pregnant again. During those early weeks I wished to protect my child from the noxious odors that might bring him harm.

"There you are. I have been searching for you." I turned as Allen walked from our lodging onto the ramparts. "What ails you, Lucy?" He stood by me, also looking out over the river. Through a lifetime of habit, he was assessing the tide and the wind and paying little heed to the colors of the sunrise.

"Nothing. It is just fancy."

He walked to the edge of the ramparts and looked down upon the wharf, where the first deliveries of the morning were being unloaded. He watched intently, absorbed in the business going on below.

"What?" He did not turn from his observations. "Today, I grant Wat liberty of the Tower, for that is all the king will yield to, and his end is inevitable. Please ensure that he and his guests are given all they request in food and drink and make them comfortable."

"I will. Does Bess come now?"

"Yes, poor woman, she is finally permitted today. I decide now who sees him and who doesn't, who he shall spend his days with during his trial. He is completely under the jurisdiction of the Tower, and I challenge any to remove that from me." His words came as a burst, emotional, and he strode back to the door and disappeared.

As time will when there is a finite amount, it trickled as sand through our fingers. Much as we tried to look beyond Walter's mortal end to his everlasting life, it was with great difficulty we watched the hours move through their inevitable course. He slept little, for many came to pay their respects as he was preparing for trial, and he was much comforted by the presence of those who had always championed him.

After Walter had written to the king his apology, it seemed his soul was at rest. Although Allen said it was not in his right voice, I believed it was, for Walter always manifested a multitude of different characters, which was both his charm and his undoing. This final act of writing cleansed his soul. A great calmness settled over him, giving him the strength to comfort Bess and those others around him who beseeched him to wage his last battle. Even Northumberland, strange, unsocial man that he was, invited Walter into his rooms of the evenings. They sat together late into the night, still discussing the philosophies and astrologies that first forged their friendship.

Will was severely affected, direly disturbed by George's demand that he be the catalyst in Walter's arrest. He did not sleep those troubled nights at the Tower, preferring instead to remain by Walter's side, a silent companion in the dark night hours when others around him dozed. It was a devastating watch he had undertaken, but one he refused to hand to anyone else. Eleanor and I let him be and brought him soups and wine to sustain him.

Walter's trial was a farce, for all who attended attested to the veracity of his words and the weakness of the king's case. Allen returned each day torn between anger that such a travesty could be taking place and hope beyond hope that reason would prevail over politics. In the end though, Walter's cause was lost, and his execution was set for White Hall, not even the privacy of the shed on the Tower Green. Allen accompanied him to the scaffold to honor his old comrade. I excused myself to stay with the children, for I could not bear the grief of watching him die.

"He died a good death, if there is such a thing." Allen returned late, his journey back from White Hall delayed by the Lord Mayor's Day and the thousands who had taken to the streets. "He read a strong speech. He commanded the axeman to dispatch him quickly." He gave a great, shuddering sigh. "'Strike, man, strike,' he shouted, prepared with arms stretched. Finally, the axe struck his head, once, twice. Even at the end, the crowd was divided, some cheering, some protesting."

I held Allen in my arms, trying to still his shaking.

"But no declaration of his being a traitor from the executioner." Allen looked up at me, his eyes bright with tears. "'We have not another such head to be cut off,' called someone from the crowd. It was a fitting launch on his final voyage."

31

Dearest Anne,

How I long for the peace of Lydiard and the quiet of the country. You and John chose the right course, and I beg you not to consider a visit now, for times are turbulent here in London. Walter's death has cast a grim shadow upon Allen, tormenting him that he was unable to save his friend from execution. As chief gaoler of the land, he thought he would be meting justice in the king's name to treacherous criminals. In this instance, Wat's crime was being too bold, too courageous, spinning stories too fantastic. What felony lies in men's dreams? Except when for others they turn into nightmares. Allen has now taken up more of his victualling business and is spending his days in the Yard or traveling to the ports. He shares my bed when he is home, but he is seldom home, and I miss him, Anne. Alas, I do not return to the Yard, for we must fill our duty in the Tower for Villiers, and with Allen gone, the burden of spying falls on me.

We cannot escape. We are prisoners.

Lucy Apsley

Tower, **1618**

I rubbed my cold fingers, stiff with chill bleyns this bitter January, and sighed as I finished my weekly report to the Earl of Buckingham.

There has been a great falling out between the Earl of Somerset and his lady, and they live separate lives, each outdoing the other in inconveniencing us in their expectations and requests for special favors and entitlements within their captivity and competing for the best rooms, the tastiest food, musicians, company, and entertainment. Their demands are excessive, and yet they continue, as if they had now made this prison their palace.

250

Alone in our chamber, I reflected on the oddity of my situation. Allen had left again, this time to Portsmouth, I hear. He does not tell me much, only that the navy victualling demands his attention and that he must supervise closely all transactions to ensure that he is not shorted in his investments. This means he spends time with us but rarely. He has left the running of the Tower's business to Sir John Keys and relies on me to watch for the needs of the inhabitants. Taking care of their welfare is a responsibility I am glad to assume. Spying on the prisoners is one I cannot bear.

The greatest burden is observing the Somersets. Reluctantly, I visit them regularly on the pretext of ensuring that their meals and medicines are distributed and to the quality they demand. In fact it is to calm the fears of George Villiers that there are no plots to topple him, no retribution planned for his own coup. I long to write to him there is nothing to fear from this broken couple, for they are so engaged in their own bitter fight that they have no heed to the greater landscape outside of the Tower. The countess has struck a peculiar friendship with the Wizard Earl, and together they now intrigue against his daughter and her secret marriage.

And now Sir Thomas Lake and his wife and daughter arrive at the Tower and join the shadow court that is established here. I understand their crimes include adultery, incest, poisoning, and murder, although I have yet to read the charge papers sent to Allen. I am so heartily sick of these people who consider themselves above the laws of God and man. They act with such impunity, as if they are not to face a judgment day where they will be condemned to the everlasting fires of hell. It makes me reluctant to even supervise their food and accede to their demands, and yet I must in this strange position of gaoler-servant.

But enough of this gossip, for the earl cares not for these tangled webs of intrigue.

I placed my quill on my writing desk. As the afternoon light withered, I called for the candles to be lit early in my parlor, wishing to dispel the winter and bring warmth to the room. The cold stone walls encircled me, and I recalled that monument on Salisbury Plain that I visited so long ago with Anne on our journey to Guernsey. Who knew what ghosts had haunted those giant stones. I wondered at the substance of rock that it encouraged these spirits to cling to the particles, for in truth, I feel the sadness and sorrows of this place embedded in the very fabric of the walls.

My fancies were overwhelming me, and I called also for my children. Their innocence and laughter would chase away the mournful humors that lingered in the corners of this house. I yearned for joy so that my own unhappiness would not taint the soul of the new baby within me and set a sorrowful future for him.

My lying-in came shortly thereafter. Allen did not return for the birth, saying I was in good hands with Eleanor by my side, and he sent me a great basket of fresh oranges and lemons. These were most welcome in that stale winter, and I ate them daily to keep illness at bay. Along with the citruses, Allen sent instructions to name our son James, for he was convinced he would have another boy, and he was proven correct.

"Better our son be called George, for that is where our fortunes derive, not the king."

I put the letter down. It was pitifully brief, no words of tenderness. Where had Allen and I lost our way?

"Now that would not be a good omen, sweet sister. Burdening your child with a reputation such as the earl's would not be an auspicious start to his young life."

"You're right. I'm just ill of temper."

"You miss Allen?"

"I know not where my life leads, Eleanor. I'm tired. I feel sad. And lonely for Allen. And this child has taken more from me than the previous."

"You have bred rapidly, Lucy." She kissed my cheek and gave me a quick hug. "This is nothing but the last of the childbirth humor leaving your body."

"I hope so. For I have little joy in me."

"So, how fares your grocer today, Lucy? All well in the Villiers's pantry?" I hesitated in my reading. Frances's voice cut through the words, falling as a shadow across them just as the watery sun threw a copy of her figure across the pale blue of my skirts. I sat on the garden bench, savoring the first spring morning that emerged from the long winter, my first venture out after birthing James.

"I am sorry? I did not hear your words." I carried on with my eyes on my page, although the words were blurred now, my focus elsewhere.

"Apsley. Lining his purse with the Villiers's commerce? Provisioning the king's ships and his pockets?"

I looked up at her, standing dark before me as I squinted into the low sun. I stood, denying her the advantage, before she could continue with her remarks.

"Are you well, madam? Is there anything I can get you?"

"Freedom. Can you purchase that today for me, Lucy? Or is that beyond the purse of your new wealth?"

I did not answer, but simply stood quietly. Over the time as her gaoler, I learned I should treat her with respect, but not feel compelled to do as she bid or pay attention to her words if they were not within my comfort.

"Or how about a new husband, Lucy? Mine troubles me beyond measure, and I tire of his whining ways." She laughed, but it was mirthless. "Perhaps that is a wish I should keep to myself, for I have not had successful conclusions with men who disturb me." She tired of her jibes and turned aside from me. She was bundled deep in beaver and sable furs. In the unkind light, there were many lines of disconsolation in her face, especially drawing down her fine mouth, and her skin was sallow from no exercise.

"What think you now, Lucy?" She turned again, her movement swift, as if to strike. "Do you still envy me? Do my looks still intimidate you, a simple country wench with your gardens and your reading?" She pulled the skins around her closer, although I did not feel the cold that she seemed to. "Breeding becomes you. I heard you have another son."

"I do," I replied cautiously, uncertain of where this next thought was heading. I felt always as a mouse played by a cat when speaking to her, not knowing if I was being liberated from her attention only to be pounced on again.

"And how does he?"

"Well, madam, thank you."

"You are blessed. I see my daughter but rarely, for she is of an age where I do not wish her to visit her mother in prison. You have sons and a husband who takes good care of you, Lucy. Theo's loss was your gain. You managed your impropriety better than most maids who lose their reputations. You have mastered your fate, my dear."

"I trust in God, madam. He holds my fate, not I."

"I seem to not have God on my side, for his choice in my fate does not appeal to me."

She crossed the path, crushing the small shoots of snowdrops that had raised their heads in the first light of spring, and tossed a command over her shoulder as she left.

"Theo has returned from the Low Countries and comes today. Please be sure that our dinner is adequate and it is served in my chamber promptly at seven this evening."

I knew she was eager for a reaction from me, anything to break the boredom of her existence, but I would not give her the satisfaction of knowing that my heart beat faster at her words. As Mary and the children came out into the garden to exercise in the fresh air, I turned my attention to them and allowed their play to push the specter of Theo aside.

As I stood with Eleanor in the hall, ready to send the servants to the Bloody Tower with Frances's dinner, the front door flew open, and Barbara swept in. The antechamber quickly filled with her presence, her expensive musk perfume overpowering the delicate scent of early freesias that I had placed in a tankard by the window.

"What brings you here, Barbara?" I asked, for her presence had been scarce since the death of Raleigh, and I had seen little of her the past winter.

"I would dine with Frances. I hear she has a companion in Theo tonight. George doesn't believe you are reporting sufficient information and has asked for my opinion."

"There is nothing to record, Barbara. You do not need to trouble yourself." I felt uncertain why I did not want her to dine with Frances and Theo, but it was my first reaction.

"I will be the judge of that. I will join her for dinner. I am interested in their conversation."

Her clothes had become even more ornate since I had seen her last, and her sumptuous velvet-and-silk dress was of a glorious emerald green, cunningly embroidered in silver and gold threads. The intricacy of the work was extraordinary, and I could not help but stare at the craftsmanship and extravagance of the stitching. She smoothed the fabric with that complacent cat smile that I knew of old from Battersey.

"I have just received this from my dressmaker in Threadneedle." She examined an embroidered falcon, our family crest, which had been woven into the panels at the front of her skirts. "George recently gave Edward the monopolies for gold and silver thread and so feels it only right that we patronize the tailors. After all, the more thread they use, the more money he makes." She laughed and continued to stroke the fabric as if it were a living thing.

Eleanor and I glanced at each other in silent communication of the extravagances of our sister.

She dropped her pretense at small talk and pushed past me, walking into my parlor.

"Call me when it is time to dine." She sat, immovable, making it quite obvious that she was not going to be deterred from her objective.

"Are you going to allow her to do this?" Eleanor whispered, sounding worried, as she was so often these days.

"I don't have a lot of choice," I hissed back. "If George were to hear that I refused his sister-in-law hospitality, it would not go well for us. I shall have to be there too. Allen has specifically commanded me to be vigilant in all that the Howards do, and this change in routine, with Theo arriving too, requires my oversight."

"You really are their gaoler, aren't you?"

I shrugged. "With Allen away, someone must step in to look after our interests. I can't let George hear that the position of constable is not being used in its best capacity to serve him. I do not know where any loyalties lie, and I must continue to observe them. Theo has not been to see Frances in a year, and my guess is that he has much to catch up on."

"What new could happen to her since she is held such a close prisoner?"

"And why did Barbara pick this of all nights to insist on dining with Frances? I do not know these inner workings, Eleanor. All I can do is write of what I see and hope that others do with this information what they may."

"Allen left you a great deal of responsibility." Eleanor's statement hung in the room, a simple observation and yet so full of meaning. I sighed, and the weight of her words lay heavily on me.

The tableaux of dinner in the Bloody Tower was an ironic mimicry of the evenings we had spent in White Hall at Frances's apartments. As if on a stage, our party assembled again, and yet the roles had been contorted to such a degree that although the players were recognizable, their parts were usurped. Within Walter's old rooms in the Tower, Frances had brought in costly furnishings and carpets, tapestries and hangings. Nothing could disguise the thick prison walls and the cramped proportions of the small stone chamber worsened by the expensive furniture that failed to replicate any palace apartment.

"Who invited you?" demanded Frances as Barbara slipped into the room behind me. "I did not ask you to attend this evening."

"Buckingham," Barbara replied simply as she settled herself at the table and gestured to the server to fill her wine.

Carr was not to be seen, and I asked Frances how he fared.

"I do not care to know how he does, for he does not concern me." She turned again to Barbara. "Why are you here?"

Barbara did not reply; she simply looked around the cluttered chamber appraisingly, her hands folded on the table in front of her. Frances stood by the small fireplace, a broad, curved stone arch weighing down the fabric of the room, hinting at the larger battlements beyond, from which this prison chamber was hewn. Only the hissing of the fire and the occasional crack of the logs disturbed the heavy silence that encumbered the room. If Carr was upstairs in his bed, no sound came through the timbered ceiling.

The candles flared as a gust of wind preceded Theo's arrival, throwing shadows dancing on the walls and creating dark corners. No longer illuminated by the lights of a palace, he appeared taller, his face thinner, his auburn hair dulled in the half-light. But he still moved with that easy grace, and as he entered the stone chamber, Frances threw herself upon him, sobbing his name. They stood embracing, their shadows mingled to make one that stretched upon a wall and the low ceiling, looming over us.

As he stroked her hair and murmured soft words, Theo glanced at Barbara sitting at the board and then looked across at me.

"You have restored old acquaintances, Sister. I have been gone too long. I did not expect to share our reunion with an audience."

"They attend uninvited, Theo. I no more want them here than you do."

"Uninvited perhaps, but maybe welcome." Barbara stood and curtsied deeply to Theo, her silver-threaded gown glimmering in the dreary chamber. "I come on behalf of the earl, who is eager to hear how you fare, Theo."

"And he could not ask for himself when I am next at court?"

"Let us just say that this is a family matter and not for the ears of those supplicants who haunt his privy chamber."

"And you, Lucy, what brings you to this reunion? Tired of your old husband's company?"

"I . . ."

"She is my gaoler," Frances interrupted, her voice cutting across mine. Another sword thrust.

"I am simply doing my duty." I was so tired of explaining, so sick of always defending my position.

"Sir Allen leaves you to tattle tales while he fills his pockets with the king's gold. One a grocer, the other a spy." Frances turned to Theo. "Do not share with her any confidences, Theo, for she is not to be trusted."

Barbara put her hand on Theo's arm and drew him closer to the fire.

"Come, drink a cup of sack with us. I would gladly offer you our hospitality, for although Lucy may be Frances's keeper, I have ordered Allen's finest wines from the cellar."

Their talk ranged wide as dinner was served. I recalled Edward Villiers, his brother George, and Theo had studied together in Angers and knew each other of old. Theo had befriended George while Carr reigned supreme in the king's favor. Loyalty was rare in the Howard family.

"So Edward has done well; his star ascends." Theo stretched back in his chair, the meal complete. He glanced at me and edged closer to Barbara. She sipped her wine, smiling as the firelight played on her bare shoulders.

"It does. He has become Comptroller of the Wards, Master of the Mint, and holds the patent for gold and silver thread. Next, we hope for Master of the Jewel House, perhaps Comptroller of the Household. All lucrative but still tied to commerce." Barbara fingered a large jewel that gleamed between her breasts.

Theo's eyes were on her. "Does Buckingham not indicate more is ahead in the way of land or titles?"

"It takes time. And he values Edward as his intermediary when men ask for favors of him that he does not wish to grant immediately. Edward has the common touch, and men fear not to approach him. It is a convenience for the earl to listen but not decide. And of course, there are many fees to collect as messenger. We amass much in the way of wealth to support our titles when they arrive." Barbara looked squarely at Theo, speaking across Frances, who was seated to her left. "But tell me, how fare your children, Theo?"

He looked down, and a shadow crossed his face. "Well, Barbara, thank you. Elizabeth breeds consistently." He did not say more, nor would he look at me.

"And you have sons? Daughters?"

"We have been blessed with both."

"And now that you are the Earl of Suffolk, I am sure there is much planning for their future and their maintenance."

Theo lifted his eyes from the table and studied her as she continued.

"My sons and daughters thrive too. They grow fast and will have many opportunities, with Buckingham as their uncle." She sipped again from her wineglass and fell silent.

Frances and Theo exchanged a swift look, and Frances nodded to Theo, her eyes fixed on him. He sat straighter in his chair.

"Are your children yet pledged, Barbara?"

"We have had discussions with many. George has plans for a title for my eldest through a reversion. But I have not yet settled on who might be an appropriate match for my second son and daughter."

"Two children, then, you seek to contract in a marriage bond."

"Yes. To the right family, to one that has an established title and lands that would make a worthwhile match."

"And in return?"

"Wealth. Influence. The king's ear . . . redemption . . ."

Frances leaned forward, and I could see a pulse in her neck throbbing. I held my breath as I watched Barbara draw them in as a spider waits on its web, prey tangled by invisible threads.

"So a promise for a marriage alliance, and in return a pledge for freedom?" Theo's hand covered Frances's, his knuckles whitening as he gripped her hand.

"It is worth considering." Barbara stood suddenly and beckoned for her cloak. "I shall let George know how pleasant our dinner has been and how I find you both. He will be delighted to hear your family thrives, Theo. Healthy children are always so beneficial to one's well-being. Captivity does not suit you, Frances, and it would be a shame for you to live the rest of your life in solitude here."

She left the chamber, the door clicking shut behind her. A log cracked loudly in the fireplace, breaking the tension. I sat in the shadows, forgotten for the moment. Frances leaned on Theo's shoulder as he stroked her hair. I recalled the courtyard of Charlton when I had first met her and thought of their closeness then, comparing them to two beautiful peacocks. Her wings may have been clipped and her plumage dulled, but there was still such a bond between the both of them that Theo had just bargained away the future of two of his children to ensure her release.

Frances lifted her head and looked at me, contempt and triumph blending in her expression.

"She foretold this." Her tone was hushed, almost reverent.

"Who? Foretold what?" I asked, not following her thought.

"Turner the fortune teller. That time at White Hall when she read your palm. She said that our families would be joined. You thought she meant you and Theo. Now I know what her true forecast was. Barbara was always the catalyst between us." A tear slid down her cheek, tracing a course into a crevice that indicated many tears had been shed before. Theo leaned over and brushed it away carefully with his fingertip.

I was sick to my stomach at the sight. Frances Howard was crying for a hanged murderess who had the evil eye and through black magic arts foretold a future that was now coming to be. I could not leave the chamber quickly enough and shake myself from the disturbing spirits that hung around her and her brother.

32.

To cause a frantic man to sleep.

The Gall of a Hare soaked in wine it will make him sleep til you give him vinegar. Valerian in all his meat and drink is good.

Tower

"I am tired, my love. That is all." Allen sat in our downstairs parlor, the fire casting his face in shadow, causing the creases from his nose to the corners of his mouth to deepen. He scratched the head of the wolfhound that had adopted me in Will's absence and now followed at my heels wherever I walked.

"You appear more than tired, Allen. What ails your spirit? There is a melancholy about you."

"Nothing. Nothing at all." He held his hand up to still any further questioning. "How fare things here? What of the Howards?"

"They carry on much as before." I looked into my lap. "Theo has returned and took supper with them."

"He did? And what came of that?"

"Barbara can tell you. There was some discussion of marriages to be arranged between his children and hers."

"Really. What is she planning now?"

I could not determine his tone.

"I think she is using this to ask a favor of George. Maybe even to ask for the release of Frances."

Allen laughed, a short burst that sounded more cynical than humorous.

"I am not surprised. She is just one on the list. George has more suits in front of him than the Court of Common Pleas."

"What do you mean?"

"Barbara wants her grandchildren to inherit the Howard lands and titles. Will hopes for new profits, for he has entered into a business with Giles Mompesson granted by the earl. Edward has been given the parliamentary position for Westminster—"

261

I interrupted him, cutting off the list of new perquisites.

"Again we put ourselves at the mercy of Villiers, Allen. What new favor has he granted you? And what moral capital have you committed in return?"

"I hear no complaints when I give you your allowance, Lucy. I don't question what you do with your money. You should not question from whence it comes."

He stood, the dog jumping up too, startled by his sudden movement.

"I am going to bed. I hope you will join me." He held out his arms to me. "Lucy, seek not to challenge me and the decisions I make. I do it for all our good."

As though a rope was being cast wide around our family, each one of us had some liability to Buckingham and his ever increasing power, which he abused with his demands for payment for every request whispered in the king's ear. I thought sometimes of my sisters and their husbands as fishes swept into a net, wriggling and leaping to survive, cast loose again by the earl to swim at his bidding, only to be reeled again when some other bait was dangled in front of them. Allen laughed at my fancies and assured me that all knew what they were doing and were not at the mercy of the Villiers' ambitions as I feared.

Much as I had hoped Allen would take up his duties at the Tower again, he preferred to rely on Sir John to carry out the daily business and left early each morning to attend the Yard, where he appeared to spend all day in pursuit of commerce. I do not know what it was that kept him so occupied, for he did not confide in me much except when he gave me my allowance on a Friday and gently bade me to spend it wisely. We spoke no more of our harsh words on his return, and in my heart, I was glad to have him back in my bed, for there we could always find ourselves.

In truth, Allen's purse was most useful, and his generosity permitted me to care for many who could not fend for themselves. For those prisoners whose families declined to enter within the Tower walls to care for them, I prepared restoratives and broths. I wanted to give them comfort in their mean surroundings so that, whatever their crime, they should not suffer more than the loss of their freedom, which heaven knows is the biggest loss that man could impose on another.

I also traveled to the city meeting houses to hear ministers preach the Calvinist doctrines. It was important to me to continue to believe that divinity was steering my fate and that my time in the Tower was guided by the Lord's watchful eye. The lecturers were often refugees from France, and it sustained my soul to hear their words. It reminded me of simpler times when I was with Anne at Castle Cornet, studying with Monsieur Montrachet.

At these moments, I often questioned my fate, for the burden of caring for the inhabitants of the Tower weighed heavily upon me.

If there is a blessing to be gained from the incarceration within the Tower—for I did feel as a prisoner myself each time I returned inside the gate and heard the watch at night call out for the keys ceremony and the locking of the prison—the blessing was the discipline that became instilled in me and the awareness that excess can generate such dissipation in mind and body. As I grew used to the rhythm of the locks and inspections, the routines of the prison carved my life into periods of time that led to great structure within my mind and home.

Although I longed at times for those days when I ran wild through the woods at Fonmon or could ride my horse free around the lanes of Guernsey, unfettered by the boundaries created by man, I embraced the structure this brought to my mind and the discipline I could impart to my children. I yearned for my past lives but embraced my present, for there was nothing I could do to change my lot, and it was better to accept with joy than deny with bitterness.

"Allen, I woke with a dream in my heart this morning."

"What, sweetheart? Did you dream of Lydiard again?"

"You know me well, my love." I reached out and touched his cheek. "I did. I always return to Lydiard."

"And what did you dream of?" He kissed my fingers gently, his voice soft and caressing.

"I dreamed we walked in the walled gardens by the moonlight, and all was still except for the nightingales in the wood."

"Go on."

"And I dreamed a star came down from heaven and fell into my outstretched hand, illuminating our world. It shone a path straight and true that led from the gardens to the world beyond."

"I know the meaning, my love," he replied softly. "The meaning is that we will have a daughter of great eminency." He pressed his finger to my lips. "Shhh. I know you are breeding again. This time, it will be a girl. And we will call her Lucy, after her beautiful mother."

I smiled back at my husband, mine for the moments that he was in our marriage bed with me. "And I will call her Luce, after the morning star who illuminates my life."

I promised that this prophecy would come true by way of education and knowledge, and not by the arrangement of marriage. I kept these thoughts to myself because some would have challenged the old ways so much that I could be called a traitor. As my daughter grew inside me, I read aloud to her from my Greek and Latin books and had my musicians play sweet melodies as we rested in our chamber, dreaming she could hear through me and develop a love of these things. And when she was born, with the fairest of sunrises on a July morning, a sunbeam pierced the dark shutters of the Tower chamber, illuminating my bed and falling on the child as she lay swaddled in my arms.

"Luce," I murmured, touching her delicate brow and drawing my finger across her smooth forehead. "My light."

A great destiny lay ahead for her.

33

Nedd Villiers has a wife
And She's a Good Un
Her dresses she doth make of cloth of gold
All financed by her brother Mompesson

All you which monopolies seek to gaines
And faire pretences turn to other straines
Example take by Giles Mompesson's fall
Lest honie sweet soone turn to bitter gall

Lucy St.John Apsley
Verses nailed by the door at the Cross Keys, Cheapside
Tower

"You must come, you must come, there is such trouble." Eleanor was crying and sobbing as she ran into my stillroom. "Will says to come now to Katherine's house, for we have to help; there is no other way out of this." She was holding my cloak and dressed for traveling. "I have a coach at the Lion Tower. Please hurry, we all have to be there."

I pushed the bottles and mixing bowls to the side and wiped my hands swiftly on a rag, grabbing my cloak from Eleanor and securing it as we walked. The children were with Mary, and I called out to her as we left the house that I was visiting Katherine but did not know what time I would return. As we crossed Tower Green, the ravens rose in a cloud of black, cawing raucously, their harsh cries echoing from the walls. In contrast, Eleanor's face was white with anxiety, and I reached for her hand as we half ran to the Bloody Tower and through to the outer ward.

A coach was waiting for us. We hastily scrambled in and sat within the dark interior. I reached for Eleanor, who was trembling with anxiety. The vehicle took off at great speed, and we bounced and hurled through the teeming city streets to Aldersgate, where Katherine and Giles dwelt, hard on the London Wall.

"Giles has been before Parliament all this week," Eleanor whispered, her voice faint beneath the great creaking and jolting of the coach. "He defends his position in the grievances against the inns along with the gold and silver thread monopolies. He protects Edward and Will and even Allen, who is joined in this scheme. And now they have issued a warrant to search his house and his papers. Barbara is there with Katherine. John and Cousin Hungerford are summoned from Battersey. She sent word for Will and us to join them."

"Dear God. Allen too. He betrays me, then, for he pledged no more dubious schemes that could cause us harm."

I was shocked to hear Allen included in the list of names. I knew with sudden clarity that he could not have been as uninvolved as he appeared and cursed my naivety in believing he had held himself apart from these dealings. There was no man free from the corruptive practices laid out by the earl. My husband was in the middle of this scandal.

Eleanor and I fell into our thoughts, our hands clasped. I prayed so fervently, so deeply for God to protect my family from their own mistakes. In truth, I could not guess what lay ahead and could only pray the same words over and over, *Jesu protect, Jesu protect.*

Katherine and Giles's house was one of the new homes pushed up to the ancient London Wall. As we arrived, I recalled his boast that time at dinner, where he predicted the amassing of wealth and the kind of house he would acquire. It was here, in front of us, a vulgar mansion, designed by greed, built on the back of other's misfortunes. This was part of my life I hitherto ignored in the hope that it would disappear.

Will was waiting for us in the hall. As we entered, he hurried us into the dining room, a chamber stuffed with cabinets, chairs, and a long table. The fireplace was burning and a lavish feast spread before it. Around the board were gathered my sisters, and in the window bay, musicians played. The room was quite dizzying to the senses between the aromas of the food, the roaring fire, the mulled and spiced wines, and the music.

"You are celebrating a special occasion. You will welcome Giles to this joyous family gathering." Will looked around the room and nodded. "Whomever he brings with him, make sure you entertain them well."

There were shouts and a banging on the front door. Katherine uttered a small cry and stuffed her fists in her mouth to prevent sound escaping. Will grasped her shoulders and spoke directly into her face.

"Do not fear, Katherine, but you must play your part. You must do as we have said."

She nodded, and Barbara, who stood by her side, put a steadying arm around her waist.

"Now is the time, Katherine. We risk all."

Before I could ask more of Will, the door opened, and Giles walked in, escorted by a serjeant-at-arms. It was a great shock to see him under arrest in this way. He appeared disoriented and certainly exhausted, his sallow skin gray with weariness.

Barbara acted as though it was the most normal happenstance. As the musicians played and the serving staff continued to lay out dishes of swan and venison, fancies, and many delicate dishes, she kissed Giles affectionately and ignored the serjeant, establishing her place as someone far above the law.

"Giles, you must be tired. I heard you have been ill," she drew him to the corner of the room where wine stood on the sideboard, "let me pour you some sack and settle you for a while," effectively separating him from the serjeant. She looked meaningfully at me and tipped her head toward the man.

Taking my cue from Barbara, I walked to him, recognizing him from previous business conducted with Allen in the Tower. He removed his hat and bowed to me, a burly man with an open country face that had little guile in it.

"My Lady Apsley."

"Sanderson, is it not?" I searched my memory for anything I knew of him. "How fares your wife? Is she recovered?"

He smiled eagerly at my conversation, obviously wishing to please his commander's wife, who took such an interest in him.

"Yes, madam, she be well again, thankee."

"I am so happy to hear of this. May I fetch you some wine? You have arrived while we celebrate my sister's birthday, and surely you can drink a toast to her." I held my hand up, and a servant came immediately with a large cup of wine, which I handed to Sanderson. In the meantime, I could see that Barbara was still holding Giles's arm and handing him a pipe of tobacco. Katherine was almost motionless at her side, but fortunately not showing any of the hysteria she was prone to.

"Eh, I really shouldn't, my lady. I'm on official duty."

"Come, Sanderson, one cup of wine will not harm you." I raised my own glass in a toast, and he followed suit, not wishing to displease me. The musicians played a little louder. My sisters laughed and chattered like magpies and even danced a few steps. The air in the room became close and the temperature heightened. I observed Sanderson was feeling increasingly uncomfortable and that his own heat was rising. Suddenly, there was a commotion in the corner by the door as Giles collapsed and vomited violently, to a shocked cry from Katherine. While Will rushed to lift him, Barbara gestured to me fiercely to distract the serjeant. I quickly put my hand on Sanderson's arm to detain him as he stepped toward his prisoner.

"Poor Giles, I fear he is most unwell. Katherine, please take him to your closet and see that he rests. He must be exhausted. Mr. Sanderson can wait here with Lady Apsley while he recovers." Barbara's voice was imperious, immediately taking control of the situation.

"Beg pardon, ma'am, I don't know that I should let him alone." Sanderson took a step forward, but it was too late for him to protest. Will and Barbara helped Giles from the room, leaving me to entertain the serjeant.

"Let Katherine tend to her husband, Mr. Sanderson, for he has been indisposed for a while. I am sure she can care for him and help him recover. Allow them a little privacy." I beckoned to a servant, who immediately filled Sanderson's glass again. "Come, I am sure you must be hungry. May I offer you something to eat? I do appreciate your mannerly behavior while Giles recovers, and I shall be sure my husband hears of this."

In this way, I entertained the serjeant for a while, encouraging him to speak of himself and his exploits, for he was not a bright man, but one who enjoyed the sound of his own voice. As he droned, I became uncomfortably suspicious that Giles had not returned, and I was filled with dread that I had been set to distract the serjeant for a reason more than Giles's privacy in his illness. I tried to catch Barbara's eye, but she avoided me and hurried from the room.

The door opened again. My brother John and Cousin Hungerford entered, both still wearing their stained riding clothes. It was a great relief to see them, for the atmosphere in the room was becoming more strained as time passed. Although I still tried to keep Sanderson at my side and distract him from wanting to retrieve Giles from Katherine's closet, I was of half a mind to attend on Giles myself. Doubt delayed me, however. Perhaps something more than just a sickness was keeping Giles away.

"Lucy, Eleanor, it is good to see you." John kissed us and gathered us on each arm. "I regret that you could only stay for so short a time and that your children require you return to them."

"We are in no hur—" Eleanor started to say before John interrupted her.

"Gather your cloaks and be on your way before curfew, dear sisters, and I shall ride by and see you in the morrow."

He almost pushed us from the room, through the hall, and out to the waiting coach, and I left Sanderson standing in the now empty room, his mouth open in an absurd way as our conversation abruptly ended. We climbed in and discovered Barbara and Katherine were already inside, Katherine weeping.

Upon a shout from John as he thumped the side, the coach jerked forward. As he stepped back, outlined by the illuminated door of the mansion, I could see the serjeant behind him, his sword out and his face wildly working in great distress.

"What happened, why are we leaving in such turmoil?" Eleanor strained to see Will but could not find him.

"We are best away from this house as quickly as we can," Barbara replied, "for I would not wish to be found an accomplice to the deed that just occurred."

I peered at her through the coach's dusky exterior. The leather blinds had been half drawn and the light was dim within. Katherine continued to moan, her keening heard over the clattering of the coach as it headed back to the Tower.

"Giles has escaped. He leaves on the night tide to France. And if it were not for us, he would not have eluded the serjeant." Barbara sat back against the seat and loosened the tie on her cloak.

"How could you do this to us, Barbara?" I was furious, realizing how she tricked us into a dangerous plot. "We will all be held to blame. What were you thinking?"

She started laughing, as if she found this situation the most amusing of all that happened to us this evening.

"Did you see that fat serjeant once he realized he had lost his prisoner?" Barbara turned on me. "Stop being so naïve, Lucy, and understand what is going on here. We saved Giles's life. Buckingham will thank us for preventing Giles from being put on the stand in his own trial. The last thing the earl needs is a lily-livered prattler who will reveal all the illegal profits from his so-called licensing venture. And we all know Giles would say anything to save his skin."

"So even this mad escape was not to save Giles's life and keep Katherine from public humiliation?" Even I couldn't believe Barbara could be so mercenary—and convince everyone else to play along with her.

"Pshaw. The only concern here was that Giles would reveal all the funds he funneled to the earl from the licensing scheme. They can't make him talk if he's not here." Barbara settled back and closed her eyes, signaling the end of her conversation. I stared out of the partially screened window at the dark streets, damp now with the river fog that had crept in with the night, obscuring all that was familiar to me.

The stakes had indeed been high, and now they had been raised again. With an arrest so close, our troubles were only just beginning.

34

Dearest Anne,

The king himself hath come to hear of Giles's trial. In our brother-in-law's absence, the Lords place an empty chair in the dock, they read the charges, they hear the witnesses, they recount his crimes. Under his cloth of state, James listens, his mind on how to appease the common people. Having given evidence and protested his innocence, the earl waits the verdict alone in his palace, noticeable by his absence.

Remain at Lydiard with John and your children. There is nothing you can do for us here.

Lucy,
Tower
March 1621

The repercussions rippled far from Giles's escape. A furious Parliament heard from the serjeant his tale of confusion and how he allowed Giles to slip from his guard. The ports were immediately ordered closed. A proclamation went from the House of Lords for none to harbor him and to bring him immediately to the Tower when apprehended, but it was too late, for Giles had many hours' start, thanks to our subterfuge. He made his escape to Sheerness in Essex, where a barque took him to a sailing ship and thence to the Continent.

At Westminster, Will, John, and our Cousin Edward Hungerford were commanded to the Painted Chamber to give an account of all they knew, and a search was immediately ordered of Giles's house and possessions. It was conducted violently and with great fury. The humiliation of his escape reflected on the men who were ordered to search, and they were not careful in their duties. The house was wrecked, chests smashed open, draperies ripped from the walls, precious mattresses slashed by swords, and every document and purse removed, leaving Katherine surrounded by the debris of her life, the richness desecrated. Her home stood open to all who could walk in and help themselves of the possessions of a hunted felon.

Allen rode to the ruins with a company of Yeomen Warders, bringing her to the Tower for safety. Katherine could not be protected on her own in the devastation of her home, and I put her quickly to bed with a sleeping draught as soon as he returned with her. It was obvious she was in great shock, her eyes fixed and staring, her voice stilled.

Buckingham, who sat with the Lords when the alert was raised, immediately spoke against Giles. It was common knowledge Villiers granted the monopolies and patents, but he declared he was no friend of Mompesson, and he would not bother the king with such matters when Parliament could decide the fate of such a man. George Villiers was aware the net was spreading, for the next matter to be brought before the Commons was the list of grievances, which included the gold and silver thread patents he had granted to his brother Edward.

The debates in Parliament raged for over a week. White with exhaustion and anxiety when he returned at night, Allen's position as Lieutenant required him to stay and observe the proceedings. He was in charge of Yelverton, the imprisoned attorney general who was also implicated with Edward and Giles in the business. Each day brought more revelations, more hatred toward the Villiers family. Allen and I talked long into each night, visiting and revisiting the few options remaining for us to survive this investigation.

"Your involvement, Allen. You must tell me the truth," my voice was imploring, for I had no pride left not to beg.

"I lent Giles money; he repaid me. I trusted him not, and I refused to go further with his schemes."

"So why such persecution now, Allen?"

"They are out to bring down the corruption which exists around the king." He summed up the day as he slumped, exhausted, by the fire in the hall of the Queen's House. He looked up as Edward and Barbara joined us, for they had not moved from the protection of the Tower for the last seven days. "Buckingham and his family represent the decayed morals of our wretched kingdom."

"The Lords can do nothing. The earl has the king's full favor, and old James will not allow these proceedings to harm him, or us." Edward was dismissive, his tone arrogant.

"Parliament called you and Giles bloodsuckers and vipers, Edward. And let me quote directly: 'Let no man's greatness daunt us, for the more we do to great men, the more we prevent in future his mischiefs.' Now do you feel secure under your brother's protection?" Allen rubbed his eyes wearily.

"My brother encourages us to let the Commons vent their anger and to stand before them as innocent investors in a bona fide business," Edward blustered. "Giles has gone and will not be recaptured, and he is the one whom all are focused on. I am above this, for George will speak for me."

"Do you not understand how the people hate him?" asked Allen incredulously. "Do you not see he is the target, and you and Giles are merely bait to land a bigger catch?"

"You are wrong, Allen, you have not the experience in court George and I do."

"This is no royal Star Chamber, but a public one of justice, for God's sake, man. The people are out to topple George, for this incident represents all they fear of power and influence and corruption. George is completely underestimating the severity of this, Edward. You are going to be fortunate to escape this one."

"What news of Giles, Allen?" I was trying to piece together all the disparate parts of this complex matter, trying to understand where our vulnerabilities could lie.

"Sentence tomorrow, and it will not be mild. The Prince of Wales sits with them to proclaim. You could not have a stronger indication that this has the king's attention."

"George and the prince are good friends. He will look out for us."

I was so frustrated with Edward's oblivion to the dangers that he and Barbara were in that I finally could not stand to be with him. I grabbed Barbara's arm, forcing her to accompany me, and left the room.

We stood, close to each other in the hall, the house the king built for Queen Anne settling around us, the Tower enclosing us in the dark night.

"Listen to me, and listen well, Barbara." I lowered my voice, forcing her to draw closer. "We cannot save Giles from this sentence, but you still have time to protect Edward from the wrath of Parliament, and from his own absurd arrogance."

Barbara opened her mouth to protest, but I continued, relentlessly honest with her.

"You've done all you can do in London. You have obtained great wealth. Arranged a marriage for two of your children to the foremost family in the land. You've secured Uncle Oliver's title to revert to your son. And enjoyed the pleasures of the court for many years. The payments from Giles and other corrupt officials have lined your purses well." I would not draw breath to let her answer me. "I see every day here the prisoners who have done less than you and who are confined at the king's pleasure for heaven knows how long, until they are forgotten and have no life left in them to fight."

"It will not happen to us." Although her words were defiant, Barbara's voice was hesitant.

"And do you not consider Frances thought the same? Do you not see the lessons from her miserable existence, and of her husband, who was the king's favorite for so many years? Do you want to be as she is now, a shadow of herself, ignored and forgotten? The Parliament is attempting to put Buckingham away forever. Unless he can distract with those minions below him, claiming no personal knowledge, you will be sacrificed to save his soul."

"He wouldn't do that to his own brother."

"He won't have an option. You need to give him one. Get Edward out of the country, and let the storm blow over. Save him from Parliament's wrath, for if they cannot have Giles stand in front of them, they will find another to blame."

"Where could he go?"

"Jesu, Barbara, you can find some reason to get him away. But act quickly, for there is little time. And make it a reason to give the king satisfaction, not just Buckingham. The closer you can be to supporting the king's needs now, the safer you will be."

She stood still, my sister who had created such havoc with my life, and for the first time, I sensed fear beneath her mask.

"Why are you advising me such, Lucy? I have done little to help you over the years."

"I do it for Allen and for my children, Barbara. I want to stop this rot from spreading further, and if I can sever you and Edward from this mess, I will. Yes, you are my sister, but it is not love for you that guides my advice. Know that Allen is not just the Lieutenant of the Tower, but the king's gaoler. His integrity is in question here, and if he is brought down, then there is no hope left for any of us. It is the love for my own family and a desire to protect them from your avarice and greed that drives me. You have no other choice but to leave."

Edward and Allen came from the chamber just then and paused to see us in such intense conversation.

"What is going on?" Edward's voice was quavering. Allen stood silently. There was a heavy moment of silence, and then Barbara spoke.

"We have matters to discuss, you and I, Edward. Come."

He followed her to the upper chamber. As they left the hall, I took a deep, shuddering breath. I had never had the courage to confront Barbara directly before. I felt such a relief of escaping from the burden of her personality. A simple conversation, and yet one on which my life had changed.

"Are you well, Lucy?" Allen knew better of me than to ask more.

"Yes." I held my hand to him. "I predict Edward will be shortly appointed to a position in Ireland, or perhaps he will be sent on a diplomatic mission to return to the Palatinate. For a long time."

Allen raised an eyebrow but said no more, and I did not tell him of my conversation with my sister.

On the 26th of March, Giles was sentenced. The winter was harsh, with a Frost Fair held on the Thames, and the chill in the air reflected the dread in my heart. It was after curfew when Allen eventually returned to the Tower, where Katherine and I anxiously waited. There were no distractions to keep her mind from the proceedings. We sat in silence for the most part of the day, my servants bringing us food left

275

untouched, Mary taking care of the children, so I heard their distant play. When Allen arrived, we both stood spontaneously. It was apparent from his face that the news was grave indeed. I caught Katherine's waist as she swayed and settled her on a stool, but I could not sit myself in the anxiety of hearing the news.

"The Lord Chief Justice, the Lords in their robes, the Prince of Wales, the Lord Chamberlain, the earls, and then the king. All in the chamber, the king under the cloth of state. I have never witnessed such a gathering."

"God have Mercy," whispered Katherine as Allen continued.

"The king spoke. He wished to reinforce that his proclamation to capture Giles was in earnest, and that failing his capture, he would ensure that sentence would be carried forth. He confirmed he had set Prince Charles among them, his beloved son, to ensure that justice was served. He spoke of Giles by name, and then spoke of Buckingham, his favorite, in the same breath, absolving him from knowledge, believing in his story that he was sore vexed by those who caused such troubles."

"So Buckingham is cleared?" My hands had been clenched so tightly that my nails were digging into my palms, and yet the pain was dull and distant.

"By the king, yes. By the people, never. So the king left the sentencing in the hands of the Lords, effectively casting it back to Parliament to decide Giles's fate, but making it apparent he believed Buckingham had little to do with these corrupt practices."

"So Edward is safe too?"

"By association, he is still linked with the man who is hated most in this land by the people. I would not recommend that Edward raise his head now. The best he could do is take his seat in Parliament to show himself a true subject of the king and then remove himself from public eye."

I thought of my conversation with Barbara and knew that my sister would ensure this would be carried out.

"And you, Allen? What of your investment?" I stood behind Katherine, gripping her shoulders lest she fall to the ground. I still needed to hear the rest that Allen had to say.

"I am not the target of these findings. I am simply the gaoler."

"And your part in this, Allen? What of your part in this?" My voice was shaking.

"It was no more than a signature on one or two pledges, Lucy. I disavowed myself of this mess a long while ago."

"What of my husband? What of Giles?" Katherine's voice trembled, and her hands were shaking terribly.

Allen turned to her.

"You must be strong, madam. He has been perpetually outlawed for his misdemeanors. He shall ever be held an infamous person. His knighthood is degraded, although your reputation is preserved. His goods and lands are forfeited to the king, and a fine of ten thousand pounds assessed. He is banished from the kingdom, and if he should attempt to return, he will be immediately imprisoned in the Tower."

35

For convulsion fits or falling sicknesses, weave five sassafras leaves into each sock and wear on your feete for five nights and days.

Blackfriars—Apothecary Schmelzle

Lucy Apsley

October 1621

Katherine and her child live now within the Tower's protection. Her home destroyed and her name ruined, there is no safety anywhere else. Our brother, John, pleaded with the king and was assigned the ten thousand-pound fine to care for her, but her devastation will take more than money to cure, and she dwells with us until her mind returns.

No word from Giles, and I care not for his fate; he can rot in France for the disgrace he brought so close to us. Allen says we are fortunate to have been overlooked in the scandal, and although Barbara still hankers for more wealth, it is within the privacy of our family she speaks of this. Edward serves on many diplomatic missions to the Palatinate, spending scant time here.

I am not surprised, for there is much to be gained, and it is safe away from the London pamphleteers who publish such venom against all Villiers now. I do not venture out beyond these walls much, for the pamphlets are everywhere, and I fear to be recognized as a Villiers relative. Although none would know me, this worry governs my life.

The sound of marching Yeomen on the gravel outside broke into my thoughts, and I went to the window to see what new prisoner was being brought to our gates. Led by Allen, the guard was directed toward the Bloody Tower, and pulling my cloak from the peg by the door, I slipped outside. Far from delivering another prisoner, it appeared they were heading for Frances Carr's apartments.

As I stood in the early spring sunshine, the Tower's familiar noises settled around me. I could hear the clink and hammering of the goldsmiths in the mint houses, and in the distance, a roar from the

Barbaries echoed from the menagerie. Closer, two ravens perched on the stone wall that separated the orchard from the path, and I shivered. I did not like these creatures, for they carried with them an evil eye, and I always thought them the keeper of the wicked souls that died within our walls. Fanciful on this bright morning, but still a shadow across the sun.

A cavalcade of horses stood by my garden gate, and I recognized the blue-and-green Howard livery. The door from the Bloody Tower opened, and Frances emerged with Theo at her side. Carr trailed behind them, his head down. Allen stepped forward and bowed and said something to her that I could not hear at this distance. She gave him her hand, and he brushed it with a kiss. Curious to know more, I found myself walking toward them and caught their conversation as I came within earshot.

"The king has shown mercy and releases you from our care," Allen said, most formally.

"I expected nothing less." Even in her pardon, Frances continued in her arrogance.

"It is thanks to Barbara and her intervention, not the king," replied Theo. He stood in front of Allen, one hand on his sword, the other on Frances's arm. "You have done little to support our calls for clemency while Lady Carr has been in your custody."

"It is not my place to intervene on behalf of a convicted murderer." Allen's response was immediate. The two men stood with little but one pace between them, shoulders tense.

"Mind your words, Sir Allen. Your position is not secure here." Theo looked from Allen to myself. "You rely heavily on the patronage of one who holds no loyalty, especially to his country cousins."

My cheeks flushed at his insolence. Allen ignored Theo and continued to address Frances.

"You have permission to retire to your lands upriver. But you must stay within the boundaries of your estate. You are not permitted to travel beyond its walls, nor return to court."

"I have no desire to return to White Hall, nor any need to travel," she replied. "Anyone I wish to see can come to me. Including Barbara. She is the only one in this family of any worth."

"And now your children are to be married to our family. I assume you will keep your side of the contract this time, Lord Howard, and not be led by temptation into one that offers more." I could not stop myself from saying the truth that lay in my heart.

Theo brushed past me without a look. He led Frances to her horse, his arm around her, a ghostly echo of their walk in the stable yard at Charlton, when I was the object of Theo's desire. She mounted her mare with exquisite grace and straightened the skirts of her deep purple riding habit. Behind her, Carr climbed onto a bay gelding, staring between its pricked ears, seemingly oblivious to his environ. The Howard retinue surrounded them, a powerful group of riders in close formation.

Frances turned her mare's head to leave and then twisted to look back at me. At a distance, on a fine horse, surrounded by the trappings of her rank, she conjured the image of her lost past.

"I leave, and you remain," she called out to me. "I wonder who now is the prisoner?"

36

A sassafras cordial

Take a scraping from the root and some of the green stem of the sassafras and pound well with anise, cloves, cinnamon. Add as much ale as will cover four times over, boyle until this reduces and strain. To be used as a tonic but sparingly, for the sassafras can also poison.

A recipe from the New World

Tower

1622

Now that Uncle Oliver is appointed Viscount Grandison and has been recalled from his position as Lord Deputy of Ireland, our family prospects ascend again. Oliver is sworn to the Privy Chamber, adding another layer of intimacy with the royal court. He has requested we attend a masque at the new banqueting hall at the palace, to celebrate the return from Spain of George Villiers, now titled the Marquess of Buckingham, and his cherished companion, the Prince of Wales.

Honoring my love of gardens, Allen commissioned the palest green silk cloth to be embroidered all over with intertwined lilies and roses. The fragile blossoms are remarkably worked into the gown with an extraordinary detail. The children quietened when I appeared, for this was the first time I had appeared in court dress to them. Young Boon was more interested in the fine ceremonial sword that his father wore, and Luce fingered the myriad of pearls on my skirts.

"You look beautiful." Allen's eyes were soft as he stroked Luce's head

I smiled. "And you are most handsome, Husband."

He reached his hand toward mine and swept a magnificent formal bow. I glimpsed traces of the young courtier that Elizabeth had favored so highly, and I realized his courtly manners were still put to use. Another side to my husband that I had not seen before.

"Shall we depart? I have a carriage waiting for us."

I took his hand and, kissing Luce and Boon, left the Queen's House. On the path, a guard was waiting for us. As they escorted us along the Green toward the Bloody Tower, the formality of my dress and the presence of Allen in his finery at my side reminded me again that we were living in a royal palace ourselves, albeit one that had fallen out of recent favor. Many of our citizens stopped to stare, and several women dropped curtsies, which I acknowledged with a smile. On other days, we prepared food together in the kitchens, our faces red with effort, sweat on our brows, but today was different. I was the Lady of the Tower.

The ramparts of the keep shouldered the gray sky above our heads. The gardens I had brought back to life stretched before me, a grove of fragrant sassafras saplings planted by Walter. They were thriving, the leaves and bark being most efficacious for medicinal treatment. As always, I had to pause to admire them, and Allen smiled, waiting patiently.

"You will always have the garden in you, Lucy, no matter what the occasion. You have taught me to look beyond the practical and admire the beauty, and I love you for that."

"I treasure these trees. They remind me of the good Walter intended from his voyages to Virginia, not the sad outcome. There is nothing like the sassafras to restore health in so many conditions, and I honor him by bringing comfort with their medicine."

"Our prisoners thrive under your care, Lucy."

"A prisoner here has already lost his freedom. There is no reason for him to lose his health too."

We walked along Water Lane, flanked by our guards, through to the Lion Tower. As they mounted their horses and we alighted into the official Tower carriage, it was one of those moments when all was right in the world. I had Allen by my side, and these recent trials had brought us close again. My children, never far from my mind, were healthy, and I was most grateful for the circumstances that had brought me to this moment. God had guided me to a good decision that day at Fonmon.

The new banquet hall at White Hall was in the Italian style, never seen before in England. Carved of palest cream stone, it appeared hewn from a foreign land and transported to our shores by Greek gods. Mr. Jones had built a glorious temple fit for the ancients amongst the midden heap that was White Hall. In the years since I last visited, the palace buildings had worsened in their cramped and noxious vapors. The recent fire that destroyed the old hall had not improved the ruinous appearance of the palace, yet the aging king continued to lodge within, as did his chief counselors and favorites.

Still accompanied by our Yeomen Warders, for Allen was determined we have a presence at the palace, we were admitted through the entry and into the palace compound. Walking by the privy gardens, resplendent with glorious statues surrounded by clipped hedges and gravel paths, we passed through the Holbein Gate. Allen took my hand and kissed it as we passed by the tiltyard, a smile passing between us as we returned to a distant memory.

I began to enjoy myself as people turned to look at us and our convoy of liveried Yeomen. Although this was not a usual circumstance for me, the power Allen carried as the Lieutenant of the Tower exuded strength and confidence, and people recognized this.

It was enlightening for me to see him so, instead of the man I knew, a husband and father and a man who managed his business affairs late at night in his gown and bedcap in the privacy of our chamber. As I entered the world of court with him guiding me, I lifted my head higher and ensured my posture was that of the Lieutenant's lady.

"The marquess will be with the king. He has asked we attend him in his Privy Chamber, so we will proceed to his apartments." As he spoke, Allen walked confidently through the maze of buildings, apparently not the first time he had visited the Buckingham at White Hall.

Buckingham's apartments, adjacent to the king's, were surrounded by a crush of common people waiting in the courtyard to gain admittance to the favorite. Our Yeoman Warders shouted to make way, and the crowd melted in front of us as the soldiers with their pikes cleared a path, escorting us through the curious onlookers. The first chamber we entered was still crammed with people of all walks of life.

As we were led through increasingly more intimate rooms, the guards on the doors became more dominant, and the people within the rooms more refined. Finally, we stopped in front of closed doors, flanked on either side by two giant guardsmen, who stood with their pikes crossed in front of the doors. The chamber hushed as a half dozen or so courtiers whispered behind their hands and shuffled as we approached. With a clatter, the guards stood to attention and moved their pikes upright, opening the door for us. Leaving our Yeomen behind in the antechamber, we stepped forward into the private rooms of the Marquess of Buckingham.

There was not a single space on the walls not covered with paintings, tapestries, and hangings of superb quality. The likenesses in the paintings were so real it was as if the room was populated with a hundred people, all ready to step from the frames and join our company, so lifelike were their images. The effect was mesmerizing, for no other way could describe the opulence except in the portraiture that surrounded us.

From a panel in the wall, which appeared as the rest of the room and cleverly disguised a door, a man stepped, and I thought him a painting that had come to life, so splendidly was he adorned. A purity and evenness about his features created a face of perfect balance, which in itself was compelling. His eyes were of a glowing deep brown, so soulful and so adoring, and his sensual lips were as full and ripe as a woman's and yet surrounded by a manly beard. Long, elegant, and athletic, his legs enhanced his graceful demeanor. His lustrous hair curled in abundance on his shoulders. He was tall and graceful, and his clothing was so sumptuous that I paled as a serving maid in my fine attire. Diamond buttons decorated his suit, and strands of pearls swept across his chest. His garb was as opulent as a woman's court gown, but there was such an air of masculinity exuding from him that no white uncut velvet and jeweled adornments could modify his virility.

"Allen! I was with the king. How are you, my friend?" He crossed the room swiftly to greet us.

"My Lord Buckingham," Allen swept his most deferential bow. "May I present my wife, Lady Lucy Apsley."

I curtsied deep, and as I stood, the marquess took my hand and raised me. His face was of such great beauty that compelled fascination, and his scent was intriguing, exotic and yet fresh. A diamond the size of my fingernail sparkled in his ear, and his eyes were luminous, as beautiful as a woman's and yet with the direct gaze of a man who knew his own power.

"Lady Apsley. Allen mentioned that he married a young wife. He did not say she was beautiful too." He grazed my fingers with his lips. "You are most welcome here, for our court benefits from the fresh life you bring into our jaded world." He released my hand and turned away.

"Allen!" He flung his arm around Allen's shoulders, surprising me at his informality. "I have a great deal to ask you about our plans for Cadiz. Stay after the masque and discuss these with me."

"Of course, my lord. I would consider it an honor."

"No honor, Allen. I respect your counsel. While others around me are new to these matters, I believe your experience will help me prepare the fleet. You are the only commander who understands my plans, for as you served under Queen Elizabeth, so shall you serve under me. We shall kindle the fire in men's hearts again, recalling the glorious exploits of old against our enemy, Spain." All shall remember those days when we torched the King of Spain's beard—only this time we shall burn his cities and devastate his economy. Come, we have a moment before we leave."

I looked at Allen, shocked at these words. This was the first I had heard of any fleet preparations. He had led me to believe his increased absences and frequent visits to Portsmouth were in the nature of his normal victualling business. They walked toward the bay window, where a table was laid out with a number of charts and documents and stacked with papers.

I was forgotten, and as their heads bowed together and they pointed to the charts, I was left to wander the chamber and examine the paintings. The work was magnificent, not only those portraitures of the Villiers family, but scenes depicting countryside and temples, biblical stories and Greek myths. All were hung with little concern for their neighbor, as if once acquired, they had been casually viewed and then put aside for the next. These gave me no pleasure, for in truth, I could not concentrate on the paintings with the words of the marquess clamoring in my mind.

The door to the chamber opened, and Allen and Buckingham turned as a party of men entered, escorting a young man of small stature, not much taller than I, who stepped cautiously with a halting gait. The marquess put down a chart and smiled with deep joy, his beautiful face alight with love.

"Here is the Commander of the Fleet! Now we have the real brains and majesty to guide us. My Lord Prince, you arrive with perfect timing, as always. We crave your insights, for without your wisdom and direction, we are but lowly mariners lost at sea!"

The young man flushed, color sweeping over his pale skin and receding just as quickly.

"George, I-I-I thought I would find you here. I w-w-welcome you, S-Sir Allen." He swallowed and made a very deliberate effort to concentrate. "Are you relaying to My Lord Admiral Buckingham your naval counsel?"

"Your Highness." Allen bowed deeply and stood before the Prince of Wales, his head respectfully bent.

"Come, Allen, I w-w-ish you to treat us as you would your own men. For we have much to learn of the ways of the navy, and who better to t-teach us than he who commanded in the first Cadiz expedition?"

I waited silently in the shadows of the room as the Prince of Wales and the Marquess of Buckingham stood with my husband, listening intently as he spoke of tides and charts, currents and landings, and jabbed his finger on the papers strewn in front of them. Allen was engrossed in his tutoring. It was quickly apparent that the marquess and the prince hung on his every word as he outlined plans for a full-scale naval expedition to Cadiz.

Presently, Buckingham glanced up and smiled at me.

"Allen, we have tarried too long planning. Time for pleasure. Let us go and see if the king is ready to attend the masque." He stretched his arms wide and draped one over the prince's shoulder and the other over Allen's. They appeared as three comrades, not as the fragile heir to the throne, the most powerful nobleman in the land, and my husband. Allen was flushed, his face excited and full of energy. I could see the meeting had rekindled old memories. He continued to talk excitedly as the three of them walked ahead of me through the doors, they both leaning toward him, their faces ignited by the tales Allen was telling. I trailed behind, excluded from their world.

King James finally appeared within the magnificent banqueting hall, and much had changed since I had last visited White Hall. He was carried in a sedan, a chair lifted onto the shoulders of four strong guards, a contraption the marquess had introduced to London society several years ago. He was mocked in the streets and cursed for putting men into slavery when it first appeared, but now it was all the rage, and men vied each other for the strongest carriers and most ornate chairs. Tonight, however, I could see that it was not just a fashion, but a necessity, for the king was so sickly and crippled with gout that he could not walk more than a step or two on his own and needed to be lifted from the sedan to his chair to view the masque.

I saw before me a dying man, for his disposition was of disassociation. Although the masque was entertaining and extravagant in its settings and costumes, it was like giving a man dying of thirst a banquet and watching him choke on the indulgencies while crying for a simple drink of water. His head lolled from side to side, and his tongue continued to escape from his lips. There remained nothing of the majesty of his person. All around, the courtiers deferred to Buckingham and Prince Charles, for although the king sat in the chair of state, no discussion included him. Most often his son and his favorite leaned across and spoke in front of him as if he were not there.

Under the noise of the gathered audience and the performers, I was able to pull Allen to a quiet space behind a column.

"What is happening, Allen? What are these plans for war you are making with the Villiers? And now the prince is involved too? What madness is this?" In the background, the music swelled and the court cheered as a particularly ornate set piece of a galleon on an ocean was towed across the floor.

"It is naval matters, Lucy. Do not trouble yourself."

"It is a family matter, Allen. I see you in a different light again, and one I do not care for. What happened to all the learnings from Giles's and Edward's experiences with the marquess? Why are you doing this?"

A storm at sea now endangered the players in the masque, and the drumming thunder competed with Allen's words.

"They command it of me." His answer was frightening in its simplicity.

"And what do you risk because they command you?" I mimicked.

He avoided my question.

"I am doing my job. Buckingham and the prince are to declare war on Spain, and they require a navy. I victual the navy. I have to serve their needs."

"But what of all this other—the charts, the planning, the stories of the times you sailed under Elizabeth?" I could barely hear his answers, and the insistent noise of the masque and its actors was giving me a headache.

"Stories, Lucy, stories to bolster their young men's egos and to validate their decisions."

"I don't understand why, Allen. Why should you need to do this?"

He hushed his voice so that it lay beneath the tumult on the stage.

"It's obvious, Lucy. The king is dying. The prince is a weakling. Buckingham holds the power. And since they returned from Spain with no infanta's hand in marriage, and no treaty, the marquess has to prop up the throne. He is recalling England's glory days, still fresh in men's memories, of when we defeated the Spanish and ruled the seas. He wants Charles to be regarded as the savior of the Stuart dynasty and the most eligible warrior prince in Christendom."

"It's a pretense, Allen, a sham. It has no more worth than this masque we are watching."

"I have to do my job. I have no choice."

The drumming rose to a crescendo, making further speech impossible, and I leaned against a column for stability. The air in the room was stifling, the stale aromas of packed bodies mingling with acrid wine fumes. The music turned discordant, the laughter raucous as the masque's players became more wild in their dancing and obscene in their gestures. A frizzed and powdered woman, her dress cut below her breasts, her breath sour with wine, stumbled into me and spilled her cup across my skirts. I stared down at the pale green silk soaked in Rhenish and had such a heart-heavy premonition of disaster that I could do nothing but stand, my hands helpless at my side, watching the stain obliterating the delicate flowers of my beautiful dress.

37

My Sweet Sister Anne,

Once more, Buckingham sails close to the winds of fate, for the City rumors now say he is in the pay of the Spanish, and the king has an investigation underway. Taking a hint from the Old queen, the newly minted Duke of Buckingham has taken to his sickbed, claiming mortal illness, which is bound to bring the addlepated king to his bedside. I also hear his plans for the invasion of Cadiz escalate, for what better way to prove loyalty than to attack an enemy? I so tire of these court behaviors, where the men who rule think only of their own affairs and not of those of the citizens of this land.

Tell me how my walled garden fares, and is John well? Please thank him for his gift of venison and fruit, for which we are most grateful. Please also pick me some of the mistletoe that grows in the woodland, for Katherine's fits are still frequent, and I should distil some cordial for her.

LA – Tower

1625

Outside the Tower walls, the plague returned to London. The death carts trundled daily with their human cargo, distorted bodies racked with more agony than any who suffered torture here. I put to use all my physicks from those days in Battersey where we had staved off the contagion, for if it breached the walls, we would be prisoners to death. I limited the traffic into the Tower from both river and road and kept the children within our house and gardens, where they could be protected.

This caused Peter especially much grievance, for he was at an age where lads need freedom to roam and discipline. The plague outbreak closed the Merchant Taylors' School, and he quickly became bored in the nursery with the younger children. Although there were many opportunities to practice his archery and to swordplay with the Yeoman trainers, he became increasingly surly, and I despaired of his influence on my younger boys. I surely loved him as one of my own, but it was a secret relief when Allen sent him from the plague to Wolverhampton at that other school of the Merchant Taylors.

Adding to my distress, the familiar sickness came upon me again. This time, I had a difficult confinement and a harsh labor. Allen feared for my life and called on Barbara and Edward, who dispatched immediately the best doctors from court to oversee the birth. I lived, but not without damage. I do not believe I will have more children, for my courses have not returned.

The little girl was born safely. Allen named her Barbara, in thankfulness, which was difficult for me, but not something I will let my child ever know. I suckled her myself, knowing that she would be my last. It brought me closer to my babe, though it made Luce mightily jealous. She is so forward for her years that she runs rings around the boys in their studies, and she soaks knowledge and erudition from their tutors in such quantities that I have to command her to play, for she would always be at her books otherwise. I trust Jocasta to distract Luce with the gentler pursuits of music and dance, for I am proud that my shy little foundling has blossomed into a beautiful young woman with many fair attributes.

After months of being within the walls, I trembled with such a restlessness to venture outside that I finally had to break free. When the plague retreated and Allen was on one of his interminable trips to Portsmouth—or Plymouth, I cared not—I left the Tower by barge and was rowed to Blackfriars, taking just Mary with me as an escort. The distance was short, but the world was different than the rarefied air of the Tower. Joyfully, I landed at the familiar steps and returned to the streets I loved. The gardens had grown since I had last stepped within, and as I passed under the arch where I had met Theo, I brushed my fingers on the flints, as if to touch the ghost of my past self who had sheltered in such heartbreak. My emotions had tempered, but I wondered, fleetingly, what would have happened if I had become his mistress and chosen a different course in life.

I made my way to the apothecary alley, where the same shops still stood, unchanged by the passage of time. Mary was used to my ways and left for her own errands as I stepped from shop to shop. Hesitant at first, I grew in confidence as the old men recognized me and made me welcome. I rediscovered the part of me suppressed for so long in the world of children and gaol.

After several hours, I came to the site of the friary house, which had collapsed with such a terrible life loss of the Catholics secretly praying there. The ruined house still stood, its upper chamber open now to the sky.

The area around had become quite disreputable, and it was no longer the fair grounds of the monastery that I had enjoyed the summer of my wedding. That era appeared tarnished now, for the local inhabitants displayed much poverty, and I heard voices in the streets that spoke terrible ill of the court and Buckingham, blaming him for all of their woes. I stopped for refreshment at the Star Inn, the cleanest and safest in the vicinity, and asked the landlord the latest news.

"It's all about the duke, ain't it?" He was abrupt in his speech, anger biting his words. "The king runs the country, the duke runs the king, and the devil runs the duke." He spat and thumped a tankard in front of me. "If his bloomin' 'ighness could've made 'im prince, he would've. Now 'es a duke, and there ain't no place higher for him to go."

"Is there nothing else that men talk about than the duke?"

"Nothing that matters. We're at 'is mercy, for 'e cares nothing of us, just wants more money till we're sucked dry. They don't care about us. They just want to play their pretty games and dances and spend our money on their court whores."

"We'll get the money when we burn Cadiz." An old man in the corner spoke up, and I turned quickly upon hearing that name again.

"What do you mean?"

"We're off to war, ain't we? We'll burn Cadiz, take the King of Spain's treasure ships, and be wealthy again." He lifted his tankard in a salute. "'Ere's to them that sailed under Queen Bess and Essex, for we was real men then, who 'ad a real majesty to serve under, not the devil's catamite."

"And when do you sail?" Allen's prolonged absences at the port cities suddenly made sense to me.

"This summer. Men are pressed from the coasts, and the ships are being victualled. It'll be a force which ain't been seen for twenty years." He drank the rest of his beer in one long draught and wiped his mouth. "I say it's time to show them Spanish bastards what good English men are made of and kick those filthy Catholics where it 'urts the most."

The landlord laughed. "If the devil sails with the duke, they'll all be saying their *Ave Marias*. It's the last chance 'e 'as to turn his reputation."

I was heartsick to hear how deep the duke's plans were rooted. If the word was on the streets of London, there was no turning back, for the populace took this cause to heart, and Allen foresaw the truth. I left quickly and hurried back through the mean streets, which no longer offered me the haven of years past. I met Mary at the Blackfriars steps, and she looked curiously at my face, for my fright must have shown.

We were sailing to war, and my husband was responsible for the welfare of the fleet.

I did not feel that the Tower would ever be as home to me, but as I returned from Blackfriars to the Queen's House and was safe behind the walls, I had a respite from the darkness in the streets and could think clearly again. I came home to a reassuring tranquility, where the children were, for once, all quite about their studies. My three boys were at the board with their Latin tutor, Luce was reading aloud from her Greek, and my baby was on Jocasta's lap, content with her doll.

I sat with them, glad to watch them preoccupied with childish things, to hear their sweet voices, and to suspend my thoughts from the gathering storms. How man could jeopardize this for the sake of plunder and pride, I could not fathom, but it was going to happen, and it was duty to protect my children and all I could from the violence of the world outside. At least Allen had given me the financial independence to secure the best tutors and guides for my children, and he also welcomed my family into our home.

In these months since Giles's escape, I had grown close to John and Anne as we cared for Katherine between the Tower and Lydiard, and it brought me great joy to have them in my life again. I reflected on Allen's merits and thought much upon his character, lodged in his early years as a soldier of fortune. He was defined by the court of Elizabeth, the Irish Wars, and the exploits of his comrades Raleigh and Essex. There was no changing his nature, and perhaps I should not try to. However, my uncertainty drove me to take on the management of our family and trust more in God's plan than I had ever before.

Resolved to spend my time where I could affect the future and my world, I let the night close in around me. In the solitude of my marriage, I found the doctrine of preordination illuminating the path forward for me through the darkness.

It was no surprise when the king died at his favorite palace of Theobolds, for I had seen the death shadow in his eyes when we were at White Hall. Determined to honor his father and inherit the full mantle of royalty on his shoulders, the new King Charles arranged with the duke for an extravagant funeral, although the plague still raged, and the country's coffers were weakened by years of dissolute extravagance and poor management. I could not imagine the sums that had been spent on the processions and mourning, but it must have been thousands of pounds, monies that could be ill afforded.

Worse, the king's death had no effect on slowing the plans for the Spanish war, and in fact, preparations were increased, for it was well known that Charles and the duke had been held back by the procrastinations of the peace-loving old king. Now, Allen was traveling from Portsmouth to Plymouth, Harwich, and to Ipswich, all across the southern ports as he provisioned the ships and men to invade Spain. At the end of each journey, he would return exhausted. I had little of him at the Tower, for he spent all his time in the Navy Yard, only returning nights to sleep and arising at three in the morning to be at his work again.

I missed him terribly, so one fine August morning I decided to take the boys over to the Yard to visit him. Peter had returned from his studies and would be able to help me with the younger ones, and as we readied ourselves, the children were giddy with excitement, for the Yard was a huge adventure for them.

Walking beyond the Tower walls gave me a sense of freedom, and I shared the boys' excitement, for I loved the Yard, and it still felt as home to me. As we strolled down the hill, the river lay before us, the wharf at St. Katherine's a forest of masts, more crowded than I had ever seen it, obscuring the south bank of the Thames. The boys shouted as they pointed at the great vessels, but a cloud had crossed the day's sun, for such intense activity only indicated to me the magnitude of the preparations that were taking place.

As we reached the brick wall surrounding the Yard, the throng of people thickened. There was much pushing and shoving as many merchants and their scribes and apprentices also approached the Yard. I held James and William closer to my skirts and protected their little faces from the roughness of the crowd while Boon and Peter pushed ahead of us and cleared a path.

As we approached the Navy House, the scene became quite frightening, for many of the men were angry and were shouting at the gate guards, demanding entry. Hemmed by the mob behind us, we had no option but to push forward, the strength of the men around us pushing us toward the steps, and we were helpless to walk on our own. As I struggled to keep the younger boys protected, Peter managed to attract a guard, who quickly knocked a couple of the crowd away with his staff and cleared a small space for us to fall into. Grabbing my arm while I held tightly to William and James, the guard pulled me up the steps and pushed me through the door into the Navy House, Peter and Boon behind me.

The contrasting quiet of the great hall plunged us into another world. The muffled shouts of the crowd could barely be heard through the thick walls. At the far end of the hall, Allen was standing with a group of men at a long table, a mass of papers spread across it, and he leaned over the documents with his back to us, deeply intent.

"'Zounds, man, if you have let one merchant in, we shall have the mob break down the doors. They will all be paid at some time, I just cannot tell them when. Damn it, keep that door closed."

I had never heard Allen shout an order with such passion, and as I took a step forward, holding the boys' hands, one of the men looked up in surprise.

"Sir Allen . . ."

"What, man, what? I am tallying. I do not have time to talk."

"Sir Allen, your wife . . ."

"What?" Allen swung around. "Jesu, Lucy, what brings you here?" His face turned white.

"I thought to bring the boys to see you. What is happening, Allen? What is going on outside?"

"Come. Leave the boys." He turned back to the men. "Continue checking in these provisions. Make a note of all stock. Issue the credit letters in my name and have them prepared for my signature within the hour. I want these merchants paid fairly, so ensure that my personal guarantee is given to all of them. Write to Bagg in Plymouth. Tell him additional credit is coming to him."

He placed his hands on the children's heads and pushed them gently toward the kitchens.

"There are new puppies in the kitchens needing some care. Go with your brothers and see if you can help. Do not go outside." His tone was stern. "You are in charge, Peter. I expect you to keep the boys with you at all times. Do not think that because you now carry a sword you will use it."

He took my arm, and we walked to the low dais at the end of the hall and sat upon a bench. The sunlight streamed in through the clerestories, and I noticed web lines of worry and weariness illuminated in his face.

"Allen, this is not good for you. This business has been your livelihood for so many years, but I see a great pressure on you now, and I worry about your welfare. You are not the young man you once were, and these are different times. Do you have to continue this? Can you not leave this to others? And why are the merchants so angry?"

He sat for a moment, his hands clasped between his knees, his face shadowed. He did not speak, but I knew he was listening.

"There is no need to drive yourself so hard. You could stop. We could leave this life and go to the country. My brother has offered Purley Manor to us to stay whenever we wish. You have enough capital

296

for us to leave this world of commerce, and you could enjoy the boys growing up and not have to live this way."

He remained silent.

"Purley is beautiful, Allen. The lawns reach down to the river, where you could fish with the boys. The air is healthy there, and it is so peaceful." I leaned forward and took his hands in mine. "Can you not stop, can you not leave this life now? I want you with me; I want you with the children."

"I share your desires, Lucy. I have a little business to finish here, and then, yes, we should consider Purley. I have a dream too, and to spend it with you would be my heart's content."

I was taken aback by the swiftness with which he agreed with me.

"You would leave all this, and London?"

"Yes, Lucy, I would. Now I must get back to work." He stood and held me, kissing me soft and long, with a tenderness that I had missed for many months. "I shall have a guard take you home. Leave by the kitchen and take the back gate through the monastery garden."

He summoned men before I could say more and turned from me, back to his table of papers and his group of officers. Gathering the boys from the puppies, but not before I allowed them to choose one to bring home with us, we returned to the Tower under an escort guard. My head was full of the new life ahead of us and the prospect of Purley Manor, its water gardens and sweet country air.

38

For the green sickness, especially effective in young women who have a weakness in their heads and shortness of breath.

Two ounces and a half of the conserve of red roses, one ounce of the conserve of scurvy-grass, eight drams of steel and sulphia, make this into an electuary with syrop of clove, July flowers. Take as much as a nutmeg morning and afternoon at 4 a clock for 20 days.

Lucy Apsley
Recipes from Purley
Summer 1626

Purley, where the willows kissed the river and dragonflies shimmered above hidden ponds. In the long dusky evenings, the boys called to each other as they returned with their fishing poles through the water meadows. Allen spoke of our dreams with John and arranged for us to spend the rest of the summer here, promising to join us when his business permitted. The amber light of this warm, waning summer embraced our family and brought us peace.

In a hired, richly canopied barge that rivaled the king's, we traveled the Thames to Purley in magnificent style, far from the plague-ridden city and the talk of war. Its location is perfect, for it sits by the main road from London to the West Country, and Allen made frequent stays on his journeys to Exeter and Plymouth. Each time he kissed me good-bye, he told me he loved me, and that this victualling for the Cadiz war would be his last. I feel he has fallen under the magic of the countryside and will at last end his obligations to Villiers.

John and Anne stayed with us on their way to Lydiard, and each night was full of laughter and joy as our musicians played till the moths appeared and the owls called across the meadows. Our meals were lavish, enriched by the fertile gardens of Purley, prepared by the cooks and served by the many staff that tend to us.

My children, who have known no other life other than behind the confines of the Tower walls, ran free and barefoot through the fields, and even Luce was persuaded to leave her books closed and make daisy chains with me in the pasture.

On the last Sunday of our stay, Anne and I sat in the garden, the fragrance of rosemary and lavender released by the warm September sun. Luce was sitting on the grass, holding a kingcup under Barbara's plump little chin to see if she liked butter. Anne's little girls sat quietly in the shade of the oak, playing with a kitten.

"Remember the rosemary wreath?" mused Anne.

"For your wedding? Of course I do. That was the first I met you. How long ago it seems."

"We weren't much older than our girls, Lucy. It is a joy to have our families together." Anne sighed and shifted slightly on the bench. I looked at her sympathetically.

"Is the baby kicking? You are carrying him high."

"Another boy, you think, Lucy? Five strong young men I have already. John is so proud of his family."

"And you too, I hope. You have borne him fine children."

She smiled, and a web of fine lines appeared around her eyes. "It has not always been easy."

"Mother, I have a friend for you to meet." Jocasta's voice interrupted our conversation.

I turned at her words, my attention caught by the young man at her side. He was of pleasant face, medium height, and possessed startling blue eyes with a sure and steady gaze.

"Who is this, Jocasta?"

"Lyster Blount, madam." He bowed as I stood up from the bench, his voice low and melodious. Anne looked at him with interest.

"From Mapledurham, across the river?" The Blounts were an old family in the area, their history intertwined with ours over several generations.

"The same." He grinned, his smile infectious. "I am Sir Richard's third son. It is my pleasure to make your acquaintance."

Jocasta beamed, her delight in our meeting obvious.

"And how did you and Jocasta meet?" I had not heard this young man's name before, but it did not surprise me. Jocasta was not a child to share her secrets easily, and now she was a young woman, her demeanor was even more challenging to read.

They looked at each other.

"We have been practicing our archery together and found a common love of the sport."

It would not have been hard for these young people to strike a friendship during the required exercise on Sundays. He seemed a mannered young man, and I did not think Allen would object to Jocasta's friendship. His father and grandfather had both held senior positions at the Tower, and Allen had always spoken with great respect of their work.

"Sup with us," I invited. "We are relaxed here in the country and dine outside in the garden. It is a fine evening. I hope you may stay."

"I would be honored," he replied and bowed again gravely. Jocasta's face lit up. As they walked together toward the house, I felt a double pang of happiness and loss.

"There's more to that than a friendship," observed Anne. "Your little cuckoo may leave her nest soon."

Our return to the Tower in October coincided with the fleet sailing for Cadiz, and a great weather change that brought squalls and gales. Ancient trees were uprooted in Smith Fields and many tiles lost from our roof, crashing to the cobbles below with a noise that resembled the very gates of hell being slammed.

As I lay sheltered in our canopied bed, the winds shrieking around our chimneys and buffeting the windows, I prayed for the mariners. Most were poor country men pressed to serve and had never left shore before. I remembered the day Anne and I left Portsmouth for Guernsey and pondered what a different city it must be now, all men fully employed, whether on board ship or provisioning from the land. There would be few vagrants sleeping in the streets at night.

The fleet had long delayed in sailing for want of money and men, and it caused Allen great worry as he continued to scrape together the provisioning for the ships. He rode relentlessly between White Hall and the ports, pushing himself hard as he received a flow of commands from the king and Buckingham, and in turn directed his victuallers in Portsmouth and Plymouth to prepare the vessels. Finally, the king and Buckingham left for Devon in September, already two months beyond a safe sailing date. When the duke sailed on the *Anne Royal*, Allen could do no more, for his work was complete, and he returned home.

There was a deep melancholy about him as he lay next to me in our marriage bed. I smelled on him a sharpness that belied an underlying anxiety such that I never witnessed before. The storm awoke him too, and in the darkness, I reached for his hand.

"All will be well, Allen. The duke has Cecil commanding; the fleet is in good hands."

"Cecil is a land man. He cannot command the seas."

"You have given them much knowledge."

"Court games, Lucy, in the safety of a palace. It is a different world on board a ship, beset by storms, fired on by the enemy, managing a crew that has no experience."

The wind gusted hard, and outside in the gardens, I heard the creaking of the sassafras trees as they were buffeted by the gales. I stroked his hand and laid my fingers on his brow to smooth the furrows from his forehead.

"You have done much to train them, Allen. And you could not have done more to provision."

"There was so little time, and yet the delays became our enemy."

I could hardly catch his words under the crash of the storm.

He sighed heavily. "The duke made the ships wait so long the meats could rot."

"There is no more you can do now, my love. The fleet will return, and Spanish treasure will fill the king's purse again. Your job will be done. Remember our time in Purley, for we will return when all this is over." I continued to murmur to him the stories of our summer there, and gradually his breathing became regular, and his hand relaxed as he fell asleep. Through the rest of the storm, I lay by him, my eyes wide in the darkness, the fear I took from him wrapped now around my heart.

At daybreak came a tremendous banging on our door that startled Allen out of bed, his usual hour of rising delayed by the first sleep he had in many nights. As he rushed downstairs, pulling on his robe, I anxiously followed him. He opened our door to a convoy of guards led by Auditor Gofton. I could not hear the exchange, but Allen shook his head and lifted his hands before dropping them at his sides and pushing past me to dress. The men stood in the entry hall, their faces impassive, and I left to tend the children, for my place was not with this official business.

Later, as I was wrapped in my cloak and in the garden, surveying the damage the winds had done, Allen approached. His step was weary and his head down.

"Allen, why did Auditor Gofton come so urgently?"

He paused and then turned and took my hands.

"He came for the Crown Jewels."

"I don't understand. They are well-guarded here. There is no place stronger in the land than the Tower to lodge them."

"It was not to guard them. It was to pawn them."

I stood in the devastation of the fallen trees, trying to understand his words.

"To pawn the Crown Jewels?"

"The Treasury is empty. This expedition has taken all the money. The duke has now commanded that the best of the jewels be taken to Holland for money to be raised against them."

"And the king?"

"King Charles does whatever the duke decrees. Our kingdom's jewels are being hawked among the Dutch moneylenders to sustain the fleet."

The devastating storms which swept over our isle blew our ships far off course. For many days, they struggled to reach Cadiz, scattered across the Narrow Sea until they lost sight of each other and their commanders. Masts broken, holds filled with water, and victuals rotted and decayed, the remnants of the glorious fleet straggled down the coast to Cadiz. Upon landing, the men were so starved of food and thirsty for water they thought of naught but sustenance. When they came across hundreds of barrels of good Spanish wine, they broke them open and drank to oblivion, the last scraps of discipline shattered in a drunken orgy.

All this Allen told me in a broken voice as he sat with me in the Queen's House, the daily dispatches reaffirming the disastrous news, accusations flying everywhere from blaming Cecil's inexperience to citing the gross incompetence of the victuallers.

"Great wrong has been done, Lucy, and I fear I am to blame for this. I should have done more to stop the duke. I should have been more realistic with him on the state of the ships, the disaster caused by the delays."

"You could not know this in advance. You could not see each day's delay and the effect it would have. The storms were not your doing. The state of the ships were not under your control. The pressed men were not yours to command. The lack of money was not your responsibility. You cannot take blame for other men's misdeeds, Allen."

I became angrier as I listed aloud all the ills that had caused this disaster.

"It seems to me that the blame should be laid at the duke's door, for without his insistence, this whole endeavor would never have happened. I despise what this wicked catamite has done, and I see why the country hates him so."

Allen put his hand on mine.

"Shhh, my love. We are sorely conflicted, but we cannot speak so. My Lord Buckingham has done much for our family to be grateful for. He is loved by the king, and it is my sworn duty to support all that the king commands, at whatever cost."

"He has brought nothing but corruption to those whom he has laid these favors upon. Look at Katherine, still vacant in mind and mourning her lost life and love. Look at Will and Eleanor, living as beggars in our home, all capital gone, and Will still dreaming of his adventuring days, which will never return. And Barbara, now a Lady of the Bedchamber to the queen, pushed into this post to guard away Catholics, her husband hiding in Ireland, her children mortgaged in marriage. Is this a life, Allen? Is this what you want for our children?"

I held his arm and turned him to me.

"Let us go now to Purley. Please, Allen, leave this behind and take our possessions, our money and children and retire to a life of peace and quiet, far from this corruption and foulness. We can leave now. Your job is done."

Allen looked at me, his hands trembling.

"Not quite, I'm afraid, Lucy. There is still more to do."

"There is nothing left, Allen. Enough of this. There is no more to do for this king, this duke, this miserable court. We must leave."

"We cannot. We have no money. I pledged my credit on behalf of the king to supply the ships on this expedition. Until he pays me back, we have no money. We have nothing but this house to live in, and this is at the king's pleasure, if none other pays more for the privilege."

I reeled as if slapped.

"No money? Nothing? You have nothing? You have pledged it all? What madness is this, Allen?"

"We all did, Lucy. We all gave our last capital, our credit, our pledges to support the king. He demanded it of us. He pawned his own jewels to finance this expedition. We could not desert him."

"He mortgaged the country and played commander in his palace while the men of this land went to war on rotten meat and stinking beer. And the duke? What of our noble duke? Tell me, Allen, how does our patron intend to help us now?"

"He has assured me that he will arrange for payment of my debts. It may take a little time, but he has a plan."

"And of what of us? What of your family that you have sacrificed to Buckingham's ambitions?" I was so angry that I forgot myself and could not hold my tongue. "Are you addled as well as blind? He cares not for you, nor us, nor anyone that he has given a favor to. He will be too busy saving his own skin. Remember Theo's words, Allen. He has no loyalty. The people want blood now. Parliament will demand a full accounting of this disaster. And you think he will remember us as he stands before England and fights for his life?"

I was so disturbed I could no longer stand to be in the same room as my husband. I left him alone in the chamber of the Queen's House with his tarnished memories of the great Elizabethan that he once was. His name was in tatters from the corruption and rot of this Stuart prince who had destroyed his character and ruined his finances.

I had no sympathy for his unswerving loyalty to the royal will, for I could see it resulted in nothing but dissolution and depravity from the king and his darling duke. And I cared not that I threw Theo's words in his face. Their absolute power brooked no consideration for the common citizens and defied God's will. Now only the divine right of King Charles and the Duke of Buckingham, Lord Admiral of the Fleet, decided the fate of the land.

Through that desperate winter, we were reminded of our dreadful circumstances in a hundred small ways, and it was only through the trickle of payments from the families of the prisoners that we were able to retrieve any income. This was our sole coin, pledges not being worth the paper they were written on. Each silver groat was carefully hoarded into a strong metal casket Allen kept locked in the stone chamber that had once imprisoned Thomas More and now kept secure our valuable possessions.

These coins were meager, for we had little in the way of affluent prisoners within our walls anymore, the Howards being gone now for more than a year and the Wizard Earl released soon thereafter. It was a poor bunch that now lived under our watch. Although my care for them wavered not, their families did not contribute to their keep as had our previous prisoners, and there was little to spare for our pains.

"I will need your allowance, Lucy."

Allen strode into the stillroom, where more and more frequently I spent my days, retreating into the comfort of my recipes and experiments. We had no income to cover additional costs of taking care of the Tower residents, and I was forever searching for ways to provide homegrown herbal curatives. My life was now divided into equal portions: children, prisoners, stillroom. There was no time for anything else.

"It has come to this, Allen? There are no other means than to deprive my relatives of our benefice, our prisoners of our care?"

305

"No. And it is not your place to question me."

He picked up and put down several of the pots that I had placed on the scrubbed bench, sniffing them.

"Is it even worth this effort? What do you gain by extending a man's life in this prison?"

"The knowledge that I have at least tried to ease pain, provide comfort."

"It would be time better spent with me, Lucy." Suddenly, his voice rose. "Your neglect of my needs at the expense of your experiments is not unnoticed." He swept a bowl from the table, and it crashed to the floor, spilling the precious contents.

"You bring your problems to my door, Allen, because you have no say in how your life is being controlled. It is not fair to accuse me of neglect when you are never here, always riding forth on some new emergency of the king's."

"You have no sense of what is happening outside these walls, do you?" He was white with anger, and yet I knew him well enough to see the fear that fueled it.

"I know enough that with one word you could end it today, and we could live at Purley with all of this behind us." I bent to the ground and started picking up the fragments of the shattered bowl.

"If I end it today, we will have nothing. Nothing. We will be destitute. Am I clear, Lucy?"

I froze, staring down on the flagstone floor, the spoiled herbs scattered within the cracks of the stones.

"God's truth, I wish I had stayed in Ireland. At least there I had only myself to care about, and a wife with a good portion of her own, and just two children to place in this world."

"I wish you had too, Allen." I shouted now, standing across the table from him, my hands full of the broken pottery, my fingers bleeding from where I had hastily grabbed the broken shards. "For God only knows I question why you thought I could bring you happiness when you refuse to heed my warnings. That day at Fonmon, you promised me you would not quench my spirit. But your ambitions have been misguided and your dreams have not included me. You have chosen material gain over love. And along the way, you have trampled my love."

39

. . . El Dorado lieth southerly in the land by the great salt lake, and in our canoes, we carried our provisions for many days as we searched for the route to the city . . .

Lucy Apsley
From my conversations with Walter Raleigh
Tower 1626

My summons to court from Barbara was completely unexpected, for I had not heard from her since her appointment to the Queen's Chamber. I knew her fair-weather friendship was that indeed, for in the storms of our financial despair, no help had been forthcoming. Her letter commanded me to meet her in the Stone Gallery, that long ago place where I had promenaded with her and Anne and met Theo. I knew she would have chosen that intentionally to remind me of the promise of the past.

The gallery itself had changed little except now there appeared more Italian paintings and tapestries until the stone walls were obscured with such ornamentation that it was impossible to see the structure beneath. Much like the court itself, I thought, where superficial trappings covered true motive. There were few people about this raw January afternoon, and I sat in an alcove and waited for Barbara.

"You look weary, Sister." Her voice cut through my musing. I looked up at her and remained sitting.

"It has been a difficult season."

"For all of us."

"You don't appear indisposed." Her gown was so thickly embroidered with gold thread that I thought it would probably stand by itself without her.

"Edward is gone to Ireland. I serve the queen. I have little choice."

"You chose your path long ago."

She tossed her head.

"Let me come to the point. We need money."

I laughed.

"And you come to me?"

"We need money. Me, Edward, George."

"Buckingham? He asks me?" I was surprised to hear he even remembered my existence. "What happened to his royal patronage? Or his noble friends?"

"The king can do little more this moment. The hatred for Buckingham seethes in the streets of London. 'Struth, Lucy, he dissolved Parliament to obstruct them from sitting in judgment upon his favorite and impeaching him for his crimes. How much more could a king prove his love for him?"

"Ah . . . divine right. Parliament answers to the king, and the king answers only to God. There is little thought for the rights of man."

"I did not command you here to discuss politics, Sister."

"Then what do you need? There must be something, for you would not call me to your side to inquire of my health." I wanted to get this encounter over, for nothing had changed between us.

"You have something of worth. He is determined to acquire it."

"I have nothing." The conversation was so absurd that I stood to leave.

"You have the map."

"What map?"

Barbara leaned closer to me, and I could see now fine lines through the paint on her face and a different light in her eyes. Her spirit was not so bold as her words made out.

"Raleigh's map." Her voice dropped to a whisper. "The one to the gold of El Dorado."

"I have no such map. I have nothing of Walter's except his recipes."

"George has been searching for this since Raleigh died. There is no other place it could be, for he would not have destroyed it. It must be somewhere with you in the Tower. Find it, and our problems will go away." She started to walk away. "The duke commands it."

"Just as he commands my husband to sacrifice his health and his family for his lost cause?"

"Hush." Barbara swirled back to me and clutched my arm. "Hush, for you know not who listens."

I looked around the empty gallery.

"There is no one here."

"There is always someone here." Her hand tightened, bruising me. "The duke has men everywhere. This is not safe. The court is no place for idle talk." Barbara glanced over toward the alcoves, and I could feel a trembling in the fingers that gripped me.

"Do not fail, Lucy. Or we will all fail with you."

As I was rowed back to the Tower in a hired wherry, bundled in a musty robe that had seen better days, it was ironic to recall what a short time ago we had been feted in a sumptuous barge on our way to Purley, musicians playing and the common folk gawking as we passed by. Now, distracted by Barbara's unsettling command, I paid little heed to my humbled surroundings except to dwell again on the precarious nature of wealth, for it treated all men with equal disdain, gripping duke and beggar equally in its bony fingers. I had seen real fear in Barbara. It was the invisible hand of poverty that constricted her throat and caused such deep anxiety.

I had heard from Allen that the duke had also been living on his credit, running monumental debts he was not held accountable for as the king's favorite, always bailed from a crisis by another monopoly granted. For Barbara to have revealed so clearly his desperation was disastrous for us.

Allen's preoccupation was with clearing accumulated paper work and sorting accounts, still assuming he would be paid his due. Now it appeared from Barbara's words that Buckingham himself was in such dire condition that he would not be caring much for other men's debts when his own estate was in such disarray. I thought over and over of Walter's last days in the Tower, as he talked with Northumberland and comforted his family. There was no occasion where he had shown a map or even spoken of El Dorado, such was his grief for his own son's death and his devastation in the failure of the voyage.

Bleakness settled into my soul as I watched the banks of the river slide by. The city presented a face of anonymity to me, so much so that in my present state of mind, I considered myself a prisoner being rowed to the Tower, with no other alternative but the life that lay before me. I was bound to Allen and the decisions he had made, and the welfare of my children depended on my abilities to navigate these unknown waters.

Tears came to my eyes as I thought of the dream I had of Luce, a star appearing in my hand, and Allen's words that she was determined for greatness. I resolved with every breath in my body to fight for the future that was hers. If I could not influence mine, I would not let the decisions of her parents divert the promise that divinity had drawn for her.

There was not time in the days after I returned to the Tower for me to search for Walter's map, for our reduced circumstance had resulted in the tutors being let go, and my boys were running wild. I eventually was able to find one Ben Tailor, who was a student himself at Lincoln's Inn. He was a patient and kind man, who did his best to beat an education into their resistant heads. I was despairing of Peter, whose London distractions had turned to dissolution. He chose to live with a crowd of other lads who had some means or credit from their fathers and spent it on swordplay and fashion rather than education and responsibility. He had turned from the sweet young boy to a man who knew little value of money. He visited infrequently except when he came to ask Allen's steward for his creditors to be satisfied.

It was all I could do to keep the younger boys focused on their own studies, for Peter appeared as a free spirit to them, always careless with a coin and full of laughter and stories of his adventures. These stories turned the heads of Boon and his brothers, and I dreaded Peter's visits, for his message was not healthy for my boys.

Jocasta had persuaded Allen to allow her to board with the Blounts in Mapledurham, where in their fine house she was tutored in music and instructed in dance, as befitting a young woman of her standing. Sir Richard and his lady were kind friends to us, and they treated Jocasta with love and care. I knew it would be happiest for her to be with them and close to Lyster when he was home from study.

In those bleak days, with Allen away at the ports, still dealing with his creditors and trying to unravel the disaster that had been Cadiz, I relied more and more upon Luce's company. As she was such a bright child with a lively mind, I encouraged Ben Tailor to continue his tutoring with her, allowing her to share lessons with Boon and James, soaking up all the knowledge she could. She was a funny little thing who had no joy in play, but always in her books, such pleasure did she take in her Latin and Greek.

When no meat purveyor within the liberty would supply us with credit any longer, and there was no food left in the buttery with which to feed the prisoners, I had to acquire coin with which to pay the merchants else we all starve. I knew that Allen used the prison that attached to our home as his strong room.

I summoned the steward to Allen's office, where I had set up my own desk amidst the dusty papers that Allen left behind.

"Master Jefferies, I wish to assess how much coin we have. Please open More's chamber."

"There is no need, my lady. I have a full accounting." He was a stout individual whose gross belly revealed a fondness for food and beer that he skimmed at the expense of both my purse and those of our prisoners, and he carried the keys on his belt in such an arrogant manner that I found him repugnant in his officiousness.

"I would see for myself your accounting." I had avoided him until now, for he was a most obnoxious man, and one that I knew Allen did despair of at times. His ways were not organized, but he held so much knowledge for so long, and he kept many creditors strung for such greater amounts than they would normally accept, that he had his own corrupt usefulness.

"It is not your place, my lady. The creditors answer to me in Sir Allen's absence."

I stood up and leaned across the desk, my voice dropping low so he had to strain to hear me.

"And I answer to the Duke of Buckingham. Open the chamber."

He gulped like a fat toad swallowing a fly. Shuffling through the jangling bundle of keys, he stumped to the corridor leading to the prison, his girth so wide that he filled the narrow passage.

I knew Allen would hear from him upon his return, but I no longer cared for consequences, so desperate were our circumstances, and I would fight that battle when it arose. As he opened the door and I stepped into the frigid chamber, a pale light illuminating the meager furnishings, despair fell upon me as if it seeped from the very walls.

"Hand me your keys. Wait outside."

My rank and the duke's name commanded obedience now, and he quickly untied them and handed his authority to me. As I weighed the heavy bunch of keys in my hand, I looked at the mess of papers, caskets, and chests that were heaped in this prison room as if to be hidden from sight, forgotten out of mind.

I picked up a paper from one of the piles and held it closer to the narrow slit window for clearer sight. It was a bill for supplies for Cadiz, and as I leafed through the documents, they revealed to be more demands, heaped upon each other, page after page outlining the preparation, cost, and disastrous outcome of the expedition.

The amounts were staggering, in the thousands, as I read one after another in the faint light. I touched the heap with trembling hands, for our financial ruin was revealed in all these piles. The debts were of such magnitude that no one man working day and night for the rest of his life could possibly redeem them.

I walked to the alcove and lay my cheek against the freezing stone, willing the sharp pain to break through my numbness, but no comfort came as I looked to the Green and the site of the scaffold. The spirits of the captive queens who had seen with their own condemned eyes a similar aspect stood at my shoulder and would not leave. Today the walls were dark gray and my trees were stripped bare, those that remained after the storm. The bleakness outside leached into my heart; More's despairing ghost crept into my soul. I stood for a while, perhaps waiting for a sign as I had witnessed in the past, but no rainbow appeared, no clouds cleared, no quiet whisper came hushed into my ear.

Gathering the documents back into heaps, I tried several keys in the casket before one opened and revealed a collection of coin. Taking a handful, I locked it again and wordlessly handed the keys back to the steward, who looked at me with contempt as he pulled the chamber door shut and waddled back toward his rooms. There was enough coin to feed us, but the papers would bury us.

Allen returned later that month, and as I greeted him at the door, I was struck by how old he appeared and a certain frailty that had crept across his being. He had lost the vigor of his bearing, and his stature, although still tall, was lean and spare. Before I could say anything, he took my hand.

"Edward is dead." The words hung between us as I struggled to understand the implications of his words. "Of the dysentery. In Youghal. He will be buried in Ireland. Barbara does not travel to be with him as he is laid to rest; there is no way for her to be there in time in this weather."

"What changes for—"

"Her? She'll need to settle his debts as well as hers. Don't fret for Barbara. She has no use for your pity. Edward's affairs were not in good order, but she has a lease for the house in Westminster, her position with the queen at court, her children betrothed to Howard's, her son inheriting the Grandison title. She has more than enough to work with." Allen's words were matter-of-fact.

"For us?" I continued. I did not need Allen to tell me that Barbara would survive.

"Little will change. Now that the duke is Lord High Admiral, he turns to me constantly for advice on how to bring his ruined navy into repair. He did not need his brother to act as intermediary and will not now."

"But satisfaction of our debts? Was Edward not helping you?" I could have screamed with frustration.

"It is each man for himself today, Lucy. Since the venture with Giles, Edward was never one to speak for others, fearing too much the spotlight. He had his own debts to manage. I hear his estate is close to bankrupt. I am pursuing my recompense with the duke, and he has promised a Star Chamber investigation before the year is out. Then I will have a chance to plead for the money to which I am due."

He left to go to the Yard, already on his way to his counting house again, and I stood alone, remembering the days at court when I first met Edward, Theo's friend fresh from the Continent, with his French manners and extravagant clothes. It seemed so long ago, and now that he was dead, it put a seal on that time for permanence, and I mourned the youth in all of us that had turned to clay.

Over the following weeks, my thoughts of Barbara returned again to her request for Walter's map to El Dorado, and now that I knew how close she stood to financial ruin—along with the rest of us—I could understand the urgency of her demand. I despaired that we should all be still haunted by the vision of a city of gold, and I dared not tell Eleanor or Will of my conversation with Barbara for fear that they would fall for yet another elusive, ruinous dream.

Will had established a regular trading business to the New World and, as part of the Virginia Charter granted him by the old king, was able to keep his family afloat with the profits of his cargoes. Eleanor did not need that disrupted with another failed expedition to El Dorado. But the thought of Walter's map would not leave me, and it niggled at my mind until I finally decided I should look for this document, for nothing else to see if it existed. Sharing it with Will and Allen would bring certain disaster, but if Buckingham desired it out of great desperation, this might be the salvation of our family.

40

The father of it is the sun, the mother the moon. The wind bore it in the womb. Its nurse is the earth, the mother of all perfection.

Its power is perfected. If it is turned into earth,

separate the earth from the fire, the subtle and thin from the crude and coarse prudently, with modesty and wisdom.

This ascends from the earth into the sky and again descends from the sky to the earth, and receives the power and efficacy of things above and of things below.

By this means you will acquire the glory of the whole world, and so you will drive away all shadows and blindness.

From my new transcript of Theatrum Capicum

on the Methodology of Alchemy

LA August 1626

Allen's appearance before the Star Chamber was upon us in the matter of the Cadiz expedition. It is a secret courtroom where no common man stands to judge the judges. Words pleaded and deeds confessed are captured behind locked doors, witnessed only by the ceiling's painted celestials that give the room its name. The highest court in the land, some say, but also the most dark and furtive.

I despaired of what might come from these proceedings, for it is commanded only by the king, and this king has made the Star Chamber his own. He has seized his father's jurisdiction of divine right and rules with it instead of government, of honest trial and jury, of the fair hearing that every Englishman is entitled to.

"How will you plead, my love? How will you tell the truth of all that Buckingham has brought about?"

"I have pledged my loyalty to the duke and to his master, the king. I have no choice in what I plead, for I stand for the truth."

"The truth?" I was incredulous. "Your version or Villiers's?"

"God's version, Lucy, for what lies in my heart is what I will reveal to the court."

"The king will defend Buckingham to the end, and so no blame will ever be found with him." My frustration was mounting with every word from Allen. Could he not see that he was the scapegoat?

"If the Star Chamber chooses to find it was my mishandling that ruined the fleet and lost the war, then so be it." He shrugged on his cloak and kissed my cheek in parting. This was the Allen that drove me to madness, for his Elizabethan beliefs led him not to question his own rights. There was no hope for changing his ways. If he was found guilty, he would surely be executed to satisfy the people's outrage. As I tried to busy myself with trivial tasks, my thoughts repeated themselves mercilessly. There is little time, there is so little time.

As Allen traveled each day to give his testimony before the peers of the realm at the Star Chamber, I frantically searched the Tower for any evidence of Walter's map. It was all I had left with which to bribe the duke to intervene and secure Allen's innocence.

There could be so few places that this document was concealed, for although Walter had the liberty, he had not ranged far, his frail health keeping him close to his bed. I thought back to that last summer, his affectionate debates with the Wizard Earl and Mr. Ruthven, his insistence on observing their experiments, his patience with my boys as they dug up his Virginia potatoes to see if they had grown, and retraced his last weeks with us.

I began in the Bloody Tower, which witnessed so much of his captivity and subsequently had been occupied by the Somersets, who modified the chamber and made it their own. He spent little time there after his last voyage, but I had to start somewhere, and since it currently entertained no occupants, it was as good a place as any. The furnishings long been dispersed, returning Frances's chamber to a prison. It did not take long to walk the perimeter of the cell, put my hand into the long-dead fireplace opening to search for a missing stone or hollowed out space, and check for any other loose bricks that could conceal a document. If there were any secrets in this room, it refused to reveal them. After a morning's work, I was satisfied that no hidden treasure map existed there.

I almost laughed at the absurdity of this thought, for I was transported back to the days at Fonmon, playing pirate with the boys, seeking treasure and capturing enemies. I was rueful how we had played a game that had transcended my fate. How innocently I had told the tales of the prisoner Elizabeth, the Tower, and the treasures of the New World. Now it had become my life story. The irony of my Calvinism doctrine of predestination did not escape me.

Allen spoke little of his days in that starry-ceilinged chamber, and each night, he spent many hours buried in papers in More's cell with our steward, preparing for the next day's interrogations. It was a torturous process, for Allen was not a man who favored clerking over action. His skill was in commanding men, in getting supplies to where they needed to be, in securing routes, in dealing with merchants, and in haggling on prices and persuading purveyors to part with their goods, all on his word and that of the king's.

That was his weakness too, for his convincing and unshakeable faith in the right of the king, the defense of the nation, and the power of the monarch and the peers was irrefutable. Although there were many that questioned and challenged his loyalty to this puppet king because of the influence of Buckingham and his corrupt ways, Allen's honesty and integrity persuaded men to throw their fate in with him.

The steward, who should have been keeping account of all that was negotiated, was too busy skimming his own share and lining his purse to manage the papers. Now it was the huge disorder that I had witnessed a few days ago. Allen was horrified at the extent of the neglect and yet was forced to depend on the steward for some understanding of the accounts. There was no choice but to try to bring to the king and the Chamber the real cost of the war, seek compensation, and maintain his innocence in the debacle that had been the expedition.

There was no point in seeking the map in More's cell, for the steward squatted all day there like a fat spider, mumbling to himself and shuffling the papers. Any document I was seeking would have long been discarded if it did not carry an accounting of beer or cider, bread or meat.

The only places remaining were the alchemy shed and my kitchens. On the morning of the third day of hearings, I sat at the stillroom's worn table, roughened by knife cuts and scrubbed clean, and thought of where else Walter may have been. Surrounded by bunches of dried herbs and lavender, the candle makings, and pots and bottles of my unguents and restoratives, it was good to sit and let the timelessness of this room wash over me. So often I had been here in such urgency, responding to an illness and seeking a curative if I knew it or a comfort if I did not. It had been a while since I had relaxed in the simplicity and taken solace in the organized and abundant medicinals that were around me.

And then it came to me. I could not believe I did not think of it sooner. I pulled Matthew L'Obel's notebooks from the shelf along with the bundles of recipes that Walter had written out for me and spread them all across the bench top. Here were his possets and notes on sassafras, his observations on other plants he had brought back from his voyages. As I turned over a page, his usual carefully sketched outlines of leaves and plant shapes were replaced by a map. I sat still, unable to believe that Barbara's story was true and that here was something of immense value that could change all of our fortunes. I traced the lines on the paper with my finger, words such as "Europa" jumping from the page, and the carefully drawn rivers, estuaries, islands, and coastline all labeled. Finally, the words "El Dorado" caught my eye, and with a shock, I put the paper down, final proof in front of me I had discovered the map Buckingham desired.

My next decision was whether to tell Barbara, and it took but a few minutes to dismiss this consideration. If, as Allen said, Edward had died leaving his estate in terrible disorder, she would not act rationally to share this information to help all of us, but would commandeer it for herself. There was no doubt in my mind that I needed to deliver this personally to the duke, and there was little time in which to do this. If I could talk to him, perhaps I would have a chance in directing Allen's fate at the Star Chamber before the peers decided that he was to blame for the failed expedition.

319

41

Sweet Anne,

Thank you for your kind delivery of the fruit from Lydiard. As I opened the basket, the aroma of the strawberries took me straight back to Castle Cornet and the gardens we planted, for in that fair air, the scents rivaled the costliest court perfumes. I wonder how our friends do, and if they are still on the island. I must confess there are many days that I wonder if I made the right decision to remain in England. But that secret liest between you and I, my sister.

With my love and longing to see you again,
Lucy

Allen had told me that Buckingham recently moved from White Hall to York House, which he spent a fortune remodeling. In this, he was encouraged by the king, for the style was that of the Italian fashion, and their shared love of the art and sculptures of that country had driven the architecture of the duke's new home. That would be where I would find him, I had no doubt, as he waited the outcome of the Star Chamber trials. He would be far enough from court not to be seen directing the proceedings, but close enough to be kept informed of every accusation raised and confession extracted.

"I have to replenish my supplies," I called to Eleanor as I swung my heavy traveling cloak around my shoulders and quickly let myself out.

"Take a guard—" Her words were cut off by the slam of the door. I did not seek her advice today. It took me no time to walk through Water Lane, the map secured tight in a purse under my cloak. As I approached the wharf, the usual Tower traffic was congesting the landing stage.

"Boatman," I called, and as he bumped up against the jetty, I climbed into the rocking wherry. "Take me to Blackfriars steps."

A Yeoman Guard on the wharf took a step forward.

"My lady, I would accompany—"

I waved him away.

"Make speed, boatman." We quickly pulled away and were soon caught up in the cluster of boats navigating the busy waterway. This was not official Tower business, and I did not want any tale of my whereabouts making its way back to Allen.

The tide was with me, and we swiftly negotiated the river traffic. As we approached Blackfriars, I commanded the wherryman to continue to the York water gate, and he did so without complaint, as I paid him another precious coin for his troubles. The marble edifice gleamed white, shining as a beacon from the dark riverside, flanked by the wooden ruins of the Savoy and the chaos of the White Hall landings. Its exquisite detailing, the lions guarding its entrances, the duke's arms above the center arch, enhanced its powerful allure.

It was not difficult to find my way into the house, for the gate led to paths through the gardens, all laid out in the Italian style. Many people were coming and going from the house, all on the duke's business, no doubt. There were a babel of different languages—Italian, French, and German, and some that I had never heard before—that were spoken by fair-haired giants, dressed all in wolf furs and leathers. It was a second royal court, for it rivaled any receiving rooms I had walked through at White Hall.

No one paid much attention to me, for the men were too busy conversing in business. What women were there did not give me a second glance, for I was not dressed in any finery, but wore my simple dark blue cloak covering my hair and clothing. I did not want to stand out. Thus, I was able to walk through the mansion until I reached the privy chamber. Guards stood before the doors, as immovable as statues, their pikes crossed and barring the way.

There approached from the outer chamber such a crowd of some fifty men and women, dressed conservatively in dark hues and working garments, speaking in a French dialect I found so familiar. As they drew nearer, I recognized them as Huguenots and took advantage of the press to join them. I blended easily, the doors were opened, and we walked through into the duke's privy chamber.

"Ah, my friends, welcome. It is my blessed honor to greet you and offer the hospitality of the English court to our Protestant allies from France." The duke's French was exquisite and his words warm.

"Please let us talk of your concerns," he continued.

I stayed at the back of the group and could not see much, for the crowd pressed tightly around me.

"Your Excellency, we are most honored to be received into your presence. We bring news from our friends in La Rochelle."

There was a striking familiarity about the voice of the speaker, and I struggled to place it for a moment.

"My family and I have witnessed firsthand the abominations of Richelieu's men and his outrages against our Huguenot community."

It was Monsieur Montrachet, my dear friend from Guernsey. I strained to hear his words.

". . . and now the perfidy of the French king threatens the safety of all good French citizens who desire to follow the Protestant faith. We crave your help, Your Excellency, for without the English intervention, our citizens in La Rochelle will be slaughtered and our cause lost forever."

There was a murmuring within the group that rose to a loud hum.

"God save us, and you too, my lord," cried a woman's voice from the front. "My babies have starved, and my parents were slaughtered on St. Bartholomew's Day. I beg you, salvation, I beg you . . ."

A babble arose around me, and much as I struggled to push my way toward the direction of Monsieur Montrachet's voice, my way was blocked.

A guard thumped his pike hard on the floor three times, and the crowd subsided into silence.

"My good people, I hear your words. I will pledge my assistance and the support of our generous king. I will muster our fleet and sail to the rescue of La Rochelle!"

"Thank you, Your Excellency, thank you." Monsieur Montrachet's voice rang clear, and the other Huguenots added their thanks to his.

"Now please avail yourself of our hospitality. I have ordered refreshments in the outer chamber for your pleasure."

There was a general shuffling, and the crowd turned and was escorted from the duke's presence. Torn, I turned to rejoin the group, wanting so much to reunite with my old friend. But a stronger need forced me to stay. I seized my opportunity to stand to one side, concealed by an ornate tapestry, as they departed without me.

The doors closed, and I was left with the duke, who stood with two of his counselors.

"It will be war, you know," he stated. "We cannot allow the French king to persecute these innocent people for their beliefs."

The men bowed their heads in agreement.

"Shall we draw up plans?" one asked.

"Yes." The duke was dismissive. It was that simple. War had been decided.

The men bowed again and departed, leaving me still in the shadows of the privy chamber. The duke stood by the window, alone, his beautiful profile sharply outlined against the bright light. I took a deep breath and stepped forward, and he whirled quickly and put his hand on his sword, a reflex against an assassin.

"My lord, I am Lucy Apsley, wife of Sir Allen Apsley, Lieutenant of the Tower and Victualler of the Navy." My words were swift before he could call his guards. "I have what you asked my sister Barbara to find."

I left the shelter of the tapestry and walked to him, conscious that I could not see him clearly, for he stood with the light behind him, and all I could do was proclaim my innocence in my openness. I held my hands wide to show that I was hiding nothing.

"What is it I have requested?" He remained still, his hand resting on his sword.

"A map."

He reached for me and drew me to the light, as if to examine me closely. His scent was evocative, and his clothing was exquisite; I had never seen such fine lacework or such delicate ornamentation. Again, I was struck by the very sensuality of his face. Under his intense scrutiny, the room around me narrowed to just his being as he held me.

"Raleigh's?"

I nodded and drew it from my purse, breaking his grip.

"You found it at the Tower?"

"Yes."

He took the sea-stained parchment and unfolded it carefully, his face expressionless except for a small movement of his cheeks as he drew breath.

"Thank you. You will be rewarded."

"Redeem our debts. Provide a warrant to support my husband's credit and proclaim his innocence. Issue a letter of credit to keep the wolves away."

He nodded.

"And what else, Lady Apsley? Surely there is more. What of Barbara? Does she not deserve compensation?"

I took a deep breath.

"Use this map wisely, my lord. And when you find the riches of El Dorado . . ."

"Yes?"

"When you find the riches, disperse a portion to Monsieur Montrachet and the refugees on Guernsey."

"No one else?"

"No."

"I will take care of my brother's wife, for the Villiers look after their own," he responded. "She did well in making you locate the map. I will see that she is richly rewarded."

"She made me do nothing. Give her what you think she deserves, Your Excellency." I dropped a formal curtsy and rose again. "I did this for Allen and for the people of La Rochelle."

He nodded, walked me to the door, opening it slightly and beckoning a guard to escort me from his chamber.

It was done. I would be happy if I never set foot in White Hall again, never heard of another scheme, never received another perquisite. Others would have kept a copy of the map or bargained for more. I could not wait to rid myself of the instrument that caused so much devastation in my family.

I had gambled it all. Now I prayed that the Duke of Buckingham would live to his side of the bargain.

A few days later, I was in the upper chamber with Luce, listening to her stumbling fingers play her harpsichord exercises, which she hated and delayed to the very last moment before her tutor arrived. I was attempting to read a discourse recently written by a Huguenot minister that I had picked up at one of the bookstalls at St. Paul's. My mind was distracted between Luce's clumsy playing and my thoughts of Allen at the Star Chamber. After reading the same sentence three times without it sinking into my dull brain, I put my reading to one side and watched from the window instead.

A fine sleet was falling, and the Tower appeared blurred in the flowing air, its walls blending with the lowering sky. The bare sassafras trees were bleak in the walled garden. I feared they were much stunted, for London clay was no fertile Virginia soil, and I despaired they would grow much more. Only those who had to be out on duty were visible on this miserable January afternoon, and mostly the enclosure was empty except for the Yeomen. With most of the jewels gone and our prisoners those who had spoken against the king rather than raise armies to challenge him, our guards were not tested much. The air was subdued, quiet, waiting.

Allen came into view as I watched through the murky glass, and from a distance, seeing him on horseback, I glimpsed the man who wooed me at Fonmon, for he rode with such grace that he appeared twenty years younger. Glancing up, he waved, his face impassive, but I sensed a change in him and flew from the room to greet him in the hall.

"You are returned early?" I dared not ask more. The next few moments would reveal our fate.

"It is done."

He held me close. "The duke has commanded the Privy Council to pay my debts. They are all to be cleared with warrants issued from the king."

"And your name? Your culpability?"

"We stay here. I continue as Surveyor of Marine Victuals. It was acknowledged that through the acts of God, the delays and storms caused the supplies to rot and the ships to be scattered. There was no way I could have provided enough to see this mission through. But there were many below me who did not do their duties and who did not supervise the quality or quantity of the provisions. In the future, I will change how our accounting tallies and ensure that more is done within the locales to ensure proper victualling." He brushed the melting sleet from his cloak and undid the clasp with stiffened fingers. I saw that his knuckles were swollen with the arthritis.

"In the future, Allen? How long will you continue?" It seemed always with good news there was a caveat that encumbered.

"It will take time for affairs to be straightened. Not all the money will be repaid at once, for the state is in poor shape. My most pressing debts will be paid immediately. The rest will come in time."

"How much, Allen? How much has the duke asked of the Council?"

"Five thousand pounds."

"That's a significant sum. Surely it will pay most of our creditors."

Allen shook his head.

"I had to pledge forty thousand pounds for Cadiz. But do not be concerned. We have the duke's word and the king's support now. The money will come."

I was sick to my heart again, for to hear such sums talked about as if they were my housekeeping budget truly sorrowed me, and I could not understand how such debts had been accumulated with no security but the word of my husband. He had pledged his own fortune many times over to supply the navy. Now his estate rested in the king's hands and not in ours.

42.

Anne,

I wish to meet you at Purley, for perhaps we can still establish our home there while Allen seeks compensation.

There is much suspicion against Barbara's brother-in-law and hatred surrounding him, for now the people accuse him of the old king's death, saying that the duke's mother, without the consent of the physicians, applied a salve to the king's wrist, after which he died. The new king will hear nothing against his hero and shuts himself away with his art and statues. Buckingham laughs in the face of the people, and I fear he is to pull my family into deeper disrepute, for all talk on the streets is of La Rochelle and war with France.

Your beloved sister,
Lucy Apsley
Tower 1627

In all, the duke had done more than just secure Allen's debts, for his intervention had also ratified Uncle Oliver's estate, who finally purchased Battersey, which had been so long in Joan's family. Barbara's position was also secured, and although Edward's debts were still tangled and in much disarray, she was given the house at Westminster. Since her children were all minors, this, along with a transfer of Edward's silver thread income to her, allowed her to continue living in comfort. Allen was right. She would always find a way to survive.

I waited to see what else would transpire and if the duke might be rumored to be financing another voyage to Guiana, but heard nothing, and so I concluded that he was keeping the map for a more judicious time. With the country in such severe financial straits, it would be foolish for the duke to raise the prospect of Raleigh's El Dorado again.

No man would back him, and many would wish him the same fate as Walter, such was the hatred in the streets for this man who controlled the king, and so controlled England.

I had bought our family some respite, but we were bound in a web of corruption and credit, for there appeared no way forward except more of the same. There were days I despaired that I had even brought the map to the duke, for his intervention had only delayed the calamity that surely awaited us. I was angry I was so helpless and could do little to manage the fate of my children except provide them with the education to think freely for themselves. Surely they would then perceive the corruption and wickedness that lurked within the royal circles and court where they might make their way in the world.

And now there came upon our country a time of change indeed, for the king, who was such a great lover of paintings and art and learning, established a court that worshipped enlightenment. The debaucheries of his father's court—the drunken masques, the whores and catamites—retreated into the dark corners of the kingdom, where their deeds were still practiced but in the cover of the private courts of the great nobility.

Instead, King Charles encouraged learning and great discourse, and he being a serious and chaste ruler, presided over a flowering of arts and buildings unheard of since the days of the old queen. On the broken backs of people such as Allen, who ruined their credit to sustain the monarchy, the king built his palaces and acquired fine arts with which to furnish them.

In his own divine right as monarch, he proclaimed himself as the father of his people, the protagonist of all culture and education, responsible for the spiritual well-being of his subjects. In his world, he was appointed by God to lead his people and was only answerable to God for his decisions and rulings. He acted accordingly, ruling directly without any Parliament, without any representation from the good citizens of the old shires of England.

I found myself at odds with many in my family, including John, for he was unwavering in his faith in the king. It was illogical that he should blindly accept that all laws should now stem from the king and his Star Chamber, and the men of England would have no voice in the governance of their own lives.

Worse still, Charles's French queen, Henrietta Maria, continued her popish practices within the palaces of England. Although the king proclaimed his loyalty to the Anglican Church, his love of the ceremonies and rituals, the clothing of the clergy in silken vestments, and even the use of incense in his sermons sounded like papacy to me. I suspected that the court was peopled by many who practiced these rituals and found favor with the king because of it.

I took some comfort in attending lectures and dissertations given by the Calvinists, whereby I was able to seek the intellectual company of those who were also appalled by the new papacy that was leeching into our country. On more than one occasion, I took Luce with me, for her bright mind should be exposed to all thoughts and not just those of her immediate family. If the country's fate would be governed by the corrupt Royalists, I would ensure that she be balanced and understand the importance of Parliament and the representation of the citizen's wishes.

43

My Esteemed Sir Allen,

I wish to thank you for your extraordinary forwardness to supply (even beyond your own abilities) the great wants of the ships. I would not press you to lend your help any further, but that His Majesty's present occasions urge it for relief of the poor mariners who have long served His Majesty without wages and are now in great misery for want of victuals. If you could find some good and present means to supply the ships in the downs with victuals, your care and help at this pinch will add much to the merit of your care of His Majesty's Service.

Geo. Villiers
Duke of Buckingham
April 1627

The duke, believing himself beyond all mortal man's harm now that the king had intervened and dismissed Parliament rather than hear his favorite's list of sins read aloud before the men of England, has taken the cause of the Huguenots public. The words I heard exchanged in his private chamber were now circulating the streets of London, written into pamphlets and illustrated into every sketch that circulated the alehouses, pinned to the boards on the street corners. There was no doubt in the minds of the people that the duke was taking them to war again, and this time against the French papists and Cardinal Richelieu, the symbol of corrupt Catholicism.

I had no strength left in my heart to question Allen as he made ready again to provision the fleet, for it was his unwavering belief that he could recoup some of his debts through the purchase and sale of victuals. Now that he had the king's warrant backing him, he was convinced he would not only supply the ships to ensure victory, he would recover his losses and restore his fortune.

On one of his infrequent returns to the Tower, we sat to dinner with John and Anne, who had been at their home in Hatfield Peverel and were staying with us now on their way to Lydiard, taking Katherine with them. Eleanor and Will also joined us, and it was as the old days in Blackfriars, when we celebrated around the table the joy of being together as a family.

"It is marvelous to see the changes His Majesty has wrought on the city. His influence is that of great taste and elegance. Mr. Jones has proven himself a much-talented architect." John had toured the new buildings at White Hall and returned full of enthusiasm for the renovations he now intended to make at Lydiard.

"He has certainly spent enough of the kingdom's money in doing so." It bothered me that all John could speak of was his amazement of the scale and design of the new buildings in the city. Destitute men lay dying on street corners, and hundreds of sailors had mutinied on Tower Hill for lack of wages, their prospects bleak, their families impoverished.

"It is his right. He is the king." John was quick to his defense, his statement all encompassing.

"It may be his right, but he does not need to exercise it."

"Why not? He is divinely appointed to rule over us. He is the father of our nation."

"If he is our father, than I would declare myself an orphan, for his abuses are greater than any I have seen a father inflict on a child or a master on his apprentice."

There was a shocked silence around the table.

"You say you would live without the king? What treasonous thoughts are in your mind, Lucy? Who has influenced you to speak so?" John was horrified to his provincial core, and I heard his country accent grow stronger in his distress. "Allen, manage your wife's tongue, for I fear she has grown too radical for our table."

"You call me radical when all I state is the obvious? There are men dying because our king would rather line his walls with Italian art than their stomachs with a hot meal. There are families homeless, turned out from their hovels for want of a penny, when he sleeps in palaces in rooms hidden so deep within that no taint of the real world will reach him. And you speak of the king as father to his people? Are we the children of this mortal man who would rather spend his subjects' monies on foreign wars than feed his own, who dismisses his Parliament like schoolboys rather than hear their voices speak the truth?"

"Enough, Lucy!" Allen's voice broke over mine, raised loud in anger and embarrassment. "You go too far. Your words are treasonous, and I will not have our king blasphemed so under my roof."

Anne, who was sitting next to me, reached for my hand under the table and squeezed it softly, her gesture reminding me of the times John and I had quarreled so violently when I lived at Lydiard.

"I am sure it is Lucy's soft heart that speaks so passionately," she said quietly. "I know that daily she prepares broths and bread for so many ill-served men who wait in lines at the entrance to the Tower. It is her concern for them which manifests itself in the words she speaks." She gave me the excuse to recover my words, as she had done so many times before. I sat for a moment, pulling my anger under control, managing my emotions into check again. The room was quiet, waiting. I took a sip of wine and swallowed my temper.

"I am sorry, John. Anne is right. I speak out of pity for the men I nurse daily and wish there was more I could do."

"Watch your words, Sister, for speaking thus outside of these walls could land you in great trouble, with or without the duke's protection." John turned to Allen. "And speaking of whom, what is next with you, Brother?"

"I leave for Portsmouth at the week's end."

I looked across at Allen, for I had not heard of his latest travels. There was little he told me now, for he knew that I did not care to hear of his next scheme for raising money through selling provisions.

"The fleet sails for La Rochelle?" John asked.

"Yes. The duke leads as Admiral of the Fleet. We will support the Huguenots in their besieged island and take on the might of France and the papacy of Richelieu. It will be a seminal moment for the Protestants in France, for they will rise to support us and restore freedom of worship back to the people of France. Our Puritans here will thank the duke, and his true character will be revealed to those who have ever questioned his motives."

"You say the duke will win this time?"

"We have provisions, men, and are organized to withstand both a voyage and a battle. And our friends in France will supply us with our needs when we arrive."

"We?" John heard the same as I, and we said the word together.

"I sail too. I will not let my men down again, and I need to be with them to ensure their safety and good health." Allen looked at me. "Perhaps now you will see that the king looks for the well-being of his people, and not just his own comfort. The duke and I sail together for La Rochelle, for freedom and for tolerance of religious practice."

"So you sail for the king and all he believes in?" I was bitter with disgust that my husband should embrace the practices of this mortal who believed himself God.

"I sail at the duke's command. And the duke sails to free La Rochelle, to open the seas to the English ships, and to bring liberty to those oppressed by the papists."

"It seems there are many reasons for declaring war, and not all are common. You confuse me, sir, with your speeches of democracy, and yet you sail under a tyrant monarch who dissolved Parliament and takes away the freedom of men's speeches."

My family remained silent as Allen and I faced each other across the table, our tension at a height.

"The tyrant is the false accusations and the lies that are put out by the king's enemies, Lucy. We fight on the same side, you and I, just under a different banner." Allen reached his hand across the table and smiled at me, his eyes crinkling at the corners, his love shining. "Come, my Puritan firebrand, hold your talk of tyrants and leave the fighting to the men."

44

November 1.

From my sick and senseless bed aboard the **Nonsuch,** *moored at*
Plymouth.

My beloved Lucy, I love you most faithfully and affectionately and
write to you in haste that you not be concerned, but I request your aid. We
are ruined, and my soul melts with tears to think that a state should send
so many men and no provision at all for them, but for my provision through
merchants they had been miserably starved long since. We have no drink
and bread for five thousand seamen and four thousand land men, and four
thousand more have died for want of sustenance and their wounds. We
have lost all our commanders, amongst the rest Sir Alexander Brett and
Sir Charles Rich. There are no billets left in all of Devon, and so we sail
for Portsmouth, where I hope you will send men to bring me home, for I
am not well.

Never was a husband more bound than the love I have for you.

Allen.

The letter arrived in the early morning without warning, stained,
crumpled, and carried by a navy man who showed such love and loyalty
to Allen that he forwent traveling home to his own family in order to
first bring news to me.

I was shocked to the core at these heartbreaking lines with a simple
plea to return home. In between the sorrow he expressed for his men
and the failure of the war, Allen's words spoke of his own condition,
and for the first time since I knew him, I heard a mortal fear.

I thanked the messenger and ensured that he was well fed and
clothed, for he was starving and ragged, before calling for Eleanor. I

held the letter out to her wordlessly, and after reading the brief lines, she looked up with tears in her eyes.

"I have never heard Allen sound so desperate, Lucy."

"In body and spirit. I am leaving for Portsmouth now."

"You go to fetch him?"

"Help me think, Eleanor. He cannot be left on board the *Nonsuch* for any time; there is no aid for him there, and the conditions on shore will be deteriorating hourly."

"Take him to Purley." Eleanor was decisive. "I shall dispatch a messenger to John now and have him send the coach from Lydiard to Portsmouth to collect Allen. He should pack it with supplies, blankets, and such medicines Anne has at Lydiard. When you have Allen ashore, take him to Purley—not here. There is too much pestilence in London, and if he is as weak as he writes, he does not need to be further endangered."

As Eleanor sent instructions to John, I ran to the stillroom and gathered all the medicines I thought I could use, packing all my precious restoratives into a padded leather pouch that would keep the bottles and packets safe. By the time I returned to the chamber, Eleanor had summoned a troop of eight Yeomen who would serve as my escort to Portsmouth. She also insisted to the steward that he open More's cell and dip into our precious reserve of coin for my journey.

Within the hour, I had pulled all of Allen's warmest clothes and supervised them packed onto the pony to be advanced to Purley. For me, my woolen cloaks and several layers of clothing, for the November weather was turning bitter. I did not need more; we would travel fastest with no baggage. If we set out now, we could be in Cobham by nightfall, where we could shelter at the White Lion, a coach house I had heard Allen speak of as being a safe place to stay on the road to Portsmouth.

"Pray for me, Eleanor, and for Allen." I hugged her closely and smoothed her sweet face. "Look after my children until we return. Be safe yourself, and do not leave the Liberty of the Tower." Uplifted by a surge of great will, my own humors awoke again after so many months of waiting and inactivity. I felt light and eager to be on the road.

Eleanor smiled. "Go, Lucy, go to your husband. If anyone can bring him home safely, you can."

By the time we reached Wandsworth, a crush of travelers clogged the road, and if it wasn't for the Yeomen, we would have struggled to make any pace at all. They cleared a path in front of me, sending people scuttling to the verges, and we were able to maintain a decent speed. Most of the traffic was drays heading to the coast as well, loaded with provisions so those men who were being landed in Portsmouth had food and ale on their arrival. These slow trundling carts took most of the road, and we had to be adroit in our horsemanship to maneuver around them while maintaining our speed. They also became mired in the November mud. Then baggage needed to be removed and stacked on the side of the path to lighten the load while the horses struggled and pulled the cart free, all of which increased the hazards of our journey.

At Kingston, the drizzle turned freezing, and a fog hung over the river. Our descent to the town pitched perilous, for it was hard to see the road ahead. As we slowed our horses, there emerged a most hideous sight which made me fear we had reached the gates of hell. A band of men stumbled along the road, their clothes in tatters, some even naked-chested in this unforgiving weather. Their hair was unbound and hung to their shoulders, and their faces were covered in sores. Worse, several had wounds clearly turned poisonous, with filthy blood and pus-stained bandages doing little to protect them. As the Yeomen closed around me and formed a tight guard, I turned in my saddle and lifted my hand to halt our small cavalcade.

"We have to help these men!" I had not seen such devastating injury and neglect in all the times we had fed the sailors upon Tower Hill.

"There is no helping them, Lady Apsley." The captain's voice was grim. "Where you see ten men now, there are a thousand behind them on this road. You cannot stop to aid them; you would be overwhelmed within minutes."

As he spoke, more ghastly figures appeared in the same ruinous state. My heart wrenched with despair at these poor, neglected sailors.

"If we stop now, we lose precious time in reaching Sir Allen." He gave a shout and forced us forward, not allowing me the chance to even protest. "We must keep going."

Thus, our journey entered a stage which I hope to never see again in my life, for such was the devastation of these men that they could hardly be called human. Such despair, such deprivation was in their starved faces and near-naked bodies that the price of this war and the cost of defeat was the ruin of so many lives. We drove onward, the tears running down my cheeks and mingling with the November sleet. By the time we reached Cobham, I had lost count of the numbers we passed who were silently walking to London, a ghastly procession of wrecked mariners, the flotsam of this wicked war. Allen's words swam before me, and I understood the helplessness of his position, for there was no food, no clothes, nothing to sustain these men, on ship or shore.

The next few days, our descent into hell continued, for the closer we approached to Portsmouth, the more congested the road became. Even the Yeomen could not clear a path through the southbound drays and the hideous foot traffic heading for London. All I could do was keep my eyes fixed between my horse's ears on just a few yards ahead of me and pray that I would arrive safely in Portsmouth and find Allen.

I didn't even recognize Portsmouth as the same city that Anne and I departed from for Guernsey. England had been fighting no foreign war, and the port was closed—no navy, no pressed men, no commerce for the city. All that was left then were a few stragglers that hoped to be put into service, and I recalled my distress at the handful of vagrants that were sleeping outside. Now there were bands of men—some angry, some desolate—on every corner. The atmosphere was of complete lawlessness, unpredictability blanketing every movement.

As we made our way to the quay, the tragedy that was the remnants of the navy filled the harbor. Broken-masted ships with tattered sails crowded the water. The stench of illness and death, despair and rotting food hung as a miasma over the harbor, mingling with the dank November air.

The waterfront was chaos, for between the raucous bands of common sailors, there hurried liveried companies of men and lines of coaches of others who shared the same idea as me, to bring masters and loved ones safely to shore. We exercised the advantage of the Yeomens' uniforms and so were able to clear a space. The captain and four men remained with me; the others went to search for John's coach and commission a wherry for Allen from the *Nonsuch*. In the forest of masts, it was impossible to recognize the individual ships, and I left this to the experienced soldiers while I waited impatiently on shore.

There was much argument and discourse around me, most of which was angry speech blaming the duke for this latest disaster. If these men organized in any way, there would be a serious uprising. We had witnessed just last summer five hundred sailors mutinying on Tower Hill. Although their protest had been quickly put down, it would not take much to assemble a more organized rebellion, and the fury and resentment that was being expressed in Portsmouth was surely repeated in ports all across England.

"There's my brother's carriage—the one with the falcon crest—there," I shouted to the captain, making my voice heard above the crowds.

"Here, man, here." The captain wheeled his horse in a tight circle and cleared a space in front of me, beckoning furiously.

The driver whipped those who would not move out of his way. The horses, straining to pull the coach as if escaping from the very mouth of hell, ignored those under their hooves and parted a path.

"Captain, we have him!"

From the quay, a shout rose above the rest, and several of my guard pushed to meet their comrades, one of whom had Allen slumped in his arms across the front of his saddle. In a few short paces, they pulled him from the horse and bundled him into the carriage.

I dismounted with no help from anyone, grabbed my precious saddlebags of medicines, and pushed my way through the noxious crowd, wrenching the carriage door open and falling inside.

With a command from the guards and escorted by the Yeoman, we pulled away. I crouched on the floor of the vehicle as the angry mob outside banged on the sides in an attempt to hold us back. The Yeoman drew their swords and slashed at their own kind, sailors who had done no wrong except to lose a war. I held my unconscious husband in my arms, shielding him from the jolting and shaking that threatened our very lives as we retreated from the harbor and rode hard for Purley.

Someone had thought to fill the carriage with blankets and provisions, and I did the best I could to pull the mantles around Allen as he lay half across the narrow seat and the floor of the coach. He was a dead weight. I had not the strength to lift him but stuffed blankets around him to cushion the worst of the impacts from the ruts and holes in the track. He still wore his leather jacket and great traveling cloak, but both were soaked with seawater. I needed to remove them quickly since he was shivering and shaking in his unconsciousness. Worse, he had no shoes, and to me, the sight of his poor naked feet, cut and bleeding, symbolized the devastation he had been through. God knows what could have happened that caused him to reach this state.

The carriage slowed to a halt, and the captain opened the door.

"How fares he, my lady?"

"Poorly, most poorly." I looked up from the floor of the carriage where I was cradling him. "Help me right him and get these clothes from him before we travel on. And I must get some medicine in him."

The captain called another guard. As I scrambled out of the carriage and stood in the rain on the side of the track, they went to work, stripping Allen of his sopping clothes, wrapping him in the blankets, and lifting him onto the seat. One man stayed inside the coach, holding Allen steady in his arms, and as I climbed back in, he smiled encouragingly at me.

"We got him, my lady. We got him."

I smiled back. "Yes, we did."

But I could say no more, for the horror of his condition choked the words in my throat. All I could do was concentrate on dripping medicine into his sore-encrusted mouth and dabbing a flannel soaked in vinegar across his forehead. We rode for Purley and did not stop for the rest of the day and all through the black November night except to feed the men and horses.

45.

An excellent Syrup for a consumption. Elacampaney rootes, 2 handfuls, boyle it in water till it be tender. Cutt it like small pieces, then boyle it again in hott water a quarter of an hour. Take coltsfoot, liverwort, agrimony, hartshorne each 2 handfuls, maidenshare one hysope a quarter handful. China rootes shredde an ounce, licorish sliced 2 ounces, annis seed and sweet fennel seed each a spoonful. Raisins a handful, 15 junipers, 8 dates, 5 figgs sliced. French barley a spoonful. Boyle this in 2 quarts of running water til more than half be consumed. Strain it and put to it a pound and a half of madera sugar almost to a syrup, then put in the elecampane and boyle it up.

Purley

LA

October 1627

The days following our arrival ran into each other until I knew not which was day or night. My place was by Allen's bed, my hourglass his breathing, my timekeeping marked by the minutes he stirred or fell into a deeper unconsciousness. There were times when he ceased breathing, only to draw a deep breath again after heart-stopping moments of silence. I refused to leave his side, although the housekeeper at Purley was a good woman who sat with me and offered to watch Allen so I could rest. I sat in a chair and left only to relieve myself and my bones, willing Allen to survive.

His fever peaked several times, to the point where he was soaked in sweat and mumbled and cried out so piteously that I knew he was reliving the nightmares of the battles. All I could do was wipe his face and hands and change his linens and pray that my medicines would sustain him. Every recipe, every method, every balm I had learned now all culminated in this moment in my life, where I now was fighting a war to keep him alive, bringing my knowledge to the fore of all that I had experienced over the years.

Eleanor had also written to Uncle Oliver, and he immediately dispatched doctors from London, and three of them arrived the same afternoon, just days after us. They stood and consulted together and with me. I have to say that I did have respect for them, for although they practiced many of the old methods, they did not want to bleed Allen and were satisfied that my medicines would help restore him. Day seeped into night and into day again. Only the guttering of the candles and the dim light behind the window hangings defined the hours for me.

Storms came and went, lashing the windows of the old house, the bare branches of the wisteria vines finger-tapping on the windows, the fire hissing from the raindrops. Christmas was celebrated by the servants, but for me, all days were the same, and although I read my devotionals and prayed daily, I had no cause to be festive.

After a while, Anne, rode from Lydiard and joined me in my vigil, with that same sweet demeanor that had brought me comfort for so many years. She helped me pass the days, for she was the only one I would trust to sit by Allen in my absence.

God must have been watching over us, for it was not Allen's fate to depart this life so soon, and gradually his fevers abated and his troubled mind calmed, and a peace descended on our chamber. The morning he opened his eyes and they were clear and focused and he smiled weakly at me was the morning I gave thanks instead of implorations, for I knew he would now survive and that his life was saved.

Eleanor's most recent letter included news of the children and their latest accomplishments along with Peter's most recent troubling episode of fighting. She also included verses that had been pasted all over the city, with her warning that it was still not a good time to be seen as the duke's follower.

Three things have lost our honor, men surmise—thy treachery, neglect, and cowardice.

I placed the verses down, the final line ringing in my head. The country had turned against the duke and all he represented in a way that left no doubt as to how people felt about him. He was hated, vilified, and despised across the land, and the final blow had been this terrible loss in Isle de Ré. And yet still Charles stood by him, was enraptured by him, did not call Parliament for counsel, but was content to rule with the duke at his side and the Star Chamber at his back.

During the past week, Allen had begun speaking of his experience, and his broken words brought the despair and disarray into our quiet room with devastating clarity.

"The duke required Bagg and me to witness his will," he whispered one morning, his voice hoarse with exertion. "Aboard the *Nonsuch*, the night before we sailed. We had come to him to express again our concern that we had no money, no credit, no means to supply the ships. The expedition was doomed before it set out. Even Bagg, in all his obsequious ways, wriggling before him as a dog to master, could not drive home our point."

He paused for breath, sweat beading again on his lined forehead. I tried to calm him, but he needed to speak.

"He called us his honest merchants and said that he would rather the two of us than a Privy Council full of politicians, for we would always find the way to support him rather than tear him down. He pushed his will toward us for signature, and we did so, among the heaps of credits and warrants. And then he bade us drink with him to celebrate the success of the voyage to Ré."

Allen quietened, and I thought for a moment he had dropped back to sleep before he opened his eyes again, the greatest sorrow in them.

"On his desk, there was a paper from Rubens, authorized by the king. It was for paintings, sculptures, artifacts that he collected just the previous month in Italy. Over twenty thousand pounds the king had spent on art for his own personal collection while my men starved. There is something wrong with this Lucy, something terribly wrong."

He stirred, trying to sit upright, his distress palpable.

"Bring me paper, pen. I must write to the king and the Council. Perhaps a word from someone who has lived through this will sway their thoughts."

"Allen, please, you must rest. There is nothing you can do from your sickbed."

I tried to protest, but my words only caused him to push himself up and summon a clerk.

"I must do something. I must stop this madness."

I stayed by his bedside as he dictated the words. It was then that the full impact of the lost war came to light.

His first, to Nicholas, Buckingham's secretary.

"Sir, I am so weak as not to be able to leave my bed, nor am I well enough to stand, and my physicians advise me to avoid any business. I will, however, make out an account of the money received from the duke, and provisions made by him, for which there must be a Privy Seal or Great Seal. The king his Majesty owes the duke much that should be repaid, and upon doing so my earnest hope is that the duke shall remember those who have extended themselves. In my absence my deputies continue my business, and I remain, sir,

The duke's loyal servant
Allen Apsley

His second, to the Privy Council.

Good sirs, I have disbursed in His Majesty's service near 100,000 pounds for which I have pawned lands and engaged myself and my friends beyond all that our common resources could bear. The order that has been given me to satisfy 20,000 pounds is most welcome, but it hath so many ifs in the order that no part can be enforced and no funds can be claimed. I pray that this could be revised into clear terms and that interest be allowed on the same sum. Likewise, I pray you clear the title of Newington Manor, which the king hath granteth me, but which another challenges ownership. My Lord Treasurer, I beg you use me with respect and not suffer me to be ruined by doing His Majesty's service.

Allen Apsley, Kt.

And there it was. Our life laid out on a parchment, all the paltry, miserable lines, our ruin inked across the page. Would the duke even read this, or would he dismiss his honest merchant as just a nuisance now? He had no need of him to provision another unpopular war, and his own credit could be more pleasurably spent with Peter Paul Rubens and Inigo Jones than in the victualling yard.

There was, of course, no response. I did not expect it, and nor really did I want it, for surely there would only be more broken promises, more useless warrants. We were sinking in a sea of credit, and no man would trust Allen further, for his reputation was ruined. Only the duke could unlock the treasury and send money Allen's way, and it was not forthcoming.

By February, as his health gradually improved, Allen insisted that we return to the Tower, for only by working his way forward could he see any light shed on the repayment by the king. The continued provisioning and resuming the feeding and clothing of the Tower prisoners were his old reliable sources of income.

John came to Purley before we left, and my brother asked that he speak with me privately. We walked outside, the sunken garden bare in the cold morning light, the fish ponds frozen with a film of ice that the herons had not yet broken.

"There have been many times that you and I have disagreed, Sister," he started carefully. "But I hope that this stay at Purley has given you time to reflect and that you will give Allen the support he needs to go forward in these difficult circumstances."

Already his words began to stir anger in me. I wished that Anne had accompanied him, for she would always keep the peace between us. But she was pregnant again and stayed quietly at Lydiard.

"I have always supported Allen. It is the duke and the king I despise."

"The king's divine right to rule is unquestionable, Lucy. All things come from him, and he is anointed by God to rule his people."

"Without Parliament, without representation, John?" Our talk was quickly turning political, as it always did. "You are a Member of Parliament. When were you last asked to bring your voice before the king to speak on behalf of your constituents?"

He was quiet for a moment.

"What's important is that Allen recovers his health and rebuilds his estate. It is just a matter of time that the Treasury will make good on its warrants, and Allen will be repaid all that is owed."

"At the last reckoning, John, it was more than forty thousand pounds. You believe that he will receive this in gold pieces this year, so he can retrieve his lands, pay back his friends, support his wife and children?"

"It is the nature of the business he chose to be in." John's words were harsh. "I have not pledged any money to him, nor will I."

"Thank you. I am indebted to you enough for sending your coach. I hope that didn't cause you to pledge too much. I wouldn't have asked for help if he hadn't been deserted by the duke, who rode to London to save his own skin the moment the ships put into port."

"Do not challenge the duke, Lucy. He is a powerful man, and one that has done much for this family. Do not bring his wrath on us by careless words. Look at how your sister Barbara has managed in her widowhood to maintain her position at court. Look at how she has brought the Earl of Suffolk to our family through the betrothal of her children to his. Seems she succeeded where you did not."

"Barbara bargained with Theo for a match with her children for a greater cause than ours." I was sick of how John always compared me unfavorably with her. "Theo had more at stake than she and was willing to pledge a child or two to free his sister from the Tower."

"And now he stands godfather to the duke's newborn. There are many political alliances to be gained if you had but the patience to see them through to conclusion."

"Theo would make an alliance with the devil if he felt it would benefit him. I would rather die than sell my soul to the duke." My words were out before I knew them. "He is nothing but a corrupt and wicked catamite, and all around him, including the king, are under his evil influence."

John bowed and strode away, his back registering anger and disapproval at my outburst. I sighed with frustration, for it was obvious that our two viewpoints would never be reconciled.

46

Place rosemary under your pillow to help you to remember your dreams and to keep away nightmares and other unwanted nighttime visitations.

Rosemary can be carried or worn by the bride to symbolize love and loyalty.

If a bride and groom plant a rosemary bush together on their wedding day, they can divine the family's fortune.

A gift of rosemary is a token of fidelity.

Recipes from the Tower garden
Lucy Apsley
June 1628

Boon and Lucy were overjoyed to see their father again when we returned to the Tower, for although Eleanor had done much to keep them occupied, they were in dread that he would not survive. I could see she was shocked at how weak he was, for upon our arrival, he went straight to his bed in the upper chamber. It was a subdued homecoming despite the excitement of the children.

"You must understand that your father has been gravely ill, and it will be some time before he recovers." I spoke with them quietly. "The physicians feared greatly for his life and despaired of his health."

"But you made him well again, Mother?" Luce's little face was pinched with concern, for she favored her father above all others in our family.

"Not just I, sweeting. Your uncles sent many fine doctors to help in his recovery, but we have a long road ahead of us to keep him growing stronger."

"I will help. Teach me the medicines that will bring him his health."

"That I will do, Luce, for you are old enough now to aid me in caring for your father and for the prisoners here. You can begin by reading the medicinal recipes that I have collected since I was your age and start understanding their efficacy."

She smiled. She was always a child that cared not for play but was more joyfully engaged in learning and study, and the thought of helping her father through reading the medicinal books was one that appealed to her greatly.

"I shall continue to protect him from the creditors that harass us." Boon placed his hand on the small dagger that I had noticed he had taken to wearing on his belt in my absence.

"What do you mean?" I asked sharply. "Who has been harassing you?"

"They arrive daily," he said nonchalantly. "I see them off, for I tell them that they betray the king by demanding of my father their measly bills."

"Allen, who has been here? What have you said to them?"

His posturing dropped at my tone and use of his given name.

"Merchants, provisioners, clerks, secretaries. They all come demanding their payment. At first, I was uncertain, but if I called on the name of the duke and King Charles to stand behind us, they went away." My young boy had grown into a man while I was gone. "They took my word and agreed to defer their demands. I believe the king will make good his promises. If Father believes that he will pay us back, then I trust in his judgment."

There now came upon us a time of gentle recovery, for as Boon had witnessed, the duke's word still had some significance in the backing of the debts. The king issued new warrants to supply the navy and victual the fleet in between his frequent visits to his horse races at Newmarket and expanding his art collection at White Hall, which I heard now rivaled those in any Italian palace. The warrants were still not coin, but they bought us time, for even the most demanding of merchants still had to accept credit drawn against the king's word.

Gradually, as spring moved to summer, Allen's health strengthened. Through my and Luce's ministrations, he was able to remove from his bed to sit in his office and receive the constant stream of traffic that required his attention. As the weeks passed, he appeared to slowly recover both his health and his spirits, although a troubling cough that first appeared during those early days in Purley never quite left him.

I was not there when the messenger arrived from Lydiard, but the moment I walked into the chamber with Allen's physick, my heart started pounding. He was motionless in his chair, hands in his lap, a paper discarded on the floor beside him. He did not turn when I entered, but continued staring out of the window.

"Allen, Allen, what ails you?" I knelt by his side and grasped his hands. "Why do you cry, what are these tears for?"

He turned to me with great effort and folded me in his arms, holding me tightly against his chest.

"My darling, I want you to be brave." He drew a great breath, and still I was bound by the strength of his arms around me. "Our dear Anne has passed away. In childbirth, three days ago."

"No!" It could not be true. It *must* not be true. "You are mistaken. She was healthy. She has never had trouble delivering." Sobs racked me, and I started shaking and could not stop. "Who says . . . what could have happened?"

"The news is from John." Allen held me slightly away from him so I could read the truth in his eyes. "She is gone, Lucy."

I sat stunned, beset by pictures of Anne, laughing in our room at Lydiard, walking the Stone Gallery at White Hall, standing by my side on the ship to Guernsey, always defending me to John. No more. No more would I see her sweet face, feel her kiss on my cheek, her hand in mine. No more would her laugh soothe me, her words comfort me. Once we declared a mother's love for each other. Now all I had left was an orphan's grief. My mother, my sister, my best friend had left me. God's grace would accompany her, for surely she would not suffer where she had gone. I should take comfort in God's choosing her to be with Him, but all I could feel was anger that He should steal her from me.

Lyster Blount had declared his intentions to Allen while my husband was convalescing at Purley, and it was with our blessing that Jocasta and he married in the Chapel of St. Peter within the Tower. Lyster's father and grandfather had also been Lieutenants of the Tower, and so the citizens of the Liberty made a special occasion of the joining of our families. I tried for everyone's sake to share the joy of the young couple, but my heart mourned Anne. The wedding was a poignant reminder of hers and mine, and our promises to each other.

We held the wedding party at the Queen's House, and as I sat in the gardens under the leafy sassafras trees, a peace stole upon me. I would always miss Anne, but perhaps my grief was mellowing to acceptance, and I knew she would want me to carry on with my life. I watched my children play with their cousins in the late summer twilight, idly listening to Allen and Will as they sat together, tankards in hand. I smiled to see them, for both still loved their soldier's ale above any French wine.

"I tell you, Allen, you know not the value of what you have in hand." Will's voice was excited, his Welsh lilt more pronounced. "I took Giles's portion of the Virginia Charter to keep it in the family rather than let it be sold to an outsider. It was the best decision I've made in years."

"The duke always thought more would come of the company than just a trade route," replied Allen. "Do you really think the New World has a possibility for habitation?"

"More than just habitation, Allen. There are rumors now that great resources exist on those shores, if we are just willing to make the effort to seek them."

"Are you going to explore these lands?" Allen's voice sounded almost wistful, and I paid close attention. I did not need to hear that he was off on another voyage underwritten by the Duke of Buckingham.

"Aye, as soon as we have the funding for the *Adventure*. That's my newest ship, Allen, and I am almost completely underwritten. I propose a trade route from here to the New England shore could be established in weeks, and within the year, I will be running ten ships each way. The duke is eager to see the proof of this plan, and then he will venture for the New World with the backing of the king. It is our way forward, Allen, our salvation."

It was the old Will, a dream in his pocket, weaving his visions for us all to share. I stood up and moved toward them.

"No commitment from us yet, Will." I rested my fingers in Allen's gray hair, still thick and curling, soft under my caress. "We do not have the means to underwrite our portion."

"You could be second to the scheme and still earn much." Will leaned forward, and I could see the excitement at this new scheme returning vigor to Allen's guise.

Allen looked up at me and caught my hand, kissing the inside of my wrist.

"Second is what I shall be, Will. By the time you return, I will have settled our debts and be in a position to join your venture."

The golden evening slowly faded into dusk as the lanterns were lit and cast a glow upon all of us. The stone walls of the Tower flared orange from the torchlight. As the stars appeared, the city around us settled as evening came upon us. Even the lions in the menagerie were quiet tonight, the soft air perhaps lulling them to dream. It was past the children's bedtime, but I was so happy to see them at play that I had not the heart to send them inside.

Our musicians struck up a pavane, and Will held out his hand, inviting me to join him. I smiled, recalling our days of old, and accepted. As we danced under the stars, Allen and Eleanor watching and laughing, the old magic sparked in me. I was wrapped in Will's arms and felt young again, my sorrow lifted.

"You look beautiful, Lucy. The years have been kind to you." Will's words were soft under the musician's strumming. "It has been long since we danced together."

I leaned back to regard him.

"You sound very sentimental, Will. That is not a humor I would say you are familiar with."

"I am conscious of the years passing, Lucy." A shadow crossed his face, and he shook his head slightly. "Call it fancy, but I feel my age. And the spirits surround me."

He glanced up at the Bloody Tower.

"I miss Walter. And all the other men I sailed with and fought with."

"You came home, Will, where many didn't. Or those who did suffered another fate."

I kissed his cheek softly and brushed his hair from his eyes, noticing that his temples were gray.

"And you saved lives as well as lost them. You saved mine. If it was not for your strength, Will, I would have run away three times over. You gave me the courage to face myself, to face my fears and to live."

"No regrets, Lucy?" He held my face between is hands. I smiled and looked across at Allen.

"No regrets."

Suddenly, the bells of the church at St. Katherine's tolled, followed by those of Barking, and then taken up by various belfries across the Liberty and into the City. We stopped still, uncertain as to what news would herald the bell ringers to sound a celebration peal.

A messenger threw open the garden gate. He stood before us, breathless with haste.

"What is it, man? Quick, out with it!" Allen lifted his hand, commanding silence from our group.

"The duke. The duke has been murdered. He is dead at Portsmouth of an assassin's blade."

We were stunned into silence. Around us, the bells pealed on, celebrating the death of the man who had commanded the love of two kings and the hatred of the people. Close crowded the ghosts of those he had sent to the Tower, some who had escaped death, others who had not. I fancied I saw Walter nodding his head, Frances Howard and Robert Carr applauding. So many lives lost, so many fortunes ruined.

"What does this mean?" I whispered my concern, the bells of the city churches drowning my voice, shouting from the streets drifting over the walls. Someone had started a bonfire on the green, and other blazes lit the skies over in Smith's Fields. "Where do we go from here? Are we free to live our own lives?"

"Great change is upon us and the nation. I cannot foretell what this will mean for the king. But for us, we are as a ship that has lost wind, rudder, and anchor. We are free from the duke's enemies, but we go into unchartered waters, Lucy, for I know not what safe harbor will welcome us."

Allen broke into a spate of helpless coughing, and it was a while before he could speak, a kerchief held to his mouth to stifle the spasms.

47

Eleanor, Allen has not risen from his bed in three weeks, his sickness returned since we heard the news of the duke. My heart is heavy and my soul is troubled, for the days are dark and our future is concealed. I know not who will protect us. Can Uncle Oliver spare you to return to us from Battersey? I must act before all is lost. I think I must return to the court.

In haste,

Lucy

The Tower

January 1629

I stood across from Barbara's house in Westminster, watching the fashionable ladies of the court accompanied by their maids as they strolled to and from the palace. Some even had dark ethnickes carrying their purses. The courtiers' dress and style was extravagant, silks and gold thread, which would never in my time have been seen in the day, glistening in the afternoon sun.

I concealed myself within the dusky shadow of the palace wall and smoothed my damp palms on my skirts, my awareness heightened as I searched anxiously for Barbara, for Allen knew not that I left the Tower. It took longer than I planned to ride through the crowded streets, for the tide was running against me, and the river inaccessible. I needed to return before dark, for his pride would be sorely wounded and his temper raised if he knew of my errand.

At last, Barbara came into sight, and I watched unseen from my hiding place as she walked with her servants. Her green silk gown, trimmed in the latest fashion with just a hint of lace, was cut low across her breasts. A piccadilly the size of a millstone surrounded her neck, and her elegant sleeves were slashed to reveal burgundy velvet. Her hair was ornately dressed with diamond clasps, and her face as beautiful as ever, age lending voluptuousness.

My fingers, roughened by the ministrations in the kitchens and stillroom, and my dress, although of fine cloth from remnants left by the prisoners, appeared poverty-stricken. As she drew near, I took a deep breath and stepped into her path.

"Barbara, I must speak to you."

She stopped and drew back as if bitten.

"Who . . . what . . . ?" She turned to a maid as if questioning who dared to intrude on her and then back to me. "'Struth, Lucy? What has happened to you? You look dreadful."

She swiftly appraised me from head to toe, her eyes flickering back and forth as she took in the details of my worn, made-over clothes, my reddened hands, and outdated bonnet.

"Come. We cannot stand in the street like domestics." She turned, and I followed in her wake.

Once inside her fashionable house, she took me to her parlor, filled with fine walnut furniture and many paintings, delicate Venetian glass, the walls decorated with embroidered hangings. It reminded me of the duke's apartments, for the same quality of artwork was apparent, and a similar extravagance in the fabrics and tapestry was evident. I was out of sorts and awkward in the warm clutter, my eye long accustomed to the stark stone of the ancient Tower and its barren cells.

I had heard that she negotiated an annuity on her gold thread perquisite, and certainly the quality of the appointments rivaled those of our wealthiest prisoners in their Tower apartments. I drew a deep breath.

"I come to ask for your help." I had practiced a speech before I arrived, but the carefully prepared words flew from my mind, and all that remained was a pleading. "I would not trouble you, but I have nowhere else to turn. You have the king's ear, you serve the queen. Perhaps you can intervene on our behalf."

"And why me, Lucy? It seems that lately you have had little tolerance for the king and our court, preferring your Calvinist sermons and Puritan congregations. What has changed your mind now to bring you to Westminster? Are you that desperate?"

My pride almost propelled me from the room. I had no option but to continue, for to leave now would slam the final door on my situation.

"When I found the map—"

"You found the map?" Her voice cut through mine, sharp as a dagger. "You did not tell me this."

"I thought it best to deliver it to the duke directly."

"You little idiot." She spat the words. "You put it in his hands? For what reason? How could you believe him capable of organizing an expedition to El Dorado? Look at the disasters that have been La Rochelle and Cadiz." She turned angrily and paced in her cluttered parlor, walking rapidly and in high humor. "When did you give it to him?"

"Last summer. Before he and Allen sailed for La Rochelle."

"And what did he say he would do?"

"Back our warrants. And the house in Westminster was put in your name. Oliver became Lord Grandison."

"Hush. I know well enough what favors have come our way. I've worked hard enough for them, and God knows I've sacrificed more than most. And I also know what opportunities were denied us." She stopped, momentarily distracted before continuing her rant. "But the map . . . who has the map now that the duke is dead? Give me the copy."

"I made no copy."

"'Od's blood, you have no idea how much you have lost us."

She walked to me and stood very close. I could see faint lines in her forehead, a slight wrinkling of her neck, but still she was so very beautiful and charismatic.

I stood my ground. "Oh, but I do. I know exactly how much I have lost you."

She raised her hand as if to strike me.

"Get out of here. Be gone. Go back to the Tower, Lucy, to your pathetic world of victuals and bills, tradesmen and merchants, and I hope you drown in those debts. Go back to your French lecturers in Blackfriars and your old Calvinist husband and your grubbing in soil and pounding of medicinals. You have no right here at court, you are a novice at these schemes, and you have no idea of the value of what you gave away to the duke. You sicken me."

"Your words no longer have power over me, Barbara. And I care nothing for your intrigues. You will never know the happiness of an honorable life."

I turned to the door, stumbling as it opened upon me, and fell behind it as a tall man walked over the threshold.

"My darling, I am so sorry I'm late. Elizabeth insisted we hear the children at their music, and the time was interminable." Theo bowed and kissed Barbara's hand before clasping her waist and kissing her mouth. "I have pined for you since I left this morning and could wait only to be in your arms again. Tell me you missed me also."

As I stood in the shadow of the door, unnoticed by him, Barbara looked over his shoulder at me triumphantly.

"I miss you each time you leave, my love, and I long for your return with each breath I take." She smiled alluringly, drawing his face to hers, and kissed him deeply back.

"You filthy betrayer." The words burst from me before I could stop them, preventing me from running, pinning me to the present.

Theo whipped round, his face startled.

"Lucy? You should have announced yourself. Why are you hiding?"

I stepped forward, propelled by my heart that was hammering furiously inside my breast.

"Why are you here, my Lord Suffolk?" I could say his title disparagingly, for he was no longer Theo to me, but just another foolish gallant. Beneath the anger, I felt as calm as a deep pool, carrying a lifetime of words said to myself but never aloud.

"Why do you embrace my sister so, when all know that you have a wife at home?"

"A wife who does not appreciate him, a woman he has no love for." Barbara's hand was on his sleeve, intimately holding his arm, keeping him by her. "You should leave now, Lucy. This does not concern you." She turned her back on me, dismissing me as she always had.

"But it does." She stood still at my words, refusing to acknowledge me but listening intently.

"Why did he marry Lady Hume, Barbara? Why did he agree to take a wife not yet twelve years of age, a girl presented for his convenience?"

"Leave, Lucy, now." Her words were low, vibrating with anger, but still she kept her back to me.

"I tell you why, Barbara. Because you tricked him. Because you said I would be his mistress. Because you told him that he could still have me. Didn't you? Your plan was to sell me to him, to gain the connection to court you craved."

"That is old gossip. You have no proof." She turned slowly, her face white with anger, almost ugly.

"I need no proof. One look at your life of sin and anyone can see your hands on so much wickedness. You are no better than a procuress, Barbara, and if it is not me you are selling, it's your own children."

"Madam, you accuse your sister, and yet no word on my decision in this?" Theo's fine features had blurred over time. A slackness now softened his jaw; his eyes were bloodshot. "Come, let us kiss and make up, for my part I would have both sisters be allies."

"Your part? Yes. A part is what you played. From the first time we met, Theo, you were playing a part."

He swayed a little, as if confused by my words. "Hold on, Lucy, we were young and amusing ourselves at love—"

"I was not playing. I have never played. And I thank God that I remained true to my soul, for I see in front of me the depraved result of portraying your courtly love."

"Madam, I deserve an apology. A forfeit by way of a . . ." Theo pressed closely to me and made as if to kiss my lips. I could smell his fine cologne, and under it the sourness of wine seeping from his very pores. I shoved him away.

"Theo, you have what you deserved all along. You have Barbara. My sister. My enemy."

"And hasn't she done well for herself." He waved his hands around the room, his gesture overly dramatic in the way of most drunks. "Why, Barbara even lends me money now, when I am hunted by my creditors."

"So not only are you a cheat, you are a procurer too, Theo? What's next, a bankrupt?"

He drew himself up proudly, and I caught a shadow of the old Theo, a watery echo of the youthful courtier I had thought my destiny. But it was just a ghost, an apparition from my youth.

"You defame Barbara and insult me."

"I think not, for you have no honor to insult, and she has no reputation to defame. You both deserve each other, and that is the greatest gift I can give you."

He stood silently, his eyes not meeting mine as he struggled to understand my words. "Once, I told you my heart was torn in two, Lucy. I thought I might find it again here, with your sister, one who is close to you."

Barbara joined him, her hand possessively drawing him away from me. "And so you have, my love, so you have. I will always fill your heart."

Theo brushed her hand away and took a step toward me. "Titania."

"You are a pitiful excuse for a man. And I don't have a sister."

I hurried from the room, slamming the door on them. Only when I reached the street did the trembling begin, and yet I walked steadily and with a purpose away from Westminster, burning the final bridge behind me.

"You have been gone a long time, Lucy." Allen's voice greeted me as I stepped into the house. I halted, for I did not expect to see him seated at the window downstairs.

"I have been looking for you," he continued. "Where have you been?"

"Out, at the apothecary's. Are you feeling better? I am happy to see you out of the chamber."

"Where else did you go, Lucy?" He stood and looked out of the window, his gaze following the movements of the Yeomen outside on the green. I crossed the room to stand by his side and look out at the now-familiar outlines against the darkening sky. *Bell, Beauchamp, Devereaux, Martin, Broad Arrow, Salt, Wakefield, and the Bloody Tower . . .*

"Barbara's."

Allen continued to look from the window, his silence commanding me to speak.

"I had to, Allen. The duke is dead. If anyone can find a way to survive, Barbara can."

"And did you find that way? Is Barbara's way your way?"

I turned to Allen, hearing the different tone in his voice.

"You know?"

"Of course."

Still, he would not look at me.

"And so is that your path forward?" I could hear something more in his voice now. I was suddenly back in the dunes at Fonmon, his unexpected proposal, the vulnerability with which he delivered it. "Is Theo and the court your destiny again? He would leave Barbara for you, there is no doubt."

There was now silence in the room, broken only by the marching footsteps of the guards outside our window, the gravel pathways crunching from the ceaseless patrols. It was a sound that had become part of my life at the Tower, and I noticed it again for the first time in years.

"Theo never was my fate, Allen." I reached up and brushed my fingers across his cheek. A memory stirred again of the first time I did so, at Fonmon. "You saved me from retreating to that course a long time ago."

"And even in these dark times, where the path I have taken you has led only to failure?"

I could not stand to hear the break in his voice, the sorrow that lay underneath the shattered pride.

"I am not sure which is worse, Lucy. I may have saved your virtue and restored your reputation by marrying you, but I have not delivered you an easy life."

"You have always done what you have thought best, and more than that no man could do."

At those words, he finally turned, his face reflecting the burden of his fears and sadness.

I stroked his hair, which I loved so much.

"There have been times when I have not been kind, Allen, or I have let slip words in anger that should not have been said. But I tell

360

you as I stand here, I would not exchange one day of my life with you for all the rewards of a life at court. You have brought me such joy in my children, my life, my independence. All you promised me you gave me, Allen." Tears were making it hard to see him, his face blurring as my heart broke at his grief.

"Never was a man more bound to a woman than I to you, Lucy." He took my hand and kissed the palm softly. "You have saved my life many times, by nursing me to health and restoring my mind to peace. Forgive me for all I have done to bring you sorrow, for you are the most virtuous woman and loving mother that any man could wish for."

We stood for a long time at the window, arms around each other. The Tower walls faded into the darkness, the guards' voices became distant as they locked the gates for the night. We were in our own world, together, a world we had created and would always have.

48

Eleanor,

You missed such a sight while away at Battersey, for the duke's funeral procession to Westminster, conducted by torches at night, was surrounded by Yeoman guards that Allen mustered. He says the coffin was empty, so in fear was the king that his beloved's remains would be desecrated by the mob. Now it is each man for himself, and we all sail under a retrograde star. The assassin, Honest Jack Felton, is hailed as a hero, such is the hatred for the slain duke. Is Will back from his voyage to Africa? I know that Allen is eager to hear more, although I am not sure of his intent. I long to see you, and I hope you will come soon to the Tower.

Lucy
The Tower,
November 1628

"Lucy, we must speak, for I can no longer hide this from you."

Eleanor took my hand and led me to a window seat in the upstairs chamber of the Queen's House. There was little furniture remaining, for we had sold most of it to raise money these past months to keep the creditors from our door. The room, which had witnessed so much over the years, was now stripped of its riches, and appeared much the same as one of the cells in the Beauchamp Tower. Indeed, what was the difference? For we were as prisoners now, our future ransomed to the debts of the king.

"What is it, Eleanor?" I sat on the hard bench, leaning back against the ornately carved oak paneling. I wondered idly if there was any worth to stripping the panels from the walls and selling those.

"Will and Allen have a plan to pay off their debts." She hesitated. "I thought you should know."

"And that is a bad thing?" I was too weary to react to Eleanor's worried tone.

"They are acting on the clauses of the charter."

"What charter?" I did not have any sense of what Eleanor was talking about. "What is Will planning now? Is he not content with his fool's search for gold in the African continent?"

"The Charter of New England, Lucy. The charter King James granted to Allen and to Giles."

"And to fifty other men along with the duke. It's worthless, Eleanor. There is no benefit to that piece of parchment. And now that the duke is gone, the charter is in the hands of many different men who squabble like fishwives over the meager profits."

Eleanor shook her head.

"You are wrong, Lucy. The charter is becoming of interest to many men now. Will moved swiftly to act as successor to Giles and take his share when he was attainted. Now his portion is equal to Allen's, and they talk daily of the new trade routes that are established."

"Trade routes? Will is trading in the Africa Company. What is he planning to sell to New England? There is no commerce or market for his goods there."

Eleanor looked at me, tears brimming from her eyes.

"There is a cargo such as none have seen before, Lucy. These routes from Africa to the Americas are transporting slaves." She gave a shuddering sob. "Allen and Will are being asked to activate their portion of the charter to join those who trade in men."

I felt the bile rise in my throat, sickened that this new venture should even be considered by our husbands.

"It cannot be true, Eleanor. You must be mistaken."

Eleanor was now crying, her tears flowing freely.

"It is. Will told me last evening he and Allen have raised the funding for the first voyage to sail in March, as soon as the winter storms cease."

"This is madness. There must be a solution. We cannot be in such straits our survival is dependent on another man's captivity." My shock turned to anger. "There is no difference between those slaves and the prisoners we keep here. Except that those men are transported beyond their shores to a land they can never return from. We must not let it go forward."

Later, on my knees in my lonely chamber, I prayed for understanding and guidance for a way forward. This latest news challenged all that I believed in. Although I knew God had a plan for all men, regardless of their nativity or station, I could not condone that snatching men's freedoms without sentence was acceptable. This was my crisis of faith, and one that I wrestled alone, for Will and Allen appeared to have no such compunction, such was their desperation.

Once more, I had to swallow my pride and ask for help where I least wanted to go. This time, there was no question that I would visit Barbara and plead for her intervention. There was nothing left between us but the ashes of our youth. She would no more receive me than I would go to her, and I would not go to her before hell froze over.

No, this time it was to Battersey I returned, to seek Oliver's counsel. I hoped his judgment would be as clear as when he ruled the Irish Parliament, but I secretly doubted. Joan still managed him, and I could hear her views on my plight influencing his clarity of thought, as it always did when it came to family matters.

My voyage along the Thames was a codicil to my past, the boatmen speedily rowing upriver with the fast-flowing incoming tide. Past the Blackfriars steps, where the steeple of St. Anne's peeked above the monastery walls. Past the duke's water gate—now daubed with paint where the apprentices had vented their anger by vandalizing his property. And past the palaces of White Hall and Westminster, the usual commerce crowding the piers and wharfs, the privy steps marked by ornate barges tied to their mooring posts.

Life moved on around and in front of me at the palace steps. "*Do you not know me?*" I wanted to shout at those people who came and went with such importance, such an air of self-satisfaction.

I walked where you do now. Here sits one who thought as you, who considered herself invincible, whose family climbed to the heights before falling to the depths. Once we feted Raleigh and his tales of gold. Now we trade in men's souls.

The river swelled swiftly with the incoming tide, seagulls screeching as the mudflats filled with salt water. Here were the marshes which froze that winter, and there was the village of Chelsea, that I had watched that long ago day when the Old queen died and the bells rang loud.

Too soon we were at the Battersey steps, and the manor lay before me in all its vulgarity. Joan had spent Oliver's Irish wealth, and the new house stuck out as a sore thumb from the land that surrounded it. The church remained, but Vicar Ridley had long since passed, and his Spanish wife had returned to Castile.

Although I sent a messenger ahead of me, there was no greeting upon my arrival. I entered the wintery grounds accompanied by just the watchman, who grudgingly left his seat by the brazier at the wharf to see me to the house. He was eager to return to his fire and left me as soon as he could. I stood for a moment under the gnarled trees of the old orchard, the November chill seeping into my bones. Taking a deep breath, I walked the familiar garden path toward the house, endeavoring to put the nine-year-old girl back in her place and act as the woman of substance I was.

"You picked your moment well. Oliver is in his study and may receive visitors for a short while." Joan turned from the window and walked toward me, her face in shadow. The room was gloomy, darker even than the mid-November afternoon warranted. The fire was meager, and the candles were thin and well burned down, the wicks trimmed low. I recalled how miserable my childhood days had been and saw how little had changed.

"He is not well?" I had not heard this news.

"He is feeling his years. The Irish climate was not conducive to his gout." Joan peered up at me. I was not tall, but she had shrunken mightily, and her eyes were rheumy. She aged poorly, and the cosmetics smeared across her face did little to conceal the sour wrinkles that drew down her mouth. "What news do you bring? Or are you here on another cause? I hear that your victualler does not pay his debts on time."

I refused to rise to her bait.

"We manage well enough. I am not here to discuss our financial condition." Not the truth, but I was not about to give Joan an opportunity to further denigrate Allen.

"I'm surprised. The duke's death has left its mark on all of us. Some more than others. We already dispense charity to Will and Eleanor." She looked at me sharply. "So what do you want, Lucy? You have never been one to call on me socially."

"I would like my uncle's advice on a business venture."

"Oh, so you now manage the business of your household? Allen is too weakened to make an appearance himself?"

"Allen is recovering well, I thank you, madam. Now please take me to my uncle." I made as though to leave the room of my own accord, and she quickly stepped in front of me.

"No asking for money or favors, my girl. Oliver has more than enough supplicants surrounding him and needs no beggars within his family." She put a bony hand on my arm, and it took all my effort not to shake it off. "Unlike my Barbara, you made your choice a long time ago. There's nothing from Oliver for you."

"Do not bring Barbara into this. I have nothing to say about her."

"You don't need to. She and I talk plenty. Especially now that her son is Oliver's heir."

I took a deep breath. "Just take me to Oliver, Joan. I really do not care to speak of this further."

She shrugged and opened the door. We walked along a gallery, which should have been hung with ornate tapestries and paintings, but which instead hosted a few sticks of mean furniture and wall hangings that were aged and worn. The edifice of the house concealed the paucity within. It did not surprise me.

As we entered the wood-paneled study, I was saddened to see the change in Oliver. His beard was sparse, and a few strands of thin hair straggled from beneath his cap.

He looked up as I entered, and a smile broke across his face.

"Lucy, my dear. What a pleasure to see you. How fare you and your family?" He struggled to push himself up from his desk, and I crossed the room swiftly to prevent him from rising.

"Uncle, do not rise for me." I kissed his wrinkled cheek. "I am well, thank you, as are the children."

366

"Sit, sit." He gestured to a stool by the desk. "Joan, you may leave us."

She snorted and left the room, chin leading. Oliver appeared to not notice.

"And Allen? How is his health?" Oliver reached his hand out and took mine in his.

"He is recovering—" I interrupted myself as a lump in my throat forced me to pause before continuing. "In truth, he's not well. His health was broken on the voyage to Ré. I do not think he will ever recover again." His touch of kindness brought back memories of my childhood, waiting for his return from Ireland.

"That is a heavy burden you bear. Do you have doctors attending him?"

"Allen has dismissed them all. He says I am the best curator of his health and that I would keep him alive where none others would." I could not tell the truth, that we could not afford to pay their fees. I was exhausted with caring for him with my other duties.

"And his commerce? Who is managing his financial affairs while you tend to him?"

"His steward, his deputy, very badly. They cheat him at every opportunity. And Will is now bringing business to him." I took a deep breath. "That is what I wanted to seek your counsel on, Uncle."

Oliver raised his eyebrows in a question. "Will? What commerce does he have that he discusses with Allen?"

"It's the charter. They have been asked to activate their share. But it is no longer supplies or materials. Will is intending human cargo."

"Slaves?" The word hung between us, Oliver's voice raised in surprise.

I nodded.

"Uncle, you have to stop them. You have to help me. I cannot in all my conscience raise my children on money that has been derived from other men's misery. It is wicked and ungodly."

"Are things so bad that Allen and Will should stoop to this?"

"Yes." I said this softly, almost under my breath. It was the most I had admitted to anyone of our miserable circumstance.

The door flew open, making us both jump. "She pleads a sorry case. She made her bed. You will not give her any money," Joan's voice cut across the room. "If you acted on the mewling of all your relatives, we'd be paupers in a year."

"Woman, leave me to attend to my own."

Joan strode to the desk and stood beside Oliver, her arms crossed as she stared at me.

"I knew I could not leave her alone with you. You have me to think of, and your own business. Do not think you have so much you can afford to give it away."

I stood with great indignation. "I am asking nothing of you. I never have, and I never will."

"Then why are you here?" She spat the words at me.

"To save the souls of the men I love."

"Enough!" Oliver's voice, although querulous with age, cut between us as a sword.

"Joan, I will not jeopardize your portion, you have always held the purse strings in this household. Nothing is changing now." He pushed himself with great difficulty to standing. Although his frailty caused him to shake as he stood, his voice still carried authority.

"Lucy, I pledge to talk to Will, persuade him to give up this idea of slavery. There must be other ways to increase his trade. And if Will is no longer pursuing this line, then Allen will not have the opportunity either."

"Thank you, Uncle." His struggle to remain authoritative racked my conscience. "I do not wish to cause you more distress. But I know Will heeds your counsel."

"I think it is time you left," Joan interrupted us again. "I will see you to the door, Lucy."

I looked at Oliver, who nodded his head slightly and made a small farewell gesture with his trembling hand.

"I will return soon, Uncle, when you are feeling better."

He smiled at me.

"You do so, sweeting. I will enjoy that. And bring your children next time. I like to have young people around me."

"This way, mistress." Joan pushed the door open. I smiled at Oliver and lifted a hand in good-bye.

In the gallery outside his study, Joan stopped me.

"Do not come begging for favors here again."

In the dim light, I saw again the woman I remembered as my stepmother.

"Why do you hate me so much?" It took courage to find those words, but I could no longer accept her cruelty.

She peered at me.

"You were the chosen child, Lucy." The words flew from her mouth.

"What do you mean?" The last thing I felt in her household was chosen.

"Oliver loved you above all others. Over Barbara, over me." Her voice was raw, angry.

"I don't understand."

"When he brought you to me, after your mother died, he said you would be the girl I had longed for, the daughter I wanted. Barbara remembered her. But you . . . I had hope you might be young enough to forget."

"What do you mean, Joan, what are you trying to tell me?"

"I nurtured you as my own, Lucy. For a year, I tried to rear you as my daughter, to take pride in your growth, reward your accomplishments, make you love me. But you wouldn't." Her voice was flat now, emotionless, as if her anger had been spent. "You refused to love me in return. You turned your back on me; you spoke only of the mother who had died."

"I was a child, Joan. I would not know I was hurting you." My thoughts flew to Jocasta and how carefully I had trod not to replace her cherished memories of her mother. "Children do not know when their honesty hurts."

"Oh, you did. You took delight in rebuffing me, in turning my attentions aside, in crying for your mother when I tried to comfort you."

"How could you think an innocent child would have those intentions? And you took your envy of my dead mother out on me?"

She ignored me.

"But as for Barbara. She knew how to keep me company; she knew what a daughter's love could be. She found the ways to engender my affection."

369

"And so you favored her above me. And were not ashamed to show it."

"There was no choice to be had. You made me do it."

"You are a sick woman, Joan. You think a child can make a choice such as that?"

Joan laughed. "It really doesn't matter, does it, Lucy? For I chose right. Barbara was the one who brought wealth and positions and perquisites to this family. She was the one who earned the title of daughter to me."

"You sicken me. I would not further call you mother than the devil." So much now became clear. "You seek to control all those around you, Joan. But you have no governance over me. Just be sure you take care of Oliver, for he is a kind man, and gentle. Do not harm him."

I pushed past her, walking swiftly through the hall and out of that sorrowful house, resolving never to return.

49

Aqua Mirabilis

3 pints of sack, one of Angelica water, one quart of the juyce of celandine, cowslip flower, mint, balm of melilot flower, rosemary flower, marygolds, and a dram of saffron, spinyworth, cynamon, cloves, nutmeg, ginger, cubebs, cardamums, galangal, each 1 dram. Bruise them, mix them, still them in a cote still. You may bang musk and ambergreis in it if you will, sweeten it with sugar. It dissolves the swelling of the lungs. Who uses it need not be let blood. It is good for melancholy, flegm, hartburning, keeps the memory. This is called Aqua Mirabalis. The Miracle Water.

Tower

May 1630

Luce carefully poured the aromatic contents of her pan into three glass flasks and corked them, her lips pursed with concentration as she tried not to spill a drop of the precious liquid. The scent of cloves and nutmeg drifted through the stillroom.

"There. That will help Father's cough, I'm sure of it." She sensed me watching her and looked up, smiling. "He says my medicine makes him feel better than anything else in this world."

"I know it does, sweetheart." Luce had barely left her father's side these past two weeks, bringing him medicines, a rose she had picked in the garden, dew-covered and fragrant, reading aloud to him from the book of sermons she was studying.

"Might he rise today, Mother? He seemed much stronger yesterday, and today's May Day, and I wanted him to watch us dance."

"We shall see, Luce."

Those words, spoken daily it seemed, promising nothing, for I could not tell Allen's health any more than each hour at a time. He was so terribly weak, and the fever he had caught in Ré had never left his chest. Now I have noticed that his fingers have Hippocratic swelling.

I fear this signs a deeper humor lurks which cannot be treated with topicals such as Luce and I brew.

"Come, let's see if he awakes."

I stepped carefully through into the main passageway of the house, picking my way across the beam dislodged from the ceiling, which we dared not touch for fear of displacing the weight of the floor above. The fallen beam revealed more than just the attic above . . . it was scratched and scored with witchmarks, some recent, judging by the color of the wood. When it fell, it had dislodged other amulets, charms to prevent the witches from harming us. I assumed the servants had placed them there, for the old ways were still practiced and fresh in memory.

Our home had fallen ill, for without the regular maintenance our monied days afforded, it began to decompose, first in small ways, but now more evident. The past winter's storms ripped many tiles from the roof, and the top floor was no longer habitable. Much damp and mold clung there from the rains, fungus sprouted on the walls, and the plaster was so soft that a finger could imprint where before only a mason's hammer would indent. I had closed off the floor, but the damp odor seeped through the boarded-up passages. It was impossible to mask it with the pungent lavender and rosemary branches I threw on the floors.

Allen now occupied the main chamber above the entry, the council room with a cavernous fireplace I could light to keep the damp at bay, although our wood supply was precious. It was convenient to the stillroom and kitchen passage, so I was able to continue to manage the feeding of the prisoners, and Luce could run and bring him medicinals as he needed. He ordered his desk and our tawny canopied marriage bed moved there, and I tried to make an adventure, as though we were living in a small cottage and had few other rooms, bringing my chair to the window to work at mending while he rested and calculating our accounts at the table. The children often came to study to keep him company too, and Boon was seated there at his Latin when Luce and I arrived.

"Here you are, Father, I have made a posset for your cough." Luce's soft voice caused Allen's eyelids to flicker, and he awoke from his doze and smiled at her, his hollowed face reflecting a shadow of his old grin that I loved so dearly. He struggled to sit up, and in the morning light, I caught my breath to see his weakness, his skin grayed and his fingers clubbed with consumption's curse.

"Thank you, sweeting, I look forward to your brew every morning. Today I will get up, for I feel stronger."

"It's May Day, and the Moorish dancers are about." Lucy lifted her arms. "Look, I have new ribbons today!" She showed the scraps I had cut from my blue court dress, the last remnants of which would give her some joy today.

"You always do love to dance, little one." Allen smiled at his favorite child.

Suddenly, a pounding outside occurred as heavy footsteps running up the stairs broke our peacefulness. The door flung open. A disheveled man burst in, a dagger in his hand, his eyes crazed.

"Where's my money? Where's my money, you dog?" he screamed, his mouth spit-flecked as he waved his weapon in front of him. "You cur, you've broken me, you've broken me."

He stood looking around wildly, breathing heavily. Boon jumped to his feet, overturning his ink flask and grabbing his rapier as he stepped in front of Luce to protect her. Allen struggled half out of bed, reaching for his breeches and the sword he kept by the chest. Luce screamed, and all was bedlam as Boon beat back the man, pushing him toward the door, while Allen grasped the bedpost in one hand and held his sword aloft in the other. Alerted by the shouts and disturbance, several Yeoman Warders clattered up the stairs and quickly subdued the man, who lost his dagger in the fight, but not his voice.

"You have broken me, broken me!" he screamed. "Give me my money, for I have nothing, nothing, you bastard! I curse you and the king, for you cost me my livelihood and have ruined my family."

Boon rushed to the top of the stair.

"Take him to the Fleet!" he yelled at the backs of the warders as they pushed the man down the stairs. "Put that scum where he belongs, and double the guard on our house. Do not let anyone in!"

I flew to Allen, who fell to his knees, his sword still in his hand.

"Luce, quick, help me get him back into bed." She darted to my side, and between us we were able to lift Allen up and half carry him across the room. His bones were so fragile through his skin that it was as I carried a child, not my husband. We lay him down and propped pillows under him, for his exertion had brought on a terrible coughing fit, which racked his thin frame.

"I hate Buckingham, I hate the king, I hate what they have done to Father and our family." Luce's emotions burst from her as tears streamed down her face. "Why is there a need for a king? He has done nothing for us except bring despair to our people and financial ruin to our family." She mopped at Allen's face with a piece of lawn torn from her own petticoat.

"There will always be a king, Luce." Boon was panting, his sword still drawn. "He is all that is England. Without the monarchy, there is no Englishman. You sound like a Puritan. Don't speak such treason."

"It is not treason, it is common sense. He is just a man, like any other. I have no—" She stopped in shock as the pale linen turned red. "Mother, look, what's happening?"

I took her place at Allen's side.

"Both of you, please, no more arguments. Go fetch some fresh water, sweetheart. And take Boon with you and ask Cook for some food. He'll be starving after his battle." She stood, uncertain, staring at her father and the bloody cloth. "Go on! Father will be fine. It is just a little sanguinity making its way out of his body."

She obeyed, much to my relief. "I'll be back shortly, Father," she said comfortingly. "And Mother can tell us again the story of Jocasta at Fonmon, when all thought her a wood fairy. I love that story."

She left the room, and I could hear her lecturing Boon as they went together to the kitchens. I said a heartfelt prayer that they would always have each other, for despite their differences, they were so close in their hearts.

I settled the curtains of our marriage bed, pulling the blankets around Allen's tired body and smoothing the damp hair from his forehead. His breathing was shallow and rapid, and the exertion had stirred the sanguinity in his chest. It was with terrible foreboding that I held the cloth to his mouth, for the blood was bright red and showed no sign of mucus spew, and I feared it signified the final progression I had been dreading.

"Lucy?" the whisper was soft but direct, bringing me from my doze. The fire had flickered out, and the afternoon turned gray. It had been two weeks from when the intruder had stormed our room. Allen had not stirred from bed since.

"Is Peter here, and Jocasta?"

"I can send for them, my love."

"I must settle their debts. They vex me with their creditors, Lucy." He took a deep, shuddering breath. "I have been more troubled with my domestic disputes than ever those in foreign lands."

His fingers were working on the heavy quilt, fidgeting with the threads that were bare from rubbing under his hands for so many months.

"Allen, they are young and foolish. Peter has a restless spirit, and Jocasta is just learning the ways of managing a household. She cannot help that her husband spends more than his means."

"It was not as I wished them to be, not as I was at their age." His voice was troubled. "I must settle their debts, for their creditors will keep returning, and when I am gone, they will haunt you, Lucy."

"Shhh, Allen, all will be well. We still have the king's warrant, and you will be well. Summer approaches, and with the warmer weather, your health will return." I turned my head so he could not see the tears filling my eyes.

"Goring. Go to Lord Goring, Lucy, when the time is upon you. I will ask for his intervention with the king, for he has influence. And Will? Does he continue with our venture? There is money to be made in the New World."

I took a deep breath, for I had not yet told Allen of the reason for my visit with Oliver.

"Will does well, Allen. Uncle Oliver formed a new syndicate. Your interest and Will's has been included. He has found a source of ores in Africa, and Will's ships sail frequently to the plantations with a precious cargo of minerals and metals."

"And do we profit, Lucy? Is there money coming?" His fingers continued to twitch and pull on the quilt.

"We will do so, Allen. The ships sail, and Oliver is a good custodian. Do not fret."

He became quiet and slipped back into a soft sleep, his fingers stilling.

"Bring me parchment and a clerk." His voice was hushed in the evening twilight, hardly more than the whisper of a leaf stirring at the top of the sassafras.

"Allen, my love, no business now. You must rest."

"Bring parchment, Lucy, and a man to hear me. It is God's business. I must make my testament."

"Later, Allen, later. You are recovering. Have patience. It just will take a little more time."

"Time I don't have, my love. Please fetch the clerk and leave me."

His eyes were clear, and although his frame was now shrunken with the consumption, there was a quiet strength that emanated from him. He had not lost his authority, even though the sickness disobeyed him.

I left him and walked downstairs to the offices, where his clerks were at work, summoning one that I knew had a clear hand and head and would serve him well.

"Sir Allen requests your help. Please gather your writing materials and come with me."

He nodded and placed his quills and parchment in his case, following me from the room and back upstairs to the chamber, where I showed him in and softly closed the door on them. Whatever Allen wished to say to God was his own private affair. I found myself at a loss, for I had been in the room with Allen for so many days I barely recognized the surroundings of my home and was lost as a stranger amongst the familiar.

I returned to the stillroom and there found consolation, the familiar aromas and instruments welcoming me. I set to work, for there was always much to be done for the prisoners, and as I sorted a bunch of rosemary that Luce had gathered and left hanging above the table, I stripped the fresh green tips from the tough branches, the oil staining my fingers with its pungent scent. Rosemary for love, for faithfulness, for remembrance.

Allen left me as gently as he had once found me, on a May morning, his hand in mine as his labored breathing gradually quietened. All through the night, I kept watch and listened, and there were many times his breath stopped, only to start again after a long pause. I could do nothing but hold his hand and count the hours, challenging God to take him from me. Death sat across the bed through that dark night, and I refused to sleep, fighting to keep Allen with me, for this time I was the soldier who defied death, who shook my fist and kept him at bay with my shield of love. But in the morning, while I looked away, death came and stole my love, and the room became quiet, and his face stilled, and his poor exhausted body rested.

I had my time alone with him, for until I left that room, he was mine; telling no others kept the truth from the world. Until I had said all I had to, I was not ready to share him. But in the end, there were no words. All I could do was kiss his cooling brow and let my heart speak for me, in thoughts and memories and reflections of our love, in my regrets for my doubts, and in my thankfulness that I had been so very loved.

I walked slowly through the garden of the Tower, the bared trees arching over me, tiny red buds concealing the leaves within, branches laced against the pale morning sky. In the east, above the stone walls, the first morning rays of sun shafted through the river mist, and a thrush greeted the light with a joyous burst of song. I bade good-bye to this garden, no longer mine to tend, these trees that were left for another Lady of the Tower to sit beneath, and Walter's vegetables to feed another family. I brushed my fingers across a damask rose, its head heavy with dew, and the drops fell as tears to the leaves below.

"I am leaving now." Eleanor's voice was quiet, her footsteps so soft that I had not heard her come behind me. "Oliver sent his barge. It waits at the wharf."

"Shall you manage, on your own, at Battersey?" The prospect of Joan's wretchedness glimmered between us, my presence forbidden, my company not welcome to visit. God forbid Allen's debts should taint her precious property.

"I have Huw. And Will should return by year's end. I have little choice. There is nowhere else to go."

"John still does not send for us?"

"He will not, Lucy. He is courting Lady Grobham. I predict they will be married by Michaelmas. We are not welcome."

I held her tight, my emotions flowing from my heart to hers.

"I wish you could come . . ." My words trailed away.

"With you? There is no room for us where you travel, and Oliver needs support at Battersey. His offer to appoint Will to manage his estate when he returns from this last voyage is one that will serve us well." She hugged me back, her arms soft around me, her cheek warm on mine.

"Remember the day we were first reunited, Lucy? We knew there was a bond that none could break. That love continues, and you will always be in my heart. We will make this uncertain world sure again one day. Do not fear, do not lose hope." She turned quickly, the tears on her face glistening like the dew on the rose. I watched, desolate, my own tears falling as she left the garden and closed the gate behind her.

Beyond the walls, I could hear the shouts of the men who were moving our marriage bed from the chamber into the cart in front of the Queen's House, piling it with my chair and the two trunks that held our other possessions, all I could recover from the bountiful times we had once lived.

The meager purse of coins I concealed in my pocket, enough to sustain us for a year, if we were prudent. Two days was all I had, two days in which to bid farewell to this home, this prison. So much had its ancient walls witnessed, now just memories, fragmented dreams. With my departure traveled the memories of Frances, of Walter, of the duke's quest for the map to the gold.

Allen's testament and his last letter to me, along with a deed to Newington Manor, were safe in my bodice, pressed against my heart. His appointment of Lord Goring as executor, his one friend who still carried great sway with the king, duly signing the will. I could hear Allen's voice from the dictated words, his final moment before God to clear his conscience.

I pulled the creased parchment, warm from my breast, and read it again, although the words were so familiar I really did not need to see them written.

My body I commit to the earth to be buried where I shall happen to dye in a silent manner. For the Lady Lucie Apsley, my wife, I do hereby declare and express that she hath been a dear, tender kind and loving wife unto me who (next unto God) hath saved my life through several tymes by her continual care and industry. For my sake she has endured many sorrows and evermore in times of my extremitie hath relieved and comforted me, for which the God of Heaven comfort her in all her sorrows. She has been a most loving, discreet and religious mother towards her children and brought them up in the feare of God and they likewise have stood in awe been obedient to her although she never corrected them. She is a woman virtuous and good. If my deare wife (unto whom never man was more bound) take any distaste I do earnestly entreat her to forgive me. I desire all the world should know that she is a religious and virtuous lady, and a most kind wife.

In his last words, Allen had proclaimed my virtue. He banished Theo's shadow, drifting across our marriage, never substantial enough to challenge, never weak enough to dismiss. His last gift to me was not of much material worth, but infinitely more, for it was my reputation. He may be entangled in all men's minds with the corruption and debts of a bankrupt king and court, but he cleared me of any association, and so restored my honor.

In the quiet of the garden, in that singular place where I had always found comfort throughout my life, I pledged my determination to go forward. I swore to embrace the changes that destiny had wrought in our lives and to fan the small ember of courage in the dark of the unknown for the sake of my children.

Once, I dreamed I walked in the garden of Lydiard and a star came down to my hand, signifying I would have a daughter who would achieve eminence.

I would live for the prophecy and fight for the future.

For further reading, please enjoy this brief extract from the next book in the series.

By Love Divided
The Lydiard Chronicles | 1630-1646

Royalist Sir Allen Apsley thinks his choice is clear, but when his mother embraces the Puritan cause, and his beloved sister Luce falls in love with John Hutchinson, a Roundhead soldier, his loyalties are tested. Is it family first? Is it country first? As England falls into bloody civil war, Allen must fight for king and country, while Luce embraces Parliament's radical views and confronts the very core of the family's beliefs. And when their influential Villiers cousins raise the stakes, Allen and Luce face a devastating challenge. Will war unite or divide them? In the dawn of rebellion, love is the final battleground.

Based on surviving memoirs, court papers and letters of Elizabeth St.John's family, By Love Divided continues the story of Lucy St.John, The Lady of the Tower. This powerfully emotional novel tells of England's great divide, and the heart-wrenching choices one family faces.

By Love Divided

The Lydiard Chronicles | 1630-1646

ELIZABETH ST.JOHN

Prologue

The fire is most fervent in a frosty season.

Luce

21st August, 1642

These were the times in which Lucy Apsley questioned if God had deserted her.

Around the table, her children gathered. When had they grown into men and women? Where went the innocent Allen, the child in Luce? These young people talked recklessly tonight.

Lucy shook the ghosts of yesteryear from her thoughts.

Be grateful for the hour at hand, the joy shared in this pleasing home.

Still, the doubts chattered in her mind. The past crept close tonight, the door ajar between dead and living.

This dinner was a happy occasion, a celebration of Allen's knighthood. A fresh carp caught in their own fishponds graced the table. Elegant clothes were unpacked from trunks, dried lavender shaken from the skirts. Even Luce, always careless with her dress, wore a fine gown of blue watered silk, dotted with moonstones.

And then, as unpredictable as a summer storm, a lightning exchange heralded dispute.

For the king. Against the king. Favored by Villiers. Betrayed by Parliament.

Those old arguments restored her husband's memory, twelve years departed from this life. And now, their past disputes echoed in her children.

"Where lies your loyalty, Allen?" demanded Luce. "Your family deserves the truth."

He shrugged, his broad shoulders strong under the fine holland shirt, the beautifully cut doublet. Court was good to her son.

"Why, Luce," he replied, "As God is my witness, I am loyal to His Majesty and faithful to the Parliament. My heart lies with the men of this country, and their wish for peace."

"By forming armed bands of Cavaliers?" cried Luce, her voice rising. "My heart is loyal and faithful too—loyal to the Parliament who represent the rights of men, faithful to the tradition of monarchy. Consider your own world order, not mine."

Allen stood too, his soldier's physique suddenly charging the atmosphere. His color rose. "The king is as a father to the people of this nation. He knows what is best for them."

"Is that why he commandeers our ammunition, leaves our towns defenseless, our woman and children vulnerable to any band of armed men?"

"Keep to your writing and notebooks, Sister, and leave the business of government to men."

Lucy prayed for the storm to subside. Thus always ranged their arguments, until one caught the other's eye, and a shared smile would appear, contagious and healing.

Please, God, let this night be no different.

"Tomorrow, we ride to Nottingham to attend King Charles," she said. "He speaks to unite our country, to stand down the armies. Tonight, let not differences divide us."

A mother knows what is best for her children. And still, they seek out their own destinies. Perhaps, once more, she could protect her children with a lie.

God save us. For again, the fate of my family and of England lies within this deceitful king's hands. And if he cannot have his way, he will destroy us all.

1

Our uncle Lord Grandison was married to a lady so jealous of him,
and so ill-natured in her jealous fits to anything that was related to him,
that her cruelties to my mother exceeded the stories of stepmothers.

Luce Apsley
16th January, 1631

Leaving sweet Chelsea for the Battersey shore, Lucy was ferried to the underworld, where Cerberus guarded the gates to Hades. Only this hell was her childhood home, and the sentinel, Aunt Joan.

"Hold tight to the side, my Lady Apsley." The Thames boatman, etched black against the lowering January sky, stood and plied his oar. "The current runs strong upon the shallows."

Lucy already gripped the weathered wood, for she knew this treacherous river of old. On the southern bank appeared St. Mary's spire, an obelisk marking the family crypt. There, her uncle would reside, laid beneath the chancel, where the flesh would fall from his bones and his spirit be exalted to the heavens.

Lord Oliver St. John, Viscount Grandison, no longer of this world. Another funeral, when her husband's death still shrouded her heart.

Would she ever be free of the melancholy? A tear stung her eye— surely from the hostile wind, unfurling silvery banners all the way from the Tower and the cold northern sea beyond.

"Do not despair, Mother. You have me to care for you," murmured her son, Allen's namesake, fourteen and caught between youth and manhood. Her eldest boy, a witness to more in the Tower than any child ought.

He huddled close to her on the rough plank bench, his threadbare cloak pulled tight across his chest. Those final years in the Tower afforded no new clothes, for the departing prisoners left but shabby pickings. At least she'd salvaged mourning silks, payment obligatory for their keeper duties.

Lucy sighed. Her husband had been so proud of his appointment. Sir Allen Apsley. Keeper and Lieutenant of the Tower of London, with all the fees and privileges that accompanied the position. Three thousand pounds he'd paid for that perquisite, moving them into the Tower to administer the prison. And so little income, after the Duke of Buckingham's death ended his favors. All had turned to dust in their last years of residence.

Her son nudged her, breaking her thoughts. Those clear glass-gray eyes. Lucy's heart clenched at the youthful reflection of her husband, before the ruinous debts and the devastating consumption had drained the life from him. Death came as a relief, his Calvinist soul content with its destiny. Who was she to challenge the doctrine that sustained her through her darkest hours? Sir Allen Apsley's time was done.

Lucy smiled and took his cold-reddened hand. "Boon—"

"Allen," he corrected her.

"Allen," she continued. So, his childhood nickname departed also. "No mother could ask more of her son, and the example you set for your brother and sisters. In these difficult times, you are still our boon."

He flushed, his young skin translucent, the down on his chin almost stubble. "Father would have wished this so. He instructed me to protect our family upon his death. My training with the Yeoman Warders will serve me well."

The wind gusted bitter at the river's center, pushing their craft upstream as the boatman struggled to steer a straight course. A fragment of muddy ice floated by, and as they approached the bulrushes, more appeared. How deep the winter gnawed.

"Eleanor is waiting for us." Lucy's heart quickened. Her beloved sister stood on the snow-covered landing, bundled in black furs and a deep hood. As the boat edged closer, Eleanor's delicate face reflected the brittle light, framed by the glossy beaver skins.

"My darlings," she called. "Praise God, you arrive safely."

Lucy stepped from the rocking boat and stumbled into Eleanor's arms.

"I have missed you sorely," she whispered.

"Sweet Lucy, your life has transformed since leaving the protection of the Tower. I am heartbroken at your suffering," responded her sister softly. Her tone lightened, "Ah, Allen, look at you—how much you have grown!"

She held her hands out to Allen as he clambered to the landing. The boatman handed up their packs and tipped his hat in thanks as Eleanor paid him.

Lucy stood silently on the dock, memories surfacing. This riverbank once was her haven, until she'd discovered the plague man, dead in the reeds. Then came the summer of change, when Uncle Oliver returned from the Irish wars, bringing with him her cousin William.

"How is Will?" she asked. "You wrote he is at sea?"

Eleanor nodded, her eyes softening. "My husband is happiest when on his ship, Lucy; you know that." She shrugged under the heavy furs, making light of her feelings as only Eleanor could. "He sails regularly to the Americas. And yet, the commerce is still not forthcoming."

Lucy glanced through the black lacework of twisted apple trees to the manor. Unrecognizable since her time here, what with Aunt Joan's vulgar adornments of turrets and a false front. Beneath, the old house she knew still rested, ancient bones settling into the ground, decay concealed behind its rendered face. Best get this over soonest.

Lucy reached for the comfort of Allen's hand. "Should we go? This cold bites to the bone."

"And even more so inside. Joan has not changed her frugal ways, despite her title." Eleanor led the way along the frosty path, her boots squeaking on the gravel. "She will expect to see you tonight at the funeral, not before. She has kept to her rooms since Oliver's death."

"And Barbara?" Lucy's voice hung with the mist of her breath in the frigid air.

"She arrives later this evening."

So Barbara attends. Of course. She was Joan's favorite. My sister. My enemy.

5

Printed in Poland
by Amazon Fulfillment
Poland Sp. z o.o., Wrocław